Zombie Jamboree

Zombie Jamboree

A NOVEL BY
ROBERT MERKIN

WILLIAM MORROW AND COMPANY, INC.
NEW YORK

For Cyndy Again and Again

Quotation from the Voyages of Doctor Dolittle, by Hugh Lofting, used with kind permission of Mr. Christopher Lofting.

Lyrics from "Zombie Jamboree," words and music by Conrad Eugene Mauge, Jr., copyright © 1955 and 1957 by Hollis Music, Inc., used by permission.

Library of Congress Cataloging-in-Publication Data

Merkin, Robert.
Zombie jamboree.

1. Vietnamese Conflict, 1961–1975—Fiction.
I. Title.
PS3563.E7413Z6   1986   813'.54   86-745
ISBN 0-688-01946-3

Printed in the United States of America

First Edition

1 2 3 4 5 6 7 8 9 10

BOOK DESIGN BY RICHARD ORIOLO

"And the Black Parrots' method of fighting was peculiar. This is what they did: on the head of each Bag-jagderag three or four parrots settled and took a good foot-hold in his hair with their claws; then they leant down over the sides of his head and began clipping snips out of his ears, for all the world as though they were punching tickets. That is all they did. They never bit them anywhere else except the ears. But it won the war for us . . .

This treatment, very painful at the time, did not however do them any permanent harm beyond the change in looks. And it later got to be the tribal mark of the Bag-jagderags. No really smart young lady of this tribe would be seen walking with a man who did not have scalloped ears—for such was a proof that he had been in the Great War. And that (though it is not generally known to scientists) is how this people came to be called by the other Indian nations, the *Ragged-Eared Bag-jag-derags*.

—HUGH LOFTING, *The Voyages of Doctor Dolittle*

I

HEISER, RICHARD A.
US51681856
0 POS
PROTESTANT

1

Becker announced once that he was conducting a worldwide search for the absolutely worst place in the entire army, so naturally I asked him why. "Because," he said, "every time I get new orders and show up at some even more godforsaken place than the last place, there's a clown in the rack next to me who says it's nothing compared to the last place he was stationed. And then the clown next to him says he's been to that one, but it wasn't as bad as some other place he used to be stationed.

"Now I believe all these guys," he went on. "They always reek of sincerity. But a process like that just can't go on forever. There has to be one absolutely worst place in the entire army, worse than which there is no other, and just once I want to know what it is, 'cause I'm so sick of hearing that my new hole is so much better than somebody else's previous hole."

Fair enough. I nominate Fort Benning, and particularly Kelly Hill. Becker and I each spent most of the same year there, so we both know it intimately. We were both in Vietnam, too, and naturally I feel obligated to say that Vietnam had to be worse than Kelly Hill, except for some guys in the brigade, maybe twenty or thirty a month, lifers and draftees alike, who used to volunteer for Vietnam to get off Kelly Hill. That's the truth, and I know because I clerked in brigade S-4, the personnel office.

I could even be more specific and nominate our enlisted Zoo, the open barracks for about seventy or eighty seething radical blacks, white college-dropout acid freaks and junkies, Minnesota farmboys, C.I.D. undercover men and other assorted lifers all frozen in a perpetual state of mutual distrust, annoyance, fear and often downright murderous hatred. The fort had a trick, of course, for making you like the Zoo at the beginning, a very smart trick. When you got orders to go to Benning, you didn't go directly to Kelly Hill and the Zoo. First you went to the Repo Depot, a transient barracks for three or four hundred uniformed refugees and outcasts waiting days and days, often the better part of a month, for some word about their permanent posting at Benning. Others were there awaiting court-martial for offenses ranging from AWOL to crimes of violence or simply theft, so instantly new arrivals knew to sleep with their wallet inside their pillowcase and their hand thrust inside the pillowcase, too. Lockers were available at the Repo Depot. Nothing of value remained in them at the end of the day, and often even the worthless items were gone as well.

It only took the first day at the Repo Depot to hear the rumor of what your permanent posting would almost certainly be, and it wouldn't be any unit on or near Main Post, with its fairly clever imitation of the basic requirements of human life. Main Post was short on support troops and permanent personnel, long on crash-and-dash temporary types, infantry officer candidates and Airborne trainees particularly. But ours were to be permanent assignments, nothing temporary, certainly nothing remotely voluntary, and we learned very quickly that would mean Kelly Hill, main staging area of the army's largest infantry brigade.

Already I have to qualify myself. Immediately worse than Kelly Hill and perhaps even worse than some accidentally never-ending assignment to the Repo Depot was the brigade's secondary staging area, Harmony Church, where about a third of the brigade was sheltered in World War II-era wooden barracks. Its location on the regional map was practically a military secret. If you had a car, it took a half hour to reach Main Post, forty minutes to reach what passed for the nearest town of size, Columbus. If you had no car, you stayed at Harmony Church. No one would pick up a hitchhiker, Harmony Church having the reputation for housing entire battalions of incipient and very disgruntled Richard Specks and Charles Mansons. An official army car or truck with armed personnel inside might feel safe enough to try, but was forbidden by regulations. Off-duty private drivers saw hitchhikers from Harmony Church and had premonitions of decomposing in the thousands of acres of woods that surrounded Harmony Church. When its soldiers were sent out on bivouac maneuvers, they hardly noticed any difference from remaining behind at Harmony Church. That was the second half of being tricked into being grateful for an assignment to Kelly Hill—getting out of the Repo Depot and then not being assigned to Harmony Church.

All of this frustrated Becker. "I agree," he whined. "Harmony Church is worse than Kelly Hill. The Repo Depot was worse than Kelly Hill. The last place I was and you were was worse than Kelly Hill. But Kelly Hill is terrible. Thirty swinging dicks a month think Kelly Hill is worse than Vietnam. Some of them have been to Vietnam once or twice already. And if we go to another place, we'll be sure Kelly Hill was worse than the new place."

"Maybe you're on the verge of a breakthrough," I suggested.

"What sort of breakthrough?"

"A relativity theory. Maybe if you're an enlisted man, wherever you are is the worst place in the army. All places are worse than all other places simultaneously."

Becker tumbled into deep thought.

"No," he said when he came back. "I reject that. It's too awful to believe. There's a place. I know there's a place. There has to be an army post so scummy, so sucky, so scum-sucky, a place that bites the hairy wazoo worse than any other army post bites the hairy wazoo. A place to despair of beyond all others. It has to be out there somewhere. I have faith."

"What would it be like?"

He smiled and savored that. "Ah. Well. There'd be three

components: the natural component, the military component and the town component. The natural component would be some barfing-forth of nature that not even Euell Gibbons could love."

"Who?"

"Euell Gibbons. *Stalking the Wild Asparagus.* He's this geek who chows down on whatever's growing in the wilderness. Lichen salad. Bark soup. Moss steak. Well, the kind of post I'm thinking of is smack-dab in the middle of a million and a half acres where the snazziest meal old Euell could snarf up would be dirt pie. And it's nothing to look at. Perfectly flat. But not even stark or austere. The army will have had decades to have fucked up any possible scenic vista with artillery targets.

"The weather's ghastly. There's something bad about every season. Eaten alive by bugs in the summer. A winter too grue-some to contemplate, and even the snow falls dirty. Spring lasts eleven days and it rains all the time. Fall has no foliage changes and is even shorter than spring. There are no birds. Just poisonous snakes.

"The military component. There's some specialty on this post that fills it full of nothing but crazed lifers with all sorts of patches and special qualifications. Everybody has to double-time twenty miles every morning in formation. Every officer is a West Point graduate."

"Oh, God!" I groaned.

"You're getting the picture. And they're all pissed off because they've pulled stateside duty, so their careers are going no-where. So they take it out on the draftees. Bivouac. Weeks and weeks of bivouac. There's an S-2 on the post who's even crazier than ours. He knows that rock 'n' roll is Communist-inspired, so by post command all four jukeboxes are filled with nothing but shitkicker music. Wherever this place is, no radio can pick up anything but shitkicker music and evangelist preachers, but if you do pick up some Chicago station at two in the morning and one of the S-2's spies hears it, you're busted.

"Every barracks has a spy from the C.I.D. There's a brigade-level inspection every week, and everybody's shit has to be per-fect. The food is just like it is here; no reason to fuck with that. You can't pay your way out of KP even if you're a millionaire, and you pull it at least twice a week. There's a meningitis outbreak every summer, just like here, so you spend four hours every night chasing down every speck of dust in the barracks."

"Tell me about the town."

"Sure, I was getting to that. It's called Lunkville. It's the only place within nine hundred miles; you'd have to own a private plane to go anywhere else on a three-day pass. Lunkville loves this post. The moment you get into town, the cops stop and frisk you. It's in some wildly Dixie-like state, so all blacks are beaten up immediately. Jews the same. Catholics too. And the post commander is so crazed on maintaining good relations with Lunkville that after they beat you up and steal your money in Lunkville, you're court-martialed when you get back to the post. The best restaurant in Lunkville is an Arby's roast beef place."

A voice, a black troop's voice, echoed over a bank of lockers. "I been there. I was stationed there. I know that place. Fort Leonard Wood, Missouri. That's the place."

"Shee-it," another voice objected. "That dude talkin' about Fort Polk, Louisiana."

"My ass. You talkin' Fort Huachuca to a tee. I been there."

"Obviously none of you people were ever stationed at Dugway Proving Grounds, Utah. That's the place he's talking about."

"Shut up, honkie. He's talkin' about Fort Sill, and that's just the fuckin' truth."

It started up again, spread to every corner and bunk, upper and lower, in the Zoo and lasted a half hour. "See? Every place in the army is worse than every other place."

"No," Becker said. "There's got to be one place worse than all the others. I just know it in my heart."

But for now, for both of us, for every beast trapped in the Kelly Hill headquarters Zoo, empty, bitter day on top of empty, bitter day, week after week and month after month, we'd landed in the functional equivalent of Becker's mythical army hole and we knew it. Only Becker could spend time trying to discover someplace truly worse; only Becker could waste his energy that way.

"What will you do," I asked, "when you find it?"

"I will be truly grateful that I'm here. That's what that place is for."

2

About a month after Becker and I started to hang out together,
I came back to my bunk after what passed for supper one
Saturday night and found Becker with his nose in one of my
magazines.

"I have a question for you," he said. "Is there life on Mars?"

"I don't know."

"The traditional answer to that one is, a little on Saturday
night. Now what's going to pass for life here tonight? If past
experience is anything to go by, we're probably going to walk
down the main drag here and hit up the movie theater. You
know what's playing there?"

"No."

He took a copy of Friday's daily bulletin out of his back
pocket. "We're in luck. It's a documentary about surfing. Of
course there are the two flicks down on Main Post. Now don't
drool. Doris Day stars in one of them. It's a heartwarming
comedy about a big family with a lot of kids. Down at the off-

brand art cinema they got a western with Henry Fonda. Real high-tone stuff. You want to hear what they got at the Harmony Church theater?"

"No. I have to confess, it sort of scares me to go to Harmony Church after dark."

"Gee, imagine what it must be like to live there around the clock. Well, anyway, if we decide to dispense with the cinema, that leaves the bowling alley up here or the big snack bar down at Main Post with its shitkicker music on the jukebox like we've been doing the last couple of Saturday nights."

"What's this leading up to?"

"Well, I was thinking that if we were to take control of our destinies right now, we could probably grab ourselves a ride to downtown Columbus and explore its marvels and delights. Now I grant you these may not rival the Great White Way or the Ginza, but it's got to beat hanging around on Kelly Hill or Main Post for yet another Saturday night. I mean, it's time you and I checked it out."

"I can't say I've been looking forward to it," I said. "I haven't been downtown on a Saturday night, but I've been to Columbus a couple of times. It's really a pit. Saturday night it's probably a pit with barfing rednecks."

"Now you haven't really given it a fair trial. And we're not just stuck with Columbus. If that should bite the big one, I hear Phenix City is one hotbed of curious activities."

"Phenix City's in Alabama," I said. "It's bad enough that I've been exiled to Georgia, but the thought of going to Alabama on purpose to satisfy any known human need sort of boggles my imagination."

"Listen, Richard, I've pretty much had it with bestowing my Saturday nights on Fort Benning. *Nada* is happening here. Zilch. Less than zilch, unless you can get shit-faced on three-point-two beer. So I say we give Columbus an honest college try. It could surprise us."

"How are we going to get back?" I wanted to know. Actually, I didn't care that much, but I was finding it hard to work up any enthusiasm about this project.

"They got buses. We could even come back in a taxi. And there are a few thousand other assholes like us, many of them with cars, who have to get their own asses back to the post. I'm sure that come Monday morning formation time, we won't still be standing on a Columbus street corner. What do you say?" He began to sing the little number about it being Saturday night and him just getting paid.

"Don't do that," I said. "Okay. Let me change. If you're ready to go, why don't you try to scare up a ride?"

"Okay! We got ourselves a thrill-seeker here! I'll see you in front of the orderly room. Don't tarry."

I didn't tarry, but I didn't exactly hustle. Two sinks down from me in the bathroom, a motor pool PFC named Hightower was slicking himself up in front of the mirror and singing an up-tempo doo-wop tune. I stopped my own unspirited preparations and looked at him.

"Hey. I have a question for you."

"Shoot, Jack. What's on your mind?"

"You act like you have a written guarantee in your pocket that you're going to get laid by Miss America tonight. Do you have some kind of guarantee like that?"

"Hey, Jack, why you want to be fucking with me on a Saturday night?"

"I'm just curious. Because if I had a guarantee along those lines, I probably wouldn't bother to slick myself up all that much."

"Oh, I get the picture," Hightower said. "No, I got no hot pussy guarantee tonight. I'm just going to take my stag self to the Soul Caverns and mix with the ladies and hope for the best. Maybe I got to come back here and get a date with Harry Palm or Sally Fingers. But I got hopes, which is more than you got any right to have with that goddam sorry-ass attitude of yours. Nobody wants to fuck somebody what's in pain, Jim. And look at those fuckin' threads! Why don't you get yourself some sharp-lookin' threads—what the hell is your name, anyway?"

"Richard."

"Okay, Jim, why don't you get yourself somethin' nasty in Italian shoes, a sharp-looking shirt, some nice slacks? You look like you goin' to a goddam Four-H Club convention. You want to get next to something nice, you got to look sharp. And you got to make like you're happy. Listen here: 'Hey, mama, you care to shake a tail-feather out on that floor?' 'Hey, darlin', that is one outstanding outfit you have poured your fine self into.'

What's that word you white people use? Tacky? Well, tacky it sure enough is, but that's just the drill if you want half a chance at gettin' a nut off with something that don't bark."

"Well, good hunting."

Hightower turned back to the mirror and started to dance while he rattailed his hair. "Good hunting is right! I may not bag nothin', but I sure as fuck goin' squeeze off a few rounds, Jim."

When I got downstairs, Becker grabbed me by the arm and dragged me out to the parking lot. We were heading right toward a smashed-up '59 Chevy. Two of the company cooks still in their stained mess uniforms, scrawny white weasels who had their own room and haunted the barracks on their own strange schedules, were leaning against it passing a bottle of Spañada back and forth.

I dug my heels into the blacktop. "Hey. I'm not driving downtown with those drunks."

"Relax," Becker whispered. "They are drunks; that's sure the truth, and that's why we're in luck. If Willie there is ever found behind the wheel of his car on this post, even if the car's up on blocks, he's going to prison for life. So that's why I'm pulling chauffeur duty. We have ourselves a ride to anywhere in Columbus we want to go."

"How are they going to get back?"

"You are so fucking fixated on everybody getting back! Fuck that! Our immediate challenge is getting downtown, don't you see that? Now go on over and make nice to the subhumans."

Becker slid behind the wheel, but in deference to the ownership of the wreck, Willie sat next to him and I got in the back seat with Willie's grinning cornhole buddy, who offered me the bottle of wine. It was the most ghastly ride I've ever had; nothing I'd ever smelled before smelled even remotely like that Chevy. Of course the rumor about career cooks was that they survived their chosen living hell very nicely by hauling off excess army food from the mess-hall loading dock and reselling it off-post at bargain rates. I could believe it. I tried to make my nose separate out the smells and thought I could identify ham and fish fillets, not to mention old spilled beer and wine, last month's vomit and of course the cooks themselves. If my backseat partner smelled anything, he called it Home.

"There!" Becker shouted as we drove along Thirteenth Street. "That's it! That's the bar I've seen in my dreams! Willie, we're getting out right here. You going to be all right?"

Willie gave a little belch, slid over to the wheel and looked out the window. "We gone be fahn. Thanks for gettin' us off the post." The Chevy careened off down the street.

We were outside the most nondescript drinking establishment on the planet. According to the window, its name was Beer.

"You've dreamed about this place?" I asked.

"Yes. Actually a guy out in Harmony Church told me about it. I just wanted some sort of reference before I gave some place my trade. The guy may show up later tonight. I told him we'd try to be here."

"What did your friend say were the big selling points for this particular tavern?"

"He said he liked it and it was cheap. All I cared about was that I'd talked to somebody who'd gone into a Columbus bar and come out again without getting knifed or rolled. That was enough for me. Let's go in."

Neither Becker nor I knew the name for a bar like this at the time, but years later when Becker started to pick up a little Spanish, he found its true name. The Cubans called it a *Punto Filipino*; you rent your beer at one end and you give it back in a hole in the wall in a little room at the other end, and for all anyone knows or cares, there's a recycling tube from the output hole back to the dispenser. I'd only seen one more-primitive drinking joint in my life, a warehouse district bar in Chicago where the all-male patrons stood at a bar about a half-block long and pissed into a trough between their feet without even bothering to leave the bar to go to the john.

The place was nearly pitch-dark. There was a crude, home-carpentered wooden bar in one corner, about twenty small round-topped wobbly tables, some booths and a coin-operated pool table that seemed to be the thrill focus for the almost all-Benning, all-enlisted, all-male crowd. You didn't sit at the bar; it was strictly a service bar for about four or five skuzzy-looking waitresses who hustled their asses back and forth bearing draft Budweiser, Miller or Schlitz by the pitcher or the glass; that's what there was, there wasn't no more. A blackboard advertised heated-up sandwiches in plastic wrap, and there were bags of pretzels and potato chips. We slid into an empty booth and Becker ordered a pitcher of Miller and two glasses. When the waitress scooted back, we got our order, a paper napkin to rest the pitcher on and two round cardboard Schlitz coasters for our glasses. "You-all have a good time now, you hear?" our waitress exhorted. If Hightower could have seen her, he'd have said she was womped with an ugly stick. I looked at Becker and found him sipping his beer with peaceful bliss written all across his face.

"You like this place?" I asked.

"Crazy about it."

"You know what this place looks like to me?"

"No, but you tell me anyway."

"Okay. You get drafted. You get your uniform. You go to basic training, AIT; then you get an assignment, a bunk, a blanket and a locker. You get three squares a day. That takes care of everything your standard enlisted man can possibly need during the duty week. But then comes the weekend, so this is the place the army issues you for your weekend pleasure. It reeks of the bare minimum. Our waitress is the civilian woman the army issued for us to look at. What more could we ask for? She's unquestionably got two breasts, she wears lipstick, she's not bald and I think she's under forty."

"You're wrong. We've already been going to those asshole places the army thoughtfully issues for our weekend pleasure. We've been hanging out at them every weekend since we came to Benning. On post. But this place is off-post. Maybe it's only two miles off-post, but it's off-post. The army doesn't have a thing to do with its management. In fact the army's declared it off-limits at least once, something about too many GIs getting beat up and rolled for their money on payday. And you're right about that woman. She is a civilian woman. But the army didn't issue her, so she's all right with me."

"And we're going to stay here all night?"

"Maybe. Maybe not. I intend to get a start on getting shitfaced while we're here, if that's okay with you. Why don't you loosen up a little and kill off half this pitcher yourself? I guarantee even that waitress will start to look attractive if you give things half a chance. You know what your problem is?"

"Tell me."

"You're so fucking shell-shocked by the army, you're so fucking blown away by the reality of being in it, that you're scared to get away from it. You're afraid something typically Southern will happen and you won't be able to get back for formation Monday, and then you'll be court-martialed for being AWOL and all that rat-shit. The army's got you brain-tethered. Well, I know the feeling. It's almost sort of safe back on the post. You're among your own kind. Nothing to explain, nothing complicated to transact, all questions answered. Well, I don't want to get used to that feeling, which is why we're experimenting with Columbus. And as soon as I scare up enough bucks and figure out someplace to go up there, I'm going to Atlanta on the weekends. I want to get used to getting the fuck out of Benning whenever I can, but you and I were starting to get used to staying there."

"I see. We're starting small."

"Yeah, but it's a start. Look. Do you have to salute anybody in here? Is anybody going to play 'The Star Spangled Banner' and yell, 'On your feet!'? Can't you feel it?" Becker made a little hand gesture like an Italian religious-painting character gesturing to heaven. "It's like a little shaft of freedom. Mix that with nine quarts of beer and you won't be a civilian again, but you'll forget a great deal about being in the army."

I poured out a glass of beer and started to work. The jukebox was squawking "I Don't Want to Play House."

"That's why I hate the South," I said. "Fucking maudlin music."

"You should love it. You're maudlin half the time yourself. Three quarters of the time."

"I'm in the army."

"Drink some more beer. Why do you always overlook the ancient remedies? Do you think we're above them?"

"We should be. Jesus, Becker, look at us. We've been to college. Good colleges, not those weird upstate and downstate places. How could we lose this much control over our lives?"

"Maybe you hadn't noticed. There's a war on. Granted, it's a silly war, but the people who run it, they're just as serious as if it were a major production number."

"Well, what the fuck happened to you? How did you get hauled in?"

"Hey. Mellow out. A man doesn't like to talk about his personal acts of patriotism."

"No, I really want to know. If I have to spend a few hours in this hole, let's trade our war stories. How did they get you?"

Becker narrowed his eyes across the table at me. "I'm warning you," he said. "It's squalid."

Becker took a long pull from his beer. "Boy, you really are a glutton for punishment. For my punishment, to boot. Okay. Here's the story. It was love. Love got me here."

"You joined the Foreign Legion to forget what's-her-name."

"Funny. No. I didn't join. You didn't join. I hope you didn't join. Did you join? Because if you joined, I don't even want to be in this disgusting bar with you. Who the fuck did join, anyway? There seem to be thousands and thousands of assholes on this post, and I still don't know a one of them who joined. They tell me there are people who joined. Whoo! Gives me the fuckin' creeps. But no, I did not exactly join. There's paperwork says I did. That's what really rankles my ass, that fucking paperwork. I mean, if I snuff it and some historian decides to make me famous, that clown will find my signature on some paperwork that says I volunteered for this. But it ain't so. It just ain't so."

"You were talking about love."

"Right. Okay, let's just slash this whole thing down to the core. What are you, twenty-two, twenty-three?"

"That's close enough."

"Right. Same deal. And you know what the black guys called me in basic? 'Old Man.' Unbelievable. Well, anyway, I was feeling young back there on the block doing something that resembled liberal arts college. That part of it's pretty much a fog, but I was keeping my grades up enough to keep my deferment. You remember those?"

"Yeah. I had one or two of those."

"That was when there were deferments. About three days after I was inducted, I was at the reception center at Bragg and some fuckhead came up to me with a newspaper and asked if I wanted to know what my draft lottery number would have been. I almost disemboweled the shmuck. Anyway, back to love. Do you happen to know what love is?"

I held out my hand flat over the table and rotated it back

and forth. "*Mezzo-mezzo.* I wouldn't want to go down on record with my ideas."

"No big deal. Okay, how I'm using love in this context is any bizarre and irrational behavior pattern that seems to involve a member of the opposite sex. For heteros. For gay people, make the necessary adjustment. Anyway, I'm not all hung up on that locker room John Wayne shit where I have to tell any fellow male that since I was nine, I've been having coitus twelve times a day. That's just not the way of the world and we all know it. I suppose guys would like to start banging their brains out when they're about fourteen or fifteen, but unless you're immediate family to a madam with privileges, June just doesn't start busting out all over on the year you get bar-mitzvahed. By the way, what happened in the year 13 A.D.?"

I pleaded ignorance.

"Jesus Christ was bar-mitzvahed. That's real old. I like you. Where'd you grow up?"

"Near Waterbury. Connecticut."

"Waterbury must have been off the joke route. You don't know any of these old ones. Okay. Well, was it different for you? Did you start popping your rocks at the age of twelve? Were you the neighborhood Lothario at fifteen? All the sex you could eat three times a day?"

"No. It seems to be important to male adolescent development to throw in four or five years between the time you could and when you finally do. It teaches patience or something."

"Yeah, right. It was worse for me. I didn't even get to go through most of the standard cock-teasing rituals. In high school, girls thought of me like the thing that pops up in the third reel of the horror movie. They used to call the cops when they saw me through binoculars."

"How do you account for this popularity?"

Becker sighed with nostalgic pain. "Ah, shit. Well, I was smart. Terrible grades, but I was smart, so dumb girls were terrified of me. They only trust sex with dumb guys. They think smart guys might be pulling something weird and unexpected on them down in the nether regions, maybe conducting a science-fair experiment or something. Who knows? And smart girls— well, they don't believe in sex just for laughs. You touch one of their tits and immediately they space out and start to wonder if you'd be a good provider, if you're going to med school, what your annual salary will be at age twenty-seven. So I couldn't get bare wrist off those honeys. I used to get a lot of smiles off them. They liked me, but at a real safe distance, everybody strictly chaperoned and clothed. When God made me the way I am, for sure He knew there was going to be a very lengthy horniness period.

"But He installed the drive. He gave me the glands and the juice. I was all dressed up glandularly; I just never had anyplace to go. I started having some misadventures, just enough to get me all steamed up and weird and to want more. Eventually I got authentically laid, but very crash-and-dash, highly irregular stuff. Regular requires some sort of relationship, and I didn't run into too many women who could take me on a regular basis. Or vice versa. I have this additional curse: I can't screw anything dumb more than once. After that first hot night of unspeakable passion and lust, they have this tendency to speak, and that's it. When they say those dumb-ass things, I can't deal with it anymore. Sometimes I can't even get stiff. It's a horror. I have to pretend to be dumb to even get a first try, and then she starts speaking that dumb stuff, and it's just a horror show. I don't come back. I can't deal with it."

"Have you sought professional help for this?"

"I don't want professional help for it. I hate dumb people. Not uneducated people. That has nothing to do with it. Education was just food that I ate 'cause I'm smart, and I know a lot of smart people, where they grew up, the food stores were all closed. They're still smart and I get along with them real enthusiastically. But I fucking-A hate dummies. Not the congenital ones who have an excuse, but the ones who have the equipment, but they just never turn their light bulbs on. You can see it in their eyes and their faces. I think they ought to be exterminated, personally. They blight up my landscape. They give me back incorrect change. They enlist in the fucking army. Some of 'em enlist in the fucking Marines, for Christ's sake, and of course the Marine Corps does its best to exterminate them, but it's not stated national policy and a lot of those jarheads are going to come back anyway. That's appalling."

"I had no idea this streak of bigotry ran so wide in you."

"There's nothing wrong with bigotry if you pick the right

target. Bigotry is healthy if you pick the right target. I have
nothing against Armenians or blacks. I just hate stupid people.
That's a class of people that even includes all bigots who aren't
exclusively bigoted against all stupid people. You follow that?"

"I think so. You were going to tell me about love, and that
was supposed to lead us to how you came to be an enlisted man
in this suck-ass Columbus bar."

"Well, I finally found her. A smart girl who put out. Who
put out for me. Regularly. And after monstrously great sex,
she'd open her mouth and smart things would come out. Not
terribly educated things—she was one of those diamonds in the
rough—but she was a smart little honey. And tough, tough as
nails, small and thin, long, willowly legs. The first time she
doffed her threads, I thought I was going to have a fatal aneur-
ism. She had small, really firm breasts. They drove me crazy.
I've really never understood the locker room fascination with
enormous gazongas. They're all right, I guess, but they give me
the creeps and it's certainly nothing I go out of my way for.
They're sort of Ripley's 'Believe It or Not' stuff, excessive. I
like small ones. Around her nipples, there were two rings. There's
a name for them. They're called areolae—"

"I know the region you're talking about," I said. "I have to
admit I never knew it had a name all its own. That must help
you a lot when you're crawling up and down a particular woman.
You'll always know just where you are and you can call from a
pay phone and tell someone where to come and get you. How
do you know things like that?"

"I don't know," Becker grunted. "I know all kinds of shit.
Sure did wonders for me, didn't it? I suppose when they finally
send me to Vietnam and I step on a claymore, my last thoughts
will be to identify every one of my parts as they go flying off:
There goes my ascending colon, there goes my appendix ver-
miformis, there goes my vas deferens . . . But anyway, she had
these areolae and they were rich, deep cocoa-brown and my
little eyes bugged out. I mean, I knew it wasn't hip to drool,
but I've never seen a woman constructed like that in 3-D and
color before or since."

"Did this vision have a name?"

"Oh, yeah. Nina. Well, I was in love. For the first time, at
least with somebody who seemed to be cooperating. It was dev-

astating. All I wanted to do was tear her clothes off and screw all day and all night and when we couldn't screw, the talking was grand. Tears used to come to my eyes sometimes when we were talking in the dark. Imagine, a thing like that next to me and it could talk, too. I didn't think they manufactured stuff like that in America."

Becker stopped talking. His eyes closed and he was breathing shallowly. I thought that he must be very close to the state mystics, psychic teleporters, achieve. There was no bar named Beer, no Columbus, no Fort Benning. I certainly wasn't there for him, except perhaps as an appointment he'd made and dimly remembered he had to keep eventually. His eyes were still closed when he spoke again.

"You know, this wasn't very long ago. No more than six or seven months ago." He shuddered a little and then his eyes opened.

"Welcome back," I said and poured him another beer.

"Thanks. Good to be back." He polished off half the glass. "I was still in school, rah rah. So maybe you think it was the old story, guy falls in with vamp, lets his grades go down the toilet, shazam, they pull his deferment and he gets the notice. I wish it were so simple. Actually, it was incredibly sloppy.

"I said that the talking was grand, and it was. I just don't remember what we talked about those first four or five days. Let me give you the picture. My father's health has been on the decline for the last couple of years, so his doctor started exiling him to Florida each winter. And my old lady goes with him. They have a little apartment on the beach north of Miami somewhere. But this was a very different year. My brother got married last summer and moved out and I was the baby of the family. So when the folks went down to Florida this time, they left me alone to guard the shack. Nice shack too. My folks have bucks. Big syntho-Tudor stone deal, big back yard, real ritzy neighborhood. I had the place all to myself all winter, with a car.

"About twelve seconds after they pulled out of the driveway I called up my buddies, and this party started. I figured it was going to last until about twelve seconds before my folks drove back up the driveway five months later. My buddies would show up every evening, some of them for dinner, the rest of them just to fuck around all night, smoke reefer, watch TeeVee. They'd bring over their regular squeezes or whatever they could manage to scare up and they'd drift on up to one of the bedrooms and do whatever it is you do in the dark under those circumstances. Downstairs we'd eat popcorn and beef jerky and make a mess, and most of them would drift off around two, three, four in the morning. Real high-tone perpetual party.

"So one night the crew drifted over and Nina walked in with them. I thought at first she was attached to Ronnie or Marvin or whatever. A little later that night we started talking, and then it got to be about about one, two, three in the morning and just about everybody else had gone home and she was still there. And we were still talking. So I asked her if she wanted a ride home and she said she was sort of having a little problem at home and wasn't officially residing in any particular place. So I said she could stay here. She said that sounded okay. So we drifted upstairs and the strangest thing leaped right out of my mouth. I mean, it was already in audible form before I even realized that I'd composed it or meant to say it."

"What did you say?"

"I think I'm positively going to swoon just thinking about it. I still to this day don't believe I said it. I asked her if she wanted to take a shower. Real matter-of-factly. I mean, the problem was clear. All she'd asked for, and all I'd offered, was a place to sleep. And we had two fully apportioned bedrooms besides mine, not to mention couches in the den and the living room. For that matter, we had two separate bathrooms, each one with its own shower. But she smiled and she said, 'Sure, that would be nice,' and a few extraordinarily long minutes later she and I were soaping one another up and I think that shower was one of my longer ones, maybe an hour, hour-and-a-half, I don't know. We were just washin' fools. Couldn't get enough of it. We decided to stop when the hot water started to run out, and we have a big-ass hot water heater. Whew!"

"You're still not in the army," I reminded him.

"Nope, not technically, but before I staggered out of that shower, I was Sam's meat. I just didn't know it yet. So, I said that I don't remember what she and I talked about for the next few days. I'll tell you what the first piece of conversation I do remember was. I asked her how old she was."

"Oh, God."

"You got it. For the past three or four days, I'd been banging the brains out of a fourteen-year-old honey. Have you ever wanted to unfuck somebody fifty or sixty times? I wanted to take her back to the shower and dirty her up, too. I knew that when the shit hit the fan, I wasn't going to get any brownie points for keeping her so immaculate and hygienic."

"What did you say to her?"

"What *could* I say, you asshole! What is there to say? You tell me! Tell me what I should have said."

" 'Go away'?"

"I didn't want her to go away. And there was this other problem."

"What?"

"I recalled something she'd said. She was a neighborhood honey. That's how she started hanging around with my buddies, those low-life shit-for-brains. She lived a few blocks away. And her old man knew my old man. I think they were at the country club together. You know how I felt? I felt the way that coyote feels when he's chasing the roadrunner and that hole opens up in the road and he looks down and he sees the river about three miles below him. Just before he starts to plummet. That's exactly how I felt immediately after she spoke the phrase 'Almost fifteen.' "

"Didn't any of your friends tell you?" I asked.

"Stupid question . . ."

"Sorry."

"So I didn't say anything to Nina. There just wasn't any use. I was fucked. Dead meat. The next day I saw Ronnie—she'd strolled in with him that first night—and I very tactfully asked him if he knew how old she was. He mumbled something like he guessed she was maybe fifteen or sixteen, he didn't know. He didn't have to know. He wasn't bopping her. They were just hanging out, going to the Hot Shoppes for a burger now and again. You can consent to a burger at any age in the District of Columbia.

"So you can imagine that the whole thing put me in a weird-ass frame of mind. And then one night she decided to put in an appearance at her own homestead. It was about three A.M. and she asked me to drive her over there. I pulled the Mustang up outside her house and she got out and shut the door and all these lights came on and this big old male parent came flying down the front steps and up to the car and he grabbed Nina by the arm and started to spit blood and hair all over the place in his pj's and his bathrobe. He was hot. He started to yell at me: 'Do you know what time it is?' I love it when they ask you that, like that's the most important thing that's happening, precision time reckoning. 'Do you know how old my daughter is?' That was a little more to the point. 'I know who you are! I know your father! I'm calling him up! I'm going to tell him what's going on!'

"Other lights started to come on up and down the street. I don't know if you get much of this shit in Waterbury, but nothing of this sort ever, ever happened in my neighborhood. This was strictly trailer-park stuff and history in the making. There's probably a plaque there now. I could see Mrs. Dad back up at the top of the stairs under the front-porch light looking out at the whole scene in curlers. Well, anyway, he got distracted hauling Nina back up toward the house by her arm and I cranked the 'Stang up and slinked out of Apple Blossom Court in reverse, 'cause it was a dead end. I got home and I developed a sincere, cold, clammy sweat."

"So that was the end?"

"Oh, no. Nina dropped on over the next night. She'd had it with home life. She'd had it with the neighborhood. She'd had it with D.C. And with junior high school, too. She wanted to go to Colorado. So, fine, I said. We threw some shit in the car and I locked up the house and we took off. Heading west."

"What about . . . ?"

"What about shit? Hey, nothing mattered. I had the girl of my dreams and my life was over anyway, and she wanted to go to Colorado, so why not? Listen, I know my epitaph. I've known for years what I want on my tombstone. You know what it is?"

"No. What?"

" 'It seemed like a good idea at the time.' That's the answer to all questions like that. It seemed like a good idea at the time. Besides, I love to drive across the country. I'm a showerin' fool and I'm a drivin' fool, so I drove my brains out during the day—there was a nonstop blizzard from western Pennsylvania onward—and when I couldn't handle it anymore, we found a motel and took another long shower, and motel water heaters never run out of hot water.

"Anyway, we were on the Indiana Turnpike somewhere near Valparaiso when I slid across the road and smashed the car into a bridge abutment. She no go no more. We were fine, just the car all messed up, one of those awesome, slow, lumbering half-mile skids where you see the end coming for ten minutes and there's not a goddam thing you can do about it. A few minutes later the whoop-whoop man showed up and started the ritual. Based on some preliminary observations and inquiries, he thought it made good sense to haul both of us back to the State Police barracks, where fate finally managed to separate us.

"I wasn't exactly under arrest. There was this sort of gentleman's agreement. If I agreed to stick around there and sleep in an unlocked cell while the detectives probed this ever-unfolding human panorama, they wouldn't actually arrest me yet, but that was clearly on the agenda. I was there for about two and a half days while the blizzard raged, mostly playing poker with a trusty. They'd whisked Nina away to a hospital with a team of juvenile matrons. And guess what they found there?"

"Oh, wow," I moaned. "There doesn't seem to be any bottom to this story."

"Soon, soon. We're going to bottom out soon, I promise. And you're right, she was pregnant. Nina and I'd been hanging out together for about three thrill-packed weeks. The detective strolled in one afternoon and told me she was about three months pregnant."

For a moment I thought the entire bar got quiet, not just Becker and I. Becker refilled his glass.

"Who was it?"

"Oh, I know who the guy was. Some neighborhood dummy. That's why her old man was so steamed. He'd been trying to keep her and this dummy apart with a crowbar for two years before I ever ran into her. It couldn't be done, but it had this aggregate effect on his blood pressure, which is why blue smoke was coming out of his ears the morning I cruised by. She never told me any of this. And I'd been good. I'd asked her about birth control that first night after the shower, a real concerned, sweet whisper while there was still time. And she'd said it was all taken care of. Turned out she was right."

"What happened then?"

"Well, the State Police detective, Detective Iverson, very kindly guy, very avuncular, soothing and thoughtful, he steered me into an interview room and laid it all out on the line. There was Nina's tender age. There was her delicate condition—I didn't even bother to try to explain the arithmetic to him, 'cause it was sort of beside the point where I was concerned. There was my car, which wasn't my car. It was my folks' car. Now if I wanted to straighten that out, Detective Iverson said he'd be glad to call them collect in Florida and chat. Oh, and there was the reefer in the car and a bottle of speed in Nina's purse. And a minor with beer . . . oh, it just went on and on.

"According to Detective Iverson, all this Sodom and Gomorrah stuff was still quite the novelty in the Valparaiso area and it was bound to raise eyebrows on the bench. Beyond that, every one of my activities had been vigorously pursued across—let's see—three state lines. The one from D.C. to Maryland doesn't count, by the way. But it only took the one from Maryland to Pennsylvania to make everything both an Indiana rap and a federal interstate commerce rap. Indiana had me by the short hairs, and when they got tired of tugging, the FBI was ready to come in and grab a handful.

"Uncle Jim—everybody in the barracks called Iverson that—paused at this moment to let me fathom my situation for myself. I fathomed it accurately. And when he spoke again, it was to introduce hope into the discussion where it had previously been wholly absent."

"Let me guess. He said you could always—"

"—go on down to see the recruiter and join up, right you are! Remember, I hadn't been arrested yet. My record was clean. Fucking Young American Golden Boy as far as the military was concerned. So Uncle Jim stepped out of the room to fetch us both a Coca-Cola and give me a little space to do some more fathoming. And I fathomed this new turn of events accurately, too. We drove from there in his unmarked brown sedan to Gary. It was late in the afternoon when we got to the federal building. The Air Force office and the Coast Guard and Navy offices were all locked. That left the Marines and the Army. Iverson strolled me down the hall to the Marines' door, but I did this vehement little dance and mime to indicate that

I wanted to try the Army door first. He smiled and said he didn't mind. And Lord have mercy! It was open! And there was a recruiting sergeant inside!"

"Did you ever find out if the Marines' door was open?" I asked.

"I have no idea to this day. Unimportant. Immaterial. Well, Iverson said he'd wait in the hall. Results were all he wanted; he didn't need to know details. When I came out he wanted to see some paperwork that said I was now an official, authentic soldier on my way to boot camp, and then and only then could I say goodbye to Uncle Jim, the State of Indiana, the FB of I, and all my recent misfortunes. He said he trusted my good judgment not to add desertion to my list.

"So I went in and talked to the sergeant. And I stumbled on a bargain of sorts. If the Air Force or Coast Guard or Navy door had been unlocked, I'd have certainly joined up. But they wanted a three-year burst. I didn't care what the jarheads were offering, even if it was ten days at Club Med. But the Army sergeant had this odd little deal. He didn't tell me about it straight off. The way he began, if I wanted to enlist, that would be a three-year minimum, too. But I asked him why the draftees only had to do two years. I pressed him on the point. It just didn't seem fair that a patriotic volunteer like me should get a shittier deal than those pinko queer hippies they had to go to all that trouble to track down and conscript.

"I must have asked the right questions, 'cause he started to get a little nervous. There are apparently limits to the lies and deceptions a recruiter can tell you, and I think he was worried that I was smarter than the average asshole and might turn around later and make trouble for him. So he dragged out his special, under-the-table Bargain Package. I could volunteer for the draft. Odd sort of phrase, but if I insisted—and he kept emphasizing that it had many significant drawbacks—I was like any other draftee and I'd only have to do two years active."

"The detective didn't care?" I wondered.

"Not in the slightest. Two years or three, imagine the paperwork and months of frustrating court appearances I'd be saving him. And he'd been through all this before. He knew just which floor the recruiting offices were on, just where to park, the whole bit. I wouldn't be surprised if he's named Recruiter of the Year sometime soon. So I signed. The sergeant scared up a notary from down the hall and administered the oath. I said goodbye to Iverson, and the sarge drove me to the AFEES station in Chicago. As you can see, I passed the physical."

"You think her old man would have pressed statutory rape charges against you?"

"Nah. The country club couldn't have coped with a scandal like that."

"Did you think about getting some heavy-duty lawyer and fighting the rest of the shit? It seems pretty piddling to me, even for Indiana."

"Do you have a family? Parents? A mother and dad? Or were you hatched?"

"I have folks," I said. "They wouldn't have been too thrilled, I guess, but they would have backed me up. You hang around in courtrooms for a few months looking contrite in a suit and tie, you pay some lawyers a shitload of money, pay another shitload to the court, pretend to be on probation for a year while you go back to college, say you're real sorry and you're home free. Youthful excess."

Becker mulled that over for a few minutes.

"I didn't know you spoke Sanskrit," he said.

"I don't. What did I say in Sanskrit?"

"I'm sorry. For a moment I thought you were speaking in some foreign tongue. You mean you'd just let the cop pick up the horn and tell your folks—collect—about your little tri-state crime, drugs and pre-pube sex spree? And they'd zip on up and hold your hand and see you through it all? Say what? Come again?"

"Something like that. We're not Ozzie and Harriet and David and Ricky exactly. We have disagreements, downright fights, I guess. But they've come through whenever I've been in a jam. It's a given."

"That's nice. That's just peachy," Becker said. "Let's just say I believe it and I don't believe it. I believe it because you say it, and I've always thought very highly of your integrity. I mean that. But then I don't know your folks and you don't know my folks and you know yours and I know mine. My folks would have been witnesses for the prosecution. It's always been like that. They've always made it crystal clear: Get out of line and they'd just as soon cut me dead. I suppose they would have written the checks and made an effort to get my corpse back, but only to flail the shit out of it. Nope. As I sat in that interview room debating a couple of years in the service during wartime versus Uncle Jim making that phone call to Florida, there was no contest. So here I am. I know the military loves families like mine. Where patriotism and conscription fall short of the quotas, families like mine have always spewed their bent and terrified little boys straight toward the recruiting office. I just didn't see any other way out."

Silence at our booth. The clattering of billiard balls, the tinkling of beer glasses, a woman's laughter in the far corner followed by a man's.

Suddenly Becker broke through his own trance, sat up straight and raised his hand to gesture for another pitcher.

"So," he said, "what's your sorry-ass tale of woe?"

3

"I don't know if you're going to find it all that interesting," I said. "I mean, look what you had—forbidden lust, car wrecks, crime . . ."

"Try your best. Don't sell yourself short."

But I wanted to tell him. I knew now that was really why I'd wormed his saga out of him in the first place. Oh, I wanted to hear his, and it had turned out to be a real pip, jam-packed as usual with Becker's curious footnotes on reproductive anatomy and the nuances of interstate commerce.

But mainly I wanted to tell *somebody* how I got here and how this had all happened to me, and I hadn't realized before how much I wanted to tell somebody. And it began to dawn on me what Becker's perverse attraction for this low-life dive was. There were no women to speak of in it, certainly no entertainment beyond the C&W jukebox, and barring a fire-bombing or an MP raid, our future was clear: From now until closing time we were going to be sitting in our corner booth staring at each other, consuming glass after glass of industrial suds and hacking away at the hours with conversation. There was even no guarantee we'd stay coherent, and no particular need to. It was elemental. Anything fancier would have been a distraction. Better liquor, edible food or a live jiggle show would have destroyed the spell.

"Did you know I'm a Quaker?" I asked him.

"Do tell? Odd crop of those we're raising this season, I'd say."

"Nothing heavy-duty. I mean, it's just how I was raised. You know they have a meeting on the post. I could go if I wanted."

"Yeah, well, it would give you something to do all those Friday nights and Saturdays while I'm praying to the God of the Hebrews. Well, of course that begs the question, doesn't it? You ain't no fucking medic, so you ain't no C.O. You planning to dabble a little in the indiscriminate taking of human life in this incarnation?"

"Are you?"

"Actually, no. You've mentioned how ordinarily, your average shmuckface G.I. Joe is a little short on control of his destiny during his stint, but that hasn't daunted me. Despite my predicament, I've decided to set personal goals for myself. No killing or maiming of little yellow people in pajamas, and no getting killed or maimed by them, either."

"And how do you intend to achieve those admirable goals? Particularly the latter. That doesn't seem to be quite so easy to arrange."

"I don't know, Richard. I really don't know. All I do know is that I have this attitude. I've been a miserable troop every day right up to now, nothing but complaints from every lifer I've ever crossed paths with, and I imagine that selfsame rotten attitude will see me through. How about you?"

"I don't know any more than you do. I know I'm going to Nam. I just know that. Everything that's happened to me is like a juggernaut. It's so much bigger than me and it keeps chasing me in just one obvious direction. I started out as a bona fide Quaker, I got drafted, I'm an infantryman—"

"You're what? You're a clerk, seal-beam. A Remington Raider. An Underwood Irregular. Clickity-click."

"My MOS is eleven-bravo," I said. "I took my light weapons advanced infantry training at Fort Lost-in-the-Wood, Missouri.

When I got here, the brigade was short on clerks. I told them I could read and they made me a clerk. It's only temporary. It vanishes the moment I go to Nam."

"Brigades are always short on clerks and no one knows how to read, let alone type. I don't think you got much to worry about."

"It's my dues for not taking a third year. God knows how you managed your dufus-ass loony MOS as a draftee."

"Connections in the Pentagon. Anyway, you were going to tell me what a nice boy like you is doing in a place like this. You can start off about being a Quaker again if you like. I find that pretty curious."

"It's how I was raised. I resent it."

"Right on!"

"I do. Look. Jew. Do Jews think they're the chosen people?"

"Heavy-duty theological discussion going down in this shit-kicker bar tonight. I don't happen to, no."

"Why not?"

" 'Cause *I* resent it. Well, there we are in the same boat of seething resentment."

"What do you resent about it?"

"Being personally picked by the Deity—although whatever for I've never been quite sure of—tends to make it difficult to mix with the common folk. Now look at me here in this setting. Just one happy-go-lucky draftee among thousands. Just like those World War II foxhole flicks, the squad marching down the road, O'Rourke, Swazinski, Eberhardt, Roosevelt T. Washington, and me, Becker, bringing up the rear. I'm happy as a pig in shit. I'm in my element."

"You're joking, but it's serious. I don't want to kill anyone. But I don't want some prepared reason, some automatic blanket to exempt me. I wasn't particularly dedicated. I went to Sunday school and meeting. I had no choice, or if I had a choice, I had no place better to go. And then one day I didn't want to keep going to college. No college, no deferment. So I started getting reclassification notices. And I went down to the board. First my folks asked me to see a lawyer who handles this kind of shit. Sort of a coach. Very hip guy. I love hip lawyers. Tweed sport jacket, leather patches, pipe. I pissed him off right away and he pissed me off right away. He yelled at me. 'This is serious!'

he said. I never know what to say when people like that tell me something's serious. So we didn't meet again and I went down to the board again."

"How did you find this panel of your friends and neighbors? Sympathetic?"

"They asked me those sister-rape questions."

"Beg pardon?"

"Oh, that's the conscientious objector's acid test, in case you happen to be some kind of a retard. What would I do if someone tried to rape my sister?"

"Do you have a sister?"

"I have four sisters. They range in age from seven to twenty-three."

"Okay, well, I'm sorry I missed your big moment. Let's replay it. You're sitting around in the living room eating some butterscotch pudding and a large bestial ethnic person motivated by a foreign power comes in and makes the phallic move on your favorite distaff sibling. So what do you do, you pacifist Quaker-face coward?"

"I walked out. I stood up and I muttered something—I thanked them. I thanked the members of my local board and I stood up and I walked out. I got my 1-A in the mail the next week."

"Okay, so you were too proud to tell them, but tell me. What would you do about that business with your sister? Jeez, they really know how to put a man of conscience on the hot seat with that little number, don't they?"

"That's just the point. I'd do what anybody would do. Which is to say, I don't know what I'd do. What kind of lunatic sits around in advance, planning what to do in case his sister's being raped? Maybe I'd shit in my drawers. Maybe I'd be outraged and bludgeon the guy into a pulp if I could. I just resented everything about the whole smarmy setup. You called me a pacifist. Well, I am. I happen to be a pacifist. A pacifist is what you call yourself. But a conscientious objector, that's a little badge the Selective Service System or the army deigns to bestow on you if you lick their ass the way they like it, which is counterclockwise, I think. You stand on one leg for a half hour and do some birdcalls, and then you give the right answer to what you'd do if foreign people aimed their units at your sister, and then you're government-approved grade-A special, exempt from dispensing death. You don't have to carry those distressing, nasty weapons. If you kiss the right ass at the right time, you don't even have to go into the army. You can be a civilian C.O. pulling bedpan detail with the Public Health Service at some V.A. hospital."

"And that's how you got drafted? You just let it happen?"

"No. I didn't know what to do. That's what I resent most of all, having to know all the sister-raping answers at twenty-two. I'm not exactly making a pitch for an extended childhood, but I don't fucking know all the cosmic truths at twenty-two; I was sort of hoping for a few dozen years of profound study and searching before I had all the answers, some time in the public library, a season in a lamasery, drive my car up Mount Washington and gaze into the sky. I resent being forced to be profound about life and death right now."

"Bang-bang, there's a war on," Becker said. "No time, no time. Move down, move down. Shit or get off the pot."

"Yeah, right. Well, so finally the real notice came. I had one month to figure it all out. So I drove off, too, into the western skies, to find somebody who had the cosmic truths. It was like having to find an emergency guru the way you have to find a plumber who'll come on a Sunday when your pipes burst. I looked up an old lady-friend of mine. She was doing heavy-duty resistance work in Tennessee. I'm not even sure what she was resisting. Capitalism. Imperialism. You name it, she and her husband were resisting it. They're Maoists, I think. That shit's all meat to me. But she and I used to be thick in school and I just needed to see her and talk to her. So I showed up at her office and her comrades unbolted and unlocked all these bolts and chains and we started to talk. I told her what was happening to me and I asked her what she thought I ought to do about it."

"And now you're here. Well, you sure went to the right radical for advice."

"We spent the afternoon in the laundromat. Nobody considers that revolutionaries need clean underwear. They do, and they wash their own clothes. So I outlined what I thought were my options. I could refuse and go to jail, or I could go to Canada, or I could show up."

"And you're here now. She chose what was behind door number three."

"No," I said. "But that's the one she recommended I chew on the hardest."

"And why, pray tell? Granted it beats going to federal prison. But Canada—it's beautiful up there, and they have their shit together. Just to give you one example, they haven't been engaged in the extermination of ideologically incorrect little yellow people in pajamas for the last seven years. That's always impressed the shit out of me. I can't begin to tell you how civilized I think that is."

"The lawyer told me not to go to Canada either. He told me not to do anything irrevocable. You know, like something that afterward you couldn't get into law school, I think he meant. I want to go to Canada. I want to go there when I want to go there. I want to become a Canadian citizen, maybe. When I feel like it, not when cops and MPs are chasing me all over the fucking continent. I like Canada, too. I have a hard time liking it the way I should when I'm being forced to like it so hard."

"Boy, you really demand a lot of breathing space, don't you?"

"All I can get. But Lucy said something finally. We were folding the towels. Listen to this, because I haven't been able to tell anybody. I listened to her and I came here and I haven't been able to tell anybody. She said if I got heroic and defied the draft and went to jail, it would have the same result as if I went to Canada or Sweden. One more upper-middle-class overeducated white boy wouldn't show up at the AFEES station, and they'd just fill his slot with the next black or Puerto Rican off the street. Because they do always fill that slot."

"Don't they ever. I've noticed."

"So I spent a couple of days there advocating the overthrow of our form of government by force, and then I drove up to Michigan. The night before my day to show up, I parked about a block from the entrance to the Detroit-Windsor tunnel and I just stood next to my car looking down at it. And somewhere between that irrevocable act that would mean I could never get an FHA mortgage, and thinking about my slot that would be filled tomorrow either with me or some swinging dick named Ortega, I couldn't go through the tunnel. So I hung an east and I drove back to Connecticut. I was a day late. I actually called the draft board from a Stuckey's to tell them. They told me there was no problem; fresh meat on the hoof doesn't spoil."

"Well, which was it?" Becker asked. "The lady or the tiger?"

"What do you mean?"

"What got to you? Ortega dying in your place or doing that irrevocable deed after which no man can ever become an orthodontist?"

"I don't know. Just life-scared, I guess. Mixed with a perverse desire to try to do something half-assed right. Don't you see? I wasn't fighting against the war. I wasn't fighting for my right not to kill or carry weapons. And I don't really feel a burning love for Ortega, who didn't have to show up after all, at least not that day. I guess he got hauled in the next day. But those are advanced courses in spirituality. I don't feel them yet so they don't set me afire yet. That's what I was so honked off about—my right just to be a spiritually lazy, sloppy, unformed, slothful guy this early on. And they took that right away."

"I'm impressed," Becker said. "A man of high principles. Fucked-up principles, but principles. So I dipped it several times into what was almost fifteen and you were fighting for your right to be your ordinary garden-variety screw-up, and here we both are. I think that's just swell. What an eye-opening evening this has been all around."

"Ah, fuck."

"Hey, don't go so wrapped up in yourself that you lose sight of the bigger picture."

"And what is that?"

Becker leaned over the table and cupped his hand over his mouth. "You and I may survive," he whispered, "or you and I may perish. But I think our side's going to lose this war."

He leaned back, lit up a smoke and blew a cloud at the rough wooden ceiling.

It was strange; he was right. I'd been terrified of the army for a year before I'd been drafted, and I'd been terrified of it for the eight months since—nearly two years of thinking constantly of nothing else—and I hadn't even considered that there was a war going on which would have to have an outcome eventually.

"We're going to lose?"

"It's nothing personal. I'm trying to be detached about it, and I have absolutely no inside information on the outcome. But I have twenty bucks down with R.J., my buddy at Harmony Church, and my money's riding on the little yellow guys."

Benning is an old post, but its history is a secret matter, a distraction, none of anybody's business. Mostly an army post's history is like the history of ocean waves: The waves that were are, remarkably like the waves that are and, if the ocean has anything to say about it, precisely like the waves that will be.

A post at war whittles time down to the strictly immediate. With the passage of less than a year, all is forgiven, and what can't be forgiven is just forgotten instead. The private or PFC is given only a year or less to act out his most memorable drunken mayhem and then he's sent on. The MPs or judge advocates who may remember his most heroic car crashes or most phenomenal collection of credit debts move on themselves within the year after that. Other drunken soldiers replace the PFC and begin their own track records of carnage. Other MPs are sent out to subdue these new miscreants and turn them over to new judge advocates who knew not Joseph. Third Army commanders and commanders of the Infantry Center, major generals and lieutenant generals, move on even more quickly; wars are short and they need combat commands, not stateside drill and ceremony centers.

So Benning's long history is obligatorily attended to, collected and preserved in some unnoticed and unknown office and simultaneously ignored and lost. Group photographs are painstakingly identified and mounted and then consigned to oblivion. The slot, not the man. Has a swinging dick been authorized to stand in that location? Yes? Then fill it with a swinging dick, and when that swinging dick gets transferred or dies of the annual summer meningitis outbreak or is rendered into red peanut butter in a jeep rollover, put some other swinging dick in that slot. A game: From lowest enlisted rank through highest commissioned rank, Becker would politely inquire if anyone chanced to know who the fuck Mister or Sergeant or General Benning was, to have had the post named after him. He'd made his way up to two lieutenant colonels and one full colonel with no joy by the time he left Benning.

That was the history of a wartime army camp. Time began the day you arrived there and all life as we know it ended when you heaved your duffel bag into the trunk of somebody's car for the ride to Columbus airport.

Or so Becker thought until he met History in the flesh, and a bad night that was for all. Becker hadn't been laid for an enormous amount of time and he'd stopped writing outgoing mail or opening the incoming for several months. He didn't contemptuously throw it away; he just narrowly eyed the letters the mail clerk handed him (once every two weeks the mystified clerk would make a special trip to give Becker his accumulated letters) and then put them into his locker unopened. There were no exceptions; no correspondent could pique him sufficiently to break the seal.

Becker in those months was as marginal a troop as any army had ever known; for much less in wages they could have had much the same results with a uniformed scarecrow on casters. But he showed up when ordered, never quite the last man there, and he produced something slightly beyond the worst output of his platoon; consequently these months went by with the army paying no heed whatsoever to him while the dork who arrived at formation just after Becker or produced a work volume slightly less than Becker's kept getting Article 15's appended to his file and spending an inordinate number of nights cleaning out the orderly room. Becker just barely managed to avoid most of that personalized harassment.

One night Becker pulled brigade staff driver duty. He showed up a few minutes past the proper time in his least funky uniform, got a nasty look from the staff duty NCO, and was given instructions to drive to the Columbus Holiday Inn to pick up some geezer named Mr. Herzog and take him to the Infantry Center. The staff car was some green American Motors piece of shit that moaned and whined every time it was asked to move forward and whose lock knobs came off in your fingers when you pulled up on one of them. Becker was actually enthused; he'd been given an army car to grind into the dust over the twenty mile stretch from brigade to Columbus and back, an unsupervised trek off-post on Sam's gas and tires.

Becker pulled into the semicircular entrance to the Holiday Inn just past sundown and walked into the lobby. Before he could announce himself at the desk, a short, fat, hairy, troll-looking civilian man with long black nose hairs and wearing a shiny, synthetic short-sleeved lime-green shirt walked up to him and put his hand on Becker's shoulder. A dog would have known from Becker's reaction to back off. "Hi," he said in an accent Becker pegged to be New Jersey. "I'm Larry Herzog. You're my ride?"

"Yes, sir," Becker said, and the two walked out to the car. Becker tried to open the rear door for him.

"Ah, I'll ride up front, if that's okay," he said. "I'm just a regular dogface myself."

Korea, maybe, Becker thought. No. Older. The Big Two. The crumbling remnants of Kilroy himself. Herzog immediately fired up a monstrous cigar. Suddenly Becker wasn't having fun anymore. There were twenty miles of potential hell to go, and there was a good chance the loathsome cigar was going to be the easy part. The passenger seemed disposed to strike up a conversation.

"What's your name, son?"

Oh, wow, he didn't really ask me that, did he? And he's blind. He can't read my fatigue name tag. Ah, fuck, I can't lie; I'm down on the log as duty driver.

"Becker, sir."

"Hey, don't call me sir. I was a tech sergeant. I came in to town late. I'm with the Newark-area Jewish War Veterans. My division's having a reunion dinner down at the Infantry Center tonight. The Rainbow Division. You Jewish? Becker?"

"Yes, sir. Sergeant."

"Hey, just call me Larry. Jesus, I haven't been here in— Christ, twenty-seven years. We trained here. At Harmony Church. Before we were shipped out to Europe."

"That must have been something."

"Yeah, it was. It must be something now. Everything must be really different. Lot of other Jewish kids here?"

Becker heard these noises in his head: Ding. Fizzle. Ka-jong.

"No, not really, Larry. Guess they've already been shipped overseas for the action."

There were about three quarters of a mile of silence while Herzog chewed this branch of the conversation around.

"No, really. Not a lot of Jewish kids in this one?"

"There are some college pricks training to be officers, sort of on the theory that if they have to be in on all this fucking, they'd rather be fuckers than fuckees. There's a psychopath named Levin who shows up at services in Green Beret threads. I stay pretty far away from him. I know another guy, he's a gravedigger. Honest to God. A Jewish gravedigger. That's about it, I think, for the whole Third Army. Maybe they got some more in the Second or First Army. But my theory is that most of the tribe seems to be sitting this one out."

Becker counted five one-tenth highway markers before more noise came out of Herzog's mouth.

"You don't sound too wild about this one yourself. What's your first name?"

"David."

"Well, look, David, I wasn't crazy about being in the army myself. But it was something we had to do. Yeah, and there were some *momzers* who weaseled out of it in World War Two, don't think there weren't. I knew a couple of 'em. But there are always *momzers* like that. And they were sorry afterward. They missed it. It was what America was doing, and they ducked it. It was sort of like a hole in their life they couldn't fill in afterward. I knew why I had to be there, so I went when I got my notice."

Becker decided to give it a rest this time.

Herzog couldn't stand it. "Look, let me tell you something. I was with a unit that liberated Bergen-Belsen. You know what that was?"

A milk bar? A Bavarian discotheque? A school for bowling pin spotters? "Concentration camp."

"You bet your ass. And let me tell you, David"—he started punctuating vividly with his forefinger—"as sick as I was to see what those goddam Nazis had done to my people, for the first time I was goddam proud to be an American soldier. I walked tall. There was nothing I'd rather have been right then and there. We kicked the shit out of those goddam Germans and we saved our own people. I was goddam proud to be an American soldier."

"So? What's the implication here?"

"Listen. You're a wise-ass. Okay. That's your right. I knew a lot of wise-asses in my company. You just have to suffer 'em. But the implication, son, is that you're in my army now, and if you can't be proud to be a soldier in my army, don't make fun of the people who were proud. Who still are proud. You understand?"

"Fuck your army. Fuck Bergen-Belsen. Fuck your Garand M-1 semiautomatic air-cooled rifle. Fuck you."

"Jesus! Don't give me that shit, son. I can still kick the shit out of you."

"Who the fuck are you—George Jessel? Let me get this straight. I have to like being in the fucking army or else I'm some kind of ingrate Communist fairy, is that the drift?"

"No. Maybe you're just an ignorant person."

"And what would happen if I wasn't ignorant? What would happen if I knew all about that Adolph Hitler shit? Listen, you superannuated dork, I got news for you. The days of G.I. Joe liberating Dachau and Bergen-Belsen in his green jeep are over. Now we're the guys that put the other funky minority groups in the concentration camps. That's G.I. Joe's job now. That's my MOS. You *versteh* MOS? Military Occupation Specialty. My Military Occupation Specialty is 94-KA, Dangler of Little Yellow People out the Doors of Huey Helicopters, and if they don't confess all their goddam Communist activities, I fucking-A let go of their little yellow feet eighteen hundred feet over Fong Plok, which coincidentally is the sound they make when they hit. That's what G.I. Joe does for Uncle Sam and the red, white and blue today. But I don't like doing it. I mean, at heart I'm just your standard freckle-faced American boy next door. Wanna see my Betty Grable pinups?"

"You're sick. There's something wrong with you."

"You said it. You're making me sick. Why don't you just go to your fucking Legion meeting and whip up some patriotic fervor?"

"Pull the fucking car over!"

Let's DO it! screamed the Full Moon into Becker's ear.

"Blow me," Becker said and kept on driving. Herzog's face was crimson.

Herzog made a determined grab at the wheel; they were doing 65 up U.S. 280. Becker rammed his right elbow into Herzog's brisket and Herzog abandoned the attempt to gain control. Herzog slid into the far corner and did some heavy-duty wheezing and gasping.

"Don't barf in the staff car," Becker said. "I have to clean it up before I go off duty."

"You're fucked. I'm going to get you court-martialed."

Becker put the accelerator to the floor and the machine lurched forward awfully. The needle slowly crept up. Somewhere between 88 and 92 it wouldn't go any farther. They passed the last exit to Fort Benning.

"Look. Okay. We had some kind of disagreement. Misunderstanding. Got off on a bad foot. You're a nice kid. I'm not going to tell anybody about this. Just take me to the dinner. We won't talk anymore."

"I want to talk. Hey—we're both dogfaces, right? Servin' our country when times get tough. Let's talk." The car had developed a sickening rhythmic whir just short of a repetitive grinding.

"Okay. You're touchy about being in the service. I can understand that. You say there aren't many other Jews. Look. In my barracks at boot camp, I was the only Jew. Crackers used to want to feel the top of my head for horns."

"I've heard that one before. Tell me a new story."

"Now look. Okay. I'm proud I did my time. You're not so crazy about it. Okay. So I learned something. Times have changed. Now slow the fucking car down."

"Take all your money out of your wallet and put it on the seat."

"Now stop it! Cut this shit out! Do you want to get into trouble? Do you want somebody to get hurt?"

Becker slammed on the brakes. The car started a fine, horrifying, long skid. Becker steered into it and managed to bring the car to a stop in the breakdown lane as prettily as if he'd decided to pull over to take a whiz. He turned the lights and the engine off and turned to Herzog, who had turned pasty white.

"Tell me more about Big Two," Becker grinned enthusiastically.

"Jesus. Look. Are you crazy, or what?"

"How many Germans did you kill? Personally?"

"Three."

"Tell me about it."

"I was a good shot. I shot one of them from behind a tree and the other two I was lying on the ground. One of them I shot in the head."

"Did you get shot?"

"No. I fell off a truck and broke my foot once. That was it."

"Souvenirs?"

"A bayonet and a Luger."

Becker lit a cigarette and looked out the windshield.

"I'm not feeling too good," Herzog said.

"I'm sorry to hear that," Becker said.

"Look, I'm sorry you don't like being in the army. I'd get you out if I could. I can't."

"You have sons?"

"One. I got one."

"How old?"

"Twenty."

"Let me guess. He's in college."

"Yeah. Look, that's the law."

"Does Snookums have a name?"

"Jeremy."

"Did you tell him to join up?"

"No. It's the law. He keeps up his grades, he's exempt."

"Nothing I love more than a scholar."

"Look, it's his life. And this isn't the same war."

"No shit, Daddyo."

"Are you going to take me to the reunion dinner?"

"Sure."

"I'm sorry if I pissed you off. I didn't mean to."

"No problem."

Becker swung the car back onto the highway and made a U-turn at the first gravel cutover. They drove onto the post in silence. After a long and pitch-dark forested stretch, they came to an intersection. Becker turned right and drove for another half mile until they pulled into a large grid of barracks; Becker stopped the car.

"This is Harmony Church," Herzog said with a little falsetto of surprise.

"Yeah. You can walk around if you want. I won't drive off and leave you."

Herzog looked at him and then opened the door. Enlisted men milled around the PX entrance. Some of them stared at him briefly. Becker could smell marijuana over the cigar smoke. Bottles of Annie Green Springs and Ripple, shattered and whole, lay at the curb. Others were being passed back and forth.

Becker got out of his side of the car. "You think I'm honked off," Becker said. "You should check out most of these guys. A lot of these guys do smack, they're so tickled to be in on this one. They're back from the Nam and they're all fucked up on smack and all kinds of weirdness."

"Jesus. That one's hair is longer than my son's."

"Fucking Harmony Church. No buses, nobody here has a car. No women. Fucking PX the size of a phone booth. Look there at the pay phones. Four fucking booths for three fucking battalions. Half these guys carry knives, stolen pistols at night. Two, maybe three stabbings and beatings a week in this goddam brigade. Real popular war, this is. Happy people. Beat the Hun."

Herzog got back in the car. Becker got in on his side, started it up and drove out of Harmony Church and down through the narrow, winding wilderness roads toward Main Post.

"Can I buy you a beer?" Herzog asked.

"No. I don't want to drink with you. I don't like you. Go get drunk with your buddies."

"Okay. I just thought I'd offer."

They came to the statue of the infantry lieutenant. Tempo-

rary stenciled signs on lamp posts pointed to the side of the
Infantry Center where reunion guests were supposed to enter.
Becker pulled up at the curb and Herzog got out.

"Look, I'm not going to get you in any trouble."

"Try it. I'll tell them you were drunk and wanted me to get
you a whore in Phenix City."

Herzog looked at him one last time and then walked to the
building entrance. Becker started the car and drove back to
brigade.

"Jesus, where the hell were you?" the staff duty NCO demanded to know.

"The guy begged me to show him Harmony Church. He's
an old World War Two vet. I'm just a sentimental fool."

5

Whether Becker could hang out in my office when he was off-duty depended on which lifers were in S-4. If Sergeant First Class Ordway was the most serious NCO in residence, Becker could spend as much time in the office as he liked. Ordway was a social drinker. Every day at lunch he'd go to the NCO Club, socially drink himself into a stupor and then come back to the office and sleep on the couch for the rest of the afternoon. He was within a few months of the end of his thirty years and profoundly didn't give a fuck. Of course lifers nearing retirement didn't give a fuck with a slightly different style from the way ordinary draftee short-timers manifested it; the lifers still had to imitate some semblance of uniform appearance and easy deference to authority. Ordway had it down to a science. When he wasn't sound asleep on the corner couch, he looked every bit the professional NCO. Lewes, the other S-4 clerk, and I kept a sharp watch for roaming sergeants major and lifer officers so we could wake Ordway up in time; it only took a nudge and a quarter second for him to sit bolt upright, grab a clipboard and appear to be studying it.

The CMFIC (Chief Mother-Fucker in Charge, Becker's lapidary abbreviation), Master Sergeant Crockett, was a different story. He'd apparently taken part in Pershing's punitive expedition to Mexico and had no intention of retiring for anything short of an authentic death certificate. While he and I got along well enough, alas, he did give several fucks. Whatever Upstairs wanted from his S-4 office, he saw to it that Upstairs got it, just so and on time. He was one of the few administrative lifers who had no notion of the usual Monday-through-Saturday-morning seven-to-four headquarters office hours. As far as he was concerned, a stateside headquarters office was no different from a line platoon in combat, with paperwork the enemy. He agreed to dismiss the office when and only when it was unconditionally victorious over the enemy.

One day I accidentally discovered this jug of relentless vinegar had a master's degree in public administration from the University of Rochester. I asked him why the hell he hadn't gone for a commission. He thought that was a very funny joke and laughed a great deal. He leaned over my desk and gestured toward Lieutenant Barnes's cubicle. "So I can be a goddam first lieutenant like him? Get laughed at and earn less to boot? I know you don't like being in the army, but you're in it, and your ignorance about it strikes me as dangerous sometimes."

At first Crockett had just been chilly and inhospitable to Becker, but one day Becker showed up and Crockett jumped to his feet and barked Becker out of the office and told him not to get caught hanging around again. Crockett was typically rude and nasty, but I'd never seen him explode before; nothing until Becker had ever rattled his cage. That night at dinner I asked Becker what that was all about; I'd been afraid to ask Crockett.

"I made a little mistake the other day," Becker said. "Stupid little mistake. The pig got all bent out of shape."

"What did you do?"

"Nothing. It was nothing."

"What happened?"

"Okay. Jesus. I was walking down the headquarters truck ramp to the basement to look for you, and he was coming out of the basement walking up the ramp toward me. Suddenly he stops, comes to attention and salutes me. He was serious. He wasn't joking. I didn't know what it was all about. I thought maybe I'd received a commission or the Congressional Medal of Honor in the mail and nobody'd told me yet. So I stopped, came to attention, saluted him back, told him to carry on, and I walked on again."

"Why did he salute you?"

"Well, that dawned on me as soon as I got to your office. It was five o'clock. They were lowering the flag in front of the headquarters building. My back was turned to it so I didn't see it, but he was facing it, so he came to attention and saluted it. That's what the book says you're supposed to do, and as you know, he tends to go by the book. Anyway, I thought he was saluting me. I felt honored."

"And you told him to carry on?"

"Yeah, yeah. I didn't want him to have to stand there honoring me all afternoon. You know me; I'm casual. So now he hates me."

After that, Becker slunk around the basement corridor and peered in cautiously to see what the complement of the office was before he ventured farther. One afternoon when it was just Lewes and me with Ordway snoring gently on the couch, he came in and did his little charade to ask after Crockett's whereabouts.

"Gone for the day," I said. "Meeting of S-4s on Main Post. Barnes is gone, too."

"Hiya, Lewes."

"Hello, Becker," Lewes said unenthusiastically and kept on typing. Lewes wasn't enthusiastic about much. I didn't blame him. He'd had it dicked with a slot in the Arkansas National Guard, a weekend warrior, but he'd fucked up and stopped going to meetings, so they drafted his ass for two years of active duty. A few weeks earlier, he'd received his orders for Vietnam, a place members of the Arkansas National Guard hardly ever saw; in fact he was likely to be the first. He registered real low on the Fort Benning Happy Scale.

Becker sat at Ordway's desk and made himself comfortable for the half hour or so before it would be time to get Ordway off the couch, send him home and lock up the office ourselves.

I kept working on some monthly brigade reports. A few minutes later, Lewes gave a loud whistle and Ordway sat bolt upright on the couch and lunged for his clipboard. A second after that, Lieutenant Sealy walked in, which made it something of a false alarm, Lieutenant Sealy being a trivial moron from upstairs, a ROTC infantry commission with a Ranger tab serving a head-quarters admin tour as he waited to fulfill his destiny, a tour in Vietnam as an infantry platoon leader.

"Afternoon, gentlemen," he said. "Look, I have a little invitation for anyone who's interested. The Main Post chapel's showing a movie tomorrow night and I have some tickets here for it, just for a little donation. We'd really like you all to come."

"Can you lock up?" Ordway asked me as if Sealy weren't even there. I nodded and Ordway took his cap and raincoat from the rack, threw me the keys and strolled out.

"What's the film?" I asked.

"It's a very good film. It stars Pat Boone. It's called *The Cross and the Switchblade*, and it's about a priest who ministers to young people in trouble, juvenile delinquents and gang members. It's very inspiring. The money goes to the post evangelical ministry."

"No thanks, sir," I said.

"How about you, Specialist Becker?"

"Jewish, sir."

"Well, that doesn't make any difference. It's a real inspiring film, about good people helping other people, showing them the way."

"I think I'll pass anyway, sir. I'm not too crazy about Pat Boone. I liked one of his earlier films, though. It was called *The Yellow Canary*. He comes home drunk one night and ends up sleeping with his sister. Something like that. It was hard to tell what really went on. I saw it on television with a lot of the hot parts sliced out and it was made a long time ago. I just remember everybody seemed real unhappy at the breakfast table the next morning. It was real downbeat."

"Well, this one won't be like that. I don't think he makes films like that anymore."

"That's a shame. No, I think I'll pass, sir."

"Mr. Lewes?"

"Uhh . . . no thanks, but good luck with the mission."

"Okay, men, but I think you're missing out on a good thing. Let me know if you change your mind." He went off to haunt the other offices in the basement.

Becker played with the platen of Ordway's 1952 Smith-Corona. "When did he say the movie was?"

"Tomorrow night, I think. It's probably listed in the— Why the fuck do you care?"

"Oh, I don't care. Just curious."

"Boy, that guy gives me the creeps," Lewes said. "He's always hitting me up for his Jesus jive. He's a real primitive. Nothin' goin' on between his ears. He tried to drag me down to a tent meeting in Columbus last month. Worked on me for days."

"Did you go?" Becker asked.

"Fuck, no. I'd rather barf all night. I had to go to those things when I was a kid. They're weird. People roll around on the dirt and speak in tongues and then people come up with canes and walkers and get healed, everybody screamin' their ass off. 'Hallelujah! Hallelujah!' Weird, just weird."

"Strange sort of hobby for a Ranger," I said.

"Oh, you should talk to him," Lewes said. "He doesn't have anything against the V.C., except that they're godless. So he has an obligation to struggle against them, which is what Jesus wants us all to do. He really is a turn-the-other-cheeker, but he's willin' to do his part as a champion of Christianity, and that's the mission of the Christian nations today, to stop godless Communism. He's a real wormy guy. I mean, I can't imagine how the hell he got through Ranger trainin', but I guess Jesus got him all psyched up for it. That's Jesus' personal warrior sellin' Pat Boone tickets there."

I blew the whistle and the factory stopped. Lewes and I put the office in order and I locked up, which meant I'd have to beat Ordway to the office in the morning or he'd be locked out without his keys. Beating Ordway to the office wasn't too difficult. Becker and I strolled across the street to change and get some chow.

"What are you doing tomorrow night?" Becker asked.

"Huh? I don't know. Until you get your motorcycle fixed, whatever I'm doing, I'm probably doing it here like always."

"Motorcycle's fixed. The Triumph strike must have ended. The parts came in. They bored out the barrels, too. Every time

I let it sit outside and rust to death for six months, they have to bore out the barrels to get it working again, so the cylinders keep getting bigger, so the motorcycle keeps getting faster and faster. I guess that'll keep up until they finally come to the wall of the engine block, but I'm in business again."

"Well, what was your idea for tomorrow night?" I asked.

"Well, it's sort of confidential, but I need a hand."

"A hand doing what?"

"Don't give me a fucking hard time," Becker said. "I don't want to talk about it now. It's not illegal and it's not dangerous. I just need your help for a few hours tomorrow night. Can you do that much for me?"

"No. Yes. Maybe. I don't know. Okay. Am I going to like it?"

"I can't promise you that. It's more along the lines of innocuous and boring. It's just a favor. I'll owe you a favor in return. I'll be deeply grateful," Becker said. "Until then, I don't want to talk about it."

"Jesus, you are so strange."

That night we went for a cruise on the resurrected motorcycle. Becker was fairly new to motorcycles. He didn't yet understand that you have to care for and feed them much more intensively than you do cars, particularly the Triumph he'd fallen in love with. He'd never bothered to buy a rain tarp for the bike, and sometimes when something minor put it on the fritz, he'd leave it standing in the parking lot in one spot for a month or two and when he finally fixed the minor problem, he'd expect the thing to start right up again and zip him around, and he'd be devastated when it failed to respond. Then he'd have to blow between two and three hundred on a new respiratory system at the local Triumph garage. He was learning, but very slowly.

The shop in Columbus, though, had done themselves proud. The machine kicked over immediately, I climbed on the back and we meandered through the back roads of the post in a full autumn moon until we hit a highway running east, a direction I'd never headed away from the post in. I thought he was going nowhere in particular at his terrifying speeds (a faded decal on the front forks claimed the machine to be the world's fastest production bike), but after about twenty miles through bare fields, he pulled the machine off to the side of the two-lane state road, shut off the engine and walked up to a low and long stone fence.

"I wanted to show you something," he said. "I found it by accident the last time the bike worked. I was just tooling around one Sunday. Look."

He was gesturing over the fence to a huge, rolling meadow. The meadow was spotted with small and spare white crosses, grave markers that gleamed in the moonlight over the rolling land as far as I could see, perhaps ten thousand of them, perhaps more.

"We can't go in at night," Becker said as he stared off in the same direction, "but you can get the picture from here."

"What is it?"

"It's a national cemetery, a military cemetery like Arlington. But it's special. Most of those graves are prisoners who died in the Andersonville prison. That was right here. It's over at that end of the cemetery, what's left of it."

"Andersonville? The Confederate prison?"

"Yeah, the very same. Andersonville is the town we just passed through. You should come here in the daytime and see it. There are no buildings left, just the foundations. And the tunnels. That's the strange part. There are dozens and dozens of little hand-dug tunnels, very ambitious ones running straight down for thirty, forty feet and out all past the foundations of the prison buildings. But they weren't really tunnels. They were wells. The prisoners were digging for water. They weren't given much food, so a lot of them starved to death. And they weren't given much water. For months at a time, most of them had to try to dig for it."

But we weren't here to look at the prison. Becker just stood. I guess we stood there for a half hour, looking out at the thousands of perfectly arranged crosses, rolling off like identical flower petals on the surface of a rolling ocean.

It wasn't all that late when we turned and left again, and Becker drove a little farther into Americus and parked outside a diner. We ordered coffee and some pieces of pecan pie. Whenever I'm in Georgia, I wouldn't think of missing the pecan pie.

"Comfortable?" Becker asked. "Enjoying your food? Relaxed?"

"I guess so."

"Then I have a surprise for you. We could get thrown in jail at any moment."

"What for?"

"The entire town of Americus is off-limits to Fort Benning personnel."

"Do tell?"

"Yeah. R.J. told me. He's from around here. Apparently a couple of years ago a whole infantry company got paid and descended on Americus and gang-raped everyone they could find with an orifice. Town's still a little steamed off about it. Until it happened, they'd been under the impression that the American forces considered them friendly civilians."

"Why did you want to go to that place tonight?"

"Just to blow the dirt out of the carburetor. And because I'm too frivolous," Becker said. "I've gotten in a bad habit of living for the instant. It's 10:17 P.M., I'll snarf up some pecan pie. It's midnight, I'll go to sleep. I'm horny, I'll try to get laid. So I wanted to look at something in the moonlight that lasts longer than an instant."

"A graveyard?"

"Numbers. I wanted to see the numbers again."

"Do you know how many there are?"

"No. When I went there the first time, I was so blown away by it that I was careful not to read any plaques that might give the numbers. That would have fixed it in a category with the number of Princess phones in Atlanta or the number of miles in the interstate highway system. All I know is that when you stand where we were, you can't see the end of the dead people straight ahead or to the right or the left.

"I think what got to me was that I ran into something like that by accident," Becker went on. "I never even knew it existed before I decided to roar down that Georgia back road. There are distractions at Arlington, buildings, amphitheaters, Kennedy's shrine, roads with traffic running through the place. No distractions here. Nothing breaks your concentration. Dead guy after dead guy after dead guy. They're not all Union prisoners. Half of them are Confederate soldiers who died trying to defend against Sherman's march to the sea. I like Sherman. Not because he fucked the South, but because he was one of the first who really understood war. He wasn't one of those bullshit gentlemen officers. He was a thug. He knew how to shorten wars. Burn all the food, starve out civilians and soldiers alike, destroy all the transportation and communications networks, make it impossible for any organized human activity to continue. When that happens to one side sooner than it happens to the other, the war ends. Mathematically. Everybody's either dead or surrenders."

"That's what Nixon and Johnson are doing to the North Vietnamese with the bombings."

"No. They're actually practicing restraint every once in a while. They're hoping their gentlemanly restraint will impress General Giap, who'll realize what swell guys we are and decide to come to terms. We stop the bombings and then we start the bombings again. That's why the war will last forever, and we're going to fill up some more endless national cemeteries again. Not like Sherman. Once he started his march, he never contacted Lincoln again. He was afraid his orders might be changed or modified. He destroyed everything in a swath fifty miles wide until he came to the Atlantic Ocean. He would have destroyed that, too, but he didn't know how."

"You know, there's a perverse apocalyptic streak in you sometimes, Becker. You don't seem to care which side wins—you have twenty bucks on the other side—but you just want them all to hustle toward some final mass carnage. Why is that?"

"Because I want the people who started the war to have to confront their war quickly. I want their own children to come back in body bags, not the children of disenfranchised strangers. I have another literate quote. Would you like to hear it?"

"Sure. Always glad for one of your quotes to class up my otherwise lackluster and pedestrian landscape."

" 'In peace, children bury their parents. War changes it around so the parents bury their children.' Something like that. It's either Thucydides or Herodotus. Maybe Pinky Lee, I don't know, but it's appropriate. Can you imagine what will happen when I win my twenty dollars and so many swinging dicks like you and me—maybe including you and me—are dead? Can you imagine what people will think? Can you imagine how our national leaders will explain away something like that?"

"They'll blame it on us," I said.

"They're going to single us out? I had no idea my weather balloons were that important."

"No. On this generation. They'll say the soldiers, the draftees, were all hippies and smoked dope and jerked off and sabotaged everything. It's obvious what they'll say about the ones who went to Canada or protested in the streets."

"Well, I guess we both have to resolve to be better soldiers starting tomorrow. I won't have our national leaders saying those vile things about me."

"Don't bother. I do my job. You loft your fucking weather balloons. We both do what's asked, no different from the guys in World War Two. Fuck, they shot an American in World War Two for desertion. He wouldn't go back to the line even after they told him they were going to shoot him if he didn't. One of your early prototype hippies, I guess. We're just like they were and the army gets the same results from us it got from them. But if we lose, if you win your stupid bet, they'll say it was us no matter what we do. You want to volunteer for the Airborne? Go Ranger, Special Forces, run around nude with a knife in your teeth behind enemy lines? It don't make no never-mind. If we lose, we're fucked. First war this country will ever have lost, so who do you think they'll blame it on?"

"I was under the impression there were generals involved calling the strategic shots."

"They'll be the first to blame it on us. Their careers are over. They know that. History will write them off as inept lame-brains. So they'll start making excuses. They'll say they had the right plans, but we let them down."

"Pretty bleak," Becker sighed. "That doesn't bode pleasantly at all for my future as a veteran."

"We have no future as veterans. The only future we have is now, trapped between now and when we get out or when we die over there. After that, we have no future. We'll be zombies. We'll be people who were supposed to have died. The living people who agreed to send us to the war won't want us around. The same thing happened to German soldiers after both the world wars. The lucky ones died. The same thing happens to every soldier who comes home from a losing war. That's the only rule for a soldier, even for temps like us: Win or die."

"Zombies. The undead. That's it? That's my declining years?"

"It is if you win that bet," I said.

"What do zombies do? They must have to do something to kill time."

"They dance in the night. They climb out of their graves and leap about and shriek and sing and try to couple with one another. They imitate the merry-making of the living. Don't you remember that song?

"Zombie Jamboree took place in Long Island cemetery
Zombie Jamboree took place in the New York cemetery . . .
Because the season was carnival
They got together in bacchanal
Back to back, belly to belly
Well, I don't give a damn, 'cause I done dead already
Back to back, belly to belly, at the Zombie Jamboree"

"That's it?" Becker asked. "We get discharged and then we party and fuck until we're dead?"

"No. You're already dead. You're done dead already. You pretend to party and you pretend to fuck, and then fifty years later you pretend to die, and then the people who pretend to have cared about you pretend to bury you. You can have a squad from the American Legion there if you want, maybe a guy playing taps. 'Cause nominally you're a war hero, right? You still betting on the little yellow pajama people?"

"I can't change my bet just because things'll go sour for me if I win. I don't bet on sentimental favorites. There's no percentage in it."

"Okay. Well, see you at the jamboree."

6

The next night after chow I was in my bunk writing a letter home when Becker appeared. "Hi," he said. "You ready to go?"

"Oh, I remember now. The mysterious favor. Do you tell me now?"

"Look, it's something that would help me out with my love life. I am allowed to have aspirations at a love life, aren't I? Well, it's wartime and the circumstances are a little strained. I ain't Hugh Hefner in a goddam smoking jacket at the door to the Playboy Mansion. I live in this Zoo where girl friends aren't allowed, and even if they were, one's style gets a little cramped with fifty other guys coming in and out all night climbing on top of you to get to the upper bunks and stuff. I don't even have an automobile with a back seat. You get the picture?"

"Not even dimly. At least I still don't see what I'm supposed to provide."

"Just come with me and I'll let you in on it when you need to know. You can bring that stuff with you. You'll have plenty of time to write home to Sister Susie."

Adventure time again with Uncle Becker, and why not? That was his trump card. Stripped of money and transportation and exiled to a wooded mountaintop a dozen miles from the nearest activity, and pretty barren activity it was at that, an enlisted man on Kelly Hill would accept an offer to watch turtles cross the highway. (The stories other guys told me about even more isolated posts like Fort Leonard Wood or Fort Polk or Fort Sill, the notion that I ought to be grateful for being on Kelly Hill, filled me with absolute horror.)

Becker headed the motorcycle in the direction of Main Post, past the post hospital. Where ordinarily we'd have kept straight as we approached Main Post, he leaned the bike to the right fork (I barely tolerated riding on the back and always instinctively fought the proper leaning motions, which drove Becker crazy and threatened to wipe us out) toward the Officers Club and post residential housing, unknown lands with strange natives and savage customs. Past the post gift shop where officers' wives bought engraved silver calling-card trays and regulation lace tablecloths for their mandated social functions, Becker turned into an entrance to the NCO family housing area. To the left was a large wooded area sloping down into a small valley with a remarkable billboard facing the street:

THIRD US ARMY
UNITED STATES ARMY INFANTRY CENTER
FORT BENNING GEORGIA
UNDEVELOPED FOREST RECREATION AREA
TREE HOUSES MAY BE BUILT IN THIS AREA

BY ORDER OF THE COMMANDER
US ARMY INFANTRY CENTER
FORT BENNING GEORGIA

It was the first time I'd ever been in the base housing area. I felt like a field slave who found himself inside the master's house for the first time; under any circumstances I could imagine, there was simply no reason for us to be here. We cruised slowly through this massive Bulgarian-style Levittown, through its grid of intersections with graph-paper addresses like L and 22 Streets, R and 51 Streets, CC and 45 Streets. At the street edge of each detached house was a little wooden painted sign announcing the military head of its household: SSG Dacon, J; 1SG Dwire, F; SGT Batista, L. The multiple housings had lower ranks and multiple listings:

CPL TARQUINO, S

SP6 FITZSIMMONS, M

SP5 HATCH, R

It was just toward the end of dinnertime and we drove through an ambush of smells, a representative menu from each of the hundreds of kitchens we passed floating out into the middle of the street to catch us: Barbecue and collard or turnip greens, pasta and tomato sauce, Chinese food, birthday cake, Irish stew, hot dogs, hamburgers, tapioca pudding. The children who'd just eaten each of these things mixed in the streets roller-skating, riding their bikes, falling down and crying, playing baseball with tennis and Whiffle balls. All the men you could see outside were wearing boots, fatigue pants and white undershirts, or regulation shoes, khaki pants and white undershirts, both ensembles featuring the blue Boy Scout web belt and brass buckle. Some of them were hosing their cars down while others sat in webbed lawn chairs and drank beer.

We crossed a wide thoroughfare with an actual name and found ourselves in officer housing, a neighborhood we had even less business in. Becker turned left, right, right, left again, slowing down and stopping every once in a while as if he were on unfamiliar turf, too, and needed to get his bearings. The housing density was slightly less here, the upkeep on the houses better and the cars newer and more ambitious. Where the wooden signs had been red in NCO and enlisted housing, now they were blue: CPT Packard, A; 1LT Kemmelman, G; WO3 Temple, P; 2LT Zlesewski, W. Pairs, trios or quartets of teenagers strolled down the streets, some of them smoking and looking around to make sure it was safe. Finally Becker parked the bike and we got off.

"We walk from here," he said.

"How far?"

"Couple of blocks. Bring your helmet."

Dogs barked as we passed and sleepy cats watched us with a

single eye raised narrowly as we passed the sidewalks in front of them. Finally Becker turned into a detached house. Its blue sign said 2LT Sealy, D. I stopped very short.

"What's going on here?"

"I'm paying a social call," Becker said.

"On whom?"

"You'll figure it out."

"I don't think I want to figure it out."

"I'm going in. Just come in with me for a minute. If you can't deal with it after a few minutes, make your excuses."

"And go where?"

"Well, it doesn't matter. If you don't stay, I can't stay either."

He was at the front door and he knocked on it. A few seconds later it opened, and a small woman about twenty with dark brown hair, somewhat of the corn-fed variety, came to the door. Her face lit up when she saw Becker.

"Hi," she said. "Come on in."

"Hi," Becker said. "This is my friend Richard. This is Corrine."

"Uh, hello," I said.

We were guided over to the living room sofa. She pointed to a three-year old boy in pajamas who was on his belly in front of the television watching something with cowboys and horses. "That's Donald Junior, and Andrea, she's fourteen months, is in bed in the back. Let me just go and check on her again. I was doing the dishes."

"What the fuck is this all about?" I hissed.

"I like her. I met her up at the Kelly Hill bowling alley a couple of weeks ago. She works at the craft center next door. You know, showing the troops how to make their own wallets and ashtrays."

"What were you doing there?"

"I broke the last clay bowl on my Moroccan hash pipe and I was trying to fabricate some new ones. She showed me how. Of course I didn't come right out and tell her what it was I was making. I told her it was chimney tiles for my little sister's dollhouse. I used the infamous red Georgia clay. The new ones look better than the old ones and they're sturdier."

"And what are we doing here? Never mind *we*. What am I doing here?"

"Well, I saw her at the craft shop today and she invited me over. I wanted to talk with her some. We sort of need a babysitter for an hour or two."

"Unbelievable. How long do Pat Boone movies last?"

"No problem. There's a fellowship meeting afterward. He won't cruise back until after eleven."

"Won't his neighbors look a little askance that two grunts are keeping company with his wife while he's off doing the Lord's work?"

"You know very little about family housing. We could be bringing circus animals through the front door and the neighbors would redouble their efforts not to notice. Half of them are passed out on the floor drunk already and the other half are with the wrong partners to begin with. Some of 'em are family men; they're trying to put the make on their stepdaughters."

"I want to tell you I don't like this setup *at all*."

"Logged and noted. Just give it a little time. I told you, I'll owe you a big favor."

Corrine came back and sat down in an easy chair. So far I'd noticed six or seven manufacturer's tags on various furniture items, ranging from Montgomery Ward to Penney's to Sears. Credit stores ate newly commissioned officers up with a spoon; they had a guarantee where to find them for the next four years, they knew just what they'd be earning, and they could petition the army to put an automatic monthly tap on their paychecks if the boys got behind on the payments. On OCS graduation day, a second lieutenant could furnish every room in San Simeon with the credit he suddenly found himself extended.

There was one item on a display cabinet against the wall that seemed a little out of place. "That's the *Britannica*, isn't it?" I asked.

"Yeah. We just got it," she said.

"How much do those things go for?"

"Well, we're paying it off in installments. Donald bought it. There was a booth selling it at the main PX, and Donald thought it would be a good idea to have for the kids."

"Can he read yet? I mean Junior?" I asked.

"Oh, no, but he likes the pictures. It has everything in it. It's already come in real handy a couple of times. Donald's reading about Vietnam and Communism in it. And there's a lot of stuff about the Bible and the Holy Land in it. And every year they'll send us a new volume with all the stuff that's changed in the world since we bought it."

"A guy sells 'em down at the main PX?"

"Yeah. He's got a booth at the front entrance. He does quite a business. You know, everybody who has kids is so concerned with giving them a good education."

"We had the *World Book*," Becker announced. "Truman was the last president in our set, but of course there was a big article about Eisenhower in it. He was the president of Columbia University then. Boy, that sucker had everything. Whenever I was bored in the den, I used to just take a volume down and hose it all in. By the time I left home, I must have snarfed up every word."

"Is that where you learned about areolae?" I asked.

"About what?" Corrine asked. Becker looked up at the ceiling.

"Areolae. They're the pigmented rings around the nipples," I explained.

"Oh," said Corrine. Thanks to Becker, we now knew more about her equipment than the owner did.

"I don't think that was in the *World Book*," Becker said. "The details of all those private organs were only vaguely outlined, like on Barbie and Ken dolls. Lumpy suggestions, mostly. Can I help you finish the dishes?"

"Sure, if you like." She turned to me. "Can I get you anything? Some coffee?"

"No, thanks."

"Just watch Donald Junior if you don't mind. Make sure he doesn't get into anything."

"Fine."

The happy couple drifted off to the kitchen out of sight. I heard water turn on and off and a few dishes rattle. After a few minutes it stayed mostly off. I heard talking and giggling. After a few minutes, that stayed mostly off, too. Junior paid no attention to me; his chin was in his hands and his eyes were on the television set. I walked over to the *Britannica* and took down a volume and started reading about camels. Things got quieter in the kitchen area. I walked toward it cautiously. By the time

I could peer into it, there was nobody in it anymore. There were still some dirty dishes in the sink.

I took a plastic tumbler with Goofy in bas-relief on it and poured some Coke into it from an opened bottle in the refrigerator and went back to the living room. Under *chrysalis*, the *Britannica* said to see *insects*, so I took down the volume that had insects in it. The color plates were magnificent photographs. From the back of the house I could hear a little indistinct dialogue going on. The rhythm had a familiar ring to it. Finally I realized what was familiar about it. It sounded like a scene from an 1890s melodrama between Nell and the landlord with the stovepipe hat alone in the cabin. A little closer to my own experience, it sounded like one of those dialogues I used to have with a girl friend during high school late on Saturday nights on the rec room couch in the basement after her parents had gone to bed.

Donald Junior finally got tired of the television and noticed me. He stood up and toddled up to me in his Dr. Dentons, eyeing me carefully. I held open the insect color plate for him to look at.

"Those are bugs," he said. "Ick."

"Some of them are pretty. Look at the butterflies."

He pointed at the book. "Is that yours?" I remembered this part from my younger sisters. Everything on earth had to be owned by somebody. Socialism is strictly an adult vice.

"No. It's yours."

He liked that news, but it confused him a little, probably because I was in momentary possession of something that was his without his express permission.

"I want it."

"How about if you just sit up here and look at it with me?"

Nothing doing. "Give it to me."

"Actually, it's not yours. It's your mommy's. When she comes back, you can ask her. My name," I said to change the subject, "is Alvin." I thought that up at the very last instant. I also remembered that children are little organic tape recorders, and if the shit got any deeper than this and he went into playback at the wrong time, I wanted to make sure his tape had nothing but misinformation on it.

"Alvin," he said.

"Alvin," I emphasized.

"Want to see the picture I made?"

"You bet. Sure thing."

He veered toward an overpowering Alhambra-style coffee table and pulled out a sheet of paper with Crayola renderings on it. It seemed to be one of those large generic protomammals that could stand for anything from a reindeer to an ox.

"Horse?"

"No, stupid. It's a cow."

"I'm sorry." I put my glasses on to indicate that it was my problem. "Yep, that sure is a cow. Very good-looking cow."

"I drew a car, too. Wanna see that?"

"Absolutely."

He went back to the coffee table and fetched another picture. This was a little clearer: the doors, hood, cab, trunk and two wheels, the antenna and smoke coming out the tailpipe. And a smiling man's head floating in the front seat. "That's my daddy. That's his car. He lets me drive it sometimes."

"Are you a good driver?"

He blushed. "Yeah. I drove it in the parking lot behind the school."

I heard a door open in the back of the house and Corrine and Becker came back into the living room and took their previous seats. "Junior's been showing me his drawings. They're pretty good."

Corrine looked a little out of breath. "Donald is a very good artist, aren't you?" He blushed again. "Was he any trouble?"

"No, none at all. Very nice guy. He thinks I'm stupid because I can't tell the difference between a horse and a cow."

"It is a little hard sometimes. He loves to use all the colors. He has this huge caddy of crayons. You should see his storybooks. He uses them for coloring books. He can write his name, can't you?" Another blush. Compliments and attention were turning him into a native American.

"I guess we ought to stroll now," Becker said. "I'll see you at the craft shop. Maybe we can have some lunch."

"Okay," she said. We all stood up. "It was nice meeting you," she said to me.

"Likewise. Take care of yourself. Goodnight." I was out the door and off into the dark. Becker lingered at the doorstep and spoke with her some more. Finally he came down the walk and joined me.

"Thanks for babysitting. I really appreciated it. Like I said, I owe you a big one."

"You don't owe me anything for that." We walked to the motorcycle without saying anything else.

Becker got on the motorcycle and kicked it over. He waited for me to climb on behind, but I didn't. I hadn't even put on my helmet.

"What's wrong?" he shouted.

"You go on," I shouted back. I attached the spare helmet to the back part of the seat with a bungee chord. "I'll get back on my own." Becker shut the engine off.

"What's wrong?" he asked again.

"Nothing. I'm just going to get back to the hill on my own, that's all. Don't worry about it."

"I'm worrying. Are you pissed off?"

"Yes. Yeah, I'm pissed off. That was a fuckhead thing to do."

"So? Have me destroyed."

"Well, that's just it. I don't mind you going off on your own to walk the tightrope over Niagara Falls, but I sort of resent it when you handcuff me to come along, too. You didn't tell me what this was all about. You just laid it on me like it was a favor, and of course I'll do you a favor, but I could have gotten fucked over this deal, too, and you didn't give me any warning."

"Hey, I was careful."

"You asshole. What if the projector had broken down? What happens if one of those neighbors who's supposed to be banging his stepdaughter wasn't? What if he was checking your—our —weird-ass act out? What if he's a friend of Sealy's?"

"Sealy has friends?"

"Probably not, but he has a community of self-interest, namely officers with wives who don't want their wives being fucked by enlisted scum. Don't you know anything about anything, Becker? Don't you have any common sense?"

His face turned sullen. "We didn't screw. She didn't want to. We just messed around a little."

"You're insane! That doesn't make any difference. This is an army post. All lifers carry guns. Sealy comes home from his Jesus meeting and finds you in the back room with his wife, he could have shot you, and they would have upgraded his marksmanship medal. That's if you were lucky. If he hadn't shot you—Jesus, I can't even imagine the shit they could have done to you for that. And that woman—I guess she's pleasant enough, but she's a moron. I thought you said you liked smart women."

"There are none. Not within a two-hundred-mile radius. The nearest smart woman is in Atlanta and she has an unlisted number. Corrine has a good soul. She's sweet. We talked. I got a kick out of her. She gets a kick out of me. We're both lonely. For Christ's sake, can you imagine what it's like married to that dipshit?"

"Sometimes you have no brains, Becker. I mean, last night we were talking about Civil War history and life and death and war and peace, and tonight you drag me over so you can try to stick your hand down some retard officer's retard wife's underwear for twenty minutes while I'm out babysitting her creepy rug rat in the living room. Sometimes you just don't have any brains."

"You're so pure and you're so well-behaved," Becker growled. "Jesus, the army's got you so shit-scared that you're not going to have any female companionship for the next two years unless you rent it in Phenix City. Okay. So I didn't do a tremendously bright thing. I lost my head. I was momentarily swept away. But at least I was trying to have some kind of a human life, someone nice to talk to. A woman to sit next to and smell. I'm tired of smelling men. They smell like men. Men men men men men. I'm sick of men. I sleep with fifty men. I shower with men. I work with men. Men tell me what to do all day. When I go out at night, I find myself with more men. When they go out at night, they find themselves with me, and they're probably just as disgusted as I am. I listen to men in the mess hall talking about trucks and guns and tanks and helicopters and NFL football. I listen to them talking about getting drunk and driving fast and getting laid. I wanted to listen to a woman's voice for a change. Even a stupid one—and I admit, Corrine's not terribly bright. If she was all that bright, she probably wouldn't have let me come over. But stop wailing on me. If it'll help, I'll admit I wasn't very bright about the whole thing. My dick got hard and my brain got soft. It's an old, sordid story. It's not like I came up with anything unique."

"I sort of thought it was unique. I was sitting there giving a false ID to a three-year-old. I told him my name was Alvin."

"Okay," Becker said. "I won't involve you in this anymore."

"Becker—the point is not to involve yourself in this anymore. You're going to get your ass in a sling."

"No promises. I got something going here. Granted it's a little on the berserk side, but it's something. I'll decide when to put it down. I'll make up my mind when to get sensible. Now you want a ride back or not?"

I stared at him. He was hard-core. If Darwin was even half right, he'd never live long enough to breed.

I took the spare helmet from the bike and put it on. "Just keep me out of it, that's all I ask," I said.

"Right. Well, she should have hired a regular sitter anyway."

7

I brood. Nothing I can do about it; I sulk and I brood. The night before, after we'd left Sealy's house, I'd felt like punching Becker. Instead I tried to reason with him. That may have had some beneficial effect on him, but it hadn't done a thing for me. He was already eating breakfast in the mess hall when I walked off the chow line with my tray, and I realized I was still enormously honked off at him. I wandered in the opposite direction and sat down with Lewes instead. At formation, I avoided Becker and managed to drift off to work without speaking with him.

When Lewes and I got to work, Crockett and Ordway were already there; they were off-post personnel and didn't have to stand formation like the barracks dwellers. We all grunted greetings at each other and I was about to pour myself a cup of coffee from the urn when Crockett told me to hold off.

"Major Jardine's inside with Lieutenant Barnes. I think they want to talk to you."

My stomach dropped out of my ass. "Oh, God, what did I do?"

"You did something good, Heiser. How's that for a change? Now go in and see the officers."

I knocked once on Barnes's door and heard him call me in. I walked to the desk, saluted and got it back. Going in to see the lieutenant was always a formal affair. Major Jardine, the brigade adjutant, a pudgy, owllike artillery officer, was sitting in a corner in an overstuffed square leatherette chair. In his office upstairs he had little framed homilies, quotations from Winston Churchill, Napoleon and other cannon freaks, about the absolute necessity of the field artillery. Barnes told me to take the other seat in the center of the room.

Beyond the standard and endless reports the S-4 office had to churn out, I'd managed to pick up a specialty in my work, the preparation of congressional responses. A congressional was the staff officer's nightmare. When a troop got ticked off about the way the army had been treating him—usually with ample reason, like the army's inexplicable failure to pay him for eight or nine months—he had four courses of action. The first, highly recommended by nine out of ten lifers, was to complain to his company officers, his first sergeant or company commander. This was the start of the infamous chain of command. (Portraits of the entire chain of command, from your lowly company captain all the way up through officers and civilians to the commander-in-chief, Richard Milhous Nixon, hung in the foyers of every army barracks and headquarters.) They listened patiently and promised to get back to him on it.

If that fizzled, and it generally did, the second method, for the ambitious, was to show up at an open-door hour the brigade or even the post commander held once a week and lay your troubles on this full colonel or general. If there was a smidgen of substance to your gripe, action usually ensued very swiftly and heads rolled. The drawback, of course, was that you had leapfrogged the chain of command and drawn shit down on your own inept company officers, who were still going to be your company officers for the next many moons and who knew many tricks to show their lingering displeasure.

The third route open was to contact the inspector general, a high-ranking, powerful officer who existed only to snoop around in the affairs of your unit and cause great grief and trouble. This route got even quicker action than the second if the I.G. found merit in your case, and had the same drawback after your initial problem was cured. First sergeants and officers had long memories about unpleasant encounters with the inspector general.

The last route was strictly for the desperate, hopeless, outraged, extraordinarily courageous or flat-out insane. Enlisted men were still technically considered American citizens, and most of them originally came from somewhere, which meant that most of them had a congressman they could call their own. From time to time, a daring trooper would pen his woes in a letter to his hometown elected representative to the Congress, and a congressman never failed to act on it with an inquiry back to the trooper's post commander. Nine out of ten brigade staff officers preferred to get live grenades in the mail. A congressional that, perish forbid, were to go unanswered or were to be botched could even threaten an entire segment of the army budget if the congressman felt so annoyed by the army response or lack of it that he held things up in committee until four-star generals came crawling to his office to beg his forgiveness. And whether your original grievance was well founded or groundless, no one involved ever forgot that you'd squealed to your congressman. At the first opportunity—and it may have been slow in coming, but come it always did—the squealer found himself transferred to a special winter combat unit in the Aleutian Islands. Or worse. And there was worse.

About a month after my temporary and fortunate elevation from light weapons infantryman to S-4 clerk, I'd stayed late in the office to type a letter when the brigade deputy commander, Lieutenant Colonel Pascelli, walked in with a worried look on his face and some paperwork in his hand.

"You're it?"

"Yes, sir."

"Okay. We have a little emergency here. Some fool at Main Post has been sitting on a congressional involving one of our men for more than a week. They were finally kind enough to drive it up here, with a little note tacked on that we better goddam get a first response on it telexed out of here by oh-nine-hundred tomorrow morning. Now I want you to start by trying to get Crockett and Barnes in here. But if you can't get them on the first try, leave a message and start making phone calls out to Harmony Church in my name. I want to see the troop involved, the company commander and first sergeant involved. I want them in here within two hours. When they show up, you'll come up to my office and take notes while I interview them. Can you handle that?"

"Yes, sir."

"I'll be upstairs. Let me know as soon as you make any progress. Son?"

"Yes, sir."

"If I haven't made it clear, this is hot. Only your best."

The telex went out at seven in the morning. With Crockett (Barnes had been off partying in Atlanta) and the DCO looking over my shoulder, I ad-libbed a concerned and reasonable-sounding militarese first draft on the typewriter directly from my interview notes. Once an acceptable first response to the congressional went out, brigade would have time to investigate the matter more fully and try however it could (short of losing the complainer in a quicksand slough) to defuse it. Crockett and I drove down to the Infantry Center signals office and personally supervised the telex to the Secretary of the Army's office. By the afternoon, a deputy assistant flunky would personally deliver it to the congressman's office. Before he went home that morning, the DCO left word with my first sergeant to let me have the rest of the day off.

After that, Crockett and Barnes routinely steered the few congressionals we had to my desk and usually let me do my own telephone interviews of the company commanders and other cadre involved; they were always pleased with the results. Of course I knew what they wanted. Without downright lying or falsification, the responses were supposed to sound as much as possible as though the original complaints were essentially groundless or, if not groundless, had already been rectified weeks or months ago. Sometimes the complaints actually were groundless, in which case the brigade was always delighted to say so in the responses. If they weren't groundless, I can say this much about complaining to a congressman: Whatever revenge the army took on your tail later, it fixed your original problem very promptly. My job was to make the original screw-up or series of them seem to have been along the lines of a short misunderstanding.

"How are you, Heiser?" Jardine inquired.

"Very good, sir. Thank you."

"I've been talking to Lieutenant Barnes about your work. It's apparently been very valuable. I understand you've put together quite a few of the recent congressionals pretty much on your own."

"I've had that responsibility. It's been interesting work, sir."

"It's also very valuable work for the brigade," Jardine said. "Doing it well makes you valuable. Have you thought much about a career in the army?"

This was a royal pain in the ass. Once a year, everyone was forced to endure a private lecture on re-upping by a company reenlistment NCO. He knew you weren't interested and you knew he knew, so both parties did their best to make it short and sweet and over. But when well-intentioned lifers bent on complimenting you thought they were doing it by asking you to become a lifer, it was embarrassing.

"I hadn't given it much thought, sir."

"You've had some college, haven't you?"

"Yes, sir. About three years. Liberal arts. Nothing very exceptional."

"No, but the results are," Jardine said. "I wasn't going to give you a re-up lecture. What we had in mind was talking to you about seeking a commission. What would you think of that?"

"I'd have to go down to OCS, sir. Please don't misunderstand, but I—I'm not very competitively oriented. I don't think I'd be motivated in the ways OCS tends to require."

Jardine nodded to pass the lecture over to Barnes. "There are other routes to a commission. The army recognizes the value of exceptional personnel. The Infantry Center offers a correspondence course. You complete the lessons, send them down there each week—it's not particularly difficult—and when that's done, staff up here writes some letters of recommendation putting you in for a direct commission. Beyond our support, the idea also has the backing of Colonel Pascelli, and when the time comes, the commander will be asked to add his approval and initiate the personnel action."

"If you're trying to tell us," Jardine said, "that you're not crazy about taking on an extra three-year obligation to become another infantry second lieutenant, we're bright enough to understand that. Your branch of commission would probably be the Adjutant General Corps. And direct commissions for exceptional personnel don't necessarily start with gold bars. There are warrants available, as well as entry as first lieutenant and occasionally captain if the army can be convinced of your value. Would you be interested enough to investigate the precommission correspondence course?"

I had a sudden urge to scream and bolt out of the room. I felt I was being taken massive advantage of in a way so sophisticated that it had robbed me of the capacity to say no. Quite frankly, I was terrified of pissing them off; I still had to work under them for the better part of a year. I wasn't sure if they realized it or not, but they were also offering me a very tempting escape from my almost inevitable fate as a draftee light weapons infantryman. For an instant I wished this were happening to Becker instead and that I could watch and listen through the window to see him handle it. What I really wanted at that moment was a quick, easy and painless way out of the interview, just something to end it for now and put its consequences off for any other day, even if it were just tomorrow.

"It's an interesting enough possibility, I suppose, sir. I'd be willing to start the course."

"Right, then," Jardine said. "I'll arrange to have the course materials sent up here. Thank you." I stood up, saluted and went back to my desk.

"There, now, that wasn't too bad, was it?" Crockett asked. I couldn't figure out what part he'd played in all this. He couldn't have opposed it or it never would have happened in the first place. It might simply have struck him as entertainment, but he worked with me every day and ought to have felt differently from Barnes, who rarely poked his head out of his cubicle and had little idea what went on. Crockett was a smart man and he read people well; I'd never made much of an effort to hide my feelings about the army from him.

A week later the mail clerk handed me Lesson One in a manila envelope. I carried it upstairs to my bunk and opened it; I found myself looking around cautiously to make sure no one in the Zoo could see what it was. It contained a form letter from the director of education of the Infantry Center, a pamphlet about four pages long and a multiple-choice examination sheet.

The lesson covered the fundamentals of military etiquette that every officer had to have down pat. Within four paragraphs, the army was showing me how to instruct my son or daughter to answer my home phone. "Lieutenant Martin's residence, Billy Martin speaking, sir." I sighed and closed the pamphlet. Jardine had lied. The course was a lot tougher than I was going to be able to handle.

I never got to the end, never filled out the multiple-choice sheet. I put the material in my locker and let it simmer indefinitely. A month after that, the Infantry Center started dunning me with form letters telling me I was falling behind in the course. I began to be afraid some asshole would start making phone calls to the first sergeant about it. I gave myself lots of good brooding time to stew on the pile of shit I hadn't had the good sense simply to say no to. It felt great.

Finally at lunchtime one day I asked Crockett if we could talk. He took me to the NCO club and set us up with a couple of beers. Ordway walked in and waved to us from the doorway but drifted off to join his regular drinking buddies.

"Shoot," Crockett said.

"I'm in some trouble," I said.

"I doubt that. Not trouble like I understand it. Trouble to me is rape or vehicular manslaughter. Or maybe desertion. Are we in that kind of a ballpark?"

"No." I stiffened up. "But it's trouble to me. It's making me sick."

"Okay."

"You know about Jardine's idea for me?"

"I know something about it."

"I can't go through with it. I didn't want it when they told me about it. I absolutely don't want it now."

"So. Tell them. Tell Barnes."

"I wanted to talk to you about it first."

"What the hell for?"

"Because as long as I was a crummy draftee with my sights on just doing my time and getting the hell out of the army, I could work everything out for myself. But they went to work on me, and when it was all over, I was all mixed up in—career stuff."

He chuckled. "Bet you started to say lifer shit. I know the drill. 'Why are lifers like flies? They eat shit and bother people.' I've seen that writ on a couple of latrine walls. Well, it serves you right. You didn't have the guts to keep yourself straight. You know, I didn't like you much yesterday, but I like you less today. You just have no idea who you are or where you stand. Sneeze and you float away just like a Kleenex. You really would have made a useless officer. Shit, you're clever. Like one of those porpoises down at Marineland. Well, I saw the major's point. Most officers are useless and not even clever, so you would have been a net marginal gain for the army for a couple of years, until the next reduction. I sure as shit don't want you as an NCO. I think we'll all be happier when you start focusing on just being a goddam draftee again."

"It wasn't my idea."

"I know, and getting drafted wasn't your idea, and when your orders for Vietnam come down, that won't be your idea either. Nothing's your idea. You are the most unmotivated fuck I know. I know how to make good use of you, and you don't give me much trouble, but that's not much reason to respect you, now, is it? Son, don't blame those nice men for offering you what they thought was a nice gift. I don't think they were smart to do it, but it's not their fault that they don't know you like I do. And it wasn't my place to pop their balloon. Part of their job is to try to get a little talent in their army. They thought you were it."

"I want you to know," I said, "that you've been really unsympathetic about all this."

"Can't help it. Got no sympathy for you. I can work with draftees. It might not have occurred to you, but that's a lifer's job and permanent cross to bear. I can even work with loons like your sick buddy Becker; I sort of enjoy keeping those types in line. I know all about him and he knows all he needs to know about me. But you? Jesus. Who are you? What do you want? You don't want to go to Vietnam, but you don't have the balls to fight it or even to grab a way out of it. Were you waiting for those officers to offer you an honorable discharge and a plane ticket back to college? Don't hold your breath."

"How about your respect for just being here and doing your goddam work?"

"Naw. You just do that so you won't go to the stockade. And

you do it well 'cause that's your curse in life. You're hard-wired that way. You take pride in work you hate. I can't get all worked up over that. I don't really mean to rub salt in your wounds, but you don't really have a problem worth my time and effort. You're just jerking off. Do something spectacular if you want my help. Rape a WAC. Burn down a barracks. Punch out an officer. I'll show you a few tricks then. But this shit? It's your pile of shit, buddy. I'm not going to wipe your nose for you."

When I got back to headquarters, I asked the clerk upstairs if I could see Major Jardine. The clerk phoned his extension and passed me in. Salute, salute, sit down, how are you, what can I do for you today?

"I've decided not to be an officer, sir. I'm sorry if it's incon-venienced you."

"No, not particularly. I'm disappointed. Colonel Pascelli will be disappointed. I think I mentioned how much he's appreci-ated your contribution to the brigade. Can I ask your reasons?"

"I'm a civilian, sir. I don't get along with the army. It gets along with me. That's okay, I guess. I don't like trouble. But I started out with the shortest route to being a civilian again, and I want it back. It was the best idea for me. I should have stuck with it."

"I can understand that. Anything else?"

"Well, just thanks, sort of. I know you and the lieutenant were just trying to offer me something you thought was a good deal."

"You know, an officer's life isn't a bad life. I was just a reserve officer, but when I was called up for this active tour, I found that I liked it. I hope I can stay on active duty. Well. That's me. Okay. Good luck."

"Thank you, sir."

I never bothered to send Lesson One back to the Infantry Center. The next time there was an inspection, I tossed it out. Every few weeks the mail clerk had another dunning letter for me, but that was as far as the Infantry Center seemed willing to go.

It never even occurred to me to tell Becker about the whole business; I was certain he'd have raked me over the coals about it worse than Crockett had. But one night he produced a chunk of hashish, courtesy of his armorer friend at Harmony Church,

R.J. Good dope actually made Becker more talkative than he normally was, if such a thing were possible. He held the blond chunk in his fingers over a flame and fluffed it into a powder, which he dropped into the red clay bowl Corrine had helped him manufacture. The ornate pipe itself was made, he said, from sections of pieces from an ancient Moroccan domino game. We were in the woods down from Kelly Hill, naughty boys doing our naughty things deep in the woods.

"I had the most curious offer last week," he said after he let out a stream of smoke. "The army has finally recognized my talents."

"They want to make you a tailor."

"No, but I was surprised they didn't when I was first drafted. The old lifers who measured me for my uniform at the reception station were Hebes. I couldn't believe it. I know a Puerto Rican with a Ph.D. in subatomic physics. He's a company cook, naturally. But you're on the right track. It has to do with my ethnic affiliation."

"No games. Get to the point."

"Well, perhaps you've encountered the DLAT."

"The language test?"

"The same. Everybody's got to take it. It's sort of in a fucked-up Esperanto. On page one they tell you that gloob means desk and flerno means pen and that you form the plural by adding wa to a noun. Then on page two they ask you how to say, 'Put the pens on the desk,' and you get the usual four choices. 'Flernowa zogzog gloob.' That sort of shit. Well, this Jewboy had four years of Latin, so the DLAT held no terrors for me. I took it about five months ago in a room with about ten of the most hopelessly confused and unhappy lifers you ever saw. And then I forgot all about it. Until last Tuesday.

"The First Pig sent word that my presence was required in the orderly room. I diddybopped my ass over there and he passed me on to Two Mysterious Strangers in crew-cutted mufti—I was fooled instantly into thinking they were civilians, especially when I saw their sharp shoes and green socks. We adjourned to the captain's vacant office and the door was shut behind me.

"These kind gentlemen introduced themselves as the bearers of my test score. They'd brought me my grades, all the way from Spook City, a.k.a. Army Intelligence at Fort Meade. Would you believe that I scored one of the most epic DLAT scores the Third U.S. Army has ever seen?"

"That's great," I said. "You're a fluent speaker of one dead and one synthetic language."

"Well, the head swine introduced himself as one Captain Ortiz. And he asked me about my Hebraic heritage. He'd been glancing over my DD-214 and said he found my religious declaration to be quite interesting. Did I chance to know any of my ancient holy lingo, he inquired? So I gave him a recital."

" 'The Shooting of Dan McGrew'?"

"Hardly. I recited my Torah portion from my Bar Mitzvah, fresh as it was on the day I got all those neat Israeli bonds and engraved Speidel ID bracelets. You should have seen their little beady eyes pop out. They thought they'd stumbled across the mother lode. Well, no sooner had I concluded the scriptural reading than they laid their cards on the table. How would I, Ortiz asked, like to leave this Georgian toilet for six months at the Army Lingo Center at the Presidio in San Francisco, after which I would be knighted an officer in Her Majesty's Intelligence Service and spend the next three or four years translating secret Israeli documents and cyphers?"

"What did you say?"

"*Kash mir tochis.* Words to that effect."

"Zionist leanings?"

"Fuck, no. Hey, I'm a nosy sucker and I'll spy on anybody, but I ain't spying on no Israelis. Those people have no sense of humor. And they're violent people. You know what they did to an American intelligence ship that strayed too close to one of their wars a couple of years ago? They just strafed the piss out of it until it didn't float no more. A Yankee Jewboy opening their personal mail? No way. You can't get life insurance rates for that kind of work. That's called uninsurable risk in the trade. Like guys with the palsy who work for the bomb squad."

It was good hash. When he finally shut up, I surprised myself. I told him my army career opportunity story.

"No shit? We could have both been officers. I finally would have learned how to put my trousers on both legs at the same time. And Crockett would have had to salute me even when they weren't lowering the flag behind my back. I don't know,

Richard. We could both have made some serious mistakes here."

"At least you knew what you wanted right away."

"That's right. Kick yourself in the nuts. Christ, you sure do wail on yourself. Listen, why do you think *Hamlet*'s such a great play? The asshole knew within five minutes who killed his old man and what he was supposed to do about it, but the play lingers on for six more hours. So you thought about it for a couple of weeks. Mox nix, Whitebread. I'd loan you a razor blade, but all I have is those cartridge jobs."

"It was real tempting for a while," I said.

"Right. Officers fuck enlisted men all day and all night. Pretty natural to want to be a fucker rather than a fucked every now and then. I still love you, even though you're enlisted scum. I'm enlisted scum, too."

"We could both have gotten out of what's coming up for us. You know what's coming up for us."

"Look. I got news for you. We each have a little more than a year left to go. And we're going to live. And come home with all our parts, and most of 'em will still work. And when it's all over, we'll certainly know we got fucked. But that's all—just got fucked, but didn't go looking for some way out so we could fuck other folks. And we'll both be out in our two years. That's an accomplishment. Sad to say, but it's the sexiest accomplishment assholes like us can hope for in this year of our Lord 1970. But it's a real accomplishment. We'll live. We'll survive. Listen to how they've twisted things around in that suggestible brain of yours—you're embarrassed about trying to negotiate your own survival. Well, stop being embarrassed, 'cause it's embarrassing me. You're making me nervous. Pass me the pipe. Be of good cheer."

8

I'd met R.J., Becker's friend out at Harmony Church, a couple of times. I hadn't been terribly impressed. Still, I understood the bond. Like me and everyone, Becker had started his time at Fort Benning at the vile and noxious Repo Depot peopled largely, as Mr. Guthrie sang, by mother-stabbers and father-rapers. But what really made the Repo Depot unlivable was its lifers and their routine for everyone. Basic training is supposed to be unbearable, and those like me who had to go to Advanced Infantry Training had another six weeks of harassment added to that. But once you were graduated from these valuable skill-acquisition schools (Becker used to threaten people with his allegedly lethal fourteen hours of hand-to-hand combat), the reward was a huge quantum decrease in lifer-bother. Your assignments were permanent, and although lifers saw to it that you accomplished whatever work was required, they stopped there; they didn't make up imaginary tasks for you to do when the real work (usually their incomprehensible definition) was done. If you didn't piss your lifers off, they dispensed three-day passes liberally and in general tried to make their office teams or platoons as happy (again, their incomprehensible definition) as possible with whatever other perks were available, your birthday off, half-days off following some particularly raunchy detail, that sort of jive.

Then you found yourself at the Repo Depot again, and the nonstop lifer harassment began all over again like a cold bucket of water, particularly unbearable if you'd already had a burst of permanent duty somewhere. There were daily barracks inspections again, and after breakfast (in the post's worst and filthiest mess hall) and morning formation (at which the lucky ones finally got their permanent assignments and were liberated), those who stayed were assigned to policing or painting or maintenance details throughout Main Post for the rest of the day.

R.J. had preceded Becker at the Repo Depot by a few days. The night Becker arrived, R.J. was in the bunk next to his and they conversed cautiously, scoping each other out for concealed weapons or hostilities or hidden agendas like wallet theft or forcible buggery. R.J. must have been satisfied with Becker's honorable intentions, because the next morning as Becker started to trudge to the mandatory forced-work formation, R.J. caught him by the back of the collar and held him back with him as the barracks emptied. "Check this out," he said, and led Becker to a small padlocked room at the end of the barracks to which he produced a key. It was a rarely used storage room. The hasp was liberal enough to allow R.J., once inside, to slip his hand between the door and the jam and return the padlock to the hasp in a way that made it look from the outside as if the room were still locked.

From slats inside one of the room's windows, they could see and hear the formation. The first order of business was to call the names only of those whose permanent assignments had arrived from Main Post personnel. Those immediately diddy-bopped back to the barracks, got their gear (or what remained unstolen of it) and headed for waiting buses. The names of those who remained weren't called, but woe be unto him whose name had been called but who wasn't in formation. After the permanent assignments were done, the rest of the unfortunates still in formation were given lifer sergeants who marched them to their work details. R.J.'s secret room (he'd borrowed heavy duty metal cutters to snip off the official army padlock and substitute his own) was close enough so that if either his or Becker's name was called, they'd have time to rush out of the barracks unseen and get their orders. If their names weren't called, they waited until the formation dispersed into the work details, then slipped out of the barracks marching as if they were on a work detail, and spent the rest of the day fucking off royally somewhere on Main Post. If I'd been the one R.J. had so honored, I'd probably have been too uptight and worried about the consequences of getting caught to have taken him up on it. Becker on the other hand was more easily led astray. His and R.J.'s consequence was a little more than a week of harassment-free paid vacation, and Becker decided that R.J., primitive though he was, was a clever and valuable pal to have around and they stayed in touch after R.J. was exiled to Harmony Church and Becker posted to Kelly Hill.

One night after chow Becker and I were in our bunks in the Zoo winding down and trying to work up the energy to figure out some way to spend the evening, when R.J. wandered in. He grinned his meaningless grin and huddled down with Becker to whisper.

"Unless you're proposing marriage," Becker said, "I got no secrets from Richard. If you are proposing marriage, you know you're obligated to get permission from your company commander first. If you can leap that little hurdle, we'll talk. What's up?"

R.J. sat down on an empty bunk. "Well, we're sort of fucked, buddy."

"In what way?"

"The guy I paid the money to done split. That's it. The motherfucker was negotiating for a compassionate early out, and it came through. He's back on the block with your money."

"Shit," Becker said.

"If it'll help, I'm sorry, but he's got my money, too, and it's all down the commode now."

"Let me guess," I said. "Dope deal."

"That's very astute of you," Becker said. "Well, all I really wanted out of it was some free dope, and it looks like I ain't getting that. It's sure going to be a spartan month till payday."

"Look, I set it up," R.J. said, "and I thought the guy was cool, so I sort of feel I owe you some kind of favor. If you can figure out what it is, I'll try to provide it."

"Where's the guy live?" Becker asked.

"Michigan, I think. I mean, when I get out, if I happen to be cruising through that neighborhood, I'll be glad to work on the guy with a baseball bat, but that's if I can find him, and I don't think that's too likely. We're talkin' about a five-hundred-dollar search for a two-hundred-dollar asshole. I think this one's just a washout."

Becker schemed for a few seconds. "Okay. I know my favor. I want to go shooting this evening. And anytime I feel like it. Richard, too, if he's interested."

"What kind of shooting?" I asked.

"Ah, you don't know what R.J.'s curious position is in our glorious brigade. Tell the man what you do for Sam, R.J."

"I'm battalion armorer. Sure, there's no problem if that's what tickles you. All we have to do is get back to Harmony Church. We can't all fit on that motorcycle of yours, but if we can get back to the weapons shed, I can use the deuce-and-a to drive us out to the firing range."

Downstairs the brigade staff car was taking the staff duty officer out to Harmony Church to check the guard details for the first round of the night. The lieutenant was an easygoing southern ROTC type who didn't see any reason to make it difficult for people to shuttle the twenty miles between the two brigade areas, so we all piled into the sedan and got our ride. The driver let us off at the darkened weapons building. R.J. pulled a heavy pile of keys from his dog-tag chain and let us in through the front door. Inside, he turned on the lights.

"Choose your weapons," he said.

The place was like a toy store. Behind locked cages were crates of grenades and portable antitank weapons. Locked in racks against the wall were M14s, M16s, over-unders, riot shotguns, .45 automatics, .38 Colt revolvers and all manner of other obscure armament jive. Each of us pointed to our selections, and R.J. dutifully unlocked the racks and closets and handed them out to us along with the complementary ammunition. We lugged the shit out to the back of the armorer's deuce-and-a tarpaulined truck and piled into the front seat. It was around 8:30 and still not quite full dark by the time we arrived at a remote and deserted firing range rigged with high overhead light poles for night firing. R.J. gave me his keys and sent me up the monkey ladder to the range officer's tower to turn on the lighting array. "Just flick everything you can find up there," he said. Within a minute, the area was awash in a huge field of near-daytime illumination that stopped abruptly at the rectangular edges and corners of the field; beyond it was the darkness of the forest.

"I'd like to declare a house rule," Becker announced as we started to set up our equipment.

"As long as it don't send me to jail," R.J. said.

"Shooting for shooting's sake only. Nobody tries to shoot anything that moves."

"Fuck, I just like the noise anyway," R.J. said.

"Suits me thoroughly," I said.

"Wonderful," Becker said. "I worry about my karma. Okay. What happens next?"

R.J. took a fat joint in tan wheat-straw paper from his fatigue blouse pocket, fired it up and passed it around.

"Of course," Becker said. "How stupid of me. I thought the range NCO was going to insist we fire lethal weaponry sober."

"You ain't going to be straight when you shoot it in Veetnam, so ain't no reason to get prissy here. Military training should always be as realistic as possible, or else why bother? Now I got my own house rule. Don't shoot yourselves and don't fire no round at the tower. Let's have a happy picnic."

R.J. handed us out noise-reducer earplugs and then dragged up a folding chair to the wooden firing deck. Becker picked up his Russian AK47 Kalashnikov submachine gun and R.J. showed him how to load its banana magazine. "Makes sense a fuckin' hippie like you wants to shoot a Roossian machine gun," R.J. muttered. "That one's actually Czech, they tell me. Well, tear ass, boy."

Becker found a clumsy way to fire the thing left-handed. He leaned into the weapon against his shoulder and started to fire short bursts on automatic into the down-range dirt; nobody'd bothered to put up targets. Bap-bap-bap-bap. Bap-bap. The barrel of the heavy weapon rose with each burst. R.J. prepared another magazine and handed it to Becker when he'd emptied the first. Then I took a few pulls off the thing. It weighed a ton, but it seemed like a solid hunk of small-arms terror. Its rate of fire was considerably slower and the noise it made was lower than the M16 I'd fired in AIT, but the rounds themselves were more massive. It would do a better job of chopping down a small tree than an M16.

R.J. wasn't interested in the Roossian gun. We put it aside, sat down and relit the joint. R.J. stood up and readied a .45 automatic. He stood with his large bulky body square behind it and steadied it with both hands. My earplugs weren't terribly effective against the cannon roar and the after-resonance the pistol made. Huge clouds of dirt kicked up in the backstop berm down-range. After the final round, the slider flew back and exposed most of the naked barrel.

"Hot damn," R.J. said. "I do love that thing."

Becker had never fired an M16—they don't stress that in balloon lofting school, and his basic had used Korean War M14s—so he readied that toy (its plastic stock pieces were actually manufactured by Mattel, which gave us a chuckle and actual combat troops the willies) and clattered away for a few minutes on automatic. This one was a little more accommodating for lefties. Then I took a turn with a .38 revolver, which was new to me. I had the feeling a person who took his time could actually hit something with one of those; the .45 I'd trained on in AIT was strictly for lucky shots at charging rhinos.

R.J.'s next pleasure was a riot shotgun, a pump gun that he blasted repeatedly until he'd emptied its magazine under the barrel, wham-wham-wham-wham. It resonated beautifully through the gorge of the firing range. He had me touch the barrel when he was done; it was painfully hot. Next all three of us turned our attention to a vintage piece, a Browning automatic rifle steadied on the wooden deck on a bipod. It sent huge packets of lead forward with a distinctive metallic ring. We ended up the night with Becker's final pick, a .45-caliber grease gun, a truly primitive weapon composed of about six parts of stamped metal. When it failed in the field, irregular forces could often manufacture their own spare parts in a cave smelting operation. It thudded slowly, much slower than the AK47, and wrought the same kind of havoc in the dirt that the .45 pistol had, only repeatedly. It was about 10:30 when we hoisted every-thing back into the truck and shut off the lights.

R.J. drove us back to Kelly Hill through the narrow mean-dering forest roads. We'd volunteered to go back to Harmony Church with him to clean the weapons, but he'd told us not to bother; it would give him something to do the next day as he handed out weapons to the companies that were going out on field maneuvers pretending to be the enemies of the OCS can-didates from Main Post. He didn't have to join them in his truck to fix the malfunctions or exchange weapons until the after-noon.

Becker and I took another joint R.J. had left us with to smoke on the bleachers behind the barracks.

"That was really exhilarating," I said. "It's the first army-sponsored good time I think I've ever had."

"Yeah. A guy could have a great time on this post if they turned it into an amusement park. Jump off parachute towers, jump out of planes in a sort of relaxed way, fly around in fast helicopters, fire cannons, throw grenades, set off detonation charges. Whoom! Bam! You know, I used to love camping. Since I had to bivouac in basic, I don't think I'll ever go camping again. It's hard to say why. They had tents, sleeping bags. The chow tasted better in the woods just like it always does. But I just hated it."

"I know why. They messed with you. You were still in the army."

"Yeah. That's it, isn't it? They just will mess with you. The drill sergeants appointed spies to creep around in the dark to try to steal your rifles and turn 'em in to the pigs, so you got chewed out for not guarding your weapon. And there was so much noise all the fucking time. I just don't know if I'll ever be able to go camping again."

"You feel bad about R.J. losing your money?"

"Yes and no. Not R.J. He's probably telling the truth about that turkey who split. I don't know who the guy was, so I can't be sure. But R.J. doesn't need to rip me off that way. He doesn't mind ripping people off, I don't think, but he values me. He adds it all up. He'd rather have my goodwill."

"You don't strike me as his kind of guy. He really is mostly redneck."

"He's a curious redneck, like a raccoon," Becker explained. "And he's an ambitious redneck. I teach him things. Money's never going to be a problem for R.J. He's always hustling, and some of the most extraordinary hustles, too. But he has no idea what to spend it on beyond food and liquor. We go into the stores in town sometimes and I show him this and that. It's just a start. He wants me to go up to Atlanta with him. We may all be in luck. I think he's thinking of renting a house up there. A place we can mess around on weekends, three-day passes."

"What kind of hustles? Where's he get that kind of money?"

Becker smiled. "Secret time," he cautioned. "Heavy-duty secret time. You're not supposed to know this at all."

"Okay. The secret dies with me."

"Well, I mentioned the spies who used to creep around bivouac, steal your rifle and turn it in to the drill sergeants. R.J. has modified that somewhat."

"How so?"

"Well, he has to be out on those overnight maneuvers a lot himself, fixing the weapons and shit. And he's got nothing in that truck of his but racks of weapons. So he does a little night scrounging, too. Mostly for M16s. Some poor bozo dozes off with his M16 propped against the other side of the tree and R.J. liberates it. He puts it back in the rack of his truck where nobody notices it. The Bozo gets court-martialed and has to pay for the goddam thing out of his next six months' wages. R.J. files off the numbers at his leisure and goes up to Atlanta and sells the M16 to some lunatic-fringe redneck pals of his. You know that civilians can't own M16s, no way, no how. The ammo's no problem, though. So they pay him five, six hundred bucks for each piece, sometimes more."

"Jesus. I hope you're not in on that with him."

"No. My contest for the worst army post on earth is only open to regular posts, not the stockade at Fort Leavenworth. R.J. can take his chances on that all by himself. But I know about it because he asked me to come in on it with him. I politely declined. He understood."

"That's crazy. Too fucking weird for me. I don't know if I like that guy."

"He's handy. He's a resource. He's always cooking something

up to improve our lives while we're here. It's always odd, but it always helps. Like tonight."

"You know, if the boiling shit ever rains down on him, they'll be interviewing his friends."

"Yeah, I suppose they will. But I don't know anything about it. You don't know anything. None of my fingerprints on any of his purloined weapons."

"If it was me, I wouldn't hang around with him at all."

Becker turned surly. "It's not you." He took a pull off the joint and handed it to me.

"I just don't think it's worth it," I said.

"Ah, shit. Look. I wouldn't do it. I'm too scared. I don't like the idea of those grunts getting busted down three ranks when their rifles disappear. That's the part I don't like the most. Also, I don't think it's just generally a good idea to put weaponry like that in the hands of the Sons of White Baptists or the United Uhuru Honkie Annihilation Squad or whoever R.J.'s unbalanced customers are. But I'll tell you why I don't run screaming into the night over it. Yes. I will tell you why if I got to."

"Okay. I'm curious."

"Fucking Goody Two-shoes. Okay, listen up. I only roll this one by you once. Maybe because I only want to roll it by myself once. Until now, I haven't wanted to scrutinize it and put it into small words. That's not good enough for you; you're the analytic type.

"You accused me of being just a tad apocalyptic some time ago. I suppose I am. Well, I hate this war. I hate it as a general proposition. I hate it for what it's done to me personally. I was only mildly deranged before all this happened to me. Now I'm seriously deranged, but I can't act much of it out, 'cause I don't want to go to jail. Just do my time and duck and go home. That's the big catch. All my actions have to be subjected to it —will it interfere with my doing my time and going home? And you know who invented that? The army. They know I hate this war. They know you hate it and about three quarters of the draftees hate it. But nobody wants to get fucked over. Nobody wants to go to jail. If we're lucky enough to do it, we want to get out with honorable discharges, because if we don't, the fucking will just go on and on for years. So when they're watching us, we do what they tell us to do. Enough to get by.

"But that doesn't mean I don't look for opportunities to kick back. In my own cowardly, vicarious fashion. Because I don't care about courage. I don't see the world that way. I see the world as something that arbitrarily sticks the green, raspy weenie up my butt when it feels like it, and that's not very courageous; I'm being held down by the entire Pentagon when it happens. That's not my idea of courage. Not once since I was drafted has just one solitary lifer had the guts to try to fuck me without the whole army behind him.

"So. I chance to discover some marginal lunatic—R.J.—who's berserk enough not to give a fuck. He sells arms to the Indians. For profit. The consequences down the line are probably grisly. So what? If it weren't for the war, R.J. wouldn't be here. There wouldn't be any mislaid M16s. There probably wouldn't be nearly as many lunatic customers out there pissed off enough to want to shell out that kind of money for automatic weapons. Well, maybe those lunatics just hide their M16s down in their suburban basements and masturbate into the barrels at night. Or maybe they take 'em outside at night and commit mayhem and carnage with 'em. Bully for them. They're certainly not killing more little yellow pajama people, and that's what would have happened with those weapons if R.J. hadn't diverted them. They're bringing a little of the terror and fear to our own city streets. R.J.'s made that an unforeseen consequence of the war. I think that's good. Maybe police chiefs will start complaining to the Pentagon. Maybe victims will start complaining. It'll all add up to another couple of tons of resistance to the war from people who otherwise were perfectly content to let the war run its course at its convenience."

"That's pretty convoluted logic," I said.

No, it's not. Right now nobody cares about the pain in this war, because it's out of sight six thousand miles away. But when some of that pain starts showing up in Cleveland and Talla-hassee, maybe in Disneyland or at the World Series or Stupid Bowl VI, people will care. They didn't want to have to be both-ered to care, but they'll care. For the first time, the war will start intruding into their business and pleasure on their block. I'm too cowardly to help it or start it, but I can get my rocks off by watching it and not standing in its way. R.J. has the capacity to be a total loser pervert scum, but he's doing something I think is very valuable, personally and functionally. He's helping to shorten the war, and making a profit to boot. That's original. I'm impressed."

"I can't see it that way," I said.

"Then don't look."

9

Rollie was the reason Becker had first stumbled across the crafts shop and one of the reasons he still spent afternoons and evenings there even on the weeks he was willing to listen to me that trying to play hide-the-salami with Corrine was Bad Idea Number Ten. R.J. tended to produce grade-Z Mexican reefer, and was unpredictable and undependable about the few good things he showed up with. Rollie, on the other hand, was a remarkable drug connection.

Rollie was a very large brother who worked in the motor pool when he wasn't being interrogated by the CID or the S-2 for revolutionary activities, which at Kelly Hill consisted chiefly of wearing a colorful bandanna as a sweatband on his forehead when he wasn't in uniform, and keeping his hair at or beyond the regulation limits that defined the proscribed Afro. Before he'd been drafted, Rollie had been seriously contaminated by our white middle class at college. He liked our styles of going radical, our music and our acid far more than he liked wine and soul. None of the other blacks in his bay would have anything to do with him, largely because he mystified them and because he tended to hold them in contempt. He'd flung one brother in his bay who'd fucked with him into a metal locker and lacerated and dislocated his shoulder, after which his Zoomates left him all the alone he wanted.

There were only three or four thousand troops on Kelly Hill in about forty companies, so naturally it hadn't taken Rollie very long to scope Becker out as his kind of wacko, and Becker discovered that in some mysterious fashion and without leaving Columbus or environs, Rollie could come up with high-grade non-Mexican reefer and all sorts of hallucinogens with great regularity and stable prices. The two needled each other ceaselessly, Rollie calling Becker a white Uncle Tom doing the massa's work without complaint, and Becker replying that Rollie was doing an admirable job of overthrowing the system by getting busted down to private no-stripe every month and pulling extra punitive duty almost every night mopping and buffing the halls and cleaning the latrines. Rollie spent most of his off-time making his own FTA (Fun, Travel and Adventure on the posters; Fuck The Army, our way) belt buckles and peace symbols and radical what-have-you at the craft shop and had finally steered Becker there when Becker broke his last hash-pipe bowl.

When we were all there, me, Becker, Rollie and Corrine, it was a hell of a dynamic. Corrine was so astonishingly corn-belt, and yet half the time she'd be straining her eyes to help Rollie construct some metallic kill-the-pigs slogan on some doodad, and nothing Rollie could utter in the realm of the violent overthrow of the government seemed to make her bat an eyelash. Late at night, after she gave the keys to Rollie, her unofficial assistant, to lock up when she had to go home to spell Donald Senior or a sitter, we'd lock ourselves in and get blasted on whatever Rollie was offering and shoot the shit.

"It's simple, man," Rollie explained. "She's never met a Knee-Grow before, so I'm defining the species for her. She has an open mind. Whatever I do or say, that's what blacks are supposed to do and say. She wouldn't flinch if I dropped my trousers and turned out to have a two-pronged dong."

"No," Becker said. "She has expectations about that. She's talked to her girlfriends in gym class. You're supposed to have this nine-foot hose."

"I do have a nine-foot hose," Rollie said. "Do you really chase Wanda Whitebread around?"

Becker glared at me.

"Uh-uh," Rollie said. "She told me. She thought it was neat. She thinks you're cute. She's flattered."

"Does she mention her husband in all this?" I asked.

"Well, that's the odd part." Rollie said. "She must be a Mormon or something. The way she talks, she seems to think there's room for the lieutenant, the two kids and ol' Becker, too. I have the feeling that not a lot of men have chased her around, and she sort of likes the feeling. Just because it's arrived a few years after the wedding ceremony and the kids, that's no reason to scream rape as far as she's concerned."

"No. She wouldn't be a Mormon," Becker pointed out. "They were into polygamy. This would be polyandry, more than one husband per wife. That's Himalayan stuff. But I'm through with her romantically. Richard pointed out the disadvantages. He brought me to my senses."

Rollie found this wildly amusing. "Shee-it. You just live by your dick and you know it. You're just waiting for the lieutenant to go on Ranger lifer maneuvers in Dahlonega for a week and you're going to move right on in. Well, enjoy yourself, Becker. How is officer snatch, anyway?"

"Believe it or not, I wouldn't know, not firsthand, as they say. I have no reason to believe it's in any way different from enlisted or warrant snatch. Of course this particular unit may have some cautionary verse from the Old Testament tattooed on it. I'll let you know if she lets me keep the lights on."

Becker told me once that he valued Rollie for another reason. He was, Becker explained, the antidote to the Kelly Hill Random Negro. Becker himself was small and scrawny, but given to saying what was on his mind in ways that stimulated people to want to eviscerate him. Left entirely to his own devices, he was convinced he'd never make it off the Hill alive between the gangs of pissed-off blacks who roamed Kelly Hill at night and the drunken rednecks staggering out of the bowling alley with its warped lanes. Becker's Random Negro theory held that for every solitary white Jewboy strolling along minding his own business, there was a predestined Random Negro, or perhaps a redneck lifer with a broken Bud bottle, waiting to pounce from the shadows to make mincemeat of him and send him down from the Hill in one of those zippered nylon bags that were so popular in the Asian theater these days. Hanging out with Rollie, on the other hand, was an effective buffer against the Random Negro. No one in any state of sobriety or drunkenness messed with Rollie.

It was symbiosis, Becker said. Rollie kept the Random Negro at bay and Becker initiated Rollie into still more mysteries of the white middle class in general and Jewish people in particular, a rare treat for Rollie, who claimed Becker was the first Jewboy he'd actually met in the flesh. On Saturday morning the Jewish Chapel on Main Post would serve lox and bagels after services, and one morning Becker showed up at Rollie's barracks and demanded that Rollie get permission from his first sergeant to attend Jewish services with him. Rollie responded because he was always running out of novel ways to keep his first pig jumping and guessing, and to the best of his knowledge, no black in the first sergeant's long career had ever demanded to attend Jewish services before. Permission was granted largely because the first pig was always looking for ways to make Rollie disappear.

The contempt Rollie had for other blacks Becker had for other Jews, most of whom were at Benning for boot camp in the reserves or National Guard, but a few dozen of them were college boys, drafted like us, who didn't intend to spend their time as enlisted swine and had volunteered for OCS. Becker liked to goad and prod them when he met them at the chapel with their bald heads and starched fatigues. If he was feeling polite, he'd call them fascists to their face, and he got the greatest kick out of knowing that if any one of them tried something in return, he'd instantly be kicked out of OCS and sent to Vietnam as a three-stripe infantry squad leader. The worst anyone fought back was a strack OCS platoon leader who hissed at Becker behind the rabbi's back that he hoped Becker would be under his command one day. Becker wished him *mazel tov* and told him to go fuck himself in the meantime. It wasn't likely they'd meet again, and Becker liked to push his luck when he saw he was bending somebody out of shape like that.

One Saturday when my office work was done I hitched a ride down to Main Post to catch the Lox-Breath Brothers, Becker and Rollie, coming out of services. Rollie seemed pleased and glutted enough, but Becker seemed nervous and distracted, looking back over his shoulder at the chapel. I glanced at Rollie.

"They imported some Jewish stuff from Columbus," he said. "Women. Sort of. College girls back on spring break or whatever. Becker here's a little glazed."

"They speak with southern accents," Becker said. "Jewish girls saying shit like 'Y'all come back and see us, now, y'hear?' That's weird. Moon Jews, that's what they are. Jews from the moon."

"Well, were they cute?"

"Yeah, yeah, I guess," Becker said. "Yeah, a couple of them were real heavy-duty. I think mostly they're here to stimulate the officer candidates' imaginations. I had a hard time getting their attention in that crowd. Lonely lowly GI away from home just doesn't cut it when there are officer candidates around. But I have this idea. I think maybe I can get laid with something you'll approve of, Richard. I think maybe I can finally mate with unmarried civilian units of my own kind."

"What's the plan?"

"There's a synagogue in Columbus, and some of the honeys are going to host the *oneg*, the feedbag, this Friday night. So I think I'll put on my dress greens and all my medals—you know, the one I got for showing up—and tool on down there on my motorcycle. Now from there, maybe the lonely lowly Jewish GI could lead to a dinner invitation later in the week, and besides some decent home-cooked food, maybe I can run into some high school or college honey whose mother will pressure her into letting me take her to the flicks as a civic gesture."

"The motorcycle's going to queer it up," I said.

"Not necessarily. You can ride a motorcycle and look as if you're about to sodomize the citizens, or you can ride a motorcycle and look like a slightly sporty grad student at Stanford. You happen to be looking at Specialist Right, a young Jewish prince from the northern provinces, trapped by circumstances and a strong patriotic drive. You're looking at the fleshy embodiment of every Jewish mother's dreams."

"I always heard Jewish honeys didn't put out," Rollie said.

"Nonsense. How do you think they get little Jewish people? The actual rumor is that they stop screwing when they get married, but it's not likely I'll be able to verify that in the near future."

So the next Friday, Becker skipped chow, transmuted himself into his greens, slicked his sorry ass up to the extent that it was possible and headed on into town to attend evening services. When he came back that night, he was pleased with himself. "I have a date for Wednesday night," he said. "Weird but true. And let me tell you about this synagogue. These people are Sephardim, Spanish Jews booted out in 1492. Real different birds from the ones up north. My date's mother gave me a tour of the bone orchard. Anyway, they had these three graves. One of them said something like 'Isaac Levi,' dates in the eighteenth century. On his right there was 'Sarah Levi, his wife.' And then there on his left to complete the cozy family there was 'Naomi, his concubine.' Weird City. Proto-Swingers."

He looked even slicker in his conservative but sporty civilian threads the next Wednesday, the image of the college debating team captain, sparked with a healthy patriotism and a little healthy, high-spirited joy for living mixed in with the proper measure of respect for elders and traditions and above all the desire to have a nice, clean fun time with a nice (clean) fun girl at some nice clean fun malt shop; I heard Jewish America sing ing. I strolled him out to the parking lot and watched him breeze off toward Main Post and Columbus.

He was sitting in his rack across from mine looking at me when I woke up. It was dark and late and the whole Zoo had shut down, punctuated here and there by troops who snored or wheezed or otherwise made noises like badly maintained machinery when they slept. "Get up," he said. He held up a reefer and motioned toward the parade ground bleachers. I put some clothes on and went with him down the stairs to the first floor, past the C.Q. manning the first shirt's phone in the orderly room. Outside there was dew on the grass and on the seats we chose high up in the bleachers; we wiped it off before we sat down and Becker lit up the number.

I could smell the reefer, but under it, especially when he handed me the number and put his hand under my nose, I could smell venery and mixed-gender musk, sweat, Pontiac up-holstery—"Her mom loaned me the family car," he explained —and I could smell hours rolling around with a young honey on a summer night. I could smell smells I'd only thought about for the better part of a year. He had the reefer back now and took an enormous pull from it, holding the smoke for what seemed like nine or ten minutes. Then he let the smoke out.

"Things went a little better than I anticipated," he said in a whisper.

10

Becker loved the movies. Not the Hollywood rejects we got to see for a quarter at the Kelly Hill theater, but the Commander's Call movies we were forced to sit through one afternoon a week in the dayroom. I honestly believe that in his perversity, Becker found them rich, dramatic, intriguing, fraught with implications. He'd stare at them from his strange diagonal posture in his folding chair with a glazed expression of disbelief and awe, and in the dark he'd latch on to particularly berserk and unexpected dialogue and start a cheering section going which would make the lifer sergeant, who was trying to sleep, wake up and suppress the hooting and clapping before it attracted someone's attention in the orderly room below us.

"Can you believe that if this had never happened to me, I'd never have seen these movies?" he whispered during one of them—whispered not because he didn't want the training NCO to hear but because he didn't want any of the other draftees to hear him; they were already convinced he was dangerously strange. It was a rare army movie that failed to keep him riveted. I think deep down he felt he was learning new skills and trades that were denied and forbidden to most people like him. These skills loomed large in his dark and confused plans about returning to civilian life and convinced him that he'd have great advantages over most of his contemporaries who'd gone straight to med or law school. He'd learned, for example, how to control urban riots and how to escape from prisoner-of-war camps. He was convinced that somehow he'd be a jump ahead of everyone else back home because he knew how to protect himself from nuclear attacks and from chemical and biological agents. He had an edge because he knew how to take prisoners and segregate officers from enlisted men immediately to prevent them from organizing escapes. He knew his rights under the Geneva Convention and expressed scorn for his friends who were missing these lessons, because enemy captors would be able to take advantage of their ignorance.

Beyond these technical skills, he felt he'd be a better man on the outside because of the invaluable moral lessons he learned from the movies. He was chilled to the bone by the movie about the brief and unhappy career of a cocky lad who hadn't gotten with the army program and had been cashiered out with a dishonorable discharge. Jobless and universally rejected by friends, family and all but the most whorish of women, he drifted into crime and drunkenness and was soon in prison. As he received his less-than-honorable discharge from his commanding officer, he sneered that it didn't bother him a bit, and the C.O. looked at him with sad eyes and wished him not well, but the best he could under the circumstances. Becker claimed to be appalled by the boy's unregenerate attitude and vowed to straighten up and fly right immediately.

But there were more horrifying movies. Another film from which Becker never fully recovered showed a beautiful Eurasian temptress sidling up to an innocent midwestern GI in an off-post bar, showing him a few acres of thigh, and pumping him for classified information.

TEMPTRESS: Hey, GI, do you know the order of battle?

Something like that. It so unnerved Becker that he spent

weeks trying to find out what the fuck the order of battle was, because he'd never heard of it before, and he was petrified that he'd meet a Eurasian temptress in an off-post bar and have to tell her that it beat the shit out of him what the order of battle was. Once at the bar called Beer in Columbus, Becker got roaring drunk and I overheard him cornering the retarded girl who posed as a waitress, asking her if she wanted to know about the order of battle. She kept telling him to leave her alone and to sit down again. "C'mon," he kept insisting, "don't you even want to know a little bit about the order of battle? I know it. I really do. I asked somebody who knew about it and he told me." Rollie and I had to pull him off her and take him back to the booth. He was disgusted.

Then he saw an Air Force movie and got pissed that he wasn't in the Air Force and couldn't be an air traffic controller, because there'd been a young and otherwise clean-cut controller in the movie who'd succumbed to college peer pressure and had taken just one LSD trip years earlier. Now, in the tower, he found himself having an *acid flashback* as he merrily directed two C-5A mammoth transports directly toward each other at ten thousand feet. Fortunately, about a millisecond before the crash, an older and wiser lifer type had scoped out what was happening and had grabbed the mike from the hopelessly emulsified lad to avert disaster. After that, the One-Tab-Kid's life pretty much emulated the pattern of the army guy with the less-than-honorable. Becker thought a lot about acid flashbacks after that, but he complained that none ever seemed to come to him even in the most stressful situations involving mass transportation or classified documents, so he faked them by taking more acid whenever Rollie scored.

But as much as he reveled in the official movies and training, he gloried in army rumors. Nowhere on earth, he said, were there such magnificently misleading rumors, and he collected them like baseball cards and took care to continue spreading them without embellishment, like the only literal party pooper in a game of post office.

The most dreadful of all the army rumors, he said, was the tale of the Black Syph, the Black Clap, and he told us about it one night while we were toking up in the woods, exactly as a storyteller around a Boy Scout campfire tells the story of "The Monkey's Paw" or "The Golden Arm."

"When you get to Vietnam," he said, "you got to watch out for the whores, whatever you do. Some of them are Viet Cong whores and they put razor blades up their boogies or ground glass, so you got to do a little finger work first, or you'll come home with the end of your dork looking like what comes out the business end of a meat grinder. But the worst thing the whores have is the Black Clap. Not just the VC whores, but any kind of whore. There is no cure for the Black Clap. Since they discovered it over there, army doctors have been working day and night trying to find some kind of antibiotic that will kill it, but it resists everything. It just laughs at penicillin and it thinks streptomycin is food and it wants more.

"Now I don't know what it does to the whores who have it, but the guys who have it, it just starts to eat on your dick and turn it black and moldy like leprosy until finally it just rots off, and then it goes to work on your balls. When you get it, you get symptoms at first like the regular clap, you know, so you go to the medics there in Vietnam and the guy looks up from the microscope slide, and he just shakes his head real sad and writes something down on your file and then he picks up the phone and calls somebody. The next thing you know, these secret MP guys come in and they take you away—the fucking doctor doesn't even give you a couple of aspirin—and they list you as missing in action forever. They ship you off to this secret island somewhere in the middle of the Pacific that's uncharted and no one knows about but the government, just a couple of guys in the government, and that's where they keep all the guys who come down with the Black Syph, because they can't take a chance on them bringing it back to the States. They can't ever chance that. Like, half the guys that get listed as missing in action in Nam really got the Black Clap and got sent to the secret island where they just wander around with their dicks rotting off, and that's the fucking truth, man, that's the truth about the Black Clap. Those guys are still there and that's where they'll be for the rest of their fucking lives."

Then there was the Black Cong. According to Becker, he was a giant radical black dude from Watts or some similarly odious ghetto who'd been drafted into the Marines and had deserted over to the VC. There he apparently became the Simon Girty of the Vietnam War. Sneaking back through American lines in his Marine uniform or an army uniform at night, he'd ingratiate himself to grunts in the foxholes and wait for them to fall asleep, and then go to work on them. His favorite trick was to slit one guy's throat but leave his buddy alone, and then split. A few hours later when the live one woke up and found his buddy, his mind would just turn into mush instantly. The CIA had put a million-dollar contract out on the Black Cong, but to no avail, and the VC had given him the rank of lieutenant colonel and a big château in Hanoi where he rested up and planned new atrocities for the boys who'd once been his countrymen.

Then there was the alarm clock. "You'll be in a foxhole in some place that's surrounded by VC and you can't get out of there and no helicopters can get near you for days and days, and the VC's ready at any time to sneak in and do their silent stuff on you, and when they get their chance, you can just hang it up. You got to sleep. You haven't had any sleep for days, nobody has, and some of you have to sleep, so the guy who's in the point hole nearest where the VC is trying to sneak in from, everybody's got to know at all times whether he's awake and watching out for the VC or asleep. So they make this guy take the pin out of a grenade and hold on to it with his fist. That keeps him awake pretty good, but if it doesn't, that's okay, too, because he nods off and the grenade slips out of his hand and goes off and plasters him all over the foxhole like cream cheese. That wakes everyone else up in the other foxholes and they send somebody else up to the point hole with another grenade."

To Becker these rumors had profound metaphysical implications, particularly the ones involving mysterious uncharted islands and mythological black traitors, items which one could never verify except an instant prior to death or permanent insanity or as one was being led away to some tropical incarceration for life without pay phones, Western Union offices or mailboxes. Anything in this category fascinated the garbage pit he used for a mind.

We were in the Zoo one night listening to music and spacing around when a trooper named Blevins, whom we both spent a lot of time and energy trying to avoid, wandered back from a week's leave. Blevins's worst sin was that he liked us and liked hanging around with us. That sin made all his others, like abject stupidity and a psychopathic ignorance about the universe, un-forgivable. His whole sorry act was sugarcoated with a grinning freckled toadiness that used to make me carsick and used to warm Becker's temper to boiling. Where Blevins originated no one seemed to know. He seemed to belong to no identifiable ethnic group and he seemed devoid of any regional accents, experiences, marks or scars. Becker guessed that Blevins was the product of a secret research project undertaken deep in the desert by J. C. Penney to produce a synthetic American goy, an all-purpose nerd who could take the place of department store manikins or fill out the crowds in those monster rally Coca-Cola commercials.

I don't think either of us asked, but Blevins started to fill us in on the details of his leave. "I went to visit my cousin in Houston," he told us, "and you know what they got there?" (No one asked.) "My cousin told me they got this drug going around in Houston, and it's sort of like LSD, but it's different. You like take it, and it blows your mind like acid, you start tripping out. You stay high for a year, a whole year. And then you come down. And then you die. My cousin says a lot of people are really getting into it."

Becker leaped off his bunk. "I *want* some of that!" he screamed, and everyone in the Zoo started looking around. "I *want* some of that stuff. What's the name of that stuff? Where can I get some? Can you get me any of that shit?"

"Well, my cousin says he hasn't really seen any, but he says a lot of people he knows have and a lot of people are getting into it."

"No shit?" Becker was hopping up and down. "You say that you come down right before you die?"

"Yeah," Blevins confirmed.

"Dynamite! What's this shit called?"

"I don't know. My cousin didn't know the name of it."

"Well, let's call it Houston Terminal. I think that's a great name for it, and you write or telephone your cousin and tell him to put in an order for me right away. Richard?"

"Oh, no, thanks. I think I'll pass."

"Well, goddam, I sure as hell want some of that shit. A whole year, huh? Right on! Spare no expense, Blevins. Money's no object. Just tell me how much your cousin wants for a tab and

I've got it here in cold cash. I want you to hunt this shit down and bring it back, you hear?"

Blevins looked a little confused. "I'll see what I can do," he said.

"You do that, and don't fuck up. I'm counting on you."

That sealed it for Becker. Blevins, he said, had proven beyond doubt that he was the stupidest motherfucker in all creation and at the same time had brought back the granddaddy of all swell rumors. "That asshole is so fucking stupid, he probably has to remember to breathe. I don't want him around me anymore. I really don't. He's dangerous. Keep him off my case."

One night we heard a loud clang in a corner of the Zoo and lights started coming on and people started jumping out of bed to see what was going on. It wasn't just a single clang but a series of them, like someone banging a locker door shut over and over again. Above the clanging we could hear someone yelling or trying to yell, and over that we could hear Hightower cursing as we rounded the corner. Hightower was in his skivvies and he was holding Blevins up off the floor and banging him into a closed locker door again and again. "What are you, motherfucker? Are you the motherfucking C.I.D., man? I think you the motherfucking C.I.D. and I'm gonna give you some motherfucking shit to write down in that little fucking notebook of yours!" He was punctuating his remarks with Blevins, who was flailing his legs around uselessly and trying to get his breath to scream for help. Ten or twelve other guys were standing around watching the show and somebody on the other side of the Zoo was yelling for everyone to shut up so he could get some sleep. Becker and I started grabbing some of Hightower's freer limbs and tried to haul him off Blevins. Hightower started putting up a fight until he saw it was us, and then he let go of Blevins, who fell to the hard tile floor and scurried away on all fours. "I caught that motherfucker in my locker," Hightower said. "I've always thought that dufus-ass motherfucker was the C.I.D. ever since he came into this motherfucking company."

"I wasn't in your locker," Blevins managed to say from his corner. "It was open and I was just walking by."

"Yeah, I know it was open, motherfucker, and from now on, you keep your fucking nose out of that locker or I'll bust your motherfucking ass." The guy in the far corner yelled for quiet again. Becker and I hustled Hightower out of the Zoo and into the stairwell, where Becker made a jay materialize from somewhere. He lit it up and we passed it around a few times.

Hightower hissed under his breath. "I don't like that motherfucker. I sincerely don't."

"I don't think he's a C.I.D. guy, Hightower," Becker said. "He's too stupid to be the C.I.D. I mean, a C.I.D. pig is stupid, but Blevins sort of transcends even that. For that matter, I think he's too stupid to try to rip you off."

"Fuck, man, I know he wasn't trying to rip me off. He was just rubbernecking in my goddam locker, and I hate that. I just don't like that motherfucker."

"Well, join the club," Becker said.

"Man, I wish to hell there *was* a fucking C.I.D. man in this fucking bay," Hightower said, "and I wish to fuck I knew who he was, 'cause I'd knock his dick upside his fuckin' head and give him a flying lesson outside that fourth-floor window."

"We're all with you there," I said. "You think there is a C.I.D. asshole in the bay?"

"Shee-it, I don't know," Hightower grumbled. "You never know about those assholes until it's too fucking late anyway. They stroll in with these dufus-assed fake orders from Fort Shit somewhere and they try to buy reefer from you and the next fucking thing you know, you're in the goddam stockade for the rest of your sorry-assed life. Shee-it, what kind of fucking life is this, anyway? What the fuck they got to mess with everybody's head for all the time? We're here, ain't we? We doing Sam's shit like he wants, ain't we? What the fuck they got to always be messing with us for?"

We finally managed to put Hightower to bed and went back to our own racks in the dark.

"That sure is a nifty question Hightower asked," I said.

"What was that?"

"Why *do* they keep messing with us? We're here, we do what they want, and they keep messing with our heads. Isn't it enough that we're here?"

"Obviously not," Becker said.

"I can understand reefer. That's illegal outside the army, too. But there's a Spec Four in the company down the hall, S-2 interrogated him for four hours because he had a peace sticker on his car. Okay, we don't do peace stickers. I know another guy, the MPs had him in an office the whole night because a civilian guy with long hair drove him up to the main gate. Okay, give up friends with long hair. There's always something else. Demonstrations of faith. They want demonstrations of faith, and no matter how many we give them, it's never enough, they want more. I think they sit up at night in meetings to think up the next one."

The 25-cent movies in the Kelly Hill theater, like movies on every military post, all began with a reel of the flag waving and the Banana playing, and when the lights went out and the flag came on and the band started playing and the Moron Tabernacle Choir or the Clean Young White People started singing the Banana, everybody had to leap to their feet and do the saluting business or the heart slap, depending on whether you'd shuffled into the theater in civvies or in uniform. *O say can you see* and you were all up there at attention waiting for it to get over so some asshole could yell *Play Ball!* and the real movie would flutter on, inaudible and out of focus—well, what the fuck did you expect for a quarter? And then one week after a series of C.I.D. raids on an artillery battalion that had netted a couple of dozen blacks for various offenses, things started getting a little warm on the Hill, and just to put a little cherry on the top of the festering racial cupcake, the brigade sergeant major started jumping down on Afros or anything he imagined was an Afro or an Afro-to-be. He'd nail the blacks wherever he found them and march them to the barbershop, and if they gave him a hard time, he'd take a 50-cent piece out of his pocket and press it into their hands to cover the cost of the haircut. Things started getting even warmer on the Hill. More people than usual started getting beaten up outside the bowling alley at night, the AWOL rate started going up, and then one night at the theater the Banana came on and a couple of dozen brothers in the front just sat there, the fiends, and we in the back were all mildly curious as to what was going to happen. A patriotic volunteer, some dickhead three-striper in the back, started yelling, "On your feet!" and the blacks just slumped into their seats further. The Banana stopped in the middle and the lights came on and we all just sat, or stood, depending on the mode of patriotism in which the lights had frozen us, waiting for the official response to the Great Banana Mutiny. It took about three minutes to materialize. The lights went down again and the Banana started again from the top. The sitters sat and the standers stood, and suddenly a phalanx of MPs with .45s in their holsters double-timed down the center aisle with their nightsticks out and at the ready. In the dark, the MPs and the brothers they started hauling into the aisle were illuminated only by red and white flag stripes from the projection booth that happened to catch the diving and flailing bodies and the striking arms. The MPs started to go to town with their night-sticks and this time an MP yelled "On your feet!" which was followed by whacks and thuds and moans and yells and cursing. The band played on . . .

And the rocket's red glare, the bombs bursting in air . . . and semi-conscious unresisting black bodies started being hauled back up the aisle by pairs of MPs, and in the front of the theater we could see the rest of the mutineers sullenly getting to their feet to acknowledge the rest of the tune.

Oh, say does that star-spangled banner yet wave . . . and indeed it did. Rollie was standing next to me and I glanced his way in the dark and he was goggle-eyed, almost catatonic. He knew none of the mutineers, ghetto kindergarten dropouts, junkies, pimps—blacks, not precisely like him, but blacks anyway. He was sweating and the sweat was cold. "Ain't that some shit? They fuckin' knocked those niggers senseless for not saluting the fuckin' flag . . . " and he started to drift out of the theater toward the sound of the siren on the Black Maria. I drifted out with him and together we watched the finishing touches as the last mutineers were kicked into the back of the van and it drove off. A few feet away next to a green sedan stood a young MP lieutenant, strack and crew-cutted in jump boots with his trousers bloused into their tops. He turned slightly and looked at us, and I saw in his midwestern heart Mr. Death's blue-eyed boy, I saw a stare that said, "What about you boys? I would gladly beat you senseless for not saluting this flag, my flag; how about it, boys? I'll run the reel again for you." Rollie wouldn't break his stare and finally I touched his elbow and I said, "Let's drift, Uncle," and he responded slightly, still not sure what he wanted to do, but when I touched his elbow I felt it shaking and I realized his whole huge bulk was shivering, and that he and the lieutenant were about a micron away from mutual mayhem and annihilation. "Come on, goddam it," I hissed a little louder, and although it still didn't break the spell, he took a step in the direction I was trying to get us both to move toward. I tried to squeeze some sense of momentum from my muscles and start a real serious getaway, and although Rollie's legs were with me, his eyes were still on the lieutenant, who rotated slightly to keep facing Rollie like some automatic security camera, and his eyes kept following us as we retreated oh so slowly into the darkness. "Ain't that some shit?" Rollie kept saying every couple of minutes along the way, and I didn't know what to say back to him. "Ain't that some fuckin' shit?"

11

We had to find a way to get away from Benning. Of course in a few months a permanent way would be arranged for us, and I wonder now how I knew so surely it would be Vietnam. People forgot that there were other places to send soldiers to, Germany, South Korea. I didn't know the European patches, but I knew the big Indian-chief patch that meant a Korean tour and you saw those every now and again on the left shoulders of people who didn't look terribly different from us. But I suppose we figured that no one would bother to train us so long ("More sweat on the training field, less blood on the battlefield!") and spend so much on our uniforms and salaries (it didn't seem like much to the individual turkey, but was obviously a lot when multiplied by a few million turkeys) only to send such expensive, highly trained and well-dressed dragoons and Zouaves to some obscure and largely peace-ridden spot. And you didn't want to seem a fool; banking on orders for Germany or Korea was like betting to fill an inside straight. And you certainly didn't want to get all worked up with hope.

But we had to find some way to get away from Benning and Columbus. Kelly Hill was a tense place now at night and on weekends, and either the Random Negro was going to happen to us or we were going to start turning into Random Negroes ourselves and happen to other people. Rollie had the color down already and was looking more and more Random every day. And Becker, born weird, was starting to pioneer new vistas in weirdness.

One day I was bringing a staff car back to the Hill from the base hospital and as I topped the hill and turned the corner onto the main drag, I spotted Becker standing in front of the dispensary. When he saw my car, he snapped to attention and saluted, a nice crisp one. I didn't like that at all. The whole thing just smelled wrong. Becker was in the wrong place, all the way across Kelly Hill from his barracks and the meteorology unit, and he was doing the wrong thing, saluting. I pulled the sedan over to the curb and when he saw it was me, he stuck his head in the passenger window.

"Hello, Becker. What are you doing?"

"Nothing. Didn't see it was just you in the car. Thought there might be an officer in the back or something."

"That was a nice salute you shot me there," I said.

"Been practicing," he said.

"You had to go to the dispensary?"

"No."

"You want a ride back to the company?"

"Nope. I think I'll hang out here for a while, if that's okay."

"Sure," I said. "You waiting for somebody, maybe?"

"No. Yes and no."

"I don't really understand that."

He seemed to be getting annoyed. "It's just something I'm doing. No big deal."

"What the fuck *are* you doing, Becker, if I can be so bold as to ask?"

"Just being respectful," he said. "You know, this is part of military courtesy. You saw the movies."

"Look, I think you're losing it, Becker. I really do. It's no skin off my nose, but it might start some talk. Of course that's nothing new for you."

"Okay, let's go to the snack bar and fuck off for a while. Buy me a hamburger. I don't have any money."

He got into the car and after I returned it to the headquarters lot, we walked to the cafeteria. Becker bought two flat greasy-burgers and we sat down at a corner table next to the Rock-ola. I had to wait for him to snarf down the burgers and that took about five seconds. I didn't want to press the man.

He cocked his face to that bent angle of his. "First, let me thank you for the burgers," he said, and belched to make his point. "However, I have to say I'm disappointed in your attitude about military courtesy. Were you implying there was something wrong with me standing on a corner and saluting officers?"

"I didn't buy you those fucking burgers to listen to this shit," I said.

"Well, you interrupted what I'd planned to be doing all afternoon, so you're going to listen. I didn't know there were any strings attached to these burgers. Maybe if you had a little fucking ambition to try to be a better troop, you might get somewhere in this man's army."

"All I want to get in this man's army is out of it."

"You know, the salute has an interesting history. It originated as a demonstration between warriors that their hands weren't holding any weapons. Did you know that?"

"Yes, thanks. We had that class, too."

"Moreover, one of my drill sergeants in basic told us that the reason Americans salute with the palm down is because we've never lost a war. Were you aware of that?"

"What are we going to do if you win your bet and we blow this one?"

"Don't know. He didn't tell us that and nobody happened to ask. I imagine there's a group down at the Pentagon looking into it. Buy me another burger."

"Fuck, no. I ain't buying you another burger. Just what the fuck are you up to, Becker?"

He considered something for a moment, some entertaining, clammy tidbit that passed for an idea in Becker's head. "Okay. Well, you already noticed that I was hanging out in front of the dispensary saluting officers. You got that much."

"Yes. I mean, those are the only dickheads you're supposed to salute. Tell me something I don't know."

"I don't have time to tell you everything you don't know. For one thing, it's obvious you don't know that you're supposed to

salute an enlisted man if that particular enlisted man is a re-
cipient of the Congressional Medal of Honor. Even generals
are supposed to salute that swinging dick first. But let's move
on. You may have noticed that because we have an officer candidate school down on Main Post, this place is crawling with
infantry second lieutenants."

"I have in fact noticed that."

"Very good. There's hope for you yet. Now, what's the very
first thing a newly commissioned second lieutenant does when
he graduates from OCS?"

"Beats the shit out of me."

"No, he's not allowed to do that. He'd like to, but it's against
regulations. Because this officer is stuck in the army for the
next three years and everyone knows where he is at all times,
this brand-new officer finds himself with unlimited credit with
every slimeball merchant in Columbus. So the first thing he
does is he runs down to Columbus and buys himself an MG or
a Triumph sports car on credit. You don't notice very much,
do you?"

"Okay, now that you mention it, a lot of dickhead second
lieutenants drive around in little British sports cars. Where the
fuck is all this leading?"

"We're getting there. So much for what the dickheads do.
Now what is it they want?"

"I don't know."

"These dickheads have spent the last six months in the living
hell of OCS. Now they want respect from enlisted men, now
that they finally aren't enlisted men themselves anymore. And
they get that respect by having enlisted men salute them."

"So you've decided to oblige. This is still rather mysterious
to me, Becker."

"I don't oblige them all the time. Not everywhere. I just like
to salute second lieutenants when they're driving their little
British sports cars onto Kelly Hill."

"Why is that?"

"Because just at that turn, the dickheads have to gear up
from second gear, which they're in to take that narrow, twisting
hill, and they have to shift into third, for the level road in front
of the dispensary. They have to shift gears with the right hand
and turn the wheel with the left hand at the same time."

I closed my eyes and tried to picture the situation. It was starting to make something that passed for sense, assuming you were Becker. "He's shifting with his right hand, turning the wheel with his left, and you're standing there saluting him at the same time, so he has to come up with a third hand to return your salute. Something like that, isn't it?"

"Something exactly like that." Becker was a little excited now. "I saw it happen by accident a couple of nights ago and it's been brewing in my head ever since. So this morning I decided to give it a try. You wouldn't *believe* it, Richard. All of them stall out. They can't fucking help it. One guy banged into the curb and jumped it with his right front wheel, and then he stalled out. Another dickhead flooded his engine trying to get it started again. I mean, he'd only had the MG for a couple of days and you know what turkeys those guys are with mechanical things. It's great. I'm still working on actual car damage, but I figure that has to come if I hang out there long enough."

"Don't the boys get a little pissed off?"

"Enormously pissed off. But what the fuck can they do? 'Sergeant, I want you to punish this man for saluting me.' I mean, there you are being a respectful enlisted man, and as long as you don't laugh at them, there's no reason why you can't keep doing it for as long as you like."

Whoa, I thought. Whoa.

"Look. Becker. We all got to get off this fucking Hill, but I think you got to get off this Hill a little more than the rest of us. You're starting to lose the short supply of brains and self-control you came up here with, and I don't mind admitting I'm a little worried about it."

"That's sweet. I appreciate your concern. What did you have in mind?"

"Do you think you can score yourself a three-day pass?"

"Sure. They give 'em out like water in the orderly room. Nobody can afford to go anywhere, so nobody asks for them. Nobody's strong enough to stand three solid days in Columbus."

"Okay. Get one and let's go to Atlanta Friday night. Rollie can go on the back of your bike. I'll take a bus or hitch or something."

"What'll we do when we get there?" Becker asked.

"Fuck if I know, but anything's better than this shit. Rollie's

in a really bad way. We all need it pretty bad. We'll find someplace to shack up and do the mess-around. Atlanta's supposed
to be a halfway decent town."

"I'm a sport. I'm willing to give it a try. I can hang around
the dispensary saluting officers anytime."

By Thursday we all had our passes in our wallets. I had to
run out to Harmony Church Thursday morning and I wandered over to R.J.'s armory where he was repairing some M14s
the troops had been using to club trees to death.

"Goin' out to the range again tonight," he said. "You want
to come?"

"Sounds like fun, but I think I'll pass. Listen, we've all scored
three-day passes and we're skating up to Atlanta tomorrow."

"You got a place to stay?"

"No. We'll probably go in on a motel room somewhere. Tomorrow's payday."

"I got a place to stay up there. You guys can stay there if you
want. How you getting up there?"

"Becker and Rollie are going up on the bike. I was going to
take a bus or hitch."

"Fuck that. I got a car, too."

"Where'd you get a car?"

"From your cook, Willie. He got caught again drinking and
driving and the C.O. told him to get rid of it or he'd court-
martial his ass. He sold it to me for a hundred bucks and I haul
him around Phenix City a couple of nights a week. It's not a
bad deal. Big fuckin' Chevy. Right side's all banged up, but it
runs pretty good. You guys want to cruise up with me?"

"Sure. Becker'll still probably want to take the bike up, but
I'll ride with you. I don't know about Rollie. He may actually
enjoy riding on the back with Becker."

"Okay. The OCS mickeymouse ends around five tomorrow
afternoon and I can probably get the arms room locked up
before six. I'll slide down to Kelly Hill and pick up whoever's
coming with me around seven."

The OCS mickeymouse was why we were all there in the first
place. Our massive infantry brigade, with its artillery and armor
battalions, was the pretend enemy engaged in a never-ending
war against the officer candidates and occasionally the Rangers
and the shake-and-bakes, the students at a six-week school that

magically transformed privates into three-stripe infantry platoon sergeants. I'd heard of other army pretend-enemy units that had whole legends made up for them, imaginary countries, political dogmas, special salutes and weird Ruritanian uniforms. Nothing fancy like that for us. Our side was just a few thousand highly pissed-off enlisted short-timers, most of them back from their Vietnam tours, hustled out of bed every morning at 4:30 to scramble over the Georgia clay and through the forests shooting blanks out of an assortment of weapons in the vague direction of the candidates.

Nevertheless, we certainly had a dogma in the absence of an officially supplied one when we played these war games. Our side was composed entirely of people who wanted no part of any of this, while our adversaries were all volunteers who wanted all we could supply, and when we could supply nothing further in the way of authenticity, the volunteers wanted a shot at leading troops into the real thing, the live bullet experience. We really wanted to sleep till noon while our adversaries kept complaining to our superiors that, at 6:00 A.M., we'd arrived late.

This dogma never motivated any of us to put on a particularly good offensive battle against the candidates, but it motivated us to inflict casualties. The regular infantry troops had a nasty trick. To fire blanks from an M14 in such a way that it reloaded itself by recycling the hot gases from the blanks back into the rifle, a metal cylinder called a flash suppressor was fixed at the end of the barrel like a bayonet. A lot of the troops would loosen theirs so the rifle gases sent these three-pound metal devices hurtling forward with a punch surpassing that of a well-pitched hardball. When aimed true, they could clang against a candidate's helmet as he charged up San Juan Hill and send him toppling backward with visions of those cartoon stars and ringed planets dancing in his enthusiastic little head. Sometimes some of our troops would be given flamethrowers filled with water; these turned out to be the granddaddy of all water pistols and could knock a candidate off his feet at fifteen paces. Even when a candidate was certain he'd been assaulted on purpose, there was nothing he could do about it. If he tried to come after one of our black dudes, he immediately found himself facing a dozen united brothers ready to show him some real war. And a candidate couldn't go official; he could never complain about something rough and nasty that happened to him on maneuvers. You could see in their eyes that although these golden boy fools and lunatics had knowingly volunteered for infantry combat against the Viet Cong, they resented the rancor and viciousness that awaited them on the hills and in the woods of Fort Benning from troops who were nominally in their same army.

I was waiting in front of the barracks when R.J. rolled up in the big Chevy with the banged-up right side the next night. He had his usual tasteful civilian threads on, a loud flowery Hawaiian short-sleeved shirt and a pair of iridescent green polyester slacks. We drove through Main Post and out the main gate and stopped at a Piggly-Wiggly, where R.J. scored a Styrofoam ice chest, some ice, a couple of cold six-packs of beer and a bottle of fruit wine, spodie-odie. I decided to pass and bought a couple of bottles of Royal Crown, Columbus being the RC Cola center of the galaxy and RC being about the only black sweet fizz shit available for miles around. We gassed up next door and with an eight-cylinder belch took off for Georgia 85 north.

The smell of Willie's ex-car hadn't changed as far as I could tell, and everything else about it was wrong. The steering was slow and unresponsive, the brakes were uninspired, the alignment was shot to shit, the shocks had given up the ghost and the only thing that worked, the AM radio, was functioning deep within shitkicker music country, which was fine with R.J. While he guzzled down the fruit wine and the beer, I rolled numbers from a bag of reefer and smoked them until the music became almost passable.

R.J. put a crack in the silence somewhere north of Callaway Gardens and looked sideways in my direction. "How long you got to go?"

"At Benning? In the army?"

"Whatever."

"A few more months here, then another year more or less."

"Becker says you're eleven-bravo."

"That's the one."

"I couldn't handle that. I took myself a third year and went to armorer's school. The army ain't so bad. I sure as hell ain't stayin' in it, but I've had some high old times. Got sent places where women do shit so strange on you I had to pay five bucks extra to ask its name. It's going to take work and money to keep that sort of thing going on the outside."

"I'm sure you'll manage."

"Lemme tell you something. This honey in Manila asked me if I wanted to try something new, and I was up for about anything that night, so I went along with it. Well, what she commenced to do, she commenced to take a red silk scarf all knotted up with these little knots, and knot by knot she pushed that scarf some distance up my ass. Felt sort of strange, not exactly nice, but it didn't hurt; I was more curious than worried. And then she commenced to get me all hot and bothered in the usual ways until pretty soon we were honey-fuckin', real slow and low, takin' our time. So I guess I started to give off noises that I was ready to pop my rocks, and just when I was about to throw off a good one, Lord Jesus and Mary! She had her hand back there and she just yanked that scarf out right quick—I don't know what it did, except I thought I was going to shoot her halfway across the room and I thought my eyeballs were going to explode and a grenade was splattering the insides of my head into mush against the outside. But that's all there is to it—a knotted-up silk scarf and some honey with a little willingness and imagination. And good timing. But you ought to get you somebody who'll help you try that."

"I'll work on it right away."

He looked at me and laughed. "You got somethin' against that, don't you? Maybe you already got something jammed up your ass which would pree-clude this particular practice, like a broomstick."

"No. Not exactly. I just—"

"You ever paid for it?"

"No."

"Well, don't you break that barrier if you don't want. We both reckon you're going to Vietnam, and there's going to be nine tons of willing teenage pussy over there per military credit, so you make sure you don't touch a bit of it for your twelve godforsaken months. That way you can return to your fee-an-say as clean and wholesome as when you shipped out."

"Maybe you never heard Becker tell his Tales of the Black Clap or the razor blades."

"Yeah, right. Oh, shit, that Becker's so full of it. They got shots for what ails you over there. And they don't even court-martial you for it like they used to do in World War Two. And you find me some lady who puts razor blades in her snatch, you do that. I'll bring 'er back here and put her in the carnival. It just boils down to gettin' your rocks off now and then while Sam's got you in a shithole. It's for sale, for rent, for lease; it's all around. You got reasons to keep it to yourself, you do that, but don't try to explain it to me. I sure as fuck ain't got time for that."

"You and I are different."

"How? You like boys instead? That may be a little tricky here in headquarters company, but it don't make no nevermind in Cholon."

"No. I don't go in for boys."

"You go in for other species, like Becker? I always suspected that's where he was at. That boy thinks he's destined to invent whole new vistas in fucking. Sideways fuckin', inter-di-men-sional fuckin', blow jobs from Venus flytraps—that boy don't know how to shut his brain off when he's balling. I think he was devastated when the second and third times were so much like the first. He don't pay for it either. You college boys are so-oo proud. You like that free love shit. Yeah, I've had some of that free love. It is *mis*-named, to say the least."

The motorcycle was parked out front of R.J.'s house when we pulled up around 9:30. Becker and Rollie were in the living room bullshitting with a couple of honeys; they knew R.J. and were pleased as punch to see him, Hawaiian shirt and all. They were young, high school stuff as far as I could judge. Annie turned out to be one of them; it was the first time I ever saw her. The other one turned out to be her squeeze, Tina.

The house was an old brick job in a section off Peachtree that was just starting to ponder about whether or not to go on the decline (and no doubt R.J.'s success in renting would help that process along considerably). I guessed it dated from the thirties or early forties; it had magnificent woodwork, moldings and parquetry and a big fireplace in the living room and another in the master bedroom, with a kitchen obviously designed for a couple of servants. The closets were cavernous. There was a back service stairway and a finished attic you didn't have to stoop in; Annie lived in it and Tina paid rent on one of the smaller bedrooms. Even though R.J. only used the place on weekends and couldn't even manage to get away every weekend, he'd engineered the deal and paid the lion's share of the rent. Tina was a little older than Annie and had a topless gig in a dive across town, while Annie had a job as a lunchtime waitress near the Omni. They kept the place safe and livable for R.J. while he was away, so when they came up short on the rent from time to time, R.J. didn't make a big deal over it.

R.J. could have survived on beer, but the ladies kept the refrigerator stocked a little better than that with some fairly substantial solids. At first I didn't think about food. I was in a living room with a big rug, sitting in a comfortable secondhand overstuffed chair, smoking reefer, talking to new people. No one was wearing a uniform. No one had any rank. I was talking to honeys, listening to their voices and to their laughter; I even thought I could smell them. At the post and in Columbus I'd just tried to block out the voices of the women I had to contend with; their drawls drove me up the wall and the thought of having anything more to do with them than tendering a bill and receiving change made my hair stand on end. These voices were different, sweet, liquid and crystalline, musical. I listened, mostly; Becker talked the most, then Rollie.

I got up to wander through the house. The bedrooms upstairs were empty, not filled with bored and suspicious soldiers. There were flower scents from one of the bedrooms, sachet and cheap perfumes. A quilt was on the bed and on the vanity were women's jars and makeup pencils, boxes and jewelry, pairs of earrings, purposeless feathers, golden chains. In the old white-tiled bathroom with the ancient clover-fist faucets there was women's underwear, stockings draped over the towel racks to dry. When I heard people walking around downstairs, I could tell the different tread of the women from the men's. Someone put a Janis Joplin record on the stereo downstairs.

I ended up at the top of the narrow service staircase and went down to the dim kitchen. Across the room Annie was putting a teakettle on the old gas stove. She turned around suddenly and saw me.

"You scared me," she said.

"Sorry."

"Richard. You're Richard."

"Yeah."

"You hungry? We got some eggs and toast and breakfast shit like that."

"That'd be nice."

She bent down and started taking pots and pans from a cupboard.

"Listen, could I cook it myself? Would you mind?"

She looked at me. "No, go ahead. You might need some help finding everything you need."

"That's okay. You can stay if you want. I just wanted to cook it myself."

She found a corner counter and boosted herself up from behind and watched me. Things weren't hard to find at all. I took butter and a couple of eggs and some milk from the refrigerator. I cracked the eggs over a cast-iron skillet; they hit the pan with a singing noise. Annie volunteered to make the toast; there was already coffee in a percolater on the stove. She sat across from me in the dinette as I wolfed it all down.

"You like to cook."

"Yeah. I haven't been able to in a year. I haven't even been able to fry an egg."

"You're down at the fort with R.J."

"Yeah. He's in another unit, but we're both down there."

"My dad's a colonel down there. Light colonel. He teaches at the Infantry Center. He's a real asshole. I think he wants to ball me. I'm a shitty cook. You can cook all you want while you're here."

"I'll cook us all dinner tomorrow night," I said. "I'll knock your fucking lamps out with dinner. I got paid today."

12

More than just me, there were a lot of northern guys who were convinced there was an army subconspiracy to exile drafted Yankee boys to Dixie just for laughs, just to bust their chops and destroy their morale without even having to work at it. The charitable ones among us just wrote the South off as another country with strange customs, like doing a tour at the remote army communications base in Ethiopia. There weren't many who saw it that way, though. I'd tried at first, but it hadn't worked out. I hated the South. If the conspiracy worked the other way and exiled southern draftees to places like Fort Devons or Fort Dix, where they suffered from the strange ways of the Yankees, well, frankly, my dear, I didn't give a damn; that was how uncharitable Fort Benning, Columbus and Phenix City had made me. I hated the Georgia accent, particularly on women—I winced when I heard it—and whenever I tried to get charitable or just oblivious to southern ways, Dixie started acting like Dixie.

There was an Upstairs infantry major named Banner, a strange bird, skinny and tough, very sharp, very motivated, who got his jobs done perfectly but never kicked his enlisted men in the balls to do it. One afternoon in the S-4 office he loosened up and started talking socially and within about five sentences I realized he was black—well, obviously not Crayola's idea of black, but what they used to call a high yellow. If what I'd guessed before that was any judge, Banner had and knew he had the ability to pass for white for any length of time until he chose to announce otherwise. He let the cat out of the bag so casually that I suspected he used passing as an intellectual tool—by not announcing otherwise over a loudspeaker, he enjoyed being a white major for the first few months in a new unit so all the nigger-loathers, officer and enlisted, above and below him, could step up and clearly identify themselves, perhaps to invite him to a cross burning. I know I felt uncomfortable when he declared himself in that bull session; I felt a wave of panic and felt my brain suddenly reviewing the text of every previous conversation I'd had with him, even though I knew there hadn't been anything untoward. It was just a weird situation and feeling.

Banner said this was his second tour at Benning. When he'd finished OCS about five years before, he'd been posted to an infantry company for his first year as an officer. "The Columbus police pulled me over twice for driving around town with a black woman," he said. "That was all. Just for thinking I was a white man driving around with a black woman next to me in the car. Lot of nasty questions, lot of ugly looks. All I had to do to make it stop was tell them I was black. Then everything was fine and we were on our way. It hasn't happened so far this tour. Maybe there were some uglier situations and the army had to lean on them. It's happened before. Usually the fort wants good relations with the town so bad that it never interferes no matter what goes on in Columbus, but every now and then something happens to a soldier that even the army won't tolerate, and a big post knows how to do a number on its army town to whip it into line PDQ. Or maybe Columbus has just made some progess. I don't know."

I knew. Either Banner was real lucky so far this tour, his lady friends were as high yellow as he was, or his first guess was right—after the Columbus cops had whipped out some atrocity on a black soldier that the commander just couldn't ignore, the army had threatened to shut down its civilian payroll by twenty percent or some such heavy-duty money threat. Banner was being charitable. Well, that was his right and probably his need; he was a lifer, after all, and he was going to have to spend the rest of his career living in places like Columbus. That obligated him to be a little on the Pollyanna side when it came to evaluating how tolerant and progressive Dixie was; otherwise he'd have to look in the mirror every morning at a black idiot who chose to live in active Klan strongholds when he could just as easily park his ass in the North or the West. He probably didn't have too many illusions about those regions, but at least the cops there don't pull you over for mixed-race front seats as often. Or maybe he was awash with purposeful and self-protective illusions and delusions. Sometimes a sharp mind can be even more adept at that than a dullard when there's a need. If Banner lived in a different Dixie from mine, it wasn't surprising; one of my goals after simply surviving was never to set foot in Dixie again. His ambitions were clearly to go for thirty years and all the rank he could get, colonel's bird or general's stars, so his ticket was punched differently.

But stories like Banner's miscegenation front-seat adventures—not from some radical honked-off northern brother, but from a lifer who needed to get along with Dixie—infuriated me. Reading about them from a distance back on the block, they would have just annoyed me, but exiled now to the heart of the place itself, where every third bumper or license-plate holder had a Confederate flag, they deepened my misery and self-pity. No matter how hard I tried to ignore it, I had a reminder every morning in the mess hall when I wasn't quick enough to stop the cook from plopping a puddle of grits onto my tray. There was no other food I hated more than grits. I had nothing personal against asparagus. Grits was my enemy.

So a benevolent God created Atlanta just for people like me. Lord knows what it meant to southerners themselves, but I'd been tipped off to it by someone back home when I was on my way to getting drafted. "Listen," he'd said, "if you're ever sentenced to do time in the South and there's no way you can get out of it, try to do your time or spend as much time as you can in Atlanta. It's a pretty good facsimile of a northern city, close enough for rock 'n' roll, anyway. You'll find places there and you'll do things where you almost won't be able to tell the difference." I'm sure that wasn't the Atlanta Chamber of Commerce's idea of a bombshell brochure (they tended to be queer for the street corner where the taxi bumped off Margaret Mitchell), but obviously I wasn't the first exiled northern boy to seek refuge there under the illusion that it might be Pittsburgh if only the natives would just stop talking for twenty minutes. If I couldn't pay it a better compliment, it sure beat the living shit out of Columbus and Phenix City.

It certainly came along just in time for me and Rollie. Becker, I think, could have stayed in any vile pesthole indefinitely, getting his rocks off organizing some kind of underground or resistance like the Patriotic Front to Make Officers Wreck Their British Sports Cars or some such bullshit; it took me to find Atlanta for him and drag him there physically before he got in over his head dipping it into officer snatch and advising R.J.'s more berserk commercial ventures. R.J., on the other hand, could luxuriate anywhere he could cook up a profit-making scheme, and most of his schemes at Fort Benning required an Atlanta base anyway, a big, anonymous city where the authorities had more to do than focus on just the jolly kinds of things R.J. tended to cook up. Atlanta gave him psychic rewards as well, though. He liked a slow, comfortable pace and surroundings where he called the shots, and there was nothing remotely resembling that in his life at Harmony Church.

But whatever each of us needed or wanted from Atlanta, we all began to chase it around merrily. Becker started serving as Tina's motorcycle chauffeur to take her to her topless dive and spend the rest of the day nursing rum-and-Cokes and rooting for his favorite dancers—he went in for small, taut breasts and little pouty mouths, his habitual junior high school look—and Rollie drifted around town by himself with few or no explanations, becoming something of a man of mystery. It was clear he wasn't sitting on park benches or dozing in libraries. Each morning and night he'd flash out of the house with obvious direction and enthusiasm, and he did subtle little dances to discourage company. Some nights he failed to come back to the house at all, and on a few weekends he failed to connect up with us for his ride back to base, but somehow managed to show up for formation courtesy of a predawn last-minute south-bound 'Hound redeye special.

"Maybe he's rediscovered Negroes," I suggested to Becker one Saturday night in front of R.J.'s fireplace. "He has so few dealings with them at the base."

"Nah. I know what he's up to. And it's a bad business."

"He told you? He's been awfully goddam close-mouthed about it to me."

"Nope. He didn't tell me a thing," Becker said. "He's more your butt-fuck buddy than mine. But it's the clothes. Haven't you noticed his evolving trousseau? That's the tip-off."

"Not to me, it's not."

"Look, the man never cared about clothes before. On a hot day at the base when he doesn't have to wear his uniform, he'd just as soon go around nude. Half the time he wears those bizarre farmers' overalls, for Christ's sake. But up here—check out those dress slacks and those casual sports shirts. Matching socks. Tasteful. He irons the fucking things before he goes out. Now where do you think he thinks an outfit like that'll make him fit in?"

"Make me wise."

"The man's going to college."

"How can a fucking draftee go to an Atlanta college on week-ends?"

"You're really a dope, aren't you? Look. Where did he come alive back on the block? Where did he get all snooty and elite? Where did his head get filled up with all those sporty Caucasian notions? Where did he learn to stop drinking Thunderbird and start doing drugs?"

"I still don't understand. Are you saying he's enrolled in some college around here?"

"Please," Becker said. "You're embarassing me. No. Of course he isn't enrolled in college. He's just back in Fantasyland. This town is laden with colleges, Emory, Mercer, junior colleges, universities, just like a real northern city. And I am betting big bucks that every weekend he comes up here, changes into his secret identity in the Bat Cave upstairs and, not content to watch the jiggling breasts of white women with me or just stroll around Atlanta pretending to be a civilian like you, he's passing for a college student. He won't be the first. Every college has a few fruitcakes who wear the raccoon coat and the beanie, take the tests, go to the prom, carry books around and enjoy every aspect of campus life except actually being enrolled. Our gargantuan *shvartzer* pal has thoroughly lost his fucking mind and has become one of these."

"What does he do there?"

"Aw, come on. Who checks? He strolls around the campus, talks to women in the cafeteria, goes to see *Performance* and *Harold and Maude* in the auditorium, hangs out in the student union buying and selling lids and tabs. He probably goes to the dwarfed little left-wing antiwar rallies even a Georgia campus can manage to barf up these days. He's probably got a rap ready for his pals about what his major is—shit, they don't interrogate one another about their classes on weekends. Shit, college students don't talk about their classes at all. For your average college meatball, that's like talking about your leprosy sores."

"You figured all this out from his clothes?"

"Okay. I confess. I found a student activities flier in the back pocket of a pair of his jeans. I shouldn't have told you. Now you'll lose all respect for my amazing powers of deduction."

"And he hasn't talked to you about it?"

"No, sir. Would you? For those first few floors as you slide down the bannister toward mental illness, you still realize that what you're doing is way over the line, and you don't like to call attention to yourself or solicit the opinions of your friends and loved ones, 'cause they might blow the whistle on you and stop all your fun."

"What can we do?"

"Nothing," Becker insisted. "For Christ's sake, leave him be. He's probably having a whale of a time. He's free, black and twenty-one. Twenty-three skidoo. Vo-de-oh-do." Becker began to sing again, this time what snatches the wandering minstrel could conjure up of the old twenties tune "Collegiate."

Becker and I were blasted out of our senses by three A.M. when Roland honored us by wandering in and pulling up a cushion. "Well, hello," Becker said enthusiastically. "Long time no see. Good to make contact with your fat ass."

"Nice to see you, too, Beck," Rollie said. "How're the nipples and tits of Atlanta?"

"And the areolae. Abso-fucking-lutely great. I got to admit,

I don't understand what I see in those bouncing sacs myself, but I do get a charge off 'em."

"Shit," Rollie said, "I know why. You like to degrade yourself. It's symbolic. You're punishing yourself for getting drafted. The army's told you you're now a lowlife, so you're living the part. Jiggle-jiggle-jiggle."

That never-ending tension between them crackled up like the dying fireplace log and I could see Becker's eyelids rising to the challenge.

"Let me guess," he said. "You, on the other hand, are elevating yourself. Improving your mind, perhaps?"

"Maybe. Oh, I'm not going celibate. But spending thirty bucks a night getting your ears blasted off by shitkicker music to look but not touch a few acres of skin and sniff beer fumes—yeah, I got something better than that."

"Oh, Roland, there's no competition here," Becker said. "We all know you're a spiritually superior being to me even when you're comatose. No contest. So why should I even try?"

"You're right that there's no contest. There isn't. But you do have a fucking mind, you know. I admire your twisted mind, Becker, I actually do. I do get a little sad at the shit you do to your spirit, though, I'll admit that. It's a generous soul. It started out decent. But the shit you put it through—it's going to get callused and mean and no good to you or anybody. And you haven't taken it anywhere decent or elevating since you've been in the fucking army. And that's your responsibility, you know. I can't take your fucking soul out for a walk."

Now Becker's eyes narrowed, but not from sleepiness. I was keeping my mouth entirely clammed. I wanted to watch the show, but no way was I taking part.

"Roland, where should I be walking my spirit? Say, on these lovely Atlanta weekends. Where do you recommend I take my karma for a shower? Where, for example, have you been gettin' yours washed and hot-waxed?"

"That's for me to know and you to find out."

"Ah, but I'll bet I have found out, you rascal you. As a matter of fact, Richard here and I were discussing this very topic earlier this evening."

"Don't drag me into this," I said. "I don't know shit about it. You're the guy with the theories."

Becker rolled a cigarette around in his fingers like Groucho's cigar. "Open up that jacket, Rollie. Let's see what's underneath."

Rollie unbuttoned his dungaree jacket. A sweatshirt was underneath that said EMORY in big letters above an emblem. Rollie smiled in the style of the Giaconda.

"Oh, boy," Becker said. "My worst fears confirmed."

"What worst fears?"

"You had to needle me, didn't you? I didn't care. I really didn't. But now I'll tell you. I am a soldier, whether I like it or not, and I am fully authorized to spend hours on end in a puddle of hot Schlitz looking up at scantily clad jiggle dancers in Dixie dives. But you? Fuckin' small-change Jekyll and Hyde—you ain't no fucking college student. Who are you trying to kid? Why are you warping your mind that way? You're someone else. You're one of us, cannon fodder, enlisted scum, Nambait. Who are you trying to kid?"

"Like I said, I'm responsible for what I subject my spirit to. In my off hours. And I am what I feel I am. I'm not a soldier. No threats or no uniforms—not even a loaded rifle in my hands on a battlefield—can make me what I don't want to be."

"And tell me: How many people every weekend are you jiving with your Joe College threads, huh? How many people are you making verbal contact with and telling 'em that you're who you're not? How many times is the real answer 'Private-first-class motor pool jockey at Fort Benning, Georgia,' and you tell somebody something entirely different? Is that your definition of soul food? I'll bet you practically believe it by now. You're probably almost ready to declare a psych major and order your goddam class ring."

"It beats the way you spend your time," Rollie snorted.

"You're one sick fuck, Rollie. I feel sorry for you. You have no idea what you're letting yourself in for."

"I'll do what I please."

"Won't we all?" Becker said. "That flat-ass goes without saying."

In those months, on the weekends I could get up to Atlanta, what I pleased was to pal it up with Annie when she wasn't working and take in the sights around town. I blew a wad on her at Six Flags over Georgia, like taking one of my little sisters to the amusement park. It was great. She wasn't getting very much in the way of fun out of Tina; the weeks between my visits were becoming more and more miserable and dispiriting for her, and she'd spend the Friday nights just singing the blues to me about Tina's latest crude remarks or behavior. I think she wanted advice from me, but I was trying to stay out of that one, too. People that age don't want romance advice; I sure as fuck hadn't wanted any. That's everyone's first roll-your-own masterpiece catastrophe, that first hot and impossible romance; it's really not any fun if it's handled too sensibly. The idea is to drag it out as long as it can thrash and gurgle, for all the really ugly final insults and parting low stabs the thing has to belch out, and Tina was an imaginative resource for them. So on Fridays, Annie would unload, work herself up to a big cry, I'd wipe the snot off her nose by around ten o'clock and then haul her out to some restaurant or late flick or county carnival, whatever we could get to on public transportation. Tina worked Saturdays, and Annie'd already had her catharsis, so those were particularly enjoyable. We'd walk for miles down Peachtree, go to museums, hang out in the big park and mix with Atlanta's small band of nervous weekend hippies. Once we were there when the Atlanta police swept the place for the youthful subversives. Two uniformed cops rousted us. I showed them my army ID and they actually apologized and went after the more vulnerable game. I was holding some joints in my pocket. A truly magical card that said so much about my good behavior and bona fides in the community.

Each week we had to spend back at Fort Benning made me understand more and more why Becker seemed so bent out of shape about Rollie's curious Atlanta maneuvers. As Atlanta comforted us more and more, Benning became more and more unbearable by comparison. For every hour we were treated decently, for every good meal, for every evening in the company of a pretty honey, Benning became a shriller, harsher, more alien place; I walked around Kelly Hill some Mondays and Tuesdays as if I'd agreed to pretend to be a soldier on a dare for a few days, and by Wednesday, when it was horrendously clear that just wasn't so, I had feelings so bleak and turgid that I felt as if my whole mind was shutting down piston by piston. On one weekend, the weekend before payday, when I was just so titanically broke that I couldn't even afford to hitch to Atlanta, I stayed in the barracks the whole two days and sulked so hard that people walked around my bunk as if there were a dead animal under it. I hadn't realized how connected I'd been with the post and life on Kelly Hill until I'd started spending time in Atlanta and breaking the connections. A barracks can feel like your home; it really can when it has to. Now it felt— well, it felt like the Repo Depot, something minimal and harsh, to be ended quickly and mercifully.

And enough time had gone by for that merciful end. It was time for us to start worrying about our orders. Rollie's came first, the classic and oft-promised Green Weenie, a week's leave and then orders to report to the overseas shipping point at Fort Lewis, Washington. It hit him hard, harder than I'd imagined it would. There wasn't much I could do for him; when my time came, there wasn't much anybody was going to be able to do for me. But I figured at least he'd want to get as much time in on campus (suddenly it was making sense to me, too) as he could before his leave started, so I'd yak it up to him about the next weekend trip up to Atlanta, but he wouldn't tumble. He was barely talking to me at all.

"Not going up there this weekend," he grunted from his bunk.

"Why the fuck not? Jesus, Rollie, staying down here isn't going to be very therapeutic for your head."

"I know what my head needs. You and Becker go if you want. I'm just going to stay here."

"Okay. Suit yourself. If you change your mind, you know where to find us."

That went on for a few weekends. We couldn't even talk Rollie into coming up to Atlanta for a big farewell blast at a good restaurant. He just wanted to spend his last days on post, pretty much alone. He'd scored a big hunk of hash and seemed determined to make it all vanish as soon as he could by toking up on it at every opportunity night and day; he was taking less care than he should to make sure no lifer caught him in the act. On the Hill with us he didn't actually avoid us, but he didn't bother to go out of his way to look us up either. He was just blithering his way through his short time.

The last weekend he was going to be in Georgia, the weekend we'd tried to get him to party with us in Atlanta, Becker and I went up alone on the motorcycle. We left the post late and got to the house around ten-thirty, eleven. Becker took the bike around the corner and put it in the alleyway and I walked up the long flight of steps to the front door. The lights were on in the living room and I could hear people talking inside. I knocked and Annie came to the door. She had the usual look on her face that she was tickled to see me, but it was mixed with something else, something mildly awry, something that needed explaining or immediate medical attention or its balance paid. I tossed my little pack in the corner and walked into the living room with her.

"R.J.'s gone out already," Annie said. "This is Alice. Alice, this is Richard."

She was lovely, whoever this Alice was. She was wearing a simple powder-blue dress with a faded red cotton sash and some funky old white saddle shoes. She had long, straight blond hair just slightly gussied up with a thin pigtail. She was smoking a menthol cigarette to add to an already filled ashtray on the old cable-drum table. She smiled at me meekly, almost embarrassed, certainly a little confused.

"I think I'd better go," she said suddenly with just the slightest Georgia accent; she pronounced things with care, educated without the heavy hand of a finishing school. She stood quickly and grabbed for her cigarette pack. I didn't know what was going on, so I didn't know what was appropriate. I looked at Annie.

"Please don't go," Annie said to her.

Alice looked around as if she were looking for danger in the room. I guess she didn't find any. She sat down again and lit another smoke. I lit a cigarette. Annie was working on some reefer in an onyx pipe. Becker started to trudge in from the kitchen behind us, making a lot of noise. Annie got up and steered him back into the kitchen. That left me out in the living room with Alice Blue Gown.

I settled back in my chair and put my feet up on the table. It seemed to make sense to let her deal the cards so I might be able to get some idea of what the game was. When she finally spoke, it was softly, almost as if she didn't want to speak at all or have me hear what she said.

"Annie said Rollie might be coming with you."

I had a feeling instantly that I wasn't going to like this game.

"No. He didn't want to come up this weekend. Are you a friend of Rollie's?"

That must have been the gin card because she stood up again, fumbled for her smokes and started to cry all at the same time, which meant that she didn't do any particular one of those things very well. I got up, I guess to block the door gently if I had to.

"Wait a second. You're among friends. Sit down."

She sat down and kept burbling, but a little less fervently. She looked uncomfortable at it, as if she didn't do it very often. I probably did it more than she did. When she looked a little more settled, I went into the kitchen to get her some coffee or whatever might be quick and at hand. Annie was talking to Becker, who was eating some slices of salami.

"What's going on out there?" I asked Annie. "Who is she?"

"I don't know." She shrugged her shoulder. "She knocked on the door about a half hour ago and asked if Rollie lived here. I told her he didn't, but that he might come in with you guys. Is she crying out there?"

"Yeah, she's crying. She's a little calmed down now, I think. You don't know who she is?"

"Beats me," Annie said.

"If you don't have any bread," Becker asked, "do you have some mustard? I don't want any of that bland yellow shit, though."

I reheated some coffee of dubious vintage and took a couple of cups back to the living room. She had a couple of sips and then looked across the table at me. Her nose and eyes were red and moist. I found some tissues for her.

"I'm really sorry," she said. "You all must think I'm really strange."

"If you get to know us a little better, I'm sure you won't worry about that nearly as much. Look, let me try it again gently. Are you a friend of Rollie's?"

She thought about how to phrase things for a few seconds. "Yes, I guess so."

"Do you go to one of the colleges around here?"

"Yes. I'm studying English at Emory. How did you know? Did Rollie mention me?"

"Not exactly. Can I call you Alice?"

"Sure."

"Alice, listen. Did you know that Rollie's not in college?"

"Well, I knew he wasn't a full-time student at Emory, if that's what you mean."

"Not exactly. Look, let me just toss it by you all at once. Rollie's in the army. Full time. We're all in the army. Well, not all of us, not Annie, but Rollie and I and Becker back there in the kitchen—we're all stationed down at Fort Benning."

"Oh."

"Yeah. Oh. That's how I feel about it. I guess you met Rollie on campus."

"Yes. Your name's Richard, isn't it? He talked about you sometimes."

"Yeah, that's me, Richard."

"He's a soldier?"

"No. He's just in the army. Drafted, like me and Becker. That's very different from being a soldier. I know it sounds like splitting hairs, but we like to think there's a distinction. It helps us get through some of the harder days."

"I really feel like a dope."

"Why?"

"I don't know. I guess this whole thing has nothing to do with whether he's in the army or not. It's just—it's just very much of a surprise, that's all. He never mentioned anything about it."

"Yeah." I looked up at the ceiling. "You'd think he would have mentioned a little thing like that, wouldn't you?"

She looked at me a little more carefully, as if she were adding numbers together and I was a blackboard. "I'm sorry. I'm not really stupid. You're from up north. You think every girl in the South is stupid a little bit. I suppose I can understand what he was doing, why he didn't say anything."

"I don't think all southern girls are stupid. Look. I don't get much opportunity to meet many of them."

"I always thought, it always seemed he was unhappy about something, but he seemed to be having a good time with me. I didn't know. I thought it was his family or something. I thought he lived here. A friend of mine gave him a ride home one night and took him here. That's how I knew to come here."

"A friend of ours rents this place. We come up here on weekends, whenever we can get passes, whenever. Columbus is a real pit."

"I suppose it is. I've been there. Is Rollie down there now?"

"Well, yes, I think. Look, are you and Rollie having some kind of a thing? I know it's none of my business and all that crap, but it might help to straighten whatever there is to straighten out."

She nodded. "I thought we were, anyway. That's why I feel like such an asshole—I'm sorry."

"That's okay. I know what it means."

"If something had happened—but nothing happened. I don't think anything happened, anyway. I don't understand why he hasn't been around."

"That's easy. Something happened," I said. "He got his orders."

"You mean he's leaving?"

"Yeah, that's what I mean."

"When?"

"Well, I think he gets a week of leave first, starting around now."

"And then what?"

"Oh. Well, then he goes to Vietnam. It's happening to a lot of us. It's been in all the newspapers. He's not very happy about it. In fact, to tell the truth, I'm a little bit worried about him. I don't mean I'm worried about something happening to him over there. I mean about the way he's taking it."

"What do you mean?"

"Well, Rollie plays everything very close to the chest. He's also, well, a little on the sensitive side. I guess the other ghetto kids forgot to beat him up as much as they were supposed to, to toughen him up. I think he's very upset about Nam and if I had to guess, I think he's upset about you. He doesn't have anybody else."

"But he doesn't want to see me."

"Maybe. Maybe he just, well, lacked the intestinal fortitude to tell you about his little white lies. Pardon me for asking, but do you drink liquor or smoke marijuana or anything? Or do you mind if I do?"

"I could use some reefer," she said.

"Glorioski." I found a number in the teak humidor and fired it up. We passed it back and forth a few times. It mellowed me out and it seemed to loosen her up a tad.

"Could I call him?" she said after a while.

"That sounds like a grand idea." I picked up the phone from under the table and dialed up the number of the orderly room.

"Headquarters and headquarters company, Specialist van Hoff speaking, sir."

Bad news; a lifer. "Hello, van Hoff. Listen, have you seen Rollie around there tonight?"

"You mean Cutler? He's signed out. He got the staff duty driver to take him to the airport."

"You sure?"

"Yeah. They left about an hour ago. There's a late flight. He had orders to Nam, you know."

"I know. Thanks, van Hoff. Hey, do you happen to know his home address, his leave address? Is that on his orders?"

"I don't have his orders."

"Okay, I'll get it later. Thanks."

"No sweat."

I hung up. "The C.Q. says he's left to go on leave already," I explained.

"I don't know what to do."

"I can probably scare you up his home address, where he'll be for the next week. We can try to get him there."

"I'm pregnant," she said.

I closed my eyes and rocked a little back and forth in the chair. People were always telling me things like that, that they were pregnant or queer or on the run from espionage raps or were just masquerading as generals. Perfect strangers. It must have been something about my face. I wondered if there'd be any way to make a buck at it after I got out of the service.

"Does Rollie know?"

"No. I don't even know why I told you."

That makes two of us, I thought.

"I'm sorry. I shouldn't have. I don't know why I did. It's not your problem. I just haven't told anyone—"

"That's all right. It is my problem, sort of. Maybe. I'll try to do what I can, anyway. I take it you're in love with the lad."

"I don't know. That makes it sound like some kind of yes-or-no question. I don't know what I am except pregnant. We were just having such good times. It was very different. I've never dated anyone very much. Yes, I think so."

"What about him? How does he feel about you?"

"I don't know. I think he—Well, how can I know?"

"Well, let's pretend it's the real stuff both ways, you and him. What would you like to do?"

"What do you mean?"

I got mad. I don't know why. Yes, I know why. I was pissed off at all the goddam shyness and self-sacrifice going around. It was pissing me off something awful.

"I mean, do you just want to slink off in the night and let the slimy motherfucker off the hook, or do you want to give the poor jerk a hand and meet him halfway? He's having a hard time dealing with things right now. So are you. Maybe you'd both have an easier time dealing with everything together. I think he's very scared. Shitfaced, in fact. To put it very crudely, I think he thinks he's going to die soon or get his groin blasted off, something like that, and it hasn't put him in much of a mood for acting sensibly. Maybe you could help him out."

"I don't think so. Not with what I'd have to tell him."

"How do you know? It just might be the jolly thing to put a sunny complexion on his other worries. I'll be getting orders like that soon. Oh, I keep hoping for the French Riviera, but it's just not going to work out that way. And I don't have anyone. I have friends, but it's not the same thing. I can't sleep with my friends. I can't whisper things in the night to them. I can't tell them I'm scared. And I am very scared, Alice."

"I haven't known anyone who's gone," she said.

"Well, now you've met a whole scout troop that's going, going, gone, and let me tell you, each of us is one very scared asshole. Me, I think you ought to fool everybody and chase his black ass down and find him and tell him. Tell him you love him and you're going to have a baby by him and all the rest of the crap that usually goes along with that. God knows it couldn't make him feel any worse."

"I don't want to go home," she said.

"That can be arranged, too. But what about Rollie?"

"Maybe I just ought to get an abortion and let him do whatever he wants to do."

"Maybe you owe it to him to talk to him about it. It's going to be his kid, too."

"He doesn't want to see me. I shouldn't have come here."

"Yes, you should have, and you did, and now you've laid it

all on me, and to tell you the truth, I'm not just going to keep it to myself. I'm going to call him up and tell him even if you won't, so the cat is definitely out of the bag. All he can tell either of us to do is to go jump, but I don't think that's what he's going to do. I don't think he's that kind of dude. I know him pretty —Jesus FUCK, what IS this insanity?" and I got mad again and stormed into the kitchen and kicked a bunch of cabinet doors around while Annie and Becker watched.

"Help you with anything?" Becker asked.

"Get screwed."

Eventually Annie calmed me down and left me with Becker while she went out to have her turn with Alice. I heard some more crying and honking and burbling and then things calmed down somewhat and Annie came back and fetched me back out to the living room for another family counseling session. It ended up with me calling van Hoff again and talking his reluctant lifer ass into rifling through the first sergeant's files until he found some personnel form with Rollie's home address on it. Then I started to do all this telephoning to Baltimore information ad I finally got this sweet-sounding woman who identified herself as the aunt of the one and only Rollie, a.k.a. Roland Cutler, presently serving in the U.S. Army. He'd called earlier that night from the Columbus Airport, and now her husband was on the way out to Friendship Airport to pick him up. The plane was due in soon and Rollie'd probably be home in an hour or so. So we all got ripped as shit and played some loud and wildly inappropriate rock 'n' roll music to kill the time and then I finally had the motherfucker himself on the horn, I suppose around one-thirty in the morning. I gave the phone to Alice Blue Gown, and Annie and I went upstairs and broke into R.J.'s stash of truly weird things. I don't know how it felt for Rollie and Alice or for Annie, but this first love bullshit was seriously bringing me down.

But it had power, I had to give it that. We put Alice up for the night in R.J.'s room (the alley cat never did wander back) and the next morning I borrowed the motorcycle and took her to the savings and loan where she took all her money out, and then I took her to the airport. She called her folks from a pay phone there and told them she was going up to Baltimore (*Where?*) for a few days to meet her fiancé (your *what?*) and that she didn't know when she'd be back, and not to worry about her (*Don't* worry *about you?*). I took her to the ticket window where she got a seat on a flight for Friendship leaving in about twenty minutes. Then I took her down to the gate and the next thing anyone knew I was raising this insane, terrific ruckus about the security machine and X-raying pregnant women and how I absolutely refused to let them do any such thing, and the poor security people tried to explain that the luggage got X-rayed but it wasn't that kind of a deal with the walk-through gate, which apparently ran on mere magnetism. Alice was by this time red with embarrassment and wondering if I was about to be arrested as a possible Cuban hijacker. When I finally calmed down, Alice kissed me on the cheek and the plucky honey headed down the hall for her plane.

I got a card from Rollie a few weeks later and it said:

Dear Richard,

Alice and I got married in Towson on the 14th. She's getting an apartment in Towson and working for a while until it's time for the baby, she'll send you her address. You can write me care of her too if you want and she can send it along. Alice says to tell you she thinks you're an okay dude, for what that's worth. Seriously, sorry if I gave you any hassle, I guess I did. Stay loose. Say hi to Becker and RJ and Annie and everybody.

Rollie

13

Becker got his orders three weeks before mine came through. I'd dreaded everything about orders: Becker's, mine, Becker's reaction to them, my reaction to them. Becker's reaction amazed me. He didn't have one. He acknowledged the orders and muttered about the things he'd have to do before he left Benning, just as if he'd scored temporary duty orders to an armed forces meteorology school somewhere in Nebraska. That he was going to Vietnam for a year right in the middle of the hottest war on the planet, and perhaps the galaxy, either hadn't sunk in or just made no impression. For once I kept my mouth shut, not because I wasn't curious or didn't think I had the right to pry, but because I figured if I showed a little patience, either he'd burst his own dam in his own time or someone else would be rude enough to ask him what he really thought about it while I was around and I'd get what I wanted without collecting the stigma for asking.

He pulled C.Q. in the orderly room one night when I had

the next day off, so I hung out with him while we listened to music on a borrowed stereo and spelled him while he crept out behind the barracks to get ripped to the tits, Charge of Quarters normally not being one of your more intellectually demanding army challenges. We played gin rummy until neither of us could remember any of the discards. "My father," he explained, "contaminated me with this useless game. It makes no sense. There's no point to it except to annihilate long blocks of time. Watching television in the dayroom on Saturday morning is more fulfilling." We played about fifty hands.

Without actually breaching any forbidden drawers, locked offices or cabinets, his hands and eyes pored over every loose document in and around the first sergeant's desk and the orderly room. Some of them he'd share with me, files of cheap company-level courts-martial or a bizarre set of Pentagon weapons maintenance manuals issued in comic book form. He also stumbled across something called "Lessons Learned," a Pentagon pamphlet with combat advice gleaned from last month's Vietnam combat disasters large and small. One of them that Becker particularly enjoyed and read out loud described a heated and enthusiastic volleyball competition between two army units who met at the same village at the same hour each week for their matches, stacking all their weapons to the side of the playing area. It didn't take long for Victor Charles to get hip to this clockwork temptation, and during about the ninth or tenth matchup, Victor dropped by in force and annihilated about eighteen of II Corps' finest unarmed volleyball players.

"What are the lessons here?" Becker asked me; it was snap quiz time.

"Volleyball causes death."

"Not so. Jesus. Do you mean to tell me that not one out of eighteen assholes could figure out they were setting themselves up as sitting ducks? I'm hardly what you'd call a master tactician, but even I don't intend to stand around unarmed in the same place at the same time every week over there punching a ball and screaming. I don't even do that over here. You remember my treasonous wager with R.J.?"

"Oh, yeah. Twenty bucks on America to place."

"Well, it's just possible that one of the reasons I'll collect is that the average imported allied dork ain't real fucking bright about combat matters compared to our foe. I get the feeling Foe's sharp as a tack, gets up real early in the morning and is real motivated. I don't get that same feeling about the average Us from what I've seen here. Hey, you went to advanced infantry training. Did you learn the profound skills necessary to stay alive and defeat the enemy?"

"Absolutely," I said. "If the Nazis or the North Koreans decide to restart World War Two or Korea, I'm completely prepared for full allied victory. These little pajama weasels, though—everyone in positions of authority I've talked to says they're really not playing fair. They don't have the guts to stand their ground or stay in one place long enough either to accept massive air or artillery strikes or to engage our larger divisions head on."

"Oh, well, that explains everything. We're winning the ethical, out-front war where men with real balls stand up and look you straight in the eye. That's something."

"Maybe you'll have a special advantage over there. You're Jewish. Those Israelis seem to be real good at kicking those third world types right smack back to the fourth or fifth world."

"Those fuckers are good, all right. They really know how to waste their hordes of untrained, undernourished, illiterate neighbors. But none of that shit rubbed off on me. I've seen *Exodus* on TeeVee a couple of times and it failed to move me the way it was supposed to."

"How was it supposed to move you?"

"I was supposed to move. To Israel."

"You ever been there?"

"No. There's a tree somewhere there with my name on it, though. You buy trees for Israel in Sunday School. Then you grow up, I guess, and you go over there to visit your tree. I do want to see that tree someday. I also want to see my square inch of land in the Klondike."

"You own a square inch of land in the Klondike?"

"You bet your sweet ass," he said. "I got major holdings all over the fucking globe. I think it was Quaker Puffed Rice. Inside each box there was this real deed to a real square inch of Klondike land. I'm going there someday. Maybe I'll probe for oil with a coat hanger."

"What are you going to do with your tree?"

"I'm going to find out once and for all why those mother-fuckers wanted all those trees. Nobody ever fully explained that to me."

"You don't seem to have much lust for returning to the land of your ancestors."

"In my book, it's not a fun place and my ancestors weren't real party guys. And they didn't worship a real fun kind of god. The closer those geeks manage to reproduce the act they used to have there—no, I think I'll pass. You got to understand. Yeah, I went to Sunday School for about thirty years or whatever, but here's how it all came out in the wash. I'm still pals with my old rabbi, nice dude, understanding sort of guy, not enormously pretentious. So one day a couple of years ago he just looked me in the face—nicely, no insult intended at all—and called me a pagan. He had me pegged with a hydraulic mallet. I'm circumcised—"

"So am I. So's everybody. Big deal."

"Not true. Pay more attention at the urinals and you'll see. Sometimes I think you're going through your entire military experience with blinders on and it worries me. But anyway, I'm circumcised and I have the correct parentage and I know the lingo—*baruch-ataw-adonoi-elohenu-melech-ha-olam*—pretty slick, huh?—but at heart I'm just an old-fashioned Hellenistic, toga-wearing, grape-snorting pagan. Check out the major attraction at that tourist trap, the Wailing Wall. They expect me to fly six thousand miles for a good wail. No, those folks are a little too austere for my taste."

"So instead of defending your biblical heritage . . . "

"Yep. It's the pajama weasels for this pagan, Jack. And yea shall I rain misery on their heads with my balloons of gloom. Yea shall I chart their secret isobars and incoming cold fronts. Yea shall I note their cirrus and cumulostratus. I'm surprised they haven't sent assassins to stop me. The war could do a major turnaround from my contribution."

"You could always volunteer for the Airborne," I suggested, "or the Rangers." Now I burst into song.

        "I want to be an Airborne Ranger
            I want to live a life of danger . . .

"You could be like Sealy."

"No," Becker said, "Sealy can be like Sealy, and I can chase his wife around the bedroom while he's off jumping down cliffs on ropes, which is what I'd have kept doing if you hadn't bad-vibed me about it so heavy."

"You really are low-rent. You won't defend Israel, you bet against our side, you do as little as possible to help out around the war, you try to alienate the affections of the wives of dedicated Christian officers. Low-rent."

"I go where they send me, just like you. You may have noticed."

"How about Sweden?"

"Oh, yeah. Great idea. A desertion rap and three weeks of combined spring, summer and fall for the rest of my life. That's why they fuck so much up there—they're freezing to death. They bang their brains out and then they go to Ingmar Bergman movies for light chuckles. Forget it. Not interested."

A clamor out in the hall. Becker and I put our cards down on the table and went outside. Two troops were standing over a third, a black with the collar brass of the engineer company at the far end of the building who was sitting with his back to the corridor wall. He was screaming incoherently, not laughing, not crying, not panicked, but very loud and very drunk. Becker went up to him and knelt down. Then he mumbled something to the other soldiers, went back to the office and dialed the phone. I looked back at the troop on the floor. The hallway was dark—I think they used fifteen-watters in the barracks—but I could see now what Becker had seen. There was broken bottle glass on the floor next to the soldier and a healthy rivulet of blood was streaming from the guy's forearm and forming a pool on the floor between his boots.

"Could we have the staff duty driver over at Headquarters Company, please? We have an injured man to transport to the hospital." Becker hung up and went back to the soldier.

Brigade Headquarters was across the street. It took about five minutes for the driver to come into the barracks. He wasn't alone. Captain Diehl, who must have been pulling brigade O.D., walked in first. Diehl was a very rare bird in brigade, army perfect, West Point, Airborne, Ranger, a Vietnam combat commander and heavy-duty lifer aiming for something along the lines of chief of staff or absolute ruler of Mongo, that sort of jive. He was also a prick.

"What's going on here?"

Becker saluted—odd thing to do, it seemed, but I knew why. That's how you got Diehl's attention, even during a nuclear attack. He wouldn't notice you otherwise. Diehl saluted back.

"This man seems to have cut himself badly, sir," Becker said. "He needs transport to the hospital."

"Shit," Diehl said.

"I just want to DIE!" screamed the soldier on the floor.

"Get up, soldier," Diehl said.

"Fuck off, you motherfuckin' lifer honkie!"

Diehl turned to Becker. "Okay, that's it. If he doesn't want to go to the hospital, I'm not dragging him. It's bad enough he'd get blood all over the sedan. I'm not getting it all over my uniform." Diehl wheeled around and marched out of the barracks. In his wake, the PFC duty driver wheeled around and followed him.

Except for the bleeding soldier, but including me, general amazement. Everyone turned from the slammed barracks door back to the bleeding soldier. The fifteen-watt bulb was reflecting a gleam on the surface of the pool of blood now.

"Let me DIE!" the soldier screamed. He kicked at the air a little. Everyone kept his distance.

"Excuse me for a second," Becker said and trotted out the barracks door. I caught the door behind him and looked out into the parking lot. Diehl was getting into the sedan as the driver started the engine. Becker skipped in front of the grille as the headlights went on and stood there. Diehl got out of the car and glared at him. They stood there talking for a few seconds; I couldn't hear what they said, but I could catch a lot of anger. Finally Diehl said something to the driver, the engine shut off and all three of them marched back to the barracks.

Diehl stood to the side as Becker and the driver tried to haul the drunken soldier up to his feet. He struggled, but not very effectively. As Diehl had predicted, blood was all over Becker's uniform and the driver's. At the car, Diehl drove and the duty driver sat in the passenger seat making sure the bleeding soldier in the back seat didn't try to dive out. Becker watched the car drive off and then came back to the barracks.

"What happened?" I asked.

"The hell with it," Becker said and went into the orderly room to collect the bucket and mop. One of the soldiers in the hall offered to take it from him and clean up. That seemed to surprise Becker.

"Thank you," he said.

"Thank you," the soldier said. He was wearing the engineer brass, too, the little castle turrets. Becker walked back into the orderly room and sat back in the first pig's chair.

"What did you say to him?" I asked.

"Jesus," Becker said. "Shit, I got to get out of this uniform. Yecch." He stripped off his bloodstained shirt. "Man the deck." He went out and came back a few minutes later in another set of khakis. The engineer troop wandered back in with the bucket and mop.

"All cleaned up," he said. "Thanks again."

"What was wrong with your friend?" Becker asked.

"All fucked up. His lady back home threw him over. The usual bullshit. He just had too much to drink. He broke that bottle and cut his arm with it. I don't even know if he meant to, but he didn't seem to mind. I don't think he'll want to die when he sobers up. I guess he's in for some shit with that captain."

"Maybe not. Thanks for doing the hall."

"See you."

"Becker. What did you say to Diehl?"

"Shit. What an asshole. I made a speech. It moved him."

"What did you say?"

"I said it didn't matter if the guy didn't want to cooperate. He had to go to the hospital. Then I got elemental. I said that guy on the floor was the O.D.'s responsibility and no two fucking ways about it, and if the good captain didn't turn around and take him to the hospital, I was calling the brigade commander at home and discussing the matter with him."

"Must have been effective."

"I guess so. Diehl said he'd take the soldier to the hospital and prefer charges against me in the morning."

"Jesus. What are you going to do?"

"Meditate. I think it's your draw from the pile."

Ordinarily you get the day off if you pulled C.Q. the night before and in the morning you go upstairs to flop out. I'd left Becker about 2:00 A.M. and at 6:00 I saw him heading for the latrine while everybody else was getting ready to fall into formation. We didn't say anything; he had a pissed-off, fixated stare. Through the window a few minutes later I could see him marching across the street to Brigade Headquarters in the same fixated way.

Later that afternoon when I strolled over to the office, I found out what had happened from the executive officer's clerk, or enough to fill in the gaps. Becker'd gone upstairs in the HQ building, found a spare typewriter and filled out a written complaint against Diehl on a Disposition Form, three paragraphs, short and sweet. He asked permission to see the brigade commander, handed it to the startled colonel—it was the very first business the colonel had enountered that day—and explained it in person. Becker got there firstest with the mostest; Diehl had already wandered home.

"What would you like me to do about this?" the colonel asked. When a colonel asks a Spec-4 that, it's completely rhetorical, but some of them like to do it for the effect.

"Whatever you feel is appropriate, sir." Becker could go for effects as well as anyone.

The colonel apparently thought it was appropriate to talk the matter over with Captain Diehl, who was back at headquarters within the hour. Diehl pulled officer of the guard every night for the next two weeks.

One morning about a week later Becker and I managed to fuck off for an hour at the Kelly Hill snack bar when Diehl goose-stepped in for a stalk of celery to stick up his ass. He was wearing the strackest, starchiest fatigues and the prettiest jump boots I ever saw—the uniform of the day for the officer of the guard. He spotted Becker and walked up to the table.

"Good morning, Specialist Becker," he said. He glared at me. I played it stupid, as if Becker was George and I was Lennie. I didn't ask about the rabbits, though.

"Morning, sir," Becker said. Enlisted men didn't have to salute indoors, and besides, Becker already seemed to have his attention.

"You were wrong," Diehl said. "You scoped it out wrong and you handled it all wrong. That's all I wanted to say."

"I'm sorry you feel that way, sir, but I suppose that's why they made you a captain and me just a Spec-4. I'll try to do it your way next time."

"My job is not to nursemaid drunks."

"I heard someone disagreed with you, sir."

"He wasn't there. An incident like that could have ruined my career."

"You threatened to fuck with mine, sir. Granted mine's just an amateur career, it's still the only career I got right now. And you know how that dishonorable will haunt a guy for the rest of his days."

"Maybe we'll have dealings again," Diehl said.

"Doubt it, sir. I'm short. Going to the Nam. You can always hope that I get blown away there."

Diehl turned around and walked off for his celery stalk.

"You shouldn't have told him you were short," I said. "Maybe he'll go out of his way to fuck with you."

"No. I fuck back in ways he finds unpleasant. And he's completely sane. He's so sane he's probably got paperwork that says so. Sane people get nervous dealing with people they think are crazy. I think he'll give me a nice wide berth. Besides, it's the law of the army. Short people are absolutely unfuckable. Short crazy people doubly so."

14

I'm short, I'm short, what a magical sound
In just a few days I won't be around
I'm here but I'm not, I'll soon say goodbye,
I'm short, motherfucker, so eat shit and die . . .

It even had a primitive little tune to it, something along the
lines of "Beans, beans, the musical fruit," which is how I knew
Becker was taking one of his Greta Garbo showers. It was a
straightforward problem, really. Becker didn't have any nudity
or mass-naked-men phobias (although some fully fledged soldiers did and never got over it; except for their induction phys-
icals, they managed to get through their entire tours, like Sally
Rand, without ever once exposing their sacred areas), but he
hated to be hustled in the latrine. He hated fast showers, fast
toothbrushing, fast shaving, fast dumping (he claimed he couldn't
even take a decent dump without something to read), fast anything the latrine had to offer, so he solved his problems most

of the time by strolling into the latrine with full kit at screwy hours on screwy days when everyone else was asleep or out on the town. Four hundred men insisting on showers and shaves within the same hour meant lukewarm to downright cold showers for most of them. One solitary man turning the tap on the same hot water tanks meant Becker's kind of shower, and the latrine was far enough away from the Zoo so that he could even sing at 3:00 A.M. without complaint, and the resonance against so much wet tile was grand.

When nothing particular was on his mind, he tended toward 1940s, standards, with a particular affinity for tunes that used to tear up the GIs during The Big Two, slow, sloppy, sentimental tunes sung by The Girl Next Door, laced with suggestions that she was keeping it on ice Just For You, and boy, were you going to get a nice surprise when Japan finally surrendered and you finally got home. While he tried to have the latrine mostly to himself, he never minded a small, appreciative audience if it chanced to wander in. Dullards would sneer, add another note to their Becker certification books and walk out or ignore it, but now and then someone at the sink rack who wasn't in a big hurry would pause and listen. Musically, I had to admit he had an adequate instrument when he wanted to sing rather than lampoon; he could carry a tune in a bucket. Nothing that could ever be made professional—but he was studied about the amateur quality of his voice, and that's what got the effect. Becker had no heart or sentiment, of course, was wildly suspicious of women, and convinced they'd invented love in a secret meeting in a large women's bathroom somewhere downtown as a scheme to make men their perpetual drooling moron slaves. But he knew how love and thoughts of love mesmerized other people, particularly horny, lonely soldiers; he knew what they wanted to hear in a sloppy, sentimental love song. He also knew something nearly everyone else seemed to have forgotten—that getting fucked is relatively easy even for warty trolls, but it has nothing to do with what men really wanted but could never bring themselves to confess that they wanted, certainly not to other men and probably never to women. Yes, obviously they wanted to get laid. But men, particularly soldiers, really wanted what came occasionally after the screwing—a soft woman's voice, soothing, reassuring, understanding, loyal, a voice Real Life had rarely if ever delivered or never would actually deliver, but a critical fantasy nonetheless, the voice that said to you and to you alone: "Oh, honey, it's so good to have you here." Umm! And in the army particularly, for every barking, nasty sergeant or rude, insulting officer (and there were an estimated four of these for every enlisted man), the yours-and-yours-alone honey-sweet midnight voice fantasy became more and more secretly important every day. And those were the kinds of songs Becker collected for his shower repertoire.

Ninety-nine out of a hundred swinging dicks could come into the latrine, hear him sing and not feel a thing but the usual fear of coming down with whatever brain disease Becker was suffering from. But that hundredth unsuspecting stranger, child of the sixties, slave to rock 'n' roll or rhythm and blues or soul or shitkicker, whatever, would stroll into the sink room intent on a quick shave, hear the hermaphroditic big-band crooning from two wars back and instantly become stupefied and heartrent. Time not only stopped, it leapt back two and a half decades; the listener became the listener's own father. Becker had the trick, he had the old Helen Morgan phrasing down. A Jewish psychopath wasn't singing in the shower anymore for that sucker. A beautiful, innocent schoolgirl was waiting back home in Nebraska, lazily dangling her meaty legs on a brick stoop in a powder blue dress on a sunny day, for him and for him alone, no matter how long the war might last, how often or rarely he wrote to her, or what condition he might return home in. The effect was amazing, especially since in this particular war, anyone asshole enough to be caught up in it was by definition a pariah to any and all women he'd known back home, not to mention that in this day and age, women waited and kept themselves for a particular man for an average of maybe twenty-four hours, thirty-six if he had a particularly interesting unit or technique. We all knew that our hottest hometown romances were now spreading nightly for motorcycle societies or the Jaycees in our absence, but the fantasy that someone clean and decent cared and was waiting—well, ordinarily it was a dangerous fantasy no one wanted to spend much time thinking about. That way lay madness and desertion. (Nearly every AWOL I'd known about could be traced to the discovery of a sweetie's betrayal, which played nicely into Becker's theories of love: a phenomenon good for not much more than getting the FBI on your ass.) Which was why Becker collected these sicko tunes about someone clean and decent who cared and was waiting, and sang them in his leisure-time showers. I never did get used to them. They were eerie and unpleasant. But I never asked Becker to stop singing them and I never walked out of earshot while the mood was on him.

But something was on his pea-brain now, his near-liberation from Kelly Hill, Benning, Georgia, Dixie.

"I'm short, I'm short, I'm so close to the ground
Call my name at formation, but I can't be found
I've ceased to exist, and come the next dawn
You lifers'll be here, but I will be gone."

Greta Garbo emerged trailing a cloud of steam behind him. "Greets," he said. "Didn't know you were in the neighborhood."

"I never miss any of your concerts. Actually, I was on leave to the Côte d'Azur, but I got word you were going to sing again, so I caught the first military transport back."

"I'm short! I just realized it tonight. You know, I've known it intellectually for a month and I've been using it as an excuse to get out of all kinds of shit, but for some reason it just smashed me in the gonads full-force tonight, and I feel great. Let's go outside—" and he pointed with his thumb toward the bleachers so he wouldn't have to announce aloud that we should fire up a reefer and get blasted. It was two o'clock on Sunday morning.

"When are you actually leaving?" I asked after we'd taken up our observation posts on the top deck of the bleachers.

"Tuesday morning. I'll be signed out by then, won't even have to make formation. I had the cycle crated up and sent home. My folks'll really eat that up with a spoon. If they sell it while I'm gone I'm going to axe-murder the fuckers and make the front page."

I tried to think about how to say what I wanted to say. There was no particular problem with that. What I wanted to say could be expressed in American English in a variety of ways that all implied I was in love with Becker and wanted to be his wife after the war was over.

What I finally chose was a good example. "I'm going to miss you."

Becker, always sensitive and sympathetic to the nuance, pursed his lips and made lewd kissing noises in the dark.

"Thank you, you fuckhead," I said.

"Relax. Same here. You helped make the time bearable. Imagine, someone else in my battalion who knew the whole alphabet. What a godsent concentration of talent."

"It's not enough," I said.

"What more do you want?"

"Oh, shit. I just hate this. We're good friends. Good army friends. Tuesday we'll exchange our parents' addresses and phone numbers, and that'll be it. You'll tell me to drop on in if I'm ever in D.C. and I'll tell you to come on by if you're ever in Connecticut. You'll forget me, I'll forget you. We'll become fond memory blurs. That what's-his-name back at Benning, real nice guy. It's just a pain, that's all. I wanted to register a public complaint about it before you left town."

"I can't change the way of the world for you, Richard. I don't like it either. But it's like you to grab onto the shitty ass-end of a year's worth of something that was nice."

"Look," I said, "let's try. There are phones. As you pointed out, we're both conversant with the alphabet. Letters." An exchange of necklaces or pinkie rings, perhaps an underwear swap . . .

"You can't force it. One afternoon you'll look down and you'll already be writing me a letter, or I'll look down and I'll be writing you. It'll happen or it won't. We both know we want to give it a try. Signs point to Yes. Answer hazy, try again later. Who the fuck knows? But we have to let what happens to us happen to us. We have no choice about it, just like we had no choice about bumping into each other in the first place. All I'm trying to say is that you're not telling me anything I don't already know. You're my friend. I want that to stay. We'll both make an effort. Maybe it'll live. If it dies, I'll say kaddish for it every year around this time."

"Shit," I said.

"Jesus, no wonder the world is so fucking hard on you. You can't let anything slide by."

"I already have let everything slide by, girls I was in love with, or thought I was, my freedom, my upbringing, maybe my ass in a few months. That's why. Our friendship was something of value. I'm tired of letting things of value just keep floating on by. I'm not interested in your Zen *que sera sera* bullshit."

"I'm not a big fan of it myself. It's just the fucking way the world operates. I don't want to waste the energy to fight it the way you do. I'll herniate something and these valuable things I grab so hard for will end up bruised and forced and not so valuable. You dig?"

"Of course I dig. It just sucks, that's all."

"Okay, look. I'm going to Vietnam. So are you, says the mystic Ouija. We will make the Grand Effort there. We'll go to Bangkok and have weird women pull knotted scarves out of our rectums together. We'll buy cheap thirty-five millimeter cameras and go to Angkor Wat if it's still standing and take its picture. I promise I'll send you my APO or whatever fucked-up secret code address I end up with. The Grand Effort."

"I would appreciate that."

"So would I. And now, good friend, I'm going to hit the rack. You do likewise."

There was something in my ear. Something wet and cold. It sucked in its nostril breath. It panted. It had big lungs. Big things have big lungs. I could smell its breath. Its breath was atrocious.

I opened the one eye that wasn't wedged shut against the pillow, but didn't dare to move my head to look around. Even in the Zoo, this was something new. My best frantically imaginative guess: a very drunk and forward homosexual or the yeti. In a tenth of a second, I was going to be raped or torn limb from limb and eaten.

"You just lie still and it won't bother you. Don't make no sudden moves," a man's voice above me in the darkness said. *It.* What was this *It*?

I raised my head an inch above the pillow, opened my other eye and turned around slowly. It was going snort-snort-snort-snort-snort. I focused on a shiny black Naugahyde ball about the size of a cherry an inch away from my nose, and then on the gray blur behind it. It was a German shepherd. Attached to the rear of the German shepherd via a gleaming silver chain was a man in starched green fatigues and polished boots. Neither object should have been hovering at my bunk sometime before dawn on a Sunday morning.

The man gave a quick jerk on the chain and It retreated and ambled off toward another bunk. Lights were going on and voices were starting to ask whiny, angry questions. I could hear other things in other parts of the Zoo going snort-snort-snort-snort-snort. I rolled out and sat up.

"Okay, listen up!" a starched voice called out. "Everybody out of the rack and stand by your lockers!"

Becker was already lazily lounging with his back to his when I got to my locker. He'd pulled on a pair of filthy, wrinkled fatigues. I was still in my shorts. He was quiet but other people were saying some really vile things.

Somebody I couldn't see in a corner of the Zoo started making cat noises. Another howled like a beagle. One of the dogs started to go crazy and his handler yelled at him. The announcer strode into our aisle. "Shut up back there! Knock it off!" It was Captain Diehl, and behind him was Lieutenant Sealy, Jesus' Ranger buddy and the husband of Becker's midnight mess-around. I noticed the dufus had a black embroidered rank patch on his collar; he'd finally made first lieutenant. A dog and handler came into the aisle with them and stopped at the first locker.

"Open it up," Diehl said to the black troop standing by it. The look on the black troop's face should at least have killed the dog, but I guess the dog wasn't looking up. The troop opened the locker door. Snort-snort-snort-snort-snort. Snort snort. It backed out and started biting the base of its tail.

"Okay, close it up," Diehl said. "You." He meant me. I opened my locker. Snort-etc. Suddenly the dog became excited, animated. "Okay, pull everything out of your locker. Now!"

When I'd spread my entire life in the aisle floor, the dog took a fancy to my duffel bag. "Dump it all out," Diehl said.

"Oh, God . . ."

"Just do it! Don't take all day!"

It was mostly dirty laundry, with a few solid objects stashed in there from the last surprise emergency inspection. A bottle of English Leather rolled out onto the linoleum. The dog made noises and signs to show it was thrilled. Diehl picked up the English Leather and smelled English Leather. "Okay, pick it all up. Whose locker is this?"

Nobody answered. The dog was brought up and instantly started going ape-shit or dog-shit, leaping up and scratching at the metal door, interspersing its excited whining with a sharp bark now and then.

"Whose locker is this?" Diehl screamed. Finally he opened it himself. It was empty of everything but dust. The dog leapt into it. The handler stuck his head into the locker and looked around. He put his hand on the coat-hanger pipe and turned it in its housing. Then he yanked it out. He stuck his finger in one end. The end of a plastic bag came out the other end. Bag of reefer. End of the world. Treasure of the Incas. "Who the fuck owns this locker?"

"Hey. Nobody owns it, surrr," the black troop said. "Up here we call it an empty locker."

Diehl glared at the troop, then took the bag and put it in his pocket. He saw Becker and stared at him. He motioned for the handler to bring the dog to Becker's locker. Becker opened the door. The dog sniffed and immediately went back to biting the base of its tail. Diehl reached in anyway and knocked the few hanging clothes off the pipe and yanked out the pipe. He pointed it to the ceiling and saw a light bulb.

"Go through his stuff," Diehl muttered to Sealy, and the first team marched on.

Becker stood by impassively, almost matter-of-factly, as Sealy bent down and frisked through Becker's monstrously slovenly locker. Each item that caught Sealy's eye was weirder and more inexplicable than the one before.

"What's this?" he asked, holding up a hard black plastic and metal contraption on hinges.

"Polar planimeter, sir," Becker said.

Sealy looked up at him as if he'd replied in Flemish. Becker said nothing more.

"What's this?"

"United States passport, sir."

There was a very long silence.

"What are you doing with that? You don't need that to ship overseas."

"It's useful for writing checks downtown, sir."

"There are no stamps in here."

"I've never been anywhere, sir."

"Then what do you need a passport for?"

"I may want to go somewhere."

Another very long silence. Sealy pulled out a heavy hardback volume about the size of a dictionary. He held it up before Becker.

"The American *Ephemeris*, sir. For 1967."

Sealy put it gently on the floor and returned to the locker. There was a tiny photograph taped to the inside of the locker door. Sealy leaned toward it until his nose practically touched it. "What's this?"

"That's a picture of a bed designed in the shape of a hamburger," Becker explained. "The headboard is the top of the bun. The box spring is the bottom of the bun. They both have the effect of being slightly toasted, and they have imitation sesame seeds. The mattress is the meat patty. The pillows are a pickle slice and a tomato wedge. The sheets are colored and contoured like lettuce. A rich guy in Texas sleeps in it."

Sealy started combing through the locker's top shelf. He saw something in the dark back of the locker hanging from a string. He pulled it out. It was a solid white paper-and-cardboard object about the size of a softball. It dangled and twirled at the end of the string.

"What's this?"

I knew what it was. I was finding this really entertaining. I hadn't even bothered to start restuffing the duffel bag.

"My short-timer's calendar, sir."

Which should have made everything crsytal-clear, Becker after all being a documented short-timer. Short-timers invariably made themselves a short-timer's calendar. Surely Sealy had seen them before thousands of times in barracks lockers.

Or at least the usual ones. They were depictions of a nude woman, sometimes home-drawn, more often the blurry fiftieth-generation photocopy of some pseudo-Vargas classic original from eons ago—perhaps experts could someday prove it had once been Betty Grable, although blacks had a model that always reminded me of Angela Davis—altered now to be in the paint-by-numbers style, the woman's body being segmented like a chart of a prime beef steer into thirty or sixty little compartments. Each day the short-timer took a pen or pencil and colored in the next lower number, sort of like a porno Advent calendar. The high numbers were the unimportant female anatomy parts like the ear or shoulder or underarm. As the numbers got lower, more interesting and valued areas were colored in, the mouth and rump being highly prized and worth holding out for. The final number, zero, was, of course, the pubic triangle; a little community locker-side festival among close friends was usually organized for coloring that in.

Becker's was different.

"This is a short-timer's calendar?" Sealy asked.

"Yes. See the numbers, sir?"

"I don't think I've ever seen one like this before."

"It's an icosahedron, sir, one of the twelve perfect solids. It has twenty triangular faces. I put a number at each corner of each triangle, which works out to a two-month short-timer's countdown. It's a very interesting construction project."

"Most men use women."

"What does pussy have to do with getting out of this shithole, sir?"

Sealy stared at Becker and at last handed him back his icosahedron.

"Thank you, sir."

Sealy started to walk away.

"Oh, sir."

Sealy turned around.

"Anytime you feel like violating my constitutional rights, you just go right ahead. Happy to oblige."

Sealy stood there as if he'd been plunged into deep thought, perhaps even sorrow.

"I wasn't violating your constitutional rights." He wasn't adamant or angry at all. He was hurt. "I was protecting you."

"Right on, sir." Becker gestured out toward the other aisles, his gracious fiat for Sealy to go fuck with the brains of the other Zoo occupants. And for Sealy to go fuck himself in the bargain.

Sealy wandered off.

The show was over. Becker and I knelt among our scattered possessions. "That wasn't nice," I said. "Sealy's a moron. Diehl enjoyed it. He probably did it to catch your ass before you get out of here. But Sealy didn't mean to fuck with you. That turkey really thinks shakedowns are for our own moral and biological good."

"Look, if a two-hundred-pound guy with a hard-on falls off

a roof and his dick ends up jammed in my ass, he fucked me, and I don't care if he meant to or not. I got fucked. That was my lesson for Sealy this morning. I don't care what's on his mind. This year he's joined the Fucker's Club and he's a full-fledged, twenty-four-hour-a-day Fucker in my book. Just because he's a retard and he gets singing telegrams from Jesus makes him no different from Diehl. I don't even feel sorry for him. God made him that stupid and that dangerous. I hope he dies."

"You lucked out."

"How so?"

"Nobody's bag of reefer in nobody's locker."

"Well, I used to keep it in the pipe in my own locker. When I discovered that pipe came loose, I just thought it was the ginchiest hiding place I'd ever seen. In fact I kept it there until about a month ago."

"What the hell made you change it?"

"Materialism. One day it just flashed on me that I was keeping it in my own locker because it was my own reefer. And I thought about that. I was right. I bought it; it was mine, all mine. Good stuff, too, cost me twenty bucks. If I put it in some common area, some lowlife could find it and take it from me. And probably hide it in his locker. I didn't like that. And then I thought about the forty shmucks a day at Benning who get popped for well-hidden reefer in their own lockers, and I realized I had something in common with them: materialism. So I decided to give it away, make it community property when I didn't need it, with all the consequences. Well, I just lost twenty bucks. I feel real bad about that. And thirty-nine other morons on this post today will get court-martialed. And they'll each be out twenty bucks, too."

"Nice hunch."

"After breakfast, let's go over to Harmony Church and see if R.J.'s got any reefer."

15

So then it was just me alone on Kelly Hill, alone in the midst of two or three thousand other green-clad boys and men, but strangers all, none of them people I'd invested anything in and there were none I wanted to invest anything in; there wasn't time to test them, there wasn't time for them to test me. Rollie was gone and now Becker, and though I knew the names of most of the guys in the Zoo and in the Headquarters building, that was all I knew or wanted to know about them. There wasn't time. I'd be gone myself soon, so no one was any use to me and I wasn't any use to anyone.

R.J. was still around. I knew where to find him in his arms room any day in Harmony Church, and he was always willing, eager to pick me up any Friday night to drive up to the house in Atlanta. Somehow, without Becker or Rollie I just couldn't do it. In the last two months I went up only twice. I enjoyed spending time with Annie, and if you asked me, I couldn't find anything specific to complain about from R.J.—there was never anything specific to complain about with R.J. He wasn't that much more vulgar than Becker. If you mistook R.J. and his accent for a shitkicker you made a big mistake. If you mistook R.J. for stupid you made a worse mistake—but of course he liked people to make both mistakes because he could manipulate and predict them easier. It wasn't that R.J. was unlike me because we came from different places and different experiences. I often had the feeling R.J. had had all my experiences and been to all my places and had simply decided he had little or no use for them, but he understood them and consequently understood me. And the strangest thing was that he went through all the motions of friendship. He knew how to cut a hard business deal, and then turned around and spent his profits on you that night. When his car worked, he drove us around. The house in Atlanta was ours to use as we pleased. In his own way he was more dependable than Becker, and I guess Becker was more likely to come up with intolerable or disgusting behavior than R.J. was. I just could never warm up to him. He reminded me of the pet lizards or snakes someone in junior high school inevitably had. They went through the motions of being petted and acting like other pets, but you could never shake off the fact that they were lizards, not pets; it always seemed to be a parody of a bond, never quite the real thing. If I had to leap at something, at one thing about R.J. that kept me at a distance, I suppose it was his aura of dedication to himself and his own welfare. Well—who isn't for himself? Everyone's for himself. But there are illusions, maybe only illusions, that some people have the capacity for sacrifice, for a brave gesture for someone else now and then. Years can go by and the occasion never comes up, but you still feel that someone—Becker or Rollie—has the capacity, and that feeling makes you feel that in return you have the capacity. I would look at R.J. and could never see it, and I kept my distance. What I saw instead was something between the lines, a caution: *Prices and policies subject to change without notice.* Looking him straight in the eyes (and he always looked you right back) you still found nothing there, no clue, no hint as to design, benignity or malignity, benevolence or malevolence. Behind his eyes no one was ever home, the jury was perpetually still out. You spoke to him and asked him a question and an answering service promised to have him paged, or the 8-Ball popped up *Answer hazy, try again later* in the little round window through the cloudy fluid.

So I spent my last days at Benning without friends, systematically letting my situations degenerate and float free in any directions they chose. I let R.J. go his own way and he made no noticeable protests. I did my duties as lifers laid them on me. I filled out my forms and appeared at my designated formations approximately on time. I was late for one and accepted my Article 15 punishment from the C.O. with dull equanimity, cleaning out the orderly room three extra consecutive nights and then being congratulated by the first sergeant and absolved of future extra duty. I got my own orders to the Nam and felt my stomach knot up but no more. *Can't complain, nobody'd listen.* I never bothered to tell anyone about them. I never wrote Dad or Betty about it. I wasn't even sure whether I'd spend my two weeks' leave at home with or near them.

Becker, on the other hand, had been gone from Kelly Hill for more than a month and was still outraging the Fort almost weekly with some insane time bomb, scores of which he'd patiently planted all over the base with his mark plainly on each m26one but never his name or fingerprints. Well, sometimes; it depended. The little psycho weasel hadn't told me about any of them. Well, a few of them; it depended. If he had, I hadn't been paying much attention at the time or I thought he'd been bullshitting me. Keep 'em guessin', keep 'em hoppin'. First there was the shriek in the morning, the first time I'd ever heard the first sergeant—or the first pig, as Becker affectionately called him—shriek. Oh, he reacted to many things, but always with restraint, great restraint, knowing as he did with the certainty of thirty years' experience as a stone lifer motherfucker that whatever ill some GI had done him, he could reach out and within minutes have the malefactor writhing with fear and pain far deeper than the petty annoyance he'd originally inflicted on Top. Top could pick up the phone and have anyone under him walking guard duty in January for weeks. He could sign his name and cancel leaves and passes for entire platoons. He could whisper a recommendation and have someone's stripes torn off within an hour. But he couldn't catch Becker, Becker the Gingerbread Man, and he knew it instantly and shrieked with rage. Thank the Lord I was in the orderly room two desks away from Top when it happened. He'd dismissed the morning formation and strode in his ass-kicking manner into the barracks and around the corner and had made his determined beeline to his desk to sit down and begin another day of making nearly a hundred poor enlisted suckers miserable by running their asses ragged with piddleshit and harassment. I saw him; he looked happy and pleased. Another great day of fucking with people who couldn't fuck back. And of course the very first thing he did every day before the general terror and ass-kicking began was to flip the next leaf on his little dorky government-issue desk calendar. He did and then he shrieked. Of course it wasn't a normal full-blown human shriek, but it was certainly without question the finest shriek Top could come up with, something between a croak, a yell, a belch and a simultaneous surprise hiccup. It sounded awful, a fearsome mix of rage, frustration and helplessness tinged with a little minute degree of fear that the world had suddenly been pulled inside-out and the American flag had suddenly sprouted a rash of little hammers and sickles. He stood up; he sat down again. He reached for the phone but thought better of it. Then he paused and if you looked very carefully at him (which by now the whole orderly room complement was doing) you could see an infinitesimal tic develop in his right eye. Finally he strode over to the commander's inner sanctum door, knocked, entered after the hollow grunt from inside, mumbled an excuse and then strode swiftly from the orderly room, around the corner and down the corridor heading for the mess hall, where the heavy-duty but do-nothing lifers spent their time between meals snarfing down coffee and doughnuts.

The rest of us were confused and mesmerized and one by one we drifted over to the abandoned desk to look for clues. Was it a personal order from Richard Nixon for Top to stick his dick up his ass and fuck himself (which Top of course would have to try to do instantaneously as best he could)? Was it a letter from Top's mother disowning him as a hopeless fascist asshole? But the mystery was easy to resolve. The new day, which only minutes before had dawned with so much promise of ass-kicking galore, had disclosed on his flip-calendar, besides the date, Julian date, day of the week (Thursday), and the space-divisions for each half hour of the working day, an enormous two-page epic mural painted with a wildly dashing and thick black felt-tip pen. The central figure was a cartoon cake with dozens of little twinkling candles and a caricatured nude with panoramic tits bursting from the top, and above that in three dimensionally shaded huge black letters was the legend:

BECKER'S BIRTHDAY!

which indeed it was, now that I thought about it. And it would be his birthday all day, because between the cake and its decorations and the nude and her tits and the candles, there wasn't a square micron of space left on that calendar day in which to write anything else, and those things which had possibly or apparently been written before were now hopelessly obliterated and distorted by the apostasy.

"Holy fuck," van Hoff whispered.

But I had to give Top credit for cutting his losses and getting back to the business of the day without even irrationally ordering someone's execution as a reprisal. It took him only eight minutes to spike himself up with some coffee and get back to his desk, by which time we'd all mindlessly returned to our duty stations and wiped the smiles or aghast fear from our faces. And he returned with a sickly little smile of his own—we, of course, didn't dare, but Top could smile in his own office all he wanted to, three or four times a month if he liked. He looked down briefly at the monstrous calendar affront and neither tore out the offending pages (he would have lost Wednesday gone and Friday to come if he had) nor moved the calendar an inch from its accustomed right angled place on his desk. He'd recovered his composure now and I imagined he didn't even have to invent a new category for Becker and what he'd done. Top had killed Germans, Italians, Japanese, Koreans and Vietnamese and who knew how many hundreds of how many other nationalities in his time, but many others had slipped away in the night, darn, and it was to the category reserved for slippery enemies beyond his reach that Top undoubtedly consigned Becker. There was still time for another round with Becker and these other slippery aliens; other wars might come. The Hun might get antsy again; there might even be another Indian uprising. Hope would only die when either Top or Becker did.

I got quite a bang out of that, but I was sure it represented the limit and the end of Becker's ability to wreak long-distance transoceanic mayhem and disorder; that's a slight indication of why I've never been particularly good at games of chance or pari-mutuel betting. By the time I actually left Kelly Hill and Benning, I'd begun to feel sorry for its 45,000 souls and certainly for the lifers in charge of them, because I'd finally begun to see how severe the disadvantage was that they struggled under when they took on Becker and his maniacal energy and fertile imagination. The next cowardly assault came a week after the birthday cake incident but it took me some time even to notice it or to realize it was the work of the twenty-four-year-old perfect master, and it took me another accident of time and place, but that same deity was obviously still determined that I shouldn't miss a moment's entertainment or a single step in this *Shivah* samba.

This one started the way the American Revolution did, with heavy-handed taxation and a response by the Committees of Correspondence. It was the month of the United Fund campaign at Fort Benning and Columbus. How the Columbus civilians were rounded up, harassed and humiliated into contributing their fair share I never exactly knew, but there was no mystery about it in the army. Each commander, from company level to the post commanding general, was bound to collect something from every last swinging dick in uniform under him without fail and to report by campaign's end that his unit had a one hundred percent contribution record, not ninety-nine, not ninety-nine and forty-four one-hundredths. Until this particular campaign, no one knew what would happen to a commander who failed to make his hundred percent, because it had never happened, or if it had, the evidence had been doctored or brutally suppressed. The pressure on post was so heavy and continuous that it seemed likely that if there was one intractable holdout in some unit, he'd be taken out and shot, not as punishment, but to prevent the unit sheet from going in with anything less than a perfect record. Privates and specialists who didn't respond to the first polite call found their leaves canceled and found themselves mysteriously saddled with extra duty night after night; they got KP more than normal, and eventually if they still failed to (the magic phrase) get with the program, they found themselves having more frequent interviews with their first sergeants, battalion sergeants major (even more fearsome creatures than first shirts) and finally personal encounters with commanding officers up and ever upward along the chain of command.

How it started to fall apart this particular go-round no one at first quite knew. Word began to spread around brigade headquarters that all was not sweetness, light and Vaseline with the drive, which was about two weeks short of the end. At first the rumors indicated that people were just being more sluggish than usual, a problem that could probably be rectified with some increased ass-kicking from above. But a few days later new rumors began to spread. The problem, it seems, was confined almost entirely to blacks, and it wasn't just the usual Stepin Fetchit foot-dragging that honkie lifers expected of their reluctant jungle bunnies, but it seemed to have an organized, even a revolutionary aspect to it. It wasn't just confined to blacks who wouldn't give or pledge. Some who'd originally signed up were showing up in orderly rooms demanding to take their pledges back again; they wanted their money back and it was throwing their commanders into fear and consternation. The commanders demanded to know the reasons behind it, and finally when the organized nature of it began to surface, the matter was discussed with considerable alarm at the Wednesday morning brigade staff conference and immediately assigned to S-2, the in-house Gestapo, to ferret out the truth of the matter and stamp out the mutiny.

But the mutiny kept growing. Blacks with the balls to demand their United Way money back were given the shuffle-and-stall by their first sergeants or C.O.'s ("Well, we'll look into the matter," the commanders would promise, "but on the other hand I'd appreciate it if you'd reconsider and just give your fair share for the time being"), but they consistently returned a few days later and were still demanding their money back.

I asked Wilson, a black who slept near me in the Zoo, what the scoop was. "Them motherfuckers takin' our goddam money and just givin' it to the goddam honkies," he said.

"Try that again," I said.

"You can read, motherfucker?" he asked with annoyance.

"Passably," I said.

"Then read this, motherfucker," he said, and reached under his mattress and pulled out a crumpled photocopy that at first looked like a kidnapping ransom note constructed from letters and words from newspaper and magazine stories, headlines and ads.

Your *$$$* for the *UNITED way* is *being GI*ven to
SUP*port* s*E*g*REG*at*ed CHA*rities WHITE-only *chaRI*ties
Jim *CROW* CHAR*ities* in COLUMBUS. *CHECK* it OUT.

"Where'd you get this?" I asked.

"None of your honkie motherfuckin' business. You want to get my ass in a sling? Shee-it, man, they even catch me with this thing they probably throw my ass in the motherfuckin' stockade. You know how hot to trot those lifers are about this shit?"

"How many of these are there?"

"Well, man, you take the number of goddam Xerox machines in this stupid motherfuckin' brigade and multiply by maybe eighty or ninety and maybe you get some rough-ass ballpark figure, motherfucker," Wilson said.

"Well, how many of them were there to start with?"

"What are you, a motherfuckin' spy?"

"No."

"Shee-it, I don't know, motherfucker. Some of the brothers got these in the goddam mail a couple of days ago, that's all I know, maybe four or five. Got mailed from someplace up north, that's all I heard. New York or Philly or Peking or Hanoi, I don't fuckin' know. How the fuck am I supposed to know? Gimme that back." He grabbed the weird little note from my hand and stuffed it back under his mattress.

"Is it true?"

"Who the fuck am I, God? I don't fuckin' know. But some of the brothers got pissed and checked it out. Yeah, they found some old Nursing Home for Ancient Coons and Spooks that gets some of the motherfuckin' money, and there's another clinic, some kind of little hospital that don't let no brothers in even if they fucked up with blood leakin' all over the place and their ears where their motherfuckin' nose ought to be. Yeah, what you think? That's the fuckin' way it is down here in Dix-ieland, except now we supposed to pay for it, too. So we pissed, man, and the brothers want their fuckin' bread back."

"Far out."

"How 'bout you, motherfucker? You pissed?"

"Yes. I'm authentically pissed. I'll try to get my money back, too."

"Well, then, you're fucked up and you gonna get *your* fuckin' ass in a sling just like all these fuckin' hophead niggers who done asked for their money back, my miserable ass included."

"I'm short. I don't give a fuck."

"Well, then, I'm more beautiful than you, because I *ain't* short and I still want my goddam money back. But maybe some of the brothers appreciate it all the same."

So the next morning I joined Fort Benning's loneliest crowd and asked the first sergeant for my United Fund money back (my platoon sergeant having harassed me some weeks earlier until I'd pledged 25 cents each pay period for a year to be deducted from my check) and Top hit the roof in his own remote-controlled way and gave me a speech about how the entire matter was being investigated by the C.I.D. and S-2 and the MPs (just to give me something to think about) but that he'd pass my request on to these agencies and to the C.O. for consideration if I'd put it in writing, which I did on a Disposition Form while he did the slow burn. I found out later I was the first honkie motherfucker to join the parade and received special attention for my efforts, but I wasn't the last, and shortly afterward a small stack of the mysterious kidnap ransom notes appeared under my pillow, apparently a gift from the tooth fairy, and I started slipping them to the white meat with whom I still maintained diplomatic relations on the Hill and around post. Inspector Erskine and Sergeant Friday and their pals never had a chance to get back to me because I was gone from the post a week later, my request apparently still struggling upstream through channels and the military intelligence community. The last rumors I heard before I left Georgia forever had the conspiracy (I heard a master sergeant who'd been afflicted with solving or suppressing the problem refer to it as a "coonspiracy" over an off-duty beer) growing throughout the brigade like wildfire and beginning to take hold and start a fad among the black community and the weirdos who frequented the foreign movie theater on Main Post. It was sweepin' the nation.

And then three nights before I was to leave the Hill, I rounded a corner of the barracks outside and ran into a small coven of blacks churning out a large cloud of reefer. "You're all under arrest unless you give me some of that," I said quietly and a hand grudgingly shot out and placed a burning number in my lips. We talked and shot the shit for ten or fifteen minutes, passing the reefer around, and then the blacks began to drift off in pairs and one by one. Finally it was just me, Wilson and Dore, the mail clerk.

"When you going?" Dore asked.

"A couple of days," I said.

"'Cross the pond?"

"Yeah."

"I'll forward your mail. Fuck, man, you know you the only asshole in the company gets the fuckin' *Saturday Review*? Why don't you get fuck magazines like everybody else, you faggot?"

"I'm not a faggot. I'm a Communist spy. All Commie spies read *The Saturday Review*."

"You laugh, motherfucker," Wilson said. "Just keep on laughin'. Don't you know that's what those fuckin' CID and security types think you are, you and your little Martian friend what started all this crap?"

"Who? What Martian friend?" I asked. "I don't know anyone from Mars."

"Oh, fuck," Wilson groaned.

"Are you talking about the United Fund bullshit? I don't know who started that."

"Oh, God, I knew you were motherfuckin' crazy, but I didn't know you were so goddam sorry-assed stupid," Wilson cursed. "Who you think sent those crazy notes to all the brothers, huh? Who you think stoned enough to think up shit like that, huh?"

"Becker?" I asked.

"Wait a second, wait a second." Wilson reached in his fatigue jacket and pulled out a new number and stuck it in my mouth. "Give that asshole a rubber see-gar. You guessed it, dickhead. You really didn't know?"

"Cross my heart and hope to die," I said. "I still don't think you know for sure."

"I tell you what we know for sure, motherfucker," Wilson hissed. "We know for goddam sure that the goddam night before Becker left he was going all over the Zoo talkin' to a whole bunch of the brothers, friends of Rollie and shit, and sayin' as how he was sure going to be sorry to leave 'em, and he'd really appreciate having their addresses so he could write to 'em. That motherfucker went around collectin' name, rank, serial number shit from the brothers just before he left, and guess who got those weird-ass stick-em-up notes a month later, huh? Shee-it, that jerkoff was plannin' this shit all the time. Who else you know wacko enough to get into shit like this, man? Your little Martian pal, that's who."

"Well, sure sounds like him," I confessed.

"Yeah, it sure do," Wilson grumbled.

"You sound like you're pissed," I said.

He thought about that for a few seconds. "Fuck, man, I'm pissed off about *everything* these days. I'm in the motherfuckin' *army*, man. 'Course I'm pissed. But I ain't pissed off about this shit, man. This shit ain't shit. This shit's just funny. Becker didn't *make* anybody do nothin' he didn't want to do. It's just Beckershit, you know, like Beckertalk, and I suppose if I was a chick I'd know all about Beckerfuckin', which is probably just as weird as Beckershit and Beckertalk. That motherfucker's prick probably lights up in the dark and honks."

"I wouldn't know."

"No, man, I didn't think you would. I didn't mean nothin' by that. Becker probably only fucks light poles and chipmunks anyway, he so weird. Jesus."

"Well," I said.

"*Well* is right. You sure pick yourself some weird-ass pals, motherfucker. You know where that asshole is these days?"

"Yeah. He dropped me a card a couple of days ago."

"Well, you tell him Wilson sure do appreciate him takin' time out from his busy schedule to write a line now and then to a poor colored soldier so far from home. You tell him that. But you tell him to keep away from me in the future, right? That fucker scares me. I'm always afraid what he got might be catchin'."

"I'll be sure to tell him."

Okay, now, certainly, I thought in those last couple of days, certainly Becker's finished now, exhausted, looking for new worlds to conquer and other populations to get into an uproar. Certainly Becker has rested by this time, looked upon his work and called it Good. Certainly the lad is pooped out. And things seemed to bear me out for those next few days. Beyond Top's nervous tic and about two dozen officers and NCOs from S-2 and the CID trying to locate the source of the insurrection against enforced charity, everything seemed to be going along in a military manner as I went from office to office around the post with my clipboard and checklist to check out of the base and complete my paperwork. I saw soldiers marching, soldiers going to the movies, soldiers saluting officers driving by in their cars, soldiers doing calisthenics, trainees learning to parachute from the giant towers. . . .

That was curious, though. There seemed to be a lot of soldiers, a lot of low-rank enlisted men standing around on street corners at bad curves and busy intersections, not doing anything or going anywhere in particular, just lounging around and then coming to attention and saluting when an officer came driving by in his car. At first I was certain it had to be a coincidence, but the more I thought about it, the more I kept noticing it. I recognized the one who had Becker's old spot in front of the dispensary; he was a guy Rollie used to sell drugs to, and he knew Becker. And some of the other faces seemed familiar, too, guys I used to see at the bent movie theater on Main Post and another guy who used to try to get a ride to Atlanta with us every once in a while. I saw them at intersections on Main Post and at the entrance to the hospital and in front of the big parking lot in front of the commissary, and another very busy saluter was standing next to the bus bench in front of the Officers Club where the cars pulled in and out.

And finally a few hours before I was through with the checklist and ready to get off the post forever, I was riding in a jeep down to the Red Cross office on Main Post and I saw it: a twisted, banged-up (but formerly brand-new) TR/6 Triumph sports car that had freshly jumped a curve at an intersection near the officer housing and had smashed headfirst into a large elm tree. The driver's door was open and even bent off its hinges, and a young, skinny second lieutenant was alternating between falling on the grass on one knee and struggling to regain his balance and stand up. He had some kind of cut on his forehead which was bleeding, just a little trickle that undershot his ear and jaw and continued in a thinner stream down his neck. The car's hood had popped open and a fierce cloud of steam was issuing into the air. Not far from the wreck was a specialist I was almost certain I'd seen before. He was looking astonished (although looking something else, something I was afraid to put my finger on). The accident had apparently happened only seconds before we'd driven up in the jeep and the specialist was still at attention saluting the officer. The officer tried to add a return salute to his tasks of regaining his balance and standing up, but that was only making things worse.

16

I never told Becker about my leave. We stayed in touch (that's a mild way of putting it), but that night on the bleachers, the reason I'd had to ask for a special effort, something more effective than the standard-issue wandering-army-buddy treatment, was that he knew and understood things, complicated and fragile things, and it's the understanding that takes away the loneliness of hard times, takes the edge off them, makes them bearable and endurable. For the army our situation was in no way complicated or fragile. They needed so much meat in these slots to do these jobs to fight this war, and we were the meat, and we were drafted and uniformed and fed and trained and sent to these places, and after so much time, if we lived (and if we didn't, that was simple, too), we were let go, discharged, and if the army needed more meat after that, they got that too and trained and uniformed and shipped it around. How blunt and simple it all was for the army amazed and terrified me when I compared it to how complex and convoluted it was for me—all questions answered for them (usually the very same day, while-U-wait), everything unanswered and un-answerable to me at the very same time. And so far, only Becker, of all the good people I met and knew inside, only Becker thoroughly understood my side of it, how complicated, fragile, puzzling and near paralyzing I found it to be. Not that he cared over-much or had much awe or respect for my view of it. He just saw it, that was enough, that was plenty; it was less important to me to simplify or find answers to it than it was to have just one other person verify it. Becker was and would be that person. Though we were separated now, sent to different assignments, I could still know that if I needed it and made a good enough effort I could find him, perhaps on a crackling and hissing long-distance telephone or in letters, and I could ask him if things were really as spectacularly confusing and twisted as I was convinced they were, and he was the one I knew now would affirm it. He wouldn't care particularly; it would never paralyze him. But he'd always know and affirm.

But I never told him what happened to me on leave. I suppose I was being tested to see how strange things could be back home without Becker around to verify and help me endure them. And he wasn't around. He was already in Vietnam hoisting balloons. And as I said, I brood, and I brooded over what happened, and I stewed that Becker wasn't around to see it with me and tell me: "Yep, you're right, that's happening; I see it too."

The leave was the way I always took leave: Surprise, I'm home unannounced, take me as you find me or hide me in the base-ment, whatever, and as usual Betty and Dad just began to cook up buckwheat pancakes and drown them in butter and Vermont maple syrup and talk to me or leave me alone as I seemed to require. Amazing—two berserk Quakers feeding their son who's in the army and not even a conscientious objector during a truly wretched American Wog-buggering adventure, and they weren't even treating me with kid gloves. It was just me, Richard, back home with the usual gaggle of nineteen or eleven or however many kids, the permanents mixed in with the temps, all scream-ing for my attention to throw baseballs at them in the backyard or to show me the dollhouse in the garage that Dad had helped them make. I was so overwhelmed with unhappiness as they fed me more pancakes and instructed me to go to the store for them and to take Angela to the orthodontist, and for the first and only time I wanted to be a fly on their bedroom wall just to figure out what the fuck they made of me and what the fuck all this meant to them, their just-visiting 11-Bravo light weapons infantryman oldest son. Not being a fly on their bedroom wall, all I could see was that I had unlimited use of the Volvo.

But it wasn't entirely business as usual; things were happening. Betty told me. The old man's ticker was sunfishing much worse than usual and the doctor had exiled him, which meant Betty, too, to Florida for the cold months which were kicking in just about then. All the gaggle was farmed out already, placed here and there with friends and relatives so they could stay in school, with a couple of the very youngest accompanying them to Florida—and all this was about to take place in about four or five days without bothering me in the slightest. The house was mine to enjoy and caretake for the rest of my leave, then lock up and go back when it was time to go back. My only responsibility was to keep the joint fairly clean in case the real estate agent called to bring over some prospective buyers, but that was pretty low-pressure at this point, no sign out front, just toe-dipping to see what kind of offers were out there. Keep the place clean, no corpses, no naked girls stomping grapes in the foyer, I knew the drill. And then there was a day and evening of packing the Rambler with little cardboard games for the kids to play in the back compartment, packing the small black-and-white TV and dishes and glassware wrapped in blankets and *Goodbye, Richard, I love you, the very best of luck, write us, have fun with the house.* And then the other bigger kids disappeared on cue, except that they kept telephoning me trying to get me to come to their foster houses to have dinner with their friends' parents, and I'd tell them, *Sorry, can't make it tonight, going to the movies* (Who with? Myself probably), *'bye.*

And it was wonderful. I could wallow and become terminally depressed to my heart's content in the huge house and roam aimlessly through the upstairs and bang up against the walls downstairs, or stand in the middle of the unheated garage in a sweater for an hour if I wanted. And I could cook; Betty had packed the kitchen with eggs and whole wheat muffins and onions and garlic, big cans of ham patties and green peppers, and I went ape-shit and cooked it all up over and over again and stacked the dishes in the sink and never took the trash out. The neighbors began to talk about the ghost haunting 19301 Palace Elm, and the little mail that came addressed to me I didn't open. Wallow, wallow, wallow—I tried out all the beds like Goldilocks or Snow White, napped on them all, very weird.

One morning the phone rang and I picked it up and there was a man on the other end who stuttered a little and asked me who this was and I told him, and he said he was sorry he hadn't given me any more advance warning—he hadn't realized I was home—but he was bringing over some suckers in about an hour, and was it possible for me to get the place looking, well, you know, and I said yes, I know, I'll have it smelling like a rose, over and out. So I rectified all the damage and insult I'd done to the kitchen and my bedroom and the bathroom and flung piles of dirty towels and underwear down the chute, and then hauled the monstrous and health-threatening trash heap out to the steel cans in the garage, and I zipped the dishes, as many as would fit, into the Norge, and waited around smoking cigarettes until the short cycle was over and then stacked the clean ones neatly on the counter and crammed the next load into it, and then I cleaned the ashtray, and all the other ashtrays I'd dirtied, and then the bell rang.

The stuttering man wasn't with them. He'd sent them on their own. It was a couple, late thirties, and two kids, older girl, younger boy, something around eight and ten. I showed them in and we broke ice in the foyer for a few minutes and shook hands and I offered them coffee, and they decided not, thank you, and then I left them alone to wander but I stayed in the living room reading a copy of *Look* to make myself available for any questions. I heard their voices and footsteps as they paused before each upstairs room and looked in and flushed the toilets and ran bathroom taps and tried the casements. I heard the kids squabbling about which would be their bedrooms and what they'd do with them.

The man had worn an open shirt under a sport jacket, and a piece of jewelry had dangled from his neck. I was thinking about the piece of jewelry.

He'd told me he was an educational consultant, a Ph.D. with amorphous and high-level responsibilities with the Connecticut

Department of Education, and it had been all meat to me as I'd nodded attentively as if I gave a fuck or had any idea what he was talking about as he spoke of determinants and criteria and curriculum evaluation. His wife clung to his side, actually looping her arm through his as the kids bounced on the love seat in the foyer. His clothes were understated to the max. He was tall, hairy on the arms, losing some of his hair on the top, fighting that like hell, Italian shoes. She was shorter, blond, possibly naturally, straight blond hair trimmed with bangs in the front. She wore a long pleated beige skirt, a simple white blouse and a lightweight green V-neck sweater.

His neck, and around it the object all sublime. Dangling from a gold chain—a thick one—was a medal about the size of a book of matches, a rough-hewn rectangle of gold metal with cheap jewels jammed into its surface, small green, red and blue stones, and in enamel writing was a compressed version of the nun's ubiquitous poster: *War Is Not Healthy for Children and Other Living Things*. At least, at the very least, this expression of heartfelt sentiment was $37.95 at G. Fox or Steiger's, more like $50. It seemed bigger than it really was as it announced that these fine people were liberals, hot damn, liberals, which made me with my short hair and circumstances the butcher of Lidice; the real estate agent had tipped them off. Opportunity of a lifetime: Good and his family, in the market for a house, confront Evil. Let me know, I'd asked them, if you have any questions. About the house.

The tour was over; they were downstairs again and we were back in the foyer for the debriefing and I made a little speech about how I'd grown up in the house and been very happy growing up in the house, and the plumbing was all copper and very sound, no PVC shit, and all the electrical outlets worked to the best of my knowledge and the yard wasn't too big to maintain, I went to that elementary school around the corner, and the library's just beyond that. Their kids were around the corner tinkling on the piano, not even Chopsticks.

Then he told me (God spare me) more about themselves and what colleges they'd gone to (Illinois, Champagne-Urbana for him, somewhere in upstate New York for her) and why they liked the county and this part of it particularly, and I went into my nod again and told them I agreed with them (whatever they were saying), couldn't agree with them more, and then the Ph.D. man droned on some more, and suddenly we were talking about These Times and What Was Happening and how reluctantly they'd felt they'd had to speak out against the military and foreign policies of our country and take a stand—

And then he looked me directly in the eyes, not disapprovingly, but rather with a righteous charm born of his sincere belief in the academic ideal and the democratic dialogue (even when it meant that white trash army scum home on leave could have their opinions too), and he said, "But of course we know not everyone feels the way we do."

It was a clumsy moment; I wasn't nodding anymore. War-Is-Not-Healthy had just met his first War Fan and was looking for the gracious thing to say. What a jerk I was to think things were complicated and fragile. Fuck, they were simple. I was home on leave from the army, so I dug wars. Everything made perfect sense to any visitor wearing a $50 gold-and-rhinestone peace fetish who might drop in. I thought briefly about losing it and doing some quick knuckle work on his teeth while his wife could run screaming for the cops and his kids could cower behind the living room drapes—a really dandy scene for ten o'clock on a Sunday morning at 19301 Palace Elm. But I just kept blinking and he said, "Well, thank you very much for letting us disturb you on your leave," and I said, "No problem, come back anytime," and she hooted for the kids who came running, and War-Is-Not and his family did a wheel-about and walked down the flagstones toward their sedate blue Mercedes sedan.

White Trash Warrior Scum went back into the living room and sat on the couch and put his feet up on the coffee table (heels carefully placed on top of *Look*) and gazed across the ivory carpeting at the dining room with its deep teak table, and I thought: Becker doesn't know about this; how can I explain it to him? Betty doesn't know about this; how can I explain it to her? Nobody knows about this; how can I explain it to anyone?

II

BECKER, DAVID C.
US49963722
A POS
JEWISH

17

Dear Richard,

Okay, here's your fucking letter. Now back off.

Un-fucking-believable: college-boy Jew lofting army weather balloons in South Vietnam. This makes no fucking sense at all. I'm not bitching about it, exactly. It's as good a way to kill one of my years on the planet as any other, I suppose, and better than a lot of other ways. As things go for Jewboys this siècle, I suppose it's really pretty good. For one thing, I'm in mortal peril, but they've given me a rifle and lots of ammunition and they've promised to help us with artillery strikes if the pajama weasels try to take this mountaintop. That's a new wrinkle for Jews; they didn't used to do that for us. We used to have to take our mortal peril unarmed, hell, naked in cold boxcars half the time. So I guess things are looking up; I'm really a very lucky guy. Now I may get blown up or shot or step on one of those feces-encrusted punji sticks and lose my foot from gangrene, but this time it won't be because anybody hates Jews.

Nobody has anything against Jews here. The blacks in my unit are just as lucky. When they die or get the hot metallic contents of a claymore in the torso, it won't be because anybody hates niggers—what a relief that'll be for them; they tell me so all the time. "Becker," one of them will say around the campfire at night while another plays the harmonica, "you don't know what a relief it is that I'm not going to be lynched here. I used to worry about being lynched all the time back home in Milwaukee. But here if I get wasted, it'll be from people who couldn't care less that I'm of Afro-American descent."

But it's still so un-fucking-believable. I'm a jerk. I used to think I had it made, born in '47, and by the time I even found out about Hitler and what he had up his sleeve for me, he was dead and gone. One time I was real stoned and these people around me started talking about Hitler and the concentration camps and the Zyklon-B gas, and I just blurted out: Ha! Missed me! Home free! And he did. He did his wurst (sorry, couldn't stop myself), but the fucker missed me completely. But not by much, you got to admit, just two lousy years and a few thousand miles. So all through my teen years, I figured I had it made in the shade with marmalade, my ass was perfectly safe, nobody with anything to back it up wants to kill the Jews anymore, except for all of Israel's neighbors, and if I wanted to take the brunt of that I'd have to emigrate and volunteer, and even then I hear they don't put recent gung-ho American immigrants right in the army; they use them to pick the oranges so they won't spoil during mobilizations when all the Sabras are out hunting their local pajama weasels. So as long as I didn't get religion, I was safe.

Well, some shmuck I was. Through a series of hazy and completely inexplicable events that seem to have something to do with, of all people, the French, I'm here in mortal peril, armed, lofting my balloons thrice daily. But in appreciation for it, I'm a sergeant now, three-striper, and I'm the CMFIC of this here metro quonset hut—so important are we that we have no resident officers, nothing standing between us and hot leaden death but me and my alleged good judgment—and you have no idea what a relief that is to my men.

I guess you've got your shipping orders by now, too, so if it's this place (and of course I'll be delighted if it's not), maybe we'll be able to get some time off together and yank the hankies or see the sights in some of the Western world's last remaining colonial enclaves in the mysterious East—cheap Nikons and reel-to-reel tape decks galore, the spoils of war. But because you brought the subject up, now you have to write back and tell me where they've stashed your prissy ass and in what circumstances. Got to go now and supervise the three p.m. lofting, or my underlings will breathe in all the helium—and when that happens, the hooch sounds like Harlem in Duckburg.

Yours,
Becker

P.S. Oh, even though I've only been here two months, I've been checking things out and I think my bet with R.J.'s still safe. I promise you as an NCO and a gentleman that I'm doing nothing to stack the odds; when the balloon goes off to the south-by-southeast, I fucking-A report that it went off to the south-by-southeast. But the weasels still refuse to stand up and face us Americans like Americans, and under those circumstances, our hands are tied, what can us poor boys do?

18

I could afford to be cheery in my letter: There was a complete absence of people killing each other in the neighborhood. Odd as it seemed, all the fighting was in and for the low ground and us Allies had the mountaintop (old Mt. 1131) all to ourselves for weather-prognosticating purposes. Every two or three days a Huey resupplied us and brought us the mail and usually wasn't averse to taking one or two of us back to the artillery post across the valley for a day or two of relative luxuries and the thrill of looking at some different assorted faces. That was my big leadership task, deciding who couldn't be spared and who could when there was a spare return seat on the Huey, but usually it resolved itself; there was always some dork with an infected toenail or a personnel problem, something that allegedly needed the attention of specialists, and for two piasters I was delighted to exile him from the mountaintop for a couple of days, provided he promised to return with something fresh and exciting for our larder, or with some hot new stroke books, or maybe a new addition to Cinema 1131. About a week after I'd arrived, Oltarsh, the commo specialist for the past year, had come to the end of his tour and I was in the hooch as he packed his things. You expect a guy going home to be tickled pink, but he seemed troubled by something, and I asked him what was on his feeble little brain.

"Fuck," he said, "may as well pass it on to someone who might appreciate it. Do you think you can get an eight-millimeter projector up here?"

"Well, sure, I guess. They're not hard to come by. Why?"

"Okay. Before I came here I was in the Hundred-and-Worst's signal battalion, and they were wrapping everything up to go home, and the commander'd put down the word that he'd have the MPs and the CID checking for weird movies in everybody's duffel bags. Everybody in that unit seemed to have some local movies, real raunchy stuff, and our captain decided to have one last film festival and then burn the shit. Lasted three nights. You wouldn't believe some of the shit. Well, you will if you want the ones I rescued. Guys like me who'd just joined the unit were reassigned, and I stole some of them before they got thrown in the fire. I don't want to try to smuggle 'em back. I've seen 'em, and I don't think they'd be a big hit back home—somehow I know they'd just get me in trouble."

"Do these things have titles? Plots?"

"No. They don't even have sound and half of 'em don't even have color. Pretty primitive stuff. You want 'em?"

"Sure. I'm in charge of morale up here, too. Let me see what you got."

Oltarsh pulled a couple of film cans out of a plastic sack and we sat on the bunk and reviewed a few of the early scenes by holding the frames up to the window light. That night I passed the hat for a projector fund, and Givens, who was taking a short-short into Saigon to get diseases and said he knew his way around Cholon, agreed to buy a projector and use whatever was left over for any assorted short subjects he stumbled over. A week later we opened Cinema 1131. The first feature involved a young, nervous Asian woman and a large, mixed-breed canine, and it turned out to be one of the more restrained, sedate films. People in the audience kept saying things like, "Shee-it, do you see that?" A social critic noted, "Jesus, they must really need money bad to be in a movie like that." No shit, Sherlock —I was surrounded by insight up there on the mountaintop. I gave the movies titles like "He Did It to Her," "She Did It to Him," "They Did It to Them," "We Did It to You," "I Did It to Me," and somehow the names stuck and more amazingly the other guys knew which movies the titles referred to. Everyone going on R&R agreed to try to pick up something new for the collection, word began to get around the valley, and infantry-men began hitching chopper rides to the metro hooch for the night on their stand-down time. I was glad to provide the en-tertainment, but the only thing that irked me was the ritual so many of the patrons seemed obliged to go through after snarf-ing up twelve or fifteen of these Barf-o-ramas: They'd stand up when someone finally turned on the lights in the hooch and say, "Jesus, that's perverted! That's sick! Disgusting! They ought to arrest those guys." I reserved my respect for the few strangers who dropped by and watched the movies without these little outbursts of indignation; they usually turned out to be good reefer-smoking companions afterward in back of the hooch to watch the 02:30 105mm artillery barrages in the valley below.

"Well, that pretty much sums up things, doesn't it?" one grunt said as we strolled out on the north face and watched the flashes and listened to the delayed muffled explosions drift up through the mists. "Vietnamese honeys getting gang-banged for our amusement while we blast the living shit out of whoever's sorry enough to be in grid niner-November right now. These folks sure must live right to get us for pals."

"They don't live right at all. Some of them want to stop mak-ing those movies. Some of them want the round-eye to go home. That's why we're punishing them."

"Yeah, right. You're quite the indifferent child, ain't you?"

"Come again?"

"Hamlet's buddies, Rosencrantz and Guildenstern. They spend their time bopping around Europe checking out the latest in plagues and thumbscrews. They're not advocates of these things, mind you, but they figure if that's what's happening, they don't want to miss what's happening—like, they're obligated to be in the know."

"Oh, goodness, no," I protested. "I'm a rabid participant in life. I loft balloons."

"Yeah, right." He fired up a number. "This shit's from Cambodia. It's like your movies—more than the human brain can tolerate, but let's tolerate it anyway."

He was right. I was here because I was just drifting, just visiting, just lofting. Richard, I always thought, hated that about himself and about me and always seemed on the verge of getting frantic enough to do something rash about it, but for all his frenzy he was on his way to the Nam, too, where'd he'd soon be checking out the latest plagues, thumbscrews and animal movies himself. We'd already consigned ourselves in our own styles to the active business of letting our potentially lethal blocks of army time slide by us, a process Richard insisted on finding humiliating and shameful; I didn't, or I wouldn't. Rat shit— they could steal two years from us if they wanted, but I was fucking-A going to steal as much back from them as I could and fart in their face if they didn't like my attitude about it. And make rank to boot. I liked the Russian attitude. I'd once read an article about how the workers there get gassed on vodka on the job and find a hiding place and sleep in the factory all day, just generally fucking off beyond all belief as the whole national economy spirals down the toilet, and someone asked one of these jolly fellows why, and he said, "They pretend to pay us, and we pretend to work." These days I felt a lot of solidarity with that dude.

I could understand Richard, though. Smart as he was, he was an ordinary guy, an ordinary victim for the Green Weenie, and the Green Weenie weighs in at eight hundred pounds and comes at your ass (from behind, by surprise) at forty miles an hour, and on most ordinary guys the anal rape that follows is just savagely overwhelming. When the smoke cleared, he and most people I knew were too devastated to recover even a fraction of their composure.

The Green Weenie? It was a mythological flying sausage, the personification, I guess, of the worst bummer surprise the army could conjure up for your destiny. Where you got sent constituted about ninety percent of the fabled Weenie. I always imagined it as a large tubular deal about the size of those kosher salamis they give away as raffle second prizes, with wings, painted green, and when you were least expecting it, when everything was going along like Vaseline and you figured you had the world dicked, the GW was forcibly thrust up your ass until the top of it popped out of your mouth and your little beady eyes bulged with pain and disbelief. Some people I talked to imagined that it had a little diamond-tipped auger up front for the actual reaming. Psychically it consisted of everyone's personal vision of hell, or the nightmares of those Commie interrogators on TV who go back to your childhood to find your unique personal terror; whatever it was you wanted least to happen, that was what was jammed into the Weenie's nose cone just before they launched it your way.

I lie—the Weenie wasn't always that way. One time out of a hundred thousand it didn't ram its way up your ass or send you to Nam or the Aleutians or Fort Polk. Sometimes instead it tapped you gently on the shoulder, kissed you lightly on the cheek, played your favorite tune and handed you some of the most astonishingly beautiful shit. One asshole I know was trained to pilot assault landing craft and when it was time to leave school and get his Reality orders, he was convinced he'd be dodging hot bullets while he tried to steer his craft through the breakers during a lightning amphibious assault on North Vietnam— D-Day, but worse. So. Just to keep him and all of us on our toes, the Green Weenie sent him to a secret little outpost on the Gulf of Mexico where his job for the next year was to pilot a giant luxury Chris-Craft fishing yacht for generals and colonels and government contractors they were giving blowjobs to that month. Most of the time he lived all alone in one of the resort cabins and because he wasn't on a military base, they gave him some vast allowance for food and other crap. When none of the cheeses were around, he had unlimited fuel for the Chris-Craft and was under standing orders to take it out in the Gulf every decent day so it wouldn't stand idle. He wore his civvies the whole year he was there, on duty or off, and when the cheeses came for the fishing or the hunting, they insisted that everything be on a nice casual first-name basis, none of that sir and saluting crap, just a nice pleasant fishing cruise on a sea of beer and label Scotch. Tales to astonish, but the Weenie had tricks like that up its sleeve. It could happen. It did happen.

Rarely. Most of the time there was that unmistakable sensation of rectal salami as you read your hot new orders for Nam or some horrifying blighted Dixieland post. And of course the first encounter with the GW came at the end of basic training when you got those swell orders telling you what job the army planned for you to do for the next two years. It came coded, but most people ended up with eleven-Bravo, which by that time didn't require a reference book or scorecard: light weapons infantryman, surprise, surprise, followed by another eight weeks of advanced infantry training, a short leave in which to kiss your ass goodbye, shipment to Nam. That was the standard Weenie gift for your basic hot-meat draftee who was gritting his teeth through his mandatory two years but hadn't freaked out and begged for a third year to avoid eleven-Bravo, anything but eleven-Bravo. With the third year, you could get your pick of any of the army's fine schools, provided you tested high enough for it, exotic shit like nuclear weapons maintenance and repair at Sandia, New Mexico (I'd been tempted, I confess) or cook's school.

Of course there's no accounting for taste; some people like a salami up their butts. When I got my orders at the end of basic, the turkey standing next to me started freaking out all over the formation and threatening to call his congressman and other assorted useless nonsense, and we all assumed some slick recruiting sergeant had promised the lad, a real dork of a seventeen-year-old loser from Baltimore, that he'd be spared eleven-Bravo if he signed up for the third year. Not so. The lad had signed up for three years, all right, but only after the recruiter had *promised* to make him a light weapons infantryman. And now, as he looked at his orders, he was freaking out to find he was going to spend the next three years of his insignificant life as a cook, sheltered from combat in some mess hall or mess tent. The mind boggles, but the kid actually felt he'd been betrayed and demanded to see the C.O. The captain sent up to battalion for a copy of the turkey's enlistment form, and it turned out the shmuck had accepted the recruiter's verbal promise (wrong move) but that there was nary a written word about his dream of the infantry, Queen of Battle. Insane but true. Still, it was all for the best in this best of all possible worlds. Many of us would have been willing to trade orders with the shmuck, but most of the ground-pounders in the Nam were of the opinion that they were glad not to have to be in the same infantry squad with anyone who purposely *wanted* to be in an infantry squad, such morons being dangerous to have around. The Weenie works in mysterious ways its wonders to perform.

My first Weenie, as far as I was concerned, was basic itself. The processing at the AFEES center lasted from about eight in the morning to seven at night, and then they piled us all into a chartered Dog and shuttled us south into the darkness. I remember one stop somewhere in Kentucky or West Virginia late at night at a truck-stop burger dive that served beer, and the old civilian bus driver practically had a tear sloshing down his cheek when he let all of us out and told us to enjoy our last beer for a month. "But don't any you guys try to run off into them bushes," he said, "or they gone call you Ay-Wall and chase after your ass and they gone be mad at me." Thanks, dad, you're a prince. If only I drank beer, this would be one of the highlights of my life.

It was Bragg we were going to; I knew it by then, of course. Every goddam base that could field a basic training brigade was in full swing, and if I hadn't been so fucking dulled out by then, I'd have hoped for Fort Dix in New Jersey. I suppose that once you got intimate with the concentration camp system and there was no way out of it, Dachau had advantages over Auschwitz if you could bribe someone to arrange a transfer.

But I'd actually missed a Weenie already, this one with splinters, and not even known it. I found out about it later. It lay in wait at the induction center I'd just left. The Weenie never sleeps and is always several steps ahead of your wildest fears. You get your notice, and if you decide not to kill yourself or shoop-shoop over the Canadian border or piss on the floor instead of taking the oath, you show up on time, merrily resigned to nothing more terrifying than two years in the army and maybe getting your scrotum blown into Laos by a tacky misstep on an antipersonnel (love that word) mine. No big deal. They take your blood and mix it with your urine and if the composite color isn't black, you pass on down to the Big Oath Room, and Surprise! This time the Weenie's dressed up as a Marine gunnery sergeant, fearsome creature, who goes through the formation tapping shoulders and muttering *you you you you*—and guess what? You're all Marines and you're on your way to Parris Island, God save your luckless asses. Yes, the fabled Army Weenie could even make you a Marine—how 'bout them apples, huh? And then there was nothing for you to do but dump in your shorts, start to burble and bawl and then board the bus for your great unexpected adventure, you lucky jarhead-to-be. Betcha never knew they was drafting *Marines*. . . .

Fortunately that was one of the rarest of all the Weenie's surprise thrills, the army being vast and the Marines being comparatively smaller and most of the time managing to scrape up its necessary good men from the dregs of high school dropouts whose town elders had convinced them that there's nothing like a good old dose of leathernecking to make men of them and even get them laid when and if they dared to come back to the old hometown on leave, although of all the many sexual perversions I've encountered in women, knowingly balling a Marine has yet to make its appearance up close, in person. But I'm sure there are some who do, at least once, those anything-for-a-thrill types who have strange dreams at night and hang out at the USO.

So Bragg was my first real Green Weenie. I had the feeling things were getting a little sour when the bus finally pulled into the outskirts of Fayetteville, the army town that was leeched to Bragg's periphery. We were passing a billboard at about eleven in the morning and the sign showed a torch-carrying gent in a white sheet, Casper the Ghost style, and above and below Mr. Birth of a Nation was the legend: *Welcome to Fayetteville—This Is Klan Country.* That was great, just dandy, just what I was in the mood for under the circumstances. I'd had my baser fears pandered to before, but this was a little on the excessive side. I remembered that after niggers and just before Catholics, the Klan was always interested in us kikes, and it looked as if I'd be spending the next six weeks at one of the Klan's favorite oases. Obviously the sign was intended to convey more information than your average Lions Club placard (and in fact it failed to mention the restaurant where the meetings were held or the weekday or time); there was the strong hint that us niggers, kikes and Catholics passing through would do well to toe the mark and be the Klan's sort of nigger, kike and Catholic. I wondered what this meant for me. Was I supposed to apply for a tailoring slot at the quartermaster's? Was I expected to tell dialect jokes? Give incorrect change? Most of the bus was black; there had to be Catholics, but no one said anything as we passed the billboard. The army had powerful magicke; no one could concentrate on a puny threat like the Klan.

The bus belched us out at the reception center, a rude but comparatively puny prelude to basic training, and for the next three days and nights, practically without sleep, we were marched from building to building for our uniforms, shots, blood tests, army IQ tests, and at one point had a lecture at which a sergeant pointed to a bucket into which we were all urged to dump whatever civilian contraband we'd managed to hold on to this long—switchblades, amphetamines, smack, reefer, hypodermic needles, hash, absinthe miniatures, autographed pictures of Chairman Mao, brass knuckles, garrotes, pistols, zip guns made from car antennas, burglary tools, whoopee cushions—and if we dumped it now, all would be anonymously forgiven and ignored. Then the sergeant turned his back. I heard a lot of thumping sounds in the bucket as we were marched out, but I couldn't see what ended up in the bucket. Then we went to a benched room where we were given a form that had the Attorney General's list of *verboten* organizations former membership in which would queer our chances to be soldiers, things like the Mendocino Area Parakeet Fancier's League, the Jersey City Society for the Advancement of Barbershop Quartets, the North Central Iowa Model Railroading Consortium. The sergeant got steamed that I took so long reading them all, but I had to make sure. On the same sheet they wanted to know if I'd ever contemplated the violent overthrow of the U.S. government and I wrote *not yet*, but I never heard anything more about that; the nuance didn't seem to impede my soldiering chances in their view.

Up to that time, I'd never been much of a fancier of topics military. I knew a Boy Scout from a British Grenadier in a pinch, but that was about all, and I imagined naïvely that one army base was going to be pretty much like any other. I didn't even have to go to a second one to figure out that Bragg was different. Headquarters of the 82nd Airborne Division, about ninety percent of its lifers and almost as many of the just-passing-throughs were loony volunteer fuckers who liked to jump out of airplanes, and when they weren't doing that, they liked to talk and scream a lot about loving to jump out of airplanes. And the freakos didn't have to be mere Airborne troopers. After Airborne, they could loiter around the John F. Kennedy School for Special Warfare and become (gasp) Special Forces types. Bragg was definitely your gung-ho installation where instead of your normal complement of goldbricks, malingerers, the pissed off and the pissed on, superannuated alcoholic lifers waiting to grab their pensions, and rejects from various state unemployment emergency programs, you had a frightening number, a majority actually, of psychopaths who liked to hop out of the rack at four-thirty in the morning and run around the fort all day until they could find something dangerous to volunteer for. The guy taking a leak at the next urinal was probably a specialist in chewing through concertina wire with his incisors while carrying a three-hundred-pound satchel charge into enemy sleeping bags as silently as an alley cat in a rubber room, and he had the patches on his jungle fatigues to prove it, so there. The lieutenant who deigned to pick you up at the authorized post hitchhiking stand (the army insisted on designating places for such practices if they couldn't eradicate them entirely) was probably the exec of an outfit whose mission was to invade and hold all Antarctica in the nude with small arms. The bar fights downtown must have been really nifty affairs rife with exotic mayhem and obscure martial arts displays, but my stay at Bragg didn't leave me a lot of time to check them out.

And then suddenly, after we'd been completely separated from our hair in a shackful of what were euphemistically called barbers (and charged money for it to boot), whistles began to blow and an enormous assembly of every confused swinging dick in the reception station was called, and the lieutenant in charge announced that we were all dismissed for the next twenty-four hours, loosed upon the base unsupervised and in conformity to the army's notion of being free. The old strange bald golfer with the addiction to the Zane Grey novels had just croaked, like Christ, just for us; he'd died to give us the day off. We watched them haul the flag down to its fly-open position while we stood in our neophyte lampoons of attention and parade rest and other positions we'd seen in TV war flicks of various periods and armies, while the lieutenant on the podium said a few words about the general and how we owed this day off to the largesse of the current Commander in Chief, who, coincidentally (this wasn't included in the announcement), had been the fellow they used to catch crimping the hose to the oxygen tent at Walter Reed back in the fifties whenever Ike took deathly ill, the other hand resting conveniently on the King James just in case, or so it was alleged in hometown sour grapes gossip by the diehard liberals, Democrats, fellow travelers and eggheads. The lieutenant dismissed us and vanished. We stood around, the formation slowly decomposing like something getting older and older in a glass bowl in the refrigerator unclaimed. We offered one another cigarettes and then searched back and forth for those of us with matches or lighters. It was early in the morning and smoke issued from everyone's breath, and for a while I realized there was the startling possibility that we'd all remain standing there and wandering around within the unfenced confines of the parade ground for the entire twenty-four-hour holiday, simply because the idea of being free but in the army on a post was such an unexpected and novel clash of alien theories, like being six years old and the winner of two weeks in a whorehouse.

But the adventurous ones, singly and then in pairs, then in squads and entire platoons, began to wander off in various unknown directions, most of us penniless, all of us without transportation. The first flock to regroup clustered around the lone public phone in the area. Others, dazed, found their attention sucked in by the company bulletin board with its dozen or so neatly tacked Disposition Forms announcing the results of petty courts-martial of meatballs who hadn't even waited for basic training to start fucking up. Next to the mess hall steps, a crap game sprang up like a fairy ring in a meadow overnight. An expedition was mounted to find the post movie theater, another to find the nearest 3.2 beer dispensary, a third to search for female life if it existed in such a place and to find the circumstances, if any, under which it might put out.

I took off on my own. I hadn't had time to meet or talk with anyone yet more than a few quick grunts, and I feared there was always the chance that on this sudden holiday for which we were all so unprepared, someone might take the lead and we'd end up in the commanding general's house raping his womenfolk and drinking up his cough syrup. An hour later I was in some place the size of a high school gymnasium, the post's version of a private cafeteria, as differentiated from an actual company mess hall. The decor was identical, but no mess clerk barred the doorway with a sign-in sheet, there was a jukebox that I parked myself next to, and you paid for the food, which was indistinguishable from mess hall swill. But the differences—there was no mistaking I'd escaped from military control and hit the free-market big time. To begin with, there were choices of different kinds of swill: hot dogs *or* Swiss steak *or* drained, reboiled and redrained spaghetti and meat sauce *or* hamburgers with sickly jaundiced French's mustard and Sexton institutional-sized can ketchup already applied, all available to me at my request in the same meal if I chose, all appetizingly loitering under infrared lamps or wasting away above steam tables. And there was a woman at the end of this Monel Metal and stainless-steel-tubing byway of culinary Oz, an ancient crone in surgical whites with a gigantic wart and a thick single black hair crowning it on her upper lip; she guarded the battered brown manual NCR cash register, her massive downy thighs racily straddling the black vinyl-tape-covered stool. I piled my tray with two hamburgers, a spherical order of bleached mashed potatoes dipped in a lard-based brown gravy, a big Coke in a Dixie cup with a slick of defeated crushed ice floating on top, and a piece of squashed cherry pie that was light on the fruit but big on red corn syrup, all in exchange for perhaps $2.40 of the mad money I'd secreted about my person.

I was back at the jukebox gazing at my traditional Eisenhower's Death Day bounty. I'd put in a quarter and punched my three selections and now I wondered where to begin this Thanksgiving meal, this warped seder. The vast auditorium was almost empty. A few lifers had scattered themselves as far from one another as they could get. A few bald and frightened fellow assholes from the reception center stood at the screen door looking in and wondering if they were permitted inside. The woman counted the contents of her register. The jukebox hissed and clunked and whirred and burped (Rock-ola, rays of colored lights extending across its belly, a Perry Como Christmas LP available for the high rollers with fifty cents), and the Beach Boys started to sing.

Hot damn. I leaned back in the chair and raised the Dixie cup and toasted Ike. I liked Ike. He moved me. Then I started in on the mashed potatoes.

19

Because I mean a man's got to eat. I suppose that's the only subject I never had too many complaints about in the army, the food. The quality of the cuisine was Shit City, of course, but the quantity was smack dab in the middle of where I liked it: all I could eat. I can recite Gray's "Elegy" and I can do the cha-cha (no shit; last man on earth, I imagine), but when they finally finish stomping me to death and take my full measure, my primary impact on this plane will have been my maw, that awesome entrance to my alimentary canal. If Oliver Twist had been too shy to stand up and ask for more, you'd all have been forced to read Dickens's *David Becker* in high school instead. It's always been that way, my first question about any novel object being whether or not I could eat it. Once in college I had to go to Boston over the weekend and I scared up a ride from the bulletin board from a pair of honeys with a car who were headed in that direction. They took me to some suburb south of the city and when we arrived around dinnertime, the mother in residence wouldn't hear of me staggering off to the bus without joining the family for dinner, so I washed up and took a seat in the dining room. A stream of fried chicken with mashed potatoes and gravy and biscuits began flowing from the kitchen to be divvied up between mom, dad, the two honeys, a brother, the maid and me, and about a half hour later all the other combatants had surrendered except me. The hostess kept calling for more, and the maid kept shlepping it out from the kitchen and placing it before me, and I kept modestly and nonchalantly making it disappear as the rest of the household watched with astonishment and what seemed a little alarm. After a while I suspect that hospitality turned into something more like the desire to make sure a potential cannibal was well fed to avoid any temptations. But after everyone else had bailed out of the dining room, the mom lingered on, casually watching this phenomenon of nutrition make short work of the poultry section at the local A&P, and it seemed to touch something very deep and wondrous in her. Geometrically, I suppose it struck her very much like the circus act in which the midget car drives into the center ring and disgorges around nine dozen clowns of various shapes and sizes, because I was then and still am an unvaryingly short, stocky type with no resemblence to Henry VIII or Warren Gamaliel Harding. Finally, after a couple of slices of her blueberry pie, I smiled and indicated I was full now, and from the look on her face I thought she wanted to whip out a set of adoption papers and call a notary. She drove me to the bus stop and finally broke down and confessed that she'd never before encountered anyone with an appetite like mine and that she was moved and impressed and that I could drop in again anytime, preferably with a little advance notice so she could slaughter a calf and lay in a few bushels of onions.

Coupled with an asbestos-lined stomach, my appetite propelled me through the army probably with a bit less distress than others accumulated. There was still plenty of light at the end of the tunnel and all the food even I could eat for free. Granted it wasn't Chambord or the Four Seasons, but places like that have always made me nervous anyway because of all the impediments they place between me and the central business of snarfing down the food—numerous forks and spoons and knives of various sizes and functions, neckties and belts that aren't supposed to be loosened in polite company, waiters and stewards who seem to be standing by not so much to serve as to observe and grade me on table manners and citizenship. Somewhere between places like that and an army mess hall, and probably closer to the latter, lies my idea of a perfect restaurant. Outside, facing the highway, is a large sign announcing the restaurant's name and simultaneously its intentions: *Eat*, in classic American garish red neon. Inside is a long lunch counter and about a dozen cramped wooden booths, each equipped with those ancient individual jukebox terminals, with menus wedged between them and glass sugar, salt and pepper shakers. Newspapers are sold by the cash register, and mints and toothpicks are also dispensed. The menu has about two hundred main course entrées, all perpetually available and in season (but fresh oysters served only in January, February, March, April, Mayr, Juner, Julyr, Augustr, September, October and November). In the unseen kitchen are giant cauldrons of chicken, beef and pork gravy. The coffee is always fresh and consultants from Atlanta are flown in weekly to fine-tune the Coca-Cola dispenser. The stools at the counter swivel, and the cook is a former inmate of a concentration camp whose one aim for the rest of his or her life is to thank America every waking hour by feeding its citizens and feeding them well, substantially, and with all the secrets of the cuisine of eight European capitals. The counter and booths are serviced by a quiet, even sullen waitress who takes your order, brings you the chow and beyond that leaves you the hell alone. Substitutions are allowed, even encouraged. The place is open twenty-four hours a day, 365 days a year, has ample parking and is located some distance from the main highway to discourage transient riffraff. Hunters surreptitiously sell poached venison and moose steaks to the cook at the back door, and the waitress tips me off about it. Drunks who don't mind their own business or keep their mouths shut are immediately vaporized, rendered into tiny black spots on the linoleum floor by hidden lasers, after which the management apologizes and serves everyone a free round of pie. The ashtrays are always clean, the jukebox up-to-date, devoid of shitkicker selections. The place is far enough out of town so that if I bring a new squeeze there for burgers, there's absolutely no chance we'll run into anyone I might know who'll blab. The bathrooms are clean and businesslike, the graffiti in the stalls reflect a liberal arts education, and there are no machines on the wall dispensing rubbers or French ticklers.

Mess halls certainly fell short of these standards, but for someone who had no choice but to be there or do a stint at Fort Leavenworth, where the food was rumored to be a lot worse, it was close enough for rock 'n' roll, particularly after basic training was over. Not that the food was bad in basic; it was the ambience. For one thing, it was all portion-controlled, no seconds. For another, there wasn't time for seconds, let alone firsts. You filed into the basic training mess hall, went down the line and got your slop dished out, jammed into a table and gorged it all down while drill sergeants roller-skated around the floor screaming at you to finish up and get the fuck out of there. Once out the back door you were obliged to double-time back to the company area where the rest of the day's fun was waiting for you. Asbestos stomach, yes, but it's always asked for just a little time to check out the latest contributions and come up with a strategy to assimilate them. The five minutes allowed for bolting down a three-course meal and then jogging back to the company area was a little too much for the sensitive works, and I got in the habit of dashing out the back door of the mess hall and down the stairs, across the road, and making it to a secluded spot between two barracks where I paused for a a couple of seconds to blow a portion of my cookies on the ground. The black street types from Baltimore who were dashing back with me took notice and gave me the only nickname I can ever remember having, The Pukin' Dude, and there commenced a little drill in my platoon after each meal in which those who knew the nickname and its origin took pains to make sure they were out of azimuth and range of any sudden stream that might issue their way.

"Hey, here come The Pukin' Dude. Shee-it, watch out he don't get any on your boots."

"Shee-it, man, I'm movin' back to the second row."

"Hey, Jack, how you get in the army with a goddam stomach like that, huh? Jesus, don't stand around here."

Eventually on long hikes to and from bivouac I developed the ability to run and puke at the same time, my head cocked to the right, with nary a speck on my weapons or shoes. The field first sergeant became curious at this and hied me off to the dispensary, where I was given an odious container of liquid whose active ingredient was belladonna and told to eat less. Some bunkmates and I did the belladonna up one night after lights-out and I ignored the other half of the advice; the goddam problem had nothing to do with how much I ate, but centered around how little time I had in which to eat it and the marathons that immediately followed, and damned if I was going to let myself shrink to nothing because of some paramedic who was too fucking stupid to see that. Because I mean a man's got to eat.

Basic was living hell for a couple of weeks until the day someone clued me in that it was all a ritualistic game, a rite of passage that any shmuck could dick by being at the right X and Y coordinates at the right time T. Even a college city Jewboy could dick it and land somewhere around the fiftieth percentile with a minimum of effort, as there were always plenty of even more pitiable basket cases, mental and physical, in every company to occupy the worst attentions of the drill sergeants, lard cases from the hills of North Carolina and freaked-out blacks who took the spotlight off everyone else by going AWOL in the first week. Then around the fifth week, we were given our weapons and things lightened up even more for me, because this particular Jewboy meatball came equipped with a wholly unexpected and unadvertised feature, the ability to throw small pieces of lead precisely into tiny black target circles with astonishing regularity, another little bennie from a wealthy and indulgent upbringing, but much more helpful under the circumstances than the ability to cha-cha—but who knows when even that may come in handy one of these days? *Do the cha-cha or I gonna slit your throat, you honkie asshole*—surely stranger things have happened. Of course the M14 was no .22 competition free rifle and the ones we were issued had probably been used to chop down trees in Korea, but the principle was the same. You put a cartridge in the magazine and charged the motherfucker somehow and it slipped into position for the firing pin. You bashed your cheek and chin up against the stock, closed your left eye, looked down the sights with the right, put the target bull on top of the front post, and after the first afternoon's adjustments, you just kept doing it again and again in various required positions until the range sergeant left you alone. There was a jarring sort of kick that was absent in the old .22's and that raised a little black bruise in the small of the shoulder after the first few days, but after all, this wasn't no goddam Jewboy summer camp, this was fuckin' war, by cracky, and you had to expect a little pain and sacrifice in the defense of things we all held dear. In the meantime, you got to relax on your stomach or leaning up against the top of a trench, and there were plenty of others up and down the line who had trouble figuring out which end of the thing the bullet came out of, let alone how to come within three or four feet of the target.

We'd been issued our steel pots and camouflage covers, which tucked into a tiny canvas band on the rim, and for some reason it became the custom for each dork to write something in ballpoint ink on the band, some little token of cooperation with the program, like *Gook Death* or *Vietnam Bound*, so in tiny little printed characters I penned *Dulce Est Pro Patria Mori*. I was the only Hebe in the company, in the enlisted hot-meat ranks, anyhow. The tac officer, a second lieutenant spending two months after OCS gearing up to command an infantry platoon in the Nam, was the only other Hebe in the area, and my quotation from Horace caught the lad's eye for the first time while I was slinging them down-range. He assumed a position behind me during a lull in the paper carnage. "You know Latin, Becker?"

"Yes, sir. Four years, sir."

"I was a German man myself, but I know that quote. You believe that?"

"You bet, sir. Sweet it is, sir, to die for one's country, sir. All the way, sir."

"You shoot pretty well. Where'd you learn to shoot like that?"

"Summer camp, sir. Intercamp championship two years running, sir."

"Where'd you go to school?"

"Maryland, sir."

"I was at the University of Pennsylvania myself. Well, keep at it."

"Yes, sir."

I almost shit my drawers—an Ivy man, *mirabile dictu*, and a Jew and an infantry officer. I had words only once more with this deranged kike one Saturday night outside the orderly room.

A bunch of the boys were whooping it up outside the Malamute Saloon, so to speak, and Levin deigned to step outside for a few casual moments for an informal and officerly chat with the enlisted swine, despite the dent it was putting in his spit-shining hour. I was on my way into town without benefit of pass but paused to get in on this newsworthy exchange. Some trainee had just popped the magic question and Levin started to reply, "Well, I don't really know what's going on over there, but the way I see it, American guys are dying over there, so I guess I've got to go over there myself." The public phone booth was a few feet away and for a moment I was seized with a violent impulse to call U-Penn and ask someone in authority if he knew what his institution had loosed upon an unsuspecting world, but I repressed it. I stuck around and joined the crowd and listened to this maniac expound what may likely have been among his last few thousand words, as basic training was almost over and he'd shortly ship off to Nam, where second lieutenants with his Dink Stover attitude were regularly gifted with a short burst of automatic fire in the back of the head for instructional purposes. He was a beautiful specimen. Later at Benning, I'd see altogether too much of the statue of the infantry platoon leader holding his rifle aloft and squealing the motto of the Infantry Center, *Follow Me!* and it struck me that Levin was the statue's spitting personification minus the pink paint around the groin area with which a few of Benning's more radical troops had improved the statue one May Day or Night. Levin was tall, athletic, thin and wiry and his fatigues were always rigid with Elmer's glue or whatever officers use so they can get into their trousers both legs at the same time. His plain spectacles belied the fact that he had terminal squash rot. I gave him three months to live and headed for the bus into town.

What little college fairy dust still clung to me by the time I was drafted earned me some temporary stripes in basic which it took me only a week to divest myself of by storing my rifle in my barracks locker a couple of times so as not to miss lunch—a serious breach of military etiquette as the M14 was a favorite with urban terrorists who used it to nail the National Guard from rooftops. That suited me fine, because stripes in basic meant about twice the bullshit, and during my brief corporalcy, I'd already been forced to coerce too many dufus rednecks into doing their share of the cleanup, and it was starting to pall. I finally called one of them a son of a bitch. He was a monstrous, lurching, postadolescent North Carolina Baby Huey moonshiner and he started looming toward me with menace in his eyes. He was coming to the right place. I turned my chin to the side and jutted it out and pointed at it for him to see unguarded and defenseless, and while he started to make a fist for his haymaker to send me into oblivion, his fellow shitkicker pals in the platoon grabbed his arms and dragged him back into a corner and tried to explain to him that while I'd called him a naughty name, smashing me with my stripes was going to get him a year in the can at hard labor. The next day the drill sergeant took away my stripes and I settled back into the routine of making the fiftieth percentile and just getting the fuck out of that place. The Carolina golem never bothered me again; I imagine my attempted sacrifice fly unnerved him after he began dimly to comprehend how it had almost worked, and he wanted nothing more to do with such devious, complicated big city ways. A Minnesota farmboy took up the stripes and life was hell for him for the rest of the term. As a reward they promoted him to one-stripe on graduation and shipped him immediately to infantry school and from there doubtless to an infantry platoon in the Nam, perhaps as point man; virtue rewarded.

I don't remember anymore how basic actually ended, only that it seemed to end on that night out on bivouac when we were all rousted from our tents with our rifles and steel pots and marched several miles to the strange naked meadow with the high wooden observation towers and spotlights at the high end. We were double-timed into a deep trench slick with mud at the low end, a half-mile down-range, drill sergeants shrieking confusing and incomprehensible commands at us as they packed us dick-to-butt in a line. Then the machine guns began firing from their positions under the observation towers and I looked behind me and all the noise and confusion stopped as I followed the hot red glowing phosphorus tracer bullet trails that converged onto the vanishing point far above and behind us in the distance as if we were scaled objects in some lesson in perspective drawing. Then we were urged up the ladders and onto our bellies in more slick mud as the machine gun bullets zipped a few inches above our heads, and as I began to crawl away from the trench, I suddenly realized that for the first moment since we'd left the bus that brought us to basic training, there weren't any drill sergeants standing over us barking and shouting at us. We were on our own. No one could clock us with a stopwatch, and I slowed down as I crawled and when I got tired I stopped entirely and rested for as long as I liked. At the barbed wire, I turned over on my back and used my rifle to hold the wire high while I pushed myself forward with my boots under the wire. Star-shell flares erupted in the black sky above me, and on both sides of me I could see the others in the company, many of them frantic and screaming, some crying and paralyzed but thank Christ not losing it and standing up, the only forbidden thing to do, as it would have been instant perforation even from the chickenshit .25-caliber machine guns mounted on wooden aiming guides that kept the never-ending fusillades just above our heads. Still on my back I stopped again on the other side of the barbed wire to gaze at the tracer rounds painting their perfect long colored lines above me that converged far down the meadow. And as everyone screamed, satchel charges exploded in a pit next to me ringed with barbed wire to prevent the ultimate fools from taking shelter in a hole with dynamite. I took the Marlboro pack from my fatigue jacket and found the reefer my friend Norman had sent me in the mail that week and I lit it in the darkness, cupping the match with my hands. Who would know, and if he knew, who would give a flying fuck, and if he gave a flying fuck, what drill sergeant would venture onto that dark and fiery meadow to reproach me? I sucked in the marvelously acrid smoke of the fat number, and when I'd taken enough, I left the roach on a sandbag by the explosives pit as a little surprise for the lifer who'd come the next day to replace and rewire the C-4 charges, and then I started crawling again. Some were passing me and others were falling behind. Some had stopped entirely, and later, as we milled around the trucks to go back to bivouac, the machine guns finally stopped and the drill sergeants raced onto the meadow and screamed at the frozen, shivering few who hadn't made it. But I had, and a roaring good time it was, the great-grandfather of all illicit cherry bomb adolescent forays, the ultimate Fourth of July fireworks display and mud flop—*boom whiz datatatata swoosh pop boom!* Machine gun by machine gun it stopped, the last satchel charge was detonated from the observation tower, the last GI who made it crawled past the machine gun line on his stomach and was told politely that he could get up now (most continued crawling for another fifty feet), and that's all I remember of that marvelous night of bitter white hot smoke and Jamaican reefer and of terrible blasts inches away that made eardrums bleed and jarred the teeth in their sockets. It was only noise and pretty colors after all, all pretend and make-believe, and fuck you if you freaked out and stood up. God bless us every one, and fuck us if we stood up.

20

That rude grunt who'd dropped by for an evening at Cinema 1131 had called me an indifferent child and compared me to a couple of loutish Danish Hebes (Guildenstern and Rosencrantz?—c'mon, of course, I have cousins with those names), and it stung, not that he was above watching a little enforced group or interspecies third world romance himself. Moreover, I just lofted balloons, but he was actively involved in rupturing the tubes of the pajama weasels when he could find them, so who was he to preach during the smoke break between "You Did It to Me" (Thailand, 1967, 22 minutes, b&w) and "It Did It to Her" (Philippines, 1969, 31 minutes, color)? I never knew his name and he never visited the mountaintop again, but I thought about that smoke break a lot in the months that went by. He seemed like a relatively stable and healthy type—I pegged him to be from the Bay Area—but pursuing his logic soon led to the way Richard dangerously and apologetically fumbled through the world, with conclusions I found horrifying: Conscripted under threat of federal prison (and in those days only tax cases had a speedier priority in the courts than draft cases), Richard could somehow arrive at the conclusion that his situation was his own fault and that he'd done something either flat-out wrong or somehow worse than what Dr. Kissinger or Mr. Rogers (not the one on the educational station), General Hershey or the Rostow boys or McNamara, Rusk or Bundy were up to, and there was nothing, no imaginative scheme leading to the deaths of hundreds of thousands of theirs or ours, that they could brew up that could possibly land them in the can. I could get into Bride-of-the-Burro movies to some extent, but Richard embraced mental perversions with a heavy masochistic component that I didn't intend ever to approach even with tongs. What I figured was that Hitler had missed me, and with just a little *mazel*, a year would go by and I'd be giving the Bronx cheer to Kissinger, too. We had a patriot in the hooch, a Nevada Mormon named Warfield, and one afternoon when my tongue and brain became a little too informal for him on these topics he got hot under the collar and demanded to know how I dared compare our American leaders with Hitler.

"How dare I? Easy. Watch me. Kissinger and Nixon are our new Hitlers. How's that? Pretty easy, right?"

"I don't believe this. What kind of an American are you?"

"A conscripted American. That buys me the ticket. You don't like it? Get me relieved of duty. Make me a disgruntled civilian again. Would that it were so easy."

"I just don't see how you can say these things. Doesn't Communism bother you?"

"Very much so. I've always been against any of it in my part of Montgomery County, Maryland, and the last time I checked, we were doing real good at controlling the insurgents. We estimate their current strength at zip. Nothing but capitalists 'round where I live."

"You don't think that if the Communists take over Vietnam, it won't spread?"

"Jeez. I envy you. Three, four fucking centuries of Europeans using this part of the world as their private toilet by force, and all of it just flew right over your head. You haven't the slightest idea why these people are so pissed off at us. You think it has something to do with a naughty book by Karl Marx."

"We were asked to help keep this country free."

"Free. God, I hate how clowns like you bugger that word up the ass. Just once in my fuckin' life, won't somebody define that for me, as long as I apparently have to spend a year facing death and jock itch for it? You'd think that wouldn't be too much to ask. Free to do what, Warfield? Free to terrorize Buddhists? Free to turn our foreign aid into private Swiss bank accounts? Free to grow rubber with cheap peasant labor for the free world's Chevies and Citroëns?"

"And you think it'll be better if the Communists take over?"

"Oh, no. It'll be just as bad, but different. At least it'll be Vietnamese fuckin' with each other for a change. Right now every time a Vietnamese gets fucked around here, I'm partially responsible; I helped and I know it. It would be a great relief to me that as long as these people insist on fucking over each other, that someday they do it without dragging my good name into it."

"I really don't think the army knows the full extent of your opinions, Becker."

"Sad news for you, Warfield: The army doesn't give a flying fuck. They got my swingin' dick here, one more armed body to add to the Presence. They got two-hundred-ninety-nine-thousand-nine-hundred-ninety-nine other swingin' dicks just like me here to chaperone the Saigon regime, and that's all they care about. You can call up G-2 in Saigon on the radio if you want. You got my permission. Call today; don't delay. You think they'll care? Don't kid yourself. I'm everything they want. What comes out of my mouth in this hooch is no more shocking to them than a case of bad breath. If you send them my tape-recorded collected sermons, they won't even deny me the Good Conduct Medal."

"I think you're a traitor."

I sucked in my breath. "Oh, my God, and me without my side arm. How about swords? Under-overs, shotguns and M16s over a folding table? Well, I got a question for you, Warfield. If you're so flag-simple, why are you lost here with me on this mountaintop monitoring the anemometer? Patriotic boy like you ought to be a Ranger, Airborne(!), up with some dufus ass-kicking unit like the Blackhorse, falling out of choppers with a knife in your teeth to eviscerate the godless Commies. If they win, I've already said I won't give a rat's ass, but what about you? Will you have done enough? Will you have done all you could to save our brave, freedom-loving allies?"

It was a powerful case of bad breath. Warfield stood up and stalked out to the instrument shack. Givens, who I'd thought was stoned into oblivion on his rack (he chipped smack, my worst leadership problem), raised his arms and started to applaud leisurely. I stood up and took a little bow.

"I like that," Givens mumbled from his stupor. "I like that fine. Craziest fucker on earth dukin' it out with the dumbest fucker on earth. And I get a free front-row seat. You know, you the first Jew I ever knew. You a very entertaining people; I had no idea. I thought all you guys did was play the Jewish piano."

"What's that?"

Givens chuckled. "Shee-it. In Hough that's what we call a fuckin' cash register, man." He raised his fingers and mimed a piano keyboard; when he came to the chorus he said, "Ding!"

"And no offense taken," I assured him.

And that was the squeeze play I was in. With Richard or the Mystery Grunt, I had to defend my innocence of any and all war crimes and my simultaneous apathy about my own situation. With dorks like Warfield (and it was amazing how, with a third of a million Americans under arms in-country, dorks like Warfield were so rare), I felt compelled to assert my complicity, whip out a soapbox and sing a few bars of "The International." It was enough to make a man want to go into town and buy a new blue movie.

I actually enjoyed Warfield's treason indictment. Until then, the worst I'd perceived myself was as a minor league disgruntled malcontent. *Ain't worth killin'* was the appropriate phrase I'd picked up among the Georgia crackers. But treason—hey, that was the big time, something to write home to mom about. I made a note to write home to Mom about it, where she could stick it on the spike and deal with it after she got through dealing with the crated motorcycle in the garage, the wrecked Mustang, the murky stories that had drifted home about my westward-ho adventures with the postmenstrual daughter of one of Dad's business associates, and worst of all, her son, America's only drafted enlisted Jew.

It was 15:30 and time to loft a balloon.

"Givens," I asked, "how'd you like to assist in the war effort?"

"Oh, shee-it. Get Warfield."

"I feel I've alienated him this afternoon. Prospects do not look good. Besides, he's punishing me by doing important national defense work with the strip-chart recorder. Would you be so kind? I'll let you have a couple of hits of the helium."

"Shee-it. That's just a inert gas, Becker. It don't do diddly-squat for you. Why don't you put in for a couple of tanks of somethin' interesting like nitrous oxide or something?"

"Because then the balloons would fall down on the ground instead of floating up in the sky. Okay. Drop your cocks and on with your socks."

Givens did a half-roll to the right, but he'd apparently miscalculated his position in the rack; he fell over the edge and crashed to the wood slat floor. He screamed in pain and hopped around on one leg holding his other knee. Eventually he pulled on his grungy trousers, picked up his M16 and followed me out of the hooch.

An indifferent child—well, yes, I suppose that said it better than traitor or war criminal. Everyone who shipped to Vietnam including Richard and the Mystery Grunt went to yet another Repo Depot, with the same function but much worse than the one at Benning, there to await his in-country orders, the authentic bad news and next Green Weenie, a function of whichever terrifying infantry, artillery or helicopter air-mobile cavalry unit needed beef that week. Everyone but me. I processed through Fort Lewis like everyone else and arrived at Da Nang much like everyone else, but as soon as I got off the plane I showed the personnel NCOs my orders, which had a thick Magic Marker legend across the top: *PROJECT HIGHBALL—DO NOT DIVERT!* While the 120 other uniformed passengers were herded across the tarmac, I was aimed alone toward a hooch in another direction and told to use the phone to contact Highball for transport. I obediently steered for that course, but once out of sight drifted around the base until I found an EM recreation center, where I had some icy-cold soda pop and played pinball machines for an hour. Eventually I made my way back to the proper office and was connected to Highball in Vung Tau. I was told to make my way to helicopter pad 40, not far away, and wait. Ninety minutes later a Huey landed and picked me

up, just me the indifferent child, and headed southeast again
for Vung Tau; the sun was setting. The last third of the flight,
over the China Sea paralleling the coast to keep out of ground
fire reach, was in darkness. I liked helicopters, particularly the
squat, strictly-business, sturdy Hueys. I liked the idea of the
army dispatching one a couple of hundred miles round-trip
just for me; it wouldn't have been nearly as much fun if it had
been picking up four or five people heading for Vung Tau. I
liked not being diverted. Clearly the challenge was not to gawk,
but to take it all very nonchalantly, as if it happened to me all
the time.

The helicopter hovered above a small converted freighter
anchored about three quarters of a mile in the harbor and
landed on the precarious pad retrofitted to the fantail; there
were three masts, each one laden with a bizarre assortment of
electronics antennae, and for a moment I was convinced that
the Huey's blades or rear rotor were certain to bash into one
of the lateral projections, but they didn't. A lieutenant on deck-
watch met me and, after the engine shut off, introduced himself
as DerHammer, the project XO. He took me downstairs—
below—to the enlisted bunks, got my gear squared away and
then brought me up to the galley for some coffee. We passed
air-conditioned cabins jammed with electronics equipment, ra-
dars, computers, specialized devices I wasn't familiar with in
burnished gray metallic rack housings, most of them manned
by buck sergeants (I wasn't one yet, still just a Spec-4), but there
were also a few slightly older men in civilian clothes. Everyone
seemed to be alert, twiddling the knobs on the machines at a
casual but determined pace.

"You'll get your indoctrination starting tomorrow," Der-
Hammer said as he poured coffee for both of us. "Welcome
aboard. You're now serving aboard the USNS *Mount Taconic*,
one of the proudest ships in the army. Any questions?"

"Nothin' much. Just what the hell is Project Highball and
what will I be doing for the next year?"

He laughed. "Well, most of that'll be made clear tomorrow,
but it's fairly simple. Highball's a special unit outside the normal
meteorology network. We're trying to get a very sophisticated
handle on the regional weather patterns. The *Taconic*'s our
operational headquarters. You'll be running one of our in-country

data acquisition stations after we check you out on our procedures here. That'll take a couple of weeks. You like the beach?"

"I don't dislike it."

"Well, you'll have some time to enjoy it. Vung Tau—the French called it Cap St. Jacques—is sort of like Malibu or I guess the French Riviera, the big vacation spot. The *Taconic* runs a launch in and out all day; when you get some time off, just sign out with the launch officer and head on in. Don't wander north, though. The Viet Cong have to have their vacation beaches, too, and they have their own stretch in some forest north of here. I suspect our beach is more fun."

"They should get up a volleyball match. Healthy competition."

"I think you'll like it working for Highball, even in-country. You'll be pretty much on your own, a small unit, not more than a dozen men. The bases are pretty secure. There'll be combat units around to protect you so you can get on with the mission, and for support services, medical stuff, a little stand-down time, you'll get choppered around to the big firebases or defensive perimeters."

"What's wrong with the normal artillery metro units?"

"Nothing, as far as they go. But all they're looking for is air density and direction for fire control. We're not really concerned with field artillery. That's a short-range, short-duration problem. We're trying to collect a very big data base to run a very big regional weather model. What it's used for—well, you'll figure out enough if you stay halfway awake while you're on board. I'm not really supposed to spell it out, and I probably don't know half of what there is to know. I do have to tell you that a lot of what goes on around here is classified. S-2 will have you sign some documents about that. It's understood you'll pick up things you're not strictly supposed to know. That's okay, but the documents cover our ass about that. You raise your right hand and agree to keep your mouth shut. What's your clearance?"

"Got none, to speak of. Just that bargain-basement one everybody gets, national agency check. Heretofore no Roosians ever tried to hit me up for weather forecasts."

"Well, I'm sure they'll put you in for a clearance. It would be nice if you passed; everybody does."

"Lord, what happens if I don't?"

"Don't know. They probably rotate you to a regular artillery unit in-country. It's not a fate worse than death, but there's probably more death associated with it."

"I'll do my best to pass."

The sleeping quarters weren't air-conditioned, but in skivvies above the sheets you got by, once you got used to sleeping in a pool of your own sweat. The morning chow was fine, little black rubber steaks with eggs, syntho-orange juice, toast, more of the surprisingly good coffee, and I met some of the buck sergeants and advanced specialists—Spec-6s and -7s, odd technical ranks you didn't see in the States much except on lifer cooks—who ran the equipment. One of them had done temporary duty running an in-country Highball station and told me a retard could do it with a broken leg. "In fact that's why I had to take over," he said. "The retard in charge got drunk and broke his leg. You can have all the beer you want at these places. It's considered essential for American morale. Letting your base run out of beer is a major leadership fuckup. Don't let it happen."

After breakfast there was an assembly on the fantail, a young black sergeant first class in charge reading notices about more things you weren't supposed to do in town anymore. There were no cleanup or kitchen details. The ship was part of the Military Transport Sea Service, a quasi-civilian outfit. Everything that had to do with keeping it floating and shipshape was done by contract employees and merchant marine personnel. The weather mission part of Highball was run by a lieutenant colonel named Eyerworth, an intense, teeth-gritting, jaw-jutting lifer whose torso seemed to be shaped like a large cardboard carton on a supermarket loading dock. Without seeming to enjoy his work or to take any pride in it, he was never satisfied with anything on the ship, not like Captain Bligh threatening that heads would roll, but more like a depressive high school principal trying to motivate his students and teachers by being perpetually disappointed in them. I didn't like him very much after the first couple of times I ran across him or saw him in action, but he didn't worry me or make me nervous. I didn't think he was very bright. If I had to, I figured I could mystify him with verbal bullshit to get him off my case.

After formation, I was detailed to follow a buck sergeant named Rice around the ship for the show-around with particular emphasis on the commo shack and the reports room to see samples of the shit they'd expect from me in an in-country station. DerHammer was right—it was nothing I hadn't learned the theory of at Metro School, but where Metro School and my metro support company at Benning had been primitive meat-and-potatoes about it, this was slick and precise. Rice took me to the instrumentation shop, where about nine guys were working on balloon packages, and I'd never seen anything like them before. The stuff I knew sent off a dumb three-channel analog signal, and the electronics tended to resemble Radio Shack model-airplane radio control modules. This was the first digital instrumentation I'd ever seen, FM rather than AM, one channel, but with sophisticated multiplexing so it could send out up to sixteen kinds of information simultaneously. The final assembly was a little cork-sized piece of C-4 rigged to blow the whole package to shit when the balloon finally failed and it began to descend. Rice showed me how to trigger the package so there'd be no chance it would blow up in anyone's fingers while we were trying to loft it. That involved a basal calibration for our station's altitude as well as a timer. But he did say one had gone off a year and a half ago, scorching two guys and blowing out one of their eardrums; they'd redesigned the package after that, but you still had to treat it with respect.

I was on the ship for four days and went into Vung Tau one night with Rice. Most everything was still very French colonial with the American honky-tonk presence downplayed, somewhat temporary-looking and transient, as if there were a master plan for the war after all—the Yanks would win it, go home, and then the French would come back and run the place again. It was early evening when the launch landed us and about twenty other soldiers from the *Taconic*, and what to my wondering eyes should appear on the main drag but a pair of full-habit nuns shepherding a dozen blue-uniformed schoolgirls (but without the wide-brimmed and beribboned bonnets) two by two across the street—Vietnamese all, but Asiatic clones of Madeleine and her associates, perhaps on their way to the zoo or to the hospital to have Madeleine's appendix removed. I wondered what thirty years of our presence would graft and leave behind; perhaps Indochinese cowboys (Air Marshal Ky to my mind already looked like one) or the Virginia reel.

We took an early launch back and Rice introduced me to the real night life aboard ship, where the lower-rank enlisted men, the inevitable cadres of disgruntled freaks and radical blacks, had somehow managed a semi-official agreement with management to reserve the fantail under and to the stern of the helicopter pad at night as their dope-smoking and muttering preserve, where the NCOs and lifers seemed to be content to let them alone provided no fires broke out and no one made a rush for the arms room. One major in the unit served as the project's provost marshal, but it was a paperwork position; he had no squad of MPs the way larger navy craft have permanent Shore Patrol or Marine police contingents to quell disturbances. While it might have been difficult to field a full chorus of happy PFCs and Spec-4s on board, neither were there whole platoons of terminally pissed-off people the way most in-country units could boast. Everyone on the *Taconic* had been DO NOT DI-VERTed and most of them had good enough educations to hold skilled technical jobs that could even dispel a lot of the boredom. Everyone had had a good enough glimpse of the alternative facing them ashore if they fucked up to want to behave himself. It was Vietnam and it wasn't; it was the army yet somehow the navy. Death lurked, but it would have to don scuba suits and float mines to them. Danger came mostly in the form of terrible sunburn, followed, if duty was missed, by a court-martial on the arcane charge, rumor had it, of damaging government property.

As Rice and I joined the midnight tribal gathering under the helicopter pad, it didn't take too long to understand one major reason why the reefer-smokers and mutterers weren't often disturbed during the night by the forces of established law and order. There were priorities to attend to, and we could hear them amidships each time the launch would return from the beach. It was the lifers, the Spec-6's and -7's and the staff sergeants and sergeants first class, drunk beyond even my experiences with them at Benning, screaming their lungs out as they staggered up the outboard ladder. Someone said that on weekends it was common for one or two of them to miss and go into the drink, which required sounding the man-overboard air horns and circling with the launch and hook-pole to fish them out. A year ago, someone else said he'd heard, a staff sergeant had hit his head taking the tumble and his body had never been found. A rumor started months later that someone had seen him dressed in civvies in Cholon. It wasn't impossible. The water was still and calm most nights and if you didn't kick too much to attract the sharks, it wasn't a bad ruse to start a shadow life away from the army and into the black market. Anyway, it was a good rumor; I liked it.

On the last morning I attended the weekly seminar for newcomers of all ranks in the wardroom. A civilian woman, the first one I'd seen aboard ship, sat in the back row chaperoned by DerHammer. When the captain had finished his slide show and we dispersed, DerHammer motioned me over and introduced me to her as one of the new in-country station leaders. Her name was Mrs. Barker from DOD, a.k.a. the Pentagon. I put her in her late forties, a scrawny bird with frizzy black Brillo hair wearing a white synthetic blouse with a safari-style khaki skirt.

"Do a good job for us out there," she exhorted me as we shook hands.

"What do you do with the stuff?" I asked her. DerHammer blanched a little. I was feeling loose. What the hell; I was leaving the comfort of the ship to go into hostile territory that afternoon and I'd never be seen again, and she was a civilian besides, so she naturally assumed all enlisted men weren't terribly bright, just the unfortunately necessary tools she and her technocrat brain trust had to work with.

"Well, for one thing, we're trying to integrate it into our operations research for long-range air and ground strategy," she said. "We're trying to get a handle on meteorology that combat commanders and planners have never had before. It's buying us important windows of movement the enemy doesn't anticipate, and it's also helping us predict his rice crop and consequently the volume of food imports he'll have to rely on for the next year from the Russians. That tells us when to bomb bridges on supply arteries—well, you get the idea."

"Pretty snazzy. Is it working?"

"All we can do is hope it will. We've already been pleased with some of the results, but it's not just for this war. We're developing techniques here and in Washington for future wars, and they can only get better. It's a field you might consider staying in, and it's really being born right here. When your tour's over, you'll have valuable field experience we could use. Ultimately we're always going to have to rely on good ground stations. Satellites won't be able to tell us what we need to know about the layers closest to the surface."

"I'm hip. I'll give it careful thought." The woman was deranged—where did they construct people like that?

So that afternoon on the way to my waiting sky chauffeur on the fantail, DerHammer gave me my last briefing and pressed a packet with new sergeant's stripes and the orders that went with them into my hand and said he hoped I knew how to sew. Some soldiers were loading beer and Coca-Cola by the case into the Huey as well as a resupply of balloons, helium cannisters and instrumentation packages. There was gasoline to run our generators, cases of LRPs rations, mail, ice cream packed in dry ice, fresh and canned fruit, smokes, boxes of socks, green skivvies and T-shirts—altogether some picnic for my hilltop, and the damnedest mess you ever did see if some hostile weasel down below got lucky with his AK47. DerHammer shook my hand, I saluted—it seemed the first time I'd saluted anyone since I'd arrived in Vietnam—and I climbed aboard and found a corner suitable for my bod while the door gunner moved back into place. DerHammer shook his finger at him under the noise of the rotors and he grudgingly harnessed himself in—well, if he wanted to go sailing out into space when the Huey made a sudden course correction, that should have been his business, but DerHammer didn't see it that way. The Huey didn't want to lift off the pad, but it did, inch by inch and then a meter at a time, and finally we were high above the harbor and the *Taconic* and moving west toward the shore and distant clouded mountaintops, one of which would be mine.

21

The most eventful thing that happened to me on the mountaintop was that I got this phone call one day. That's just the fucking truth. Again I found myself getting the special treatment due me for no other reason than that I was Becker and that I'd learned long ago to expect the universe to treat me not exactly better or worse than anyone else, but just differently. Laugh, clown, but chuckle quick, because there you are pinned down in a rice paddy while the international Communist conspiracy is trying to perforate you along the dotted line, while your old buddy and pal Becker's been chosen among all the other contestants to serve the same cause but in an entirely different manner (with an offer now for post-military employment with the weather spooks) with his HIGHBALL—DO NOT DIVERT tattoo. In fact, clown, while you were laughing at Becker a few months ago, maybe you were among the hapless grunts commissioned with the task of assaulting Mount Becker in the first place and making 1131 safe for his weather balloons and strip-chart recorders by clearing out fixed NVA artillery positions in the caves—well, they were gone by the time you got there, their crews leaving behind only four or five thousand booby traps as signatures. So now that the giggling had died down, Becker was installed as the new High Lama to wait for his in-country year to be over and to pass the sacred metro traditions on to the next high priest in the lineage.

But meanwhile, a lama's got to have his basic needs attended to, so the crew chief of the Huey or Chinook, whatever machine was making the milk run that week, would somehow manage to have a bag or two of Cambodian reefer mixed in with the suds and the LRPs boxes with their P-38 can openers dropping out of the freeze-dried and canned food parcels and onto the floor until we were sick of how clever the tiny little key ring suckers were (so many arrived one month that we had to stop walking around the hooch barefoot), but these weren't nearly as clever as the LRP heat tabs. Never cook again, madam! Just stick a match to one of these wonders of science and Hot Damn! it's white-hot, and in twenty, thirty seconds your soup or stew or gruel is boiling away, yumyumeatemup.

From time to time we'd also be gifted with additional weapons and crates of NATO-stenciled ammunition, with mortars and claymores with their helpful painted hints: THIS SIDE TOWARD ENEMY, and even a starlight scope, an amazing advance over the infrared scopes of the last war because now the enemy didn't even have to give off heat to be seen (very useful for enemies who don't radiate heat); now as long as there was a star or two in the night sky, the gadget's astonishing photomultiplier tube could make the field of vision and all the crawling, scheming, politically objectionable objects in it as clear as high noon on the high school football field. In the minds of the unseen support officials who shipped us these weapons, there seemed to be some kind of direct relation between how little use we made of them and how many of them and the kinds we were sent. In fact we did use weapons now and then. Under the guise of the periodic target qualification practice officially mandated for every soldier in or out of combat, I encouraged the other metro members to borrow or appropriate whatever weapons they took a shine to (except the mortar) and sling whatever ordnance pleased them in most any direction for recreation. But for Victor Charles to get to our mountaintop chalet, he'd first have had to overrun or bypass a network of actual combat unit CPs, OPs, DPs, firebases, what-have-you that ringed 1131 from base to just below us, the cherry on the cloudy whipped cream; we were in sight and almost within shouting distance of two of these armed camps. Since the day the final Allied infantry charge to take 1131 had commenced, no sign of Victor Charles or his NVA buddies had been seen, but MACV was clearly taking no chances, and the strategic thinking seemed to involve holding the mountain for our side by sheer weight of personnel, in case it might display a tendency to float off toward Rangoon. That sucker was Ours, and before They could get to Us at the tippy-top of the Christmas tree and make it Theirs again, they'd first have to encounter and defeat every other Allied ornament on the lower branches, a prospect we never considered likely. Givens fancied that the equivalent of eight combat battalions below him on 1131 were there to give him plenty of warning to flush his "brown opium" (what the street vendors called the smack they sold—"Hey, GI, brown opium, sweet dreams, brown opium!") and his works down the toilet (which we didn't have) in case army narcs decided to march up to the villa.

But the weapons that support kept sending us were strange even for a squad that had almost no need for them. They loved to send us .45s, .38 revolvers and holsters, belt as well as shoulder contraptions, which we regarded as the kiss of death. Since rank insignia had changed some years ago from bright, shiny metal thingies for officers and giant yellow shoulder stripes for NCOs to tiny dull black metal or black sewn-on collar tabs for all, pajama weasel snipers now had to rely on second-best evidence to annihilate our field leadership selectively, and the second-best evidence was which dork packed a pistol rather than a rifle, pistols being the traditional side arm of officers. Americans loved pistols, though, and the liberal dissemination policy in Nam allowed just about any enlisted fool who wanted one to have and wear one, so sometimes the snipers would never know they'd wasted their efforts on a PFC or Marine lance corporal instead of a lieutenant or captain.

Of our squad, the only taker was Warfield. When we unwrapped the unwelcome side-arms shipment from its cosmoline paper in the hooch and he appropriated a snazzy Smith & Wesson .38, a sudden pall descended on the other troops, most of them blacks, none of them terribly crazy about Warfield; you could hear breezes outside; I imagined I heard a bird. He found a dashing canvas shoulder harness for it and started adjusting its straps, and I thought to myself, *Isn't there a single decent man in this hooch, isn't there a spark of the Jewish mother here to suggest to Warfield that sporting that thing may shorten his life?*

It was triply perilous for Warfield. Not only would he wear the pistol, but he was very Caucasian, and of all the squad, he kept himself, his uniform and jungle boots the most immaculate of any of us. He was always clean-shaven; once a month he'd ask for a day off the mountain for no other reason than to visit a nearby brigade barber. But no one spoke up. Everyone looked, but no one spoke. Not even me, and I wasn't just his sergeant but had a strong genetic grounding toward Jewish motherhood. Okay, so there weren't any pajama weasel snipers in the vicinity; that was no excuse. Somebody should have said something, the way some good-hearted asshole now and then (even in Vietnam) would tell me I shouldn't smoke. But no one spoke, not even the otherwise thoughtful and solicitous Sergeant Becker. I felt as if Warfield had walked by, I'd slapped him on the back and in the process Scotch-taped a sign between his shoulder blades that said *Shoot this officer here.*

Without regular assaults by the hostiles, how did we occupy our time on 1131 beyond the balloon loftings and the monitoring of their signals? Well, there were sentry rosters to create and supervise, not to look out for the Little Yellow Guys so much as to watch for the dreaded approach of uninvited sergeants major or other neighborhood party poopers who might assess penalties if they found rusted hypos lying in the corners or chanced to barge in during a particularly critically acclaimed screening of "It Did It to Those" (Macao, 22 minutes, color). Then there was the jeep to be revved up for a few minutes each day to blow the tropical crud out of its carburetor and then drive it around like wild men up and over the bumps and slopes and ridges or to take it a few miles down-slope for a picnic or just some private masturbating time with a stroke book. There was the radio to maintain because there weren't yet any land lines and maybe never would be because you never knew when it might be necessary to give the mountain back again and who wanted to leave the hostiles a telephone exchange? Sometimes all these odious chores required as many as two or three people to be awake and coherent all at the same time, although it should have been clear even to Ms. Frankenstein from DOD that a chimpanzee or Helen Keller could have run the place just fine from month to month and still had time to compose *Beowulf* on the side.

So after I'd put in about five or six months as *El Queso Grande* and keeper of the flame, the news from the commo shack that there was a phone call waiting for me was a heavy eruption, a Big Bopper 6.2 on the Richter scale as things went in Cloudland. Waiting for me, because the phone call was on the MARS army-amateur radio system into which we weren't linked and into which they said they weren't allowed to patch us directly; if I wanted to talk to Sister Susie or my Metropolitan Life representative or whoever the fuck it turned out to be (the relay message didn't say), I'd have to relocate my whole body from here to a command post twenty-one klicks down the mountain and then up another mountain on the other side of the valley.

I got this major news event around 01:00, my commo chief waking me up out of my rack in the hooch to make me crawl over to his shack and respond to this incomprehensible garble and heterodyning speech which was allegedly coming from the CP where the MARS station was. I identified myself over the radio with the usual gobbledygook of phonetic spellings (Bravo Echo Charlie Kilo Echo Romeo, put them all together that spells Becker) and unit code designations, and the radioman on the other end told me the situation, that the phone call was coming in for me from the States somewhere and that the calling party would try again in three hours to give me a chance to get across the valley and be there. The ionosphere would also be a little more forgiving by that time, he estimated; the first time the party had reached his MARS station, the radio propagation conditions had had all the clarity of peanut butter.

"Three hours. I'll be there. That's an affirmative," I said.

Back in the hooch, Givens was on his rack in his green skivvies snoring away when I shook him by the shoulder. He popped up like a garden rake.

"What? Who? Huh? Oh, fuck. What you want, man?"

"You want to go for a cruise?" I asked softly.

"A cruise? What the fuck wrong with you, motherfucker? What you up to now?"

"Nothing. There's a phone call for me over at the command post. I'm going over there, or I'm going to try. I thought you might like to come along for the ride."

"Come along for the ride, you say? Shee-it, no. You crazy, motherfucker."

"No, seriously," I sweet-talked him. "We're getting low on reefer, and you must be getting low on you-know-what, and we can score what we need over there. With any luck when we get there, there'll be some shit going on in the valley and we'll have to stay over there for a couple of hours before we can take the jeep back. Or maybe they won't let us take the jeep back at all and we'll have ourselves a few consecutive fully cooked fresh meals, and then they'll fly us back when there's a chopper going across."

"Well, that's great," Givens said. "Of course if there's shit going down in that motherfuckin' valley to prevent us from gettin' back here, maybe there's shit going to prevent us from making it to the CP to begin with. Maybe shit to prevent us coming home at all with both testicles. You thought about that, Socrates?"

"Yeah, I thought about that. I was just talking to the dude at the command post and he says the valley's pretty quiet, not counting the artillery free-fire zones."

"Oh, he mean that Charles done give up and went home and made peace, huh? Well, why din't you *say* somethin', motherfucker? That's great news. Charles done surrendered and give us the valley for a Christmas present. That's just swell. Go 'way from me, buck sergeant. You dangerous."

"Come on, Givens. They get fresh steaks over there, man. We got to get at least one real meal off those turkeys, something better than burnt LRPs, and most of the time we don't have an excuse. You're always bitching about the chow here."

"Yeah, but I don't complain about people up here tryin' to shoot me in the brain, which is what goes on down in the valley. No, thank you. I stay here and eat LRPs."

"Okay, I'll tell you what. While we're down there, I'll try to score you a quick pass or some temporary duty back at Vung

Tau so you can pop your rocks and come back up here with a better attitude. There's an S-4 lieutenant over there I'm tight with. I just don't want to go over there alone, that's all."

"I can certainly see why," he whined. "We safe up here, man, even if I can't get no poontang, and you safe up here even if the phone is for you."

"Come on. I'd do the same for you."

He reached for his flak jacket on a nail over his bunk. "Don't give me no Jew guilt shit, man. I'm goin' over there, but not for your dufus-ass phone call. I'm goin' over there to get me some steak and some eggs and shit, and to get that fuckin' pass to Vung Tau and that poontang—and don't you forget or I bust your fuckin' head—and to talk to my brothers, 'cause I'm tired of the same dark meat *and* white meat in this fuckin' hole, but I ain't goin' for you. Shee-it."

So while I went outside to blow the crud out of the jeep's carburetor for a few minutes and make sure there was gas in the thing, Givens scrounged around for a couple of M16s and cartridge belts and grenades and swords and shotguns and mortars and what-all for the crosstown trip—anything but pistols. Eventually he piled it all in the jeep and got in the passenger seat. We put our steel pots on, lit up a joint and started down the mountain slowly because the mists were heavy and the turns on the thing that passed for a road were pretty hairy, especially for a jeep's dumb-fuck center of gravity which made the things flip over just for laughs at almost any speed or any moderately sharp turn. Far off down the valley there was some thudding going on, what sounded like 175s pounding the living shit out of the Surprise Grid of the Night.

"Great," Givens said. "They gonna turn those fuckin' things around and pound our asses?"

"I don't think so," I said confidently. Actually, I didn't have the slightest idea. By the time I could have asked to be patched through to the fire control center, it would have been tomorrow.

Givens started taping M16 magazines together with black electrical tape as the other junk in the back seat bounced around. He took the joint from my mouth and took a pull on it. When he let it out again, he hissed, "I don't see why you bother to smoke that shit. You was fuckin' permanently stoned the day you was born."

Somewhere down on the valley floor in the opposite direction from the shelling I heard automatic weapons clatter that wasn't returned. It seemed to have the different, sluggish rhythm of Russian AK47s, but if it was, I hoped Givens wouldn't notice. Anyway, it was too faint to have much to do with our neighborhood, us in a jeep and Charles being the pedestrian type that he was. Givens pulled back the charging handle on his M16.

"Who the fuck calling you, anyway?" he asked. "The United Jewish Appeal?"

"Beats me."

"Aw, fuck. I'm going to die and you don't even know who it is you going to talk to. You stoned crazy, man."

"Look at it this way. If we get snuffed, at least we'll be doing something for ourselves, my phone call and your diseased poontang and steak and eggs. Now isn't that better than getting snuffed following some jerk from Indiana State who thinks he's John Wayne?"

"Not really. You splittin' hairs. Not when you get right down to it."

"Well, that's your opinion and you're entitled to it."

"Thank you. You sure are one tolerant mother."

That's about when the first mortar shell slammed into the hillside above us. "Oh, God!" Givens shrieked and stood up in his seat, holding on to the windshield with one hand and leveling the M16 all around with his free hand. It was a pretty good lob for a crew that probably couldn't do more than hear us every once in a while, the engine noise distorted through the fog. Clods of dirt rained down on the road and the jeep's hood. "Oh, God, keep drivin'! Hit it, motherfucker!"

"Okay!" I gunned it a little and tried to stand up myself to see as far as I could in front of me. We weren't running any lights. I was looking for a little side path coming up somewhere off to the left. When I got to it, I switched off the engine and coasted down the hill silently.

"What the fuck you doin'?" Givens hissed.

"What's it look like? Those guys are throwing that shit just out of guesswork, and they guess we'll keep driving down the main road. Let's hang out here and let 'em throw a few more at us until they get tired of not hearing anybody scream anymore. You don't mind not screaming anymore, do you?"

"I screamed 'cause I'm not fuckin' insane like you." He was craning his neck and his eyes and his body around in all directions, looking for the mortar position or at least a good hint.

A second round came in, about fifty meters to the left of the first, high above us; we didn't even get any dirt. I hadn't heard the muffled thud of the shell leaving the mortar. I found the roach on the floor of the jeep where Givens had dropped it. Fortunately it was still glowing. I cupped it and took a pull.

"Hey, Sarge, you mind staying straight while we die?"

"They're too far away to smell us," I said, "and without the engine they can't guess our position. Let's leave the jeep here and start walking."

"Oh, God," Givens moaned. "I don't want to fuckin' walk, man. There's booby traps out there, mines and shit. At least I had a little steel under my ass in the jeep."

"There's a main road a couple of klicks down the hill. We can hang out there and hitch a ride when a convoy comes through."

"If I live, I'm going to kill your jive-talkin' ass, I swear."

"That's good. Gives you something to live for."

We got out of the jeep and loaded ourselves down with enough armaments to take out a Brink's truck, and started humping it. The temperature was probably in the low eighties and we were sweating from the humidity and the fear before we got out of the jeep. Givens, he of the dread of mines, took the point. He noticed I was looking at him a little surprised.

"I don't trust you, motherfucker."

"But I'm behind you," I said.

"I mean I don't trust you not to fuck up. You could fuck up a wet dream. I assume you ain't going to kill me, 'cause I'm the only thing keepin' your ass alive."

"I hadn't noticed, but if you say so."

"I know so."

The next part wasn't so bad, especially since Givens insisted on going first. I was pretty sure it wasn't far to the road; I'd seen it often enough from the mountaintop on clear days. Not far from where we left the jeep we descended onto level ground without the slightest hint of vegetation, just pothole after pothole where both sides had spent the last couple of years demonstrating their artillery wares to each other. In each pothole was a collection of slimy, muddy, lukewarm water that gushed in and out of the canvas webbing on both sides of our boots, sloosh, sloosh, no matter how carefully we stepped. I caught my foot on something—something soft and forgiving, thank God—and stumbled forward on my knees, catching myself with the butt of my rifle. Givens turned around and tossed a few more oaths at me. Then we walked up a little rise toward a copse of something that probably used to be trees. We dropped down into the mud when we heard the noises from up ahead. They were far off but so consistent and loud and confused that after a few seconds we were certain they were Americans, friendlies. I caught a strong whiff of burning rubber, diesel fuel and cordite, the smell of fresh weapons fire. We duck-walked a few hundred meters farther until we could make out American voices. Then we stood up and walked up the rise to the road.

There were three trucks on and angled off the road. The deuce-and-a-quarter in the front was burning where it had tripped a mine or caught a mortar round. Propped up against the wheel of the rear truck was a GI, with another GI standing next to him cradling an over-under and looking around nervously. Givens and I crouched behind the tree stumps and I yelled something at the soldier who was standing. He leveled the over-under our way.

"What do you want me to say?" I called to him.

"The password."

"Fuck that. We're not from your unit. Ask me about Donald Duck or something."

"Are you Americans? I'll blow your fucking heads off if you're not."

"Hamburgers and french fries," I said. "Ketchup and mustard."

"Okay," the nervous GI said. "Come on."

We stood up and showed ourselves and he didn't blow us away. By the time we could smell his breath, he'd even lowered the over-under. I squatted down by the soldier sitting against the wheel. He was holding his hand inside his shirt like Napoleon. He was a white boy and he looked pretty pasty.

"Man's cruising into shock," I said. "You got a blanket or something?"

"I think he's got a sucking chest wound," the nervous type

said. I looked up at him and so did the pasty-looking soldier.

"I don't have a sucking chest wound," the pasty one said.

"Here's a blanket," Givens said and pulled one from the deuce-and-a-quarter's tailgate. We put it over the pasty soldier. He nodded a little blearily.

"What happened?" I asked the nervous one.

"That truck tripped a mine or something and then there was some kind of an ambush. I guess he got it jumping out of the truck. The rest of the platoon went after them." He pointed to the rear of the convoy.

"Go down there and play sentry," I told Givens. He diddy-bopped down the road a few meters and dropped into a gully by the side of the road. He was very good about taking orders. I made it a point to give him one or two each month just to keep him in practice.

"I don't know how to treat a sucking chest wound," the nervous GI said.

"I don't have a sucking chest wound," the pasty soldier said again.

I turned to the nervous type and shifted my weapon a little, nonchalantly. "If you don't stop telling this guy he has a sucking chest wound," I said quietly, "I'm going to give you one just so we'll have something to compare. Now go up to the front truck and take a position there." He looked at me for a few seconds and then went up the road and stood next to the truck so snipers could see him outlined against the flames better or something. There was a lot of gear on the ground where people had dropped it in the confusion. I rummaged around in it until I found a belt kit with a morphine Syrette and shot the man up in the leg. That was probably the wrong thing to do, but if I'd looked the way he did, I would have wanted some of that. A few minutes later I heard him start breathing a little easier. He was crying gently.

"Thank you," he said.

"You're welcome. Can I take a look?"

"Okay." I parted his jungle jacket with both hands carefully. The cloth was sticking to his chest where the blood, a lot of it, had already started to dry. He had a flashlight on his belt. I put it up an inch from his body and flashed it on the area for a second.

"You're not going to believe this," I said, "but I don't think you're fucked up all that bad." I fished around in the belt kit for a gauze compress and managed to rig it up over the wound under his T-shirt.

"Honest?"

"I'm not a medic, but assuming we get you a ride out of here fairly soon and pump some more good stuff in you, I think everything's going to be copacetic. Your buddies did promise to come back, didn't they?"

"Yeah. The lieutenant just wanted to chase the gooks around a little bit before he tried to drive out of here. He called for choppers, but they can't fly around in this soupy shit."

"Nice of him to leave you with that asshole."

"He's okay. He's my buddy."

"Far out."

We'd heard a firefight going on to our left when we'd come up to the trucks, but it had died out now and soldiers started humping back to the two trucks that hadn't been hit. A sergeant started yelling for the men to board the trucks and another one of those skinny, tall, crew-cutted second lieutenants was bending over me with a couple of GIs to lift the man into the truck.

"Who the fuck are you?" he asked.

"Becker, sir, from the metro station on 1131. Me and my troop had to get to the brigade CP up the road."

"How's Pfansteel? The wounded guy."

"It just looks like a lot of meat got peeled away and a rib crushed. I gave him some junk. Anyone else get hurt?"

"Dead truck driver. He's a real mess. We got to get the fuck out of here now and send someone after him later today. Thanks for looking after the kid."

"No problem." Givens trotted back to us and we piled into the back of the truck and the driver started to haul ass.

It took us about twenty minutes to get to the CP. Something like dawn was starting to burn through the mists in the valley. We followed a sergeant to the mess tent, where some off-duty sentries were having breakfast, and gave the sergeant our names and our lame stories. I left Givens there and went in the direction of the MARS shack. I knocked and went in. There was a magnificent blast of air conditioning inside running off some generators and compressors in the back. Thank God for electronics; GIs sure as fuck would never have rated air conditioning by themselves.

"Yeah?" the commo man asked.

"Becker. Some kind of phone call for me."

"Oh, yeah. Sorry. Whoever it was tried again about an hour ago and then had to split. Shame, too, because we had a good link for a change. The link originated in Cincinnati."

"Cincinnati? I don't know anybody in Cincinnati."

"That doesn't mean anything. That's just where the first MARS station that could get through to us was. The person who called could have been anywhere, probably in the Midwest but not necessarily. That's just where he made the long-distance call to. Anyway, the MARS guy over there said he might try again later."

"That's it?"

"That's it, buddy."

"Far out."

I strolled back to the mess tent and found Givens shoveling about a dozen eggs and some muffins down his maw. "Who was on the phone?" he asked.

"Don't know. They hung up."

"Shee-it."

I hung around the CP shooting the shit with a couple of guys I knew for the rest of the day, scoring some reefer and stuffing canned goodies into my pants pockets to take back to the rest of the guys in Cloudland. I rang up the metro station on the radio and told them where we'd left the jeep, and they said they'd trudge down the hill to find it if things loosened up. Then Givens and I found a couple of vacant racks and slept for a few hours until a crew chief woke us up and said there was a Huey waiting to take us back across the valley. On the way across the CP, a lifer sergeant stopped us.

"Got something for you," he said and gave us each some kind of little red package.

"What's this?" Givens asked.

"We're cutting orders on them. CIB. You don't have one, do you?"

"Not me. You got one, Sarge?"

"Nope. Well, thanks, I guess," I said.

We opened them in the chopper. There was an enameled

blue metal one, a little rifle with a laurel wreath slung under it for our khakis and greens and a black patch version of the same thing for our jungle threads. I was hooked up to Givens on the chopper's intercom.

"I'm deeply moved," I said.

"Shee-it, they give those things out like water. That just means somebody done shot at us. I'm going to throw mine away."

"You might as well keep it. It's in your record and some lifer's going to hassle you for not wearing it one of these days."

"All this fuckin' hassle for a goddam Combat Infantryman's Badge and a goddam mystery phone call you never got. You crazy. Hey, I'm sorry if I gave you a hard time back there."

"No problem. I appreciated the company."

"You get me my pass?"

"I'm workin' on it. You been without nookie for a few months now. Another couple of days'll be okay."

"Hey, Becker."

"What?"

"I was scaa-ared! Was you scared?"

"No. I don't know the meaning of fear."

"It means you shit in your drawers."

"Oh, that. Well, then, I guess I must have been scared."

III

HEISER, RICHARD A.
US51681856
O POS
PROTESTANT

22

The first JAG officer I had was named Cuddahy, Captain Cuddahy. I saw him on Tuesday, I think. The MP woke me up inside my Conex box with his nightstick around two in the afternoon and then unlocked it and let me crawl out. As soon as I was on my feet, he started pushing me through the perfect little streets between the perfectly arranged Conex huts, but I could hardly see any of them because my eyes still weren't used to the sunlight. A couple of times I banged into the sharp corrugated edges of the Conexes as I stumbled past them, squinting my eyes and trying to coordinate my leg muscles through the cramps. We went through a wooden and wire gate and across a field to a permanent bunker-style building, up the steps, through double glass doors, down a wide corridor—we were in air conditioning now, and it was harder to adjust to than the sunlight had been—and finally came to a large room with benches along a table that was split in half by a Cyclone fence. The MP sat me down at the bench and left the room.

There were some stubby pencils without erasers on the table and some stacks of cheap, plain, rough paper. I was alone in the room except for a black dude all the way down the bench by the wall talking to a black officer in fresh jungle fatigues. I couldn't see from where I sat whether he was JAG or what. It didn't look like a very friendly or hopeful interview. I had the feeling that was pretty much the tone of most of the interviews in the room. I didn't know how long I'd have to wait for my JAG officer. There was a water fountain behind me. I went to it and took a pull of water and then doused my hair and face with it. I didn't want to drink much more because there wasn't a pisser in the room.

He came in through the door on the other side of the Cyclone fence about fifteen minutes later, saw me, figured out I was his man by a process of elimination and came over and sat down in a chair on his side of the table. He had a black vinyl folder with a snazzy Judge Advocates General insignia sticker on the front and a couple of tan cardboard folders sticking out of it. I stood up and saluted him. I don't know why. That seemed to surprise him a little, but he saluted back and started looking at me a little harder. He sat down. I sat down.

"My name's Captain Cuddahy," he said. "I take it you're Heiser."

"Yes, sir," I said.

"I was just assigned this case this morning. Just wait a few minutes while I look over the folders again." So I sat there while he did his homework. He started with my DD-214, my service record. That was pretty nondescript, even pretty good, assuming they hadn't got around to putting the news of the last couple of weeks on it. Then he moved on to the other papers, the current events, and his eyebrows arched every once in a while. Still, I couldn't read his face very well. That was the way a young lawyer who didn't want to be in the army but ended up in the JAG corps played officer, expressionlessly. I guess it was also the way a young lawyer maintained a professional aura with his clients, to keep everyone at arm's length and in his place, the young and the old, the dumb and the smart.

The Law is the true embodiment
Of everything that's excellent.

It has no kind of fault or flaw,
And I, my Lords, embody the Law.

Doctors and lawyers. People minded their own business and tried to stay out of their way until terminal illness or capital indictments dragged them into waiting rooms and hospitals, and there their lives stopped, were put on hold, given over to these special people who'd spent all those years cramming in school in order to graduate and get their tickets. Once that happened, they knew they'd have the rest of the populace by the nuts sooner or later and could orchestrate their victims' lives for capricious lengths of time while the meter ran. Litigate. Operate. And now it had happened to me. I'd wait and the JAG officer would pull my strings for a while, a couple of months, a couple of years, what the fuck did he care? And when he got tired of me, he could step aside and another JAG officer would pop up in his place and start it all over, have me wait at the table across the Cyclone fence from him while he acquainted himself with my file. I was the nominally necessary silver iodide crystal around which the professional rain cloud formed, the continuous, never-ending storm of hassle and trouble that gave lawyers meaning and substance.

He looked up at me.

"I'm sorry. Do you smoke?"

"I did a month ago."

"Here." He slipped me a couple of Viceroys through the fence. I put one in my lips. He had a Zippo lighter with another JAG corps silver crest on it, and he lit the tip of my smoke from the other side of the fence. He didn't say anything until I'd puffed away for half a minute.

"Your record's pretty good. Most of the ones I see in here don't look like this at all. How'd you get in this mess?"

"I don't know."

"Well, take a guess. Try to flesh it out for me. I'm your lawyer and I have to know."

"I don't know what to tell you. Somebody got fragged and when they came looking for the people who did it, I was one of the ones they rounded up. Things had been pretty hairy in my outfit for a long time before this."

"How so?"

"Well, our battalion, our company was the one they sent in to bring out those stiffs that went down in a chopper Charlie shot down. Charlie shot down the chopper so we'd go in after the stiffs. We took eight casualties on the first day and we still couldn't get to the helicopter with the stiffs. Then on the third day we took two casualties in the morning and Charlie got another chopper, a medevac that was trying to get the new casualties out. That's pretty much when all this bullshit started."

"Yes?"

"People just sat down. I was trying to get my squad on its feet to go in again and about a dozen guys in the LZ just wouldn't move. At first I thought they were exhausted, but then I realized what was going on. It was happening in the third platoon, too. I guess you could call it a sit-down strike. I think the other word that was used was *mutiny*."

"Who called it a mutiny?"

"Well, our platoon leader, the lieutenant, he just got very uptight about the situation and called it in over the radio to the battalion commander's helicopter, and then all shit let loose. The command chopper came down on us and the sergeant major ran over and started reaming assholes. He was the first guy I heard use the word. But I could see the same kind of thing was going on between the battalion CO and our platoon leader and the third platoon lieutenant. And all of a sudden they got back in the command chopper and a couple of captains showed up from somewhere else in the jungle and took over our platoons. And then I wasn't a squad leader or a sergeant anymore, but a couple of lifer types showed up and started getting everybody on their feet, kicking a few of them on the ground and shit. And then we started to move in again. Things changed a little. I think they diverted another infantry battalion from a stand-down and flew them in to take the heat off our flank, but Charlie didn't leave completely. I mean, that was what the whole thing was about—more targets—so there were still a lot of snipers and the closer we got, the more we got pinned down. It was really crazy."

I closed my eyes and tried to blank it out. Now that I'd told that much to him, there was no reason to think about it anymore. It didn't work very well, but I still needed a breather. The JAG officer probably thought I was pretty miserable being locked up here in the Long Binh Conex Hilton. Actually, it was a relief. You got pushed around by the MPs, and if you gave them any lip, you got roughed up. But actually it was pretty safe. Nothing happened. They fed you and walked you around enough to keep you alive, so if you didn't fuck up too bad, you were guaranteed to come out of the Conex Hilton alive. No one was shooting at you.

"Did you get to the choppers?"

"No, sir. Two of the squads in the third platoon got there first and we gave them covering fire. That's not really true. We went through enough of the motions to keep the captain and the sergeant major off our ass, just like the other platoon. I could see them across the clearing taking the bodies out of the chopper. There were two bodies. It was one of those little Hughes observation jobs, quick and maneuverable, but a sneeze'll make it go down. I could see arms and faces, and the jungle'd done a number on them. And a few more of our own men had been hit again, and a few more of the third platoon. But they got the bodies out of the clearing and then we withdrew far enough to pound the area with artillery strikes so we could get the fuck out of there."

"Did you know the lieutenant who was killed?"

"Yes, sir. A couple of hours after the guys wouldn't go into the jungle again, one of the headquarters captains gave our platoon over to him. His name was Gishy. I knew him from headquarters. And he just wouldn't listen to anyone from the start, and when I tried to tell him what the tactical conditions were, he told me to shut the fuck up because I was an ex-sergeant and an ex-squad leader and probably a mutineer, and fuck if he was going to take advice from me. And then he just started with all these impressive West Point maneuvers and getting some more of our asses shot up. I gave up on him and just concentrated on covering my ass and keeping out of his way, but a lot of the other guys, particularly the black dudes, they didn't concentrate quite so hard, and Lieutenant Gishy was saying a lot of ugly things to them. Racial things. To motivate them, I believe."

"Gishy was killed that night?"

"Yes, sir. As soon as we got back to the defensive perimeter, he looked at us all as if we were so much dog waste and then stalked off. The lifer sergeant tried to cool us out and said we'd probably get some stand-down time and everybody'd try to forget what had happened that morning, but it didn't go down that way. The battalion sergeant major kept walking around the perimeter making noises like we were all going to go out again in the morning, or maybe just pick right back up again and bop out on a night patrol. He was really steamed off. Finally we were dismissed. That's really all I know, until I heard the frag go off on the far side of the perimeter that night. I was sitting in my rack not doing much of anything. I figured it was incoming, but I waited a few seconds for more of it to come in before I scrambled. But I didn't hear any more come in. Then about a half hour later, all these lifers and MPs came in and hauled me and about six other guys out of their bunks. That's it."

"Do you know what you're charged with?"

"Yes, sir. Murder, complicity in, conspiracy to commit. Other stuff. They told me at the interrogation."

"But you didn't do it."

"No, sir."

"Are you glad he's dead?"

"That's something entirely different, sir."

"I want to know."

"Look, sir, that's just bullshit. There are a lot of people I wouldn't mind seeing snuffed, but I just suffer them all to live because snuffing them's not my act. It's not my job."

"What if one of them's trying to get you killed?" Cuddahy asked. "What if you think one of them is leading you into dangerous combat situations and not exercising caution?"

"I cover my own ass, and if things get really weird, I write my congressman."

"Bullshit," he said.

"Look, are you my lawyer or maybe the prosecutor? Maybe I forgot to ask. It could make a difference."

"I'm your lawyer, but I think you can hang it up. They have an excellent case. I'm going to advise you to plead guilty to a lesser charge. They may be willing to make a deal. They have the niggers who did it cold, but they're not quite so sure of where you fit in. Maybe you just helped plan or instigate it, or maybe you loaned them the grenade. They'll be satisfied to give you a year in Leavenworth and then kick your ass out."

"Gee, that's really swell," I said. "Thanks a lot."

"What's that supposed to mean?"

"It means you'd better start preparing something a little heftier than that, sir. I'm not pleading guilty to anything. I'm sorry if that puts anybody to any additional trouble, but that's just the way it's going to be."

"Don't be an asshole. If you go to a general court-martial, it's for capital crimes. You could be shot. That's not very likely, but they'll be happy to settle for twenty years to life at hard labor. They don't give a fuck about you, and to tell you the truth, they get real annoyed if you put them to the trouble of a general court-martial. These aren't even judges. They're what you call lifers, and you're somebody who's giving their army trouble, a lot of it. You're also someone they assume had something to do with killing one of their own, another officer, with a fragmentation grenade, and it splattered him all over the inside of a bunker. Would you like to see the photographs?"

"Sure."

That caught him off guard. He stiffened up in his chair. "Why?"

"Because you asked me if I wanted to see them. I'm going to pay for it anyway, according to you, even though I didn't do it. I want to see what I'm buying."

"I'm not giving you a cheap thrill like that."

"Fine. You asked," I said. "I'll get to see them at the trial, I'm sure."

He thought for a second. I don't think he was used to having to shift gears in these situations.

"Look," he said, "your records say you're a smart guy. But you're not acting very smart. You're not trying to get along with me, for one thing, and I'm on your side. I could be the only thing between you and a life term in Leavenworth. I'm trying to give you some damned good advice and you keep telling me to stick it up my ass. I don't think that's very smart."

"The records say I'm smart. I never told you I was smart. If you want to go home thinking I'm dumb, that's fine with me. I still want to plead not guilty. That is allowed, isn't it? They do make provision for that somewhere in the Code, don't they?"

"Fine," he said. "Fine. Okay, the first thing that means is that you go back and sit in your little tin shack for another month. That's what it means. Do you want that?"

"Yes, sir. I'm very hard-core."

"I'm telling you, you're doing everything to get really fucked over. I'm just telling you the truth."

"I'm sure you are, sir. In the meanwhile, you will try to work up some sort of half-assed defense for me, won't you? I mean, nothing heavy. Nothing to piss anyone off or anything. But something that suggests that maybe I didn't frag the lieutenant. I'd appreciate that very much, sir."

He stood up and picked up the files and stuffed them in his black folder. "I can only help you so much that way. I'll do what I can, but I wouldn't expect jack-shit, Heiser."

"Just my day in court, sir."

"That won't get you shit, Heiser."

"You never can tell, sir."

He sighed or grunted and looked at me a last time. Then he left the room. The MP came in a few seconds later and motioned me to my feet and out of the room.

When they locked me back in my Conex, one of about three hundred, maybe more, that made up the Long Binh jail—LBJ, the guests called it—it took me about twenty seconds to get used to the dark again. There were air cracks at the top of the box that let a lot of light stream in, and the whole effect gave me enough light to see some details in my fingers, the nails and the fingerprint whorls, without having to stand up by the light that was streaming in. I reached down in my trouser leg and pulled out the sheaf of paper and the pencils I'd ripped off before Cuddahy had shown up but after the MP had left me alone in the room. I drew a thick line on the paper and stared at it. I was probably going to go blind trying to write, but I could see it. Then I started writing the numbers 1 2 3 4 5. I could just about tell them all apart. Things were looking up.

First there was the quadratic formula. That was a good choice, because I'd completely forgotten how to take a general quadratic equation equal to zero and solve it in general terms for X. And I'd also forgotten most of the algebra I'd need to reconstruct it. I rationed my eyes and my time on it, just going back to it whenever I felt bored or weird or bummed out. I also had two Viceroys and I rationed puffs on them according to the half-pack of matches I'd found in a corner of the Conex. It took me four days to work out the quadratic formula from scratch, and the flash I had when I remembered the trick of completing the square had to be one of the most satisfying things that ever happened to me. I could solve the problem in thirteen elegant little steps. I was sure there were wizards or junior high school worms who could do it in eight or six, but they weren't locked in a Conex in LBJ.

By the time the MPs hauled me out of there again for another interview, I'd used my dimly remembered high school trig to work out the value of pi using regular polygons with more and more sides until I had a general formula for a regular polygon with any number of sides. Then the trick was to compute the values of some sines and cosines. That involved computing a few square and cube roots. That wasted a shitload of time. Finally I cranked out pi to 3.142 using that method, close enough for government work, and then went on to something else.

There was the quickie about the farmer, the fox, the chicken and the grain trying to get across the river in the canoe in the least number of trips, with the stipulation that the fox and the chicken couldn't be left alone on the bank together and neither could the chicken and the grain. And I remembered a problem about Buddhist monks moving stacks of discs one at a time from one of three pegs to another. At a second per move, with sixty-four discs, that worked out to something around 584 billion years to shift the pile from one peg to another if they did it the fastest possible way. I seemed to remember lots of little problems like that I'd never bothered to work out in detail before. I could always hear the MPs a few sheds down when they came to feed us or let us out for exercise, and I stuffed the paper and pencils back into my trousers.

My favorite time killer was how fast an object had to move laterally in a given time to counteract the downward pull of gravity to the earth so it could remain in orbit. That one was a real bitch, especially because I'd forgotten the gravitational constant. It was either eight, sixteen or thirty-two feet per second squared. I dropped pencils from the roof to the floor of the shed and tried to time them to settle on the one I liked best. And as I got more and more used to the work, I could save paper by writing the formulas and diagrams smaller and smaller. And when the paper finally ran out, I was ready to start doing all the problems over again, but this time in my head. I sharpened the pencils with my teeth.

At night when I couldn't sleep I tried to remember old songs and sing them softly to myself. I sang "This Is Dedicated to the One I Love," the Mamas and the Papas' version, over and over again maybe two hundred times when the nights were still and quiet, and it seemed to cut through the oppressive heat a little, at least to take my mind off it. And of course I imagined the one I loved was back home singing it back to me in soft focus, heartfelt, while I sang the harmony in my Conex. She was clean. She was wearing a pair of pink summer shorts. She'd just shampooed her hair. She knew my name and she missed me.

I was working out the long-division style for extracting square roots without a table or trial and error when the MP rousted me out of the Conex for another interview. He didn't see the paper and pencils, but I hadn't had much time to stuff them back in my boot and I was afraid they were going to drop out on the ground while I walked. They didn't. Anyway, if I was going to the same place, I could glom some more.

There was another captain, this one in khakis, waiting on the free side of the Cyclone fence when I walked in. He looked a little like Groucho or Chico Marx, I couldn't figure out which. He had a fat black moustache and thinning hair on his head, but a mass of black hair on his arms and the part of his chest that showed above his T-shirt. The MP left us alone and I sat down. His black name tag said HART.

"Do you have any smokes?" I asked.

"No, sorry. There's a machine out in the hall. What kind do you smoke?"

"I'm not sure. Winstons, Marlboros. Marlboros. The red ones. In the box if you can."

"Just a second." He got up and walked out the other door. He didn't exactly walk; he sort of stomped, leaning forward, very quickly. When he came back he slid a whole fresh pack of Marlboros and a brand new pack of matches under the Cyclone fence. I grabbed for them and took the cellophane off them, then pulled off the foil, then lit up a smoke.

"My name's Hart," he said. "You can see that. Are you okay?"

"So-so. What happened to Cuddahy?"

"Nothing. Do you want him?"

"I don't know. Do I have a choice? They could send me somebody worse, if that's possible."

"It's probably not, and you do have a choice. Wait a second." He went groping in his pocket and took out a piece of paper. He slid that through the fence. I opened it and recognized the scrawl.

Trust this guy. He can finagle the bagel. B

This was getting interesting.

"Don't tell me. You're the stereotypical Jewish lawyer I've always heard about. I thought that was like believing in Negroes who are born dancers or Polish people not being able to count to ten."

"Actually," Hart said, "I know a lot of Jewish lawyers I wouldn't let handle my belly-button lint, much less my ass. A mutual friend asked me to look you up. How long you been here?"

"Is Nixon still President?"

"Yeah."

"First or second term?"

"First."

"Not too long, I guess. What's the score?"

"Well, first you got to sign this that says you want a new lawyer. I'll fill in the rest."

"Then what?"

"Then you go back to the little box for a while and I see what I can do."

"According to Cuddahy, all you can do is maybe get me some barbecue sauce when I fry."

"Cuddahy's an ass. Did he try to make you plead guilty?"

"Yeah."

"That's because he's a lifer. He can't cut it as a lawyer on the outside, so he stays in the JAG corps. He stays in, he doesn't want to piss the other shmucks off. It's not really an ideal arrangement for someone in your position. Me, I don't give a fuck. I'm not going to get my ass court-martialed, but I don't have to. I got drafted just like you, I want to get the fuck out of here just like you. Along the way, I give the shmucks a run for their money."

"Where'd you go to law school?"

"Columbia. Why?"

"Just curious. Our mutual friend only sends the best."

"I went to college with his brother. Give me the note." I gave it to him. He took my matches and burned the note in the ashtray. Then he pushed the form across for me to sign and I signed.

"Is there hope?"

"Sure. These guys couldn't prosecute their way out of a paper bag against a real lawyer."

"Aren't you going to ask me if I did it?"

"What? Kill the lieutenant? Suit yourself. Did you do it?"

"No."

"Did you have anything to do with it?"

"No."

"Did you know about it in advance?"

"No."

"Fine. Are you making out all right in there?"

"I think things just improved a lot."

"Do you want me to get in touch with your folks back home?"

"No, not if you can help it."

"Fine. Okay. I'll try to see you again in a day or two. I'll bring you some more smokes. Don't get in this kind of trouble when you get out. I charge a fucking fortune in civilian practice."

"I can imagine."

"Stay loose." Then he took his papers, stood up and stomped out of the room. The MP came back on my side and took me back to the shack. I still rationed the cigarettes, but this time I smoked a whole cigarette at a time. There were still four left in the pack when the MP brought me back for another interview a couple of days later.

"They want to offer you a deal," Hart said.

"Shoot."

"You take a bad conduct discharge and they fly you home. No jail, no criminal charges."

"What do you think?"

"I asked you first," Hart said.

"Would you think I was crazy if I said I didn't like it?"

"No. It just means you'll have to go back to the box again for a couple of days while I work on something else."

"Do you mind?"

"Look, I'm the guy who gets to sit in an air-conditioned office all day. I got nothing better to do. You're the guy who has to sit in the can all day like Boston baked beans. I don't mind."

"I'd like my honorable discharge. The movie said if I don't get it, I'll have to spend the rest of my life sleeping in bus stations and begging respectable people for quarters."

"I know. I saw that one, too. Great movies they got in the army. Did you see the one with the kid from *The Rifleman?*"

"Yeah. I didn't like that one too much. No romantic interest. No tension."

"Okay, I'll see what I can do. Oh, here's another couple of packs of smokes."

"Thank you."

"Don't mention it."

I was losing all interest in reconstructing mathematics. I still sang at night, but the songs were getting a little cheerier. I had half a pack of cigarettes left when they took me to the next interview and I hadn't even been rationing them.

"Hi," I said.

"Okay, here's the best I could do. General discharge under honorable conditions, same as you'd get if you were a WAC and got knocked up. You get all your bennies, back pay, veterans' rights. It won't dazzle the world on employment applications, but like I said, it's about the best I can do. Also, you get to go home now. They just want to get rid of you."

"I'm starting to feel sorry for them. I'll take it."

"Okay, hang tight. Back into the fray." He stood up.

"Wait a second. I know this sounds sappy, but if you're not just fucking with my head and you can really pull this off— well, is there anything I can do to pay you back?"

"Fuck, no. It wasn't exactly fun, but at least it was different. Sam pays the tab. You don't owe me anything. If it means that much to you, take me out to dinner sometime when you get out. I'll be practicing in Washington."

"What kind of food do you like?"

"Any kind. Actually, I love Korean food but I can't get anybody to go with me. You can buy me some *kimchi*. I'll be home in about eight months."

"Okay."

"I'll look forward to it."

"So will I."

And that was about it. The next day they took me out of my

Conex for the last time and shuttled me off to the air base. I found a poker game to while away the hours—they'd already given me some of my back pay in Allied military credits—until they put me on a commercial jet heading home. I fell asleep on the plane a couple of times, talked to a couple of guys, smoked some reefer someone had smuggled aboard in the can, and then we landed at Fort Lewis in the middle of the night and were led off to some transient barracks. We were rousted out of the rack in the morning, fed breakfast and then sent around to the eight or nine different offices and windows we had to check out with to get our discharge.

The last window was the pay window, where they figured out how much you were owed in back pay, travel pay, vacation time you hadn't used up and all that bullshit. The months I'd spent in LBJ didn't count; part of the deal Hart had cooked up for me was that it was bad time. Still, the ticket I took up to the guy, a Spec-5 with finance corps brass, said that Sam owed me something like $280. The clerk took the paperwork, rubber-stamped it and then dug into the cash drawer. He pulled out a stack of fifties and counted out fourteen of them, a couple of singles, some loose change, and pushed it all under the cage window.

"Thank you," I said.

"Good luck," he said. "Next."

I strolled to the latrine and in the privacy of a stall calculated the whole thing over again. He'd fucked up large, and all in cash. The shit probably wouldn't hit the fan until the end of the day, and there were a couple of hundred swinging dicks between my fuck-up and then. I was that masked man.

I found an invitingly dark and cavernous restaurant in Tacoma and ordered their prime ribs, rare, with a bottle of Poppe de Poppe '59 or some other such killer vintage off their wine list. They served the roast the way I liked it, big hunks of roast potatoes and roasted onions with a little char on the edges. The rib slices were each three-quarters of an inch thick, both of them. The creamed spinach had little hard-boiled egg wedges on top. After I'd cleaned the plate, I had three very slow cups of coffee and some blueberry pie with a scoop of vanilla ice cream on the side.

My cab driver knew where there was a big clothing store open on the way to the airport and said he wouldn't mind waiting while I picked up a few things. I found a pair of blue jeans and a shirt that wasn't too odious. Then I picked up a package of real underwear, not those *verdammt* o.d. boxer shorts, and a couple of pairs of socks. Finally I found a pair of tennis sneakers I could live with. I paid for it all with one of the fifties and got change back.

The driver took me to the airport where I showed the airline counterman my travel orders. I was still in uniform, so the trip back to the East coast was half-price. He booked me on a flight that was leaving for the Apple in about an hour, with connections from there up to Hartford.

I found a pay phone and dialed the big number. One of the kids answered. "Hello?" the kid said.

"Hi. Is Betty there? Is Dad there?"

"Who is this?"

"It's your brother Richard."

And then I heard her squeal *It's Richard!* out into the living room or the kitchen and I could hear this kind of pandemonium going on (on my dime), but finally Betty cut her way through the midget savages and trolls and got to the phone. "Is that you, Richard? Be quiet, everybody!"

"Yeah, Betty, it's me. How are you?"

"Fine, dear. We've been terribly worried about you. Where are you? Are you all right?"

"I'm fine. I'm at the Seattle Airport. I'll be in Hartford tomorrow morning at six. Do you think someone can pick me up?"

"Of course, Richard. I'll be there. Do you mind if some of the kids come along?"

"Well, could you keep it down to maybe three or four?"

"Certainly, dear. I won't bring any of them if I can find someone to watch them. Ellen would, but she's off at music camp this summer."

"Whatever. How's Dad?"

"Well, please don't worry because he'll be so happy to see you, but he's in the hospital again."

"Bad?"

"Well, you know, more of the same. I'm not too worried and he's looking very spry. But I'm so delighted—oh, Richard, I was so worried."

"Yeah, so was I. It's good to hear your voice."

"It's wonderful to hear yours."

I gave her the flight number and hung up. There weren't very many people on the flight, a sort of businessman's red-eye express, and I had a rack of three seats to myself. After we'd taken off and the seat belt sign went off, I took my paper sack back to the john and locked myself in. I took off my khakis and my black shoes and all the other weird shit and put on the blue jeans and the sneakers and the nice cotton underwear and the socks. I'd forgotten to buy a belt, so I put the blue Boy Scout belt with the brass buckle on the blue jeans. That didn't bother me too much. I could get around to that at my leisure.

I stretched out on the three seats with the armrests up and smoked a cigarette. The stew brought me a pillow and a Coke and then realized I'd boarded in uniform. She thought that was pretty funny.

"Do you always change on the plane?" she asked.

"No. This was the first time."

23

I didn't live in the house long. Dad had changed his mind about selling it. Even with the big extra strain of another household in Florida half the year, all he could think about was that he still had the passel of kids in school, his and Betty's, and he saw the house as the centerpiece of family normalcy. With it, he felt he could give the ones who were left stability. Without it, he just saw a black, vague doom cloud of transience and renting surrounded by dubious, undependable strangers masquerading as neighbors. I certainly didn't take a stand one way or the other, but still he and I didn't see eye to eye on it when I talked to him alone in the hospital.

"Kids are tougher than you give them credit for," I said. "You and Betty are the family, not a big house or a familiar neighborhood. As long as you're there for them, it doesn't matter where they are, whether it's a new place or the old place."

"You don't know much about kids," he said. "You haven't been paying much attention to them. You and I are older. We've knocked around a little bit and found out that we won't melt or die or go crazy because we're in a strange place. They'll find that out, too, in a few years when they're strong enough to want to try it. But they're kids right now, and you don't understand how conservative kids are. They're terrified of unfamiliar things and people and places. They get upset when we change brands of margarine. They actually did get upset when Betty threw all the butter out of the house and said we're only using margarine from now on. They didn't complain. They knew it was for me, and they're all terribly frustrated about what's happening with me and how little they can do about it. But it was a change, and they hate change. The things they're used to are the best things in the world and everything else is wrong. I caught Barry smoking last year. He hadn't filched the cigarettes from me. He bought them from a machine on his own, but they were my brand. I asked him about that. He said those were the best. Dad's poison is the best poison."

"Change is life. I read that in a book."

"But it's my job to shield them from as much of it as I can for as long as I can. Because change is also pain for them. They're going to get all the pain they want in a few years. I'm trying to keep it down to a dull roar now, and it's frustrating for me that I'm a big source of change and pain for them."

"The doctor said this wasn't a big deal."

"It's not getting any better, Richard."

"Worrying so much about Betty and the kids isn't helping. Betty's made of steel. I'm on my own, more or less, or if I'm not, there's nothing else you can do to make me handle it better. The older ones still at home look out for the young ones and keep 'em from playing on the railroad tracks. You've still got good commissions coming in from your sales. I'd cool out a little if I were you and do what's good for you."

"Can't," he said amiably. "I don't know how to explain it to you. The habits of a lifetime, I guess."

A couple of weeks after Dad came back from the hospital, I moved out as quietly and unceremoniously as I could, during a school day, and took my things over to Rudy's apartment. Not a big mistake, really, but it was an episode I could have done without. Rudy was just crazy to have me back in town. He couldn't stop phoning me up as soon as he found out I was back; he was like an amputee who gets his original foot back unexpectedly after two years. He dragged me out to bars every night and whenever he looked at me he broke into a huge grin, saying things like "Hey, everything's great again. You'll even have your hair back soon." He dragged me around to see all our old mutual friends and dragged me around to see all his new friends. I felt like a twelve-year-old's new puppy. I didn't mind the visits to the new friends; I just endured them and smiled through the evenings and made what pleasant conversation I thought would make the clock advance. It was the field trips to old friends and their new spouses and homes and apartments I wish Rudy hadn't forced me into at that pace. Well, I'm blaming something on him that was my problem, not his; I should have had the strength to tell him to chill out and let me set the pace.

What he didn't understand, what he was cheerfully and moronically oblivious of, was that, like him, none of the guys had been drafted. Some of them had held out just a little after me until the lottery system had started—I was the last shipment of meat not subject to the whims of the lottery, protected only by whatever protection I'd forged for myself, and I'd neglected to forge any protection for myself—and the others had just stayed in school and kept up their C's or B's or whatever the academic cutoff level was. A few of them had married and their wives had become pregnant in time to put them in a more protected Selective Service category before the lottery. One of them, Dan, had managed to get a slot in the Connecticut National Guard and hadn't been able to handle basic training—and NG and Reserve basic training was always forty percent sillier and easier than Regular Army basic. He'd had some kind of mid-course breakdown or titanic freakout and they'd sent him home, immunized for the duration. Roger's dad had arranged with another factory owner pal to get him a shift supervisor job on a contract that made the back-flap assemblies of amphibious personnel carriers, the ones the drivers always forgot to put down when they tried to drive the suckers across rivers, so the amphibs promptly sank with all hands aboard. That put Rog in the national defense work category. He had two kids now and was back working at his dad's paper products factory in middle management.

I didn't resent any of this shit, and I was glad to see them again. They just weren't all that delighted to see me. There were barriers now, the way they have these glass walls between the customer and a beautiful young naked woman in the backs of the San Francisco skin joints where they have the live sex acts out front on the bar—after you put in the $5 token, it's just you alone with your beautiful naked girl, who's on the other side of bulletproof glass. Plus, Rudy was forcing it on everyone; I think some of us could have worked out something better if we'd just bumped into one another by accident on the commons and played it gradually from there.

In his own way, Rudy was hip to a tiny bit of this, and one night I came back to the apartment to find the antidote, old Art—which was stretching a point about old mutual friends, but he'd hung around us back in high school—in the living room working on a third beer. Art had joined the Marines for a burst of three and was back now working in one of the factories. He'd been back for eight months and still had a crew cut. He was delighted to see me. Within five minutes he was telling me about the American Legion post he was an officer of and demanding I go over there tonight and get shitfaced with him; Rudy could come too. I begged off for both of us, which didn't seem to disappoint Rudy. Art and I traded war stories; it was our only common ground, and I knew it wasn't going to last long. He was convinced we were now and forever blood brothers, comrades in arms. I could see fantasies in his eyes of the years rolling by and him and me marching hand in hand in Armistice and Veterans' Day and Fourth of July parades, a fantasy I found horrifying beyond description. Somehow I realized—you always seem to know, it's not much of a trick—that I'd have to wait until he left before I could light up anything besides tobacco. He kept pushing a Michelob at me and I kept politely turning it down, which seemed to mystify him. At one point as we talked about other people we'd known in high school, he leaned conspiratorially over and said in a low whisper, "You know, I think some of those guys are using marijuana now."

"Nah, I don't think so," I assured him. "Not them."

And then some time later, the same hushed tone about a girl we'd known. "I ran into her not long after I got back," he said.

"I asked her out for a beer. She was nice about it, but she said she couldn't make it. You know what I heard?"

I knew what he'd heard. "No, what did you hear?"

"She's like a lesbian. That's what I heard. She's got this steady girl friend, they live together, everything."

"No shit? Well, I guess it had to happen to somebody."

"But jeez, somebody we know. I couldn't believe it. That's weird."

"Art, did you know any BAMs?"

"What's a BAM?" Rudy asked.

"Broad-Assed Marine. A woman Marine," I said.

"Sure, I knew some of 'em to talk to."

"Well, the rumor always was that a few of them—well, that was the rumor. Didn't you pick up on any of that?"

"Well, yeah. A couple of 'em got court-martialed and booted out at Pensacola when I was there, but I didn't know 'em. There was a lot of talk about that. It's just weird, that's all."

I wanted to clue him in that it was just life, reality, the weather, 1971, boys dancing with boys, girls dancing with girls, teachers smoking and selling marijuana, vets coming back and not joining the American Legion, vets not being terribly crazy about being vets in the first place, but I didn't waste my breath. I think even Rudy was getting a little embarrassed at the primitive dialogue he'd imported into the living room. That night after Art had left (and extracted a sacred oath from me that we'd get together again and again real soon, which I saw to it we never did), I cornholed Rudy in the kitchen so he couldn't escape and said, "Please don't do that to me again."

"Oh," he grunted. "You mean Art."

"I mean anything even remotely resembling that creep. Look. He has the right to be like he is. He was that way six years ago. He hasn't changed a fucking bit. He's drifted into what he thought was swell, and he'll keep going that way. Fine. There's room for him and me in the world. But not in the same room, for Christ's sake."

"I just thought—"

"I know what you thought. Okay. Nice try. Stop trying so hard. I'm trying to grab back on to my life, and you're making it hard—you keep putting loose clay and crumbly gravel where I'm trying to put my hands and feet."

"You haven't looked real happy since you been back," he said.

"I haven't *been* really happy since I've been back! I'm working on it! You're making it hard."

"Okay. I'll leave you alone." He sulked.

"Look. Have you ever shared quarters with anybody before since you moved out of your house?"

"No. I didn't have to, but I thought you needed a place."

"I do need a place, and this is a great place. It's got two rooms, a kitchenette, a shitter, a shower, a laundry room in the basement. It's paradise. But in a lot of ways I'm a wreck right now. That's just the way I am right now. Your old buddy's a mess. He's glad to see you, glad to be here, but he's having troubles. He wants to work 'em out at his own pace. Happiness, love, marriage, a dog, kids, all that'll come in time, I'm sure, and you can be best man and get your pick of the litter—the dog's, not my wife's. But right now things are just a little—edgy! Dig it?"

"Yeah, okay, I dig it."

So the social whirl tapered off considerably, and I was grateful for that, but that still left Rudy being Rudy and me being me, and to be fair to Rudy, he could have been a cuddly talking teddy bear with button eyes that month and there still would have been sparks. Not that I want to be too fair to Rudy; he handled me and my weirdnesses with all the thoughtfulness and nuance of a gym teacher, and his own day-to-day living style had an amazing capacity to drive me up the wall. I'd drift in around dinnertime and Rudy'd come back from work and turn the television on and watch all these situation comedies and reruns, and the canned laughter would laugh and Rudy'd laugh too. A character would come into the room and say, "Hi, everybody!" and the mechanical audience would go into peals of laughter, and Rudy'd join in with them. Finally one night we had a big duke-out about his favorite, *Hogan's Heroes*, and I stalked out and the next day managed to scare up some other place, somewhat less mine, less permanent and less friendly than Rudy's, but I couldn't deal with Rudy anymore.

I don't know why I was so raw about *Hogan's Heroes*. I knew that it was just the camel-back-breaking-straw at the time, but when I realized it had driven me out of a secure place to stay and caused me to say some pretty vile things to my host and old friend—and he was a good friend, good friend with a good heart, one I valued—I thought about it and tried to figure it out afterward.

What I figured out was that there used to be real guys in real World War II prison camps—well, why be picky? There are still lots of guys, lots of guys and gals, in somebody's prison camps somewhere; shit like that never goes out of style. And I had a very strong feeling that most of them who lived through it didn't think much of that experience was very funny. I imagine they didn't have much to eat, they were sick a lot, they were always worried that they might be snuffed in a big economy move, they didn't get much news and so didn't have too good an idea of who was winning the war, and they were pretty fucking hot in the summer and cold in the winter. The way I hear it, people in prison camps don't get a whole hell of a lot from the material plane's cornucopia. Oh, and they didn't have women, either. I asked a sailor buddy of mine once what sailors do when they have to be out on those ships for six, eight months at a time; I was feeling very naïve that night, I guess. And my squid buddy said, "You see your old friend Rosie Fingers." And a couple of suggestions beyond that which get into the sodomy statutes.

So what do POWs (who never have a nice day, according to the bumper stickers that were starting to appear around town) and sailors with no shore leave for half a year or more, and assholes like me canned up in the Conex Hilton for three or four months, and people in the Black Hole of Calcutta, and veterans of Dachau and so forth—what do all these folks have? What's left after they're cold and sick and hungry and naked and incredibly horny and sexually unsatisfied? What's left, assuming they're left after all that?

I thought on this for a time and it seemed to me that the only thing people like that have is their memories, their perceptions of these experiences. That's all they have, and because it's all they have, they get pretty hot under the collar when somebody fucks with those experiences and perceptions. I certainly would, anyway.

First somebody saw fit to take away your mail and your food and your heat and aspirin and your fuck magazines and your chances of getting laid, and then later, when some clown decides to take the only thing you have left, your experiences, your memories of them, and make them into a TV situation comedy with funny-looking and funny-*gespraching* Nazi guards and commandants and lots of laughs and lots of opportunities to get a little nooky from the thousands of friendly farm maidens who belong to the vast anti-Nazi underground just down the road from the *stalag*—well, then, it seems appropriate and fitting to get a little ticked off, maybe even to feel a little paranoid when a whole bunch of canned laughing people start rolling around on the rug over those wacky, zany, crazy, madcap times back there in the pits. A little paranoid, because your memories of how it really was were all you managed to take away from there besides lice and malformed bones and rotting teeth, and now you get the feeling someone's taking your memories away and changing them to sell Mr. Bubble or Tab or Preparation H. And this makes you nervous. You keep hearing that old song in your head about how they can't take that away from me, but yes they can and they did. There it goes, and there was nothing you could do to stop it. And by the time you catch up with your memories again, they've changed and become a situation comedy. The Nazis have become conscientious objectors who stumbled into this line of work by accident. The better part of a ghastly year on the USS *Bumfuck* has suddenly become an MGM musical starring Donald O'Connor, Mickey Rooney and (Hey! How'd *she* get on board?) Judy Garland. Four years waiting for your number to come up for the Zyklon-B showers has somehow popped up in the Thursday night lineup as *Tonight's Episode: Fritz and Franz meet their wacky, unpredictable Uncle Velvel hauling bodies to a mass grave (9:00 P.M., 7).*

And if I let it, if I watched that stuff and laughed along with the cans, what would they eventually do with my memories? *Tonight's Episode: The new West Point lieutenant calls down an artillery strike on his own position to impress the brass, but a lot of the enlisted men get sore (8:30 P.M., 2). Tonight's Episode: President Nixon decides to invade Cambodia, and the guys in the platoon are surprised (10:00 P.M., 14). Tonight's Episode: Heiser gets tired of seeing all those starving Vietnamese refugees, but doesn't know what to do about it (8:00 P.M., first of two parts, 9).*

Because, after all, the tendency with memories like that is certainly not to take them straight, as they are. That's an epic pain in the ass, even for me, certainly for the Dachau retiree, the POW, the Joe in Attica. No one likes memories like that. No one takes Instamatic pictures of places like that. Nobody who gets out of places like that wants to go back. Nobody tells his kids about memories like that during bedtime story hour.

So there you are with all those swell memories that you don't want to remember and don't want to talk about, and because you're hiding them and not doing anything with them, somebody else comes around to see what *he* can do with them. You weren't selling any oatmeal or automobiles with the goddam things, so why the fuck should you mind if he takes a stab at it? Put a laugh track in the background, change the kinky sadist guard to a bumbling Bavarian, cool it down for the kids and the young-at-heart, soft-pedal the politics and *voilà!* You got yourself a hit series there.

And people like me end up at night in little rooms armed and always on the defensive, guarding our little bags of stale and vile memories against these revisionist thieves who would sweeten our memories with saccharine and change and repackage them and compress them into thirty minutes and thirteen weeks. We force ourselves to stay awake and guard our little bags of terrible times and loony tunes, but we ourselves never open these bags. We have no secret rituals for them; we never share them with others. They're our parched, alkaline, useless, personal treasures, and our greatest fear grows and grows that someone will come and steal our horrid, useless, frightening bag of shit and open it in some other unknown room and dump the contents out and play with them, rearrange them and varnish them, discarding the parts he doesn't like or understand and substituting other bright new parts which he thinks will improve the whole package and make it more palatable to the consuming public. The fear of having your memories stolen and rearranged and misunderstood, the fear of having your private and personal experiences stolen and played with in an alley by laughing teenagers . . . It's the fear of contact with the brink of the void, that permanent bug-eyed mouth-agape freakout when you discover that thousands of Xerox copies of your most singularly terrifying and uniquely Richard Heiser experiences are now in circulation as office jokes all over the country, with some of the secretaries saying, *I don't get it,* and others saying, *I don't think it's all that funny,* and the rest thinking it's really boffo socko and laughing, their laughter reverberating through the company hallways and out the front door and somehow faintly echoing back to you in your little room where you wonder: *Who has taken my bag of memories away and what have they done with it? Who's got my golden memories? Who's got my golden memories?* . . .

So as I unpacked my belongings—I still used my army duffel bag, handy sucker—in a much less comfortable, much less convenient room of a much less friendly apartment than Rudy's, I realized I was beginning my Lost Years, the Zombie years I'd warned Becker about, because I found myself guarding my memories, my priceless, exhausted memories, but never peeking or looking at them, frightened out of my ever-fucking-loving wits that somebody would grab them and run with them and be faster than I was, take them somewhere and say, *Fuck, these aren't worth shit; why would anybody guard memories like this?* and then dump my memories into the garbage disposal or flush them down the toilet. Swoosh.

Lost Zombie Years keep you a little on edge, a little raw. It's hard to make the connections during Lost Years. It's really hard to do a lot of long-range career planning when you're having Lost Years. You act strange. You snap at people. You need a lot of quiet. People call you on the phone only to find that you're out of town and you've been that way for three or four days and nobody has the slightest idea where the fuck you are, but you'll probably be back.

I took a lot of odd jobs, real odd jobs. I drifted into retail, looking for a product I could sell all day that wouldn't grate my nerves and sensibilities every time I rang up the cash register. I took jobs as a messenger and then odder jobs than that. The people I worked for thought I was very strange (and they were right, by God) and sometimes they tolerated me and other times they found me entirely intolerable and fired me. A lot of that was because I was working there but never going to any of the picnics or wandering over to any of their after-work bars to get juiced up with them and talk about the Patriots or the Whalers with them. I was there but not really there, and they knew I wasn't really there, and they thought, *Goddamit, we have to really be here, so why the fuck doesn't he have to really be here?* and one thing would lead to another and I'd be hitting the bricks again to find another job to pay the rent, because I had to live somewhere during the Lost Zombie Years.

It was particularly rough trying to do it in my hometown. The people I grew up and went to school with thought I was even stranger than the people I was trying to work with had thought. I'd meet these old acquaintances on the street and they'd try to sell me tax-free municipal bonds and wonder why I wasn't buying; no, they'd wonder why I didn't seem to be there at all. They wondered why they had dog and wife and home and all that shit and I was still living in an apartment without an air-conditioner in a neighborhood they didn't like to drive through anymore.

They weren't really bad people. Once upon a time they seemed as nice as anyone I knew, as nice as I used to be, so I wished I could come up with some easy answers for their unspoken questions about whatever happened to Rich Heiser. *It's really very simple, Ted. First I became a hopeless smack freak and then I completely burned out my brainstem taking six tabs of acid a day for three straight years. Or, I don't know why I never married, Susan; maybe it's because my dick and nuts got shot off in the war.* If I'd had easy answers to unspoken questions like that, it would have made these chance meetings during the Lost Years so much simpler for me and them, so much easier for everyone all around. But even if there were any fairly good and moderately concrete answers to be found back at the shack in my tightly tied memory bag, that was the ultimate thing I could never do, I could never open that bag and pull from it some reasonable explanation about what had become of me. There were answers in there. No way was I going to pull them out and display them to anyone. No fucking way. *Well, you see, John, I guess things started to go sour when I kept having to crawl into this patch of jungle day after day after day after day after these smelly, rotting, dead helicopter crewmen while all these little invisible Asian men and women kept spraying the place with AK47 fire, and then somebody fragged the lieutenant, so I had to spend three months locked up in a hot corrugated steel box about the size of the shed you keep your garden tools in while they were deciding whether or not to court-martial me for murder and mutiny.* No, that kind of shit just won't do; it had no place either for me or for my old high school chums or old flames. So finally after the

first ten or twelve of these chance meetings I simply stopped
having chance meetings, if I was lucky enough to see those
cocksuckers before they saw me. I'd duck into an alley or a
tobacco store. I'd hide in the magazine rack behind *Popular
Mechanics* while they were down at the other end of the store
buying Pampers or shoelaces.

*If feelings of evaporation and becoming transparent persist, try re-
turning to college.* I tried that again. After all, I had all these
V.A. bennies Hart had finagled for me and I couldn't let them
go to waste. And it was still oh so very hard to make the connections even there. The strangest things kept happening. I'd
engage a honey in idle conversation on the patio outside the
student union and without reaching into the memories grab
bag, I'd mention where I spent the last few years, innocently
assuming that she must have met *someone* like me before or
heard *something* about people like me on the *CBS Evening News*,
and/but she'd say something like (something exactly like) *Oh,
you must have been for the war, you must have liked the war.*

Or *Oh, you one of those baby killers?*

And gosh, all of a sudden I had some swell new memories
to stuff in the bag, the bottomless, magic, expanding bag.
Memory after memory goes in, but none ever comes out.

Of course there were better moments of idle chatter with
strange new honeys, and sometimes they led to more idle chatter
and dates and getting laid and even some strange skeletal arrangements resembling relationships between human beings.
Sometimes things seemed to work out for months at a time. Of
course half the time it turned out they were virgins and when
you'd get too close to them after a swell meal and a great flick,
they'd jump for the window or the phone to dial 911, and
perhaps the other half weren't virgins anymore but they'd decided that all things considered, that had been a mistake, so
while I tried to make love to them, they gave me stares and
noises that gave me the distinct impression I was no longer a
boyfriend, but a member of Satan's Gangbangers M.C. who'd
bound and drugged them and forever dashed their hopes of
regaining a state of grace and life everlasting with Mother Church.
So sooner or later one of us, her or me, it didn't much matter
who, would run off screaming into the night, and even what
little pleasure I could remember of bodies and soft and forgiv-

ing flesh in dark bedrooms at night would meld with the bitter memories of the unforgiving talk in the bright daylight, so that if I had memories at all, they were just more items for the bag.

School itself, which I'd seen as a painless and magical way of getting through and beyond the Zombie Years, was getting stranger, curiouser and curiouser all the time. First there were the lines, and for the first time I discovered what the army had done to my brain about waiting in long lines. At least two or three times a month in the army my whole company would be marched to some table or window and assembled single file in front of it for some injection or dispensing or form-filling or test-taking (and by platoon, not even in alphabetical order), and when I'd driven out of the gates of Fort Lewis, something very foolish and unauthorized in my mind had added waiting in long lines to the list of certified things I'd never again have to submit to or endure. College turned out to be nothing more than another rhythm of occasions for long lines, most of the most necessary ones very much longer than army company length. None of the post-high-schoolers in the lines seemed to mind, but there I was, waiting and waiting to get up to the registration tables and systematically losing it there on the gymnasium floor or finally just blowing my morning's investment of three or four hours and leaving the line to go outside and sit down on the grass somewhere to do some deep breathing or cigarette smoking or reefer puffing, whatever happened to be the strongest palliative or hypnotic I had on me.

And then, in the middle of the second semester, the money, the V.A. checks stopped coming and the rent was due and I didn't have any fucking money in my wallet anymore and I didn't know where to get any and I was seeing the campus V.A. counselor and he was saying he was checking into what the problem was, and then I was calling these odd, disembodied, treacly male and female voices on the far end of the phone at the V.A. regional office in Boston (my dime), and they were saying that they didn't know what the problem was, either, but that if I'd just be patient a little longer, they were certain they'd find out what the problem was, but that in the meantime they were sorry but there was simply no way to send me any money until they could find out what had happened to the checks they were supposed to have been sending me, and I was screaming

YOU STUPID MOTHERFUCKERS I AM DEALING DOPE
TO PAY THE RENT AND EATING CAT FOOD WHAT IS
THE FUCKING MATTER WITH YOU PEOPLE AND WHY
THE FUCK WON'T YOU SEND ME THE GODDAM MONEY
YOU PROMISED ME and they were saying, *Please, Mr. Heiser,
we're doing everything we can, but talking like that won't help things. . . .*

Time sure flies when you're having fun. I finally scratched
going back the third semester, not having found a satisfactory
way to subsist on air and promises, and I was readying myself
for the high dive back into Odd Job City when I got the phone
call from Annie. She wanted to know whatever happened to
Rich Heiser, too, but in a different way, not as if I were so
much used Kleenex that hadn't quite made the free throw into
the corner trash can. "Yeah, well," I told her, "I came back from
the Nam and I was never heard from again."

There was fizzle and pop and hiss on the phone and I asked
her where she was calling from and she told me she'd been
living in Key West for about a year, year and a half. "Where?"

Key West, she said, south of Miami, and I said, Yeah, I know
where that is—hey, listen, would you mind if I came down there
and hung out for a while?

And that seemed to make her happy—and it seemed that it
was the first time since the army that my going toward someone
rather than walking away had made anyone happy in the slightest. Sure, she said, that would be great. And she was sure I'd
really dig it down there. And R.J. was down there. She didn't
see that much of him these days, but he was down there too.
Could I bring her anything? No, she said, nothing that she
could think of. Just come on down.

IV

BECKER, DAVID C.
US49963722
A POS
JEWISH

24

The morning sunlight was behind him in the hooch doorway.
I could tell he was tall and blond in a USC basketball sort of
way, and at first that was about all.

"I'm looking for Sergeant Becker," he said.

"That is I. I am he. Who are you?"

He walked in and stood at the foot of my bunk. He was in
jungle fatigues, but he wasn't a soldier. No rank, no fruit salad
except for that screwy triangular civilian shoulder patch I'd seen
a couple of times aboard ship. He was wearing reflective sun-
glasses; I couldn't see his eyes. I suspected he was a good deal
younger than me, which would have made him eleven. "Arkwright," he said and shot out a hand. I sat up in the bunk and
shook it. It seemed like the thing to do. Then he handed me a
large manila envelope and sat down on the bunk next to mine.
Apparently I was supposed to open the envelope. I opened it
and read it.

"No shit?" I asked.

"No shit," he said.

"What did I do wrong?"

"Not a thing. Your operation of this station's been outstanding, a model for the system. As a matter of fact, we wouldn't mind if you stayed on. We can get you down to our group in Saigon, you can take your discharge there, take some R & R and get assigned to another station. The pay's good and there's a career future in this work. I think you had a little talk with Mrs. Barker about it when you came in. But we're taking over the stations now."

"Who is we? Are you by any chance a spook?"

"I beg your pardon?"

"A spook. I don't mean like a Negro spook. I mean a spook."

"I'm a contract employee of the Defense Department."

"Right. Well, the joint's yours whenever you want it, I guess. I assume you'll want me to break you in on the routine."

"Nope, not really. I just got in a few minutes ago on a Chinook with some new commo equipment. It's waiting to take you and two others whose tours are just about over back to Vung Tau."

"This is a little bit sudden. I hadn't even started a short-timer's calendar yet. Could you just give me a little clue what's going on?"

"Sorry, the details are on a need-to-know basis," Arkwright said. "It's just a new phase of things in the program. I guess you could say you and your people were the pioneers, the groundbreakers. But now it's gotten a little bigger than that. There's a different command and control structure now. Progress. As each of the army personnel rotates out, he'll be replaced by a member of our group. How soon do you think you and the others can get ready?"

"Half hour. That okay?"

"That'll be fine. I'll be in the commo shack."

"I'll join you."

"What for?"

"Oh, nothing. Civilian drops in on my mountain with no warning and takes my command over—I just have this niggling desire to ask someone about it on the radio before I do the shazam. Nothing personal."

"That's not authorized," Arkwright said. "There's a reason. We have a new communications protocol. I told you, new equipment. From this moment, nothing goes out from this mountaintop on the old channels."

"No, one more message goes out, or me and the boys don't leave this here Lazy-D Ranch, *versteh?*"

"You have your written orders and they're very clear. They're the ones you go on."

I'd pulled guard duty last night—it helped cut down the boredom and showed what a regular guy I was—and Adonis had shown up before I'd had all my beauty sleep. I was barefoot and in my skivvies. Adonis was packing a rod. Well, what the fuck—so I couldn't pull my power play with firearms. All I had was my charm.

"All right, let's get down to the nitty-gritty. If you want it that way, are you prepared to toss me and the other guys into your whirlybird at gunpoint? You don't know much about the army, Jack. The name of the game is called Cover Your Ass, and before I vacate this mountain, I want someone I know, love and trust to tell me that's what I'm supposed to be doing instead of my usual tea and scones this morning. Otherwise, you may as well draw that there lethal weapon and make me leave under threat of death."

"I'm prepared to do that."

"You dumb motherfucker." I got up and walked out of the hooch. Six of the troops were busy unloading a sling next to an Air Force Chinook with about ten times the communications equipment we had. I walked past them to the commo shack. I could hear Arkwright marching a few steps behind me. He wasn't yelling anything or shooting. That was a good sign.

Warfield was asleep on a cot next to the commo equipment racks. Besides letting him demonstrate his unswerving round-the-clock devotion to duty, he had the only air-conditioned rack in the unit and he didn't have to mix with the Commie pinkos and the Afro-American junkies. That suited me fine. He rolled over and looked up at me and Arkwright.

"What's going on?" he asked.

"Get me the boat on the horn, please," I said. "Quick like a bunny." I turned around and stared at Arkwright. "You still have objections?"

"No, do what you want. I intend to cover my own ass by filing a report about this incident."

"Great. Don't forget to mention I was in my underwear. Go to it, Warfield. Get me somebody on that horn that I know."

Warfield rolled out of his rack and hit the transceiver switches for a transmission. He started calling for the ship with our standard unit codes.

"Cash Bar, Cash Bar, this is Highball Niner, this is Highball Niner, do you copy?"

"Highball Niner, Highball Niner, this is Cash Bar, go ahead."

I looked at Warfield. "That's Adamek, one of the commo tweets," he said.

"Okay. Slide over." I sat down at the mike. "Cash Bar, this is NCOIC Highball Niner. I have a new arrival and some written orders to turn over command. I'd like verbal confirmation, do you copy?"

"Affirmative, NCOIC Highball Niner. Wait one."

We waited one, two, three, about five minutes. I glared at the spook and the spook glared back at me. Warfield just looked at us both, wondering what the hell was going on. Finally a voice came back over the speakers. It was Lieutenant DerHammer.

"This is XO Cash Bar, go ahead NCOIC Highball Niner."

"Morning, XO. I'd like confirmation on some written orders signed CO Cash Bar dated yesterday."

"Affirmative, NCOIC. Do what the man says. Have a nice flight. See you soon."

"Affirmative, XO. We're down."

"Satisfied?" Arkwright asked.

"Absolutely. Specialist Warfield, please shut these machines down and join the formation in five minutes."

"Formation?" Warfield asked. Fair question; it would be the first one on the mountaintop except for the time the inspector general dropped in.

On the way back to the hooch to get dressed I passed the word to the rest of the troops. "Nothing formal," I said. "Come as you are. But it will be in five minutes and everyone will be there."

I wanted to put on a little show for Arkwright. And I had good news for two of my people; I wanted to break it to them right. Curiosity was enough to bring them out in a reasonable facsimile of five minutes. Just to see if they remembered, I called them to attention and called for the report. Warfield had just made Spec-6 two weeks ago, so he gave the report. Amazingly, everyone was present, although Givens was nodding and weaving a little.

"Stand—at ease!" They remembered how to do that, too. "Listen up! Two of you are rotating out of here a little early, a little birthday present from Sam. Pauli and Ebersoll—we're moving out ASAP, going back to Vung Tau. Personal gear and unloaded M16s only. Steel pots, full ammo clips in your belts. In twenty minutes exactly I want you two and all the rest of you swinging dicks here for one more formation. I'm turning over command of this station to this civilian gentleman who just arrived, Mr. Arkwright. He may not be a GI Number One Sweetie-Pie like me, so watch your ass and try to get along with the man. Any questions?"

No questions.

"Fall out!" They fell out.

Back in the hooch, I stacked up the film cans from Cinema 1131 and put them in a corner far from my bunk. I didn't bother taking any with me; next to dope, the naughtiest thing you could get nabbed with in your kit on your way back to the States was pole 'n' hole flicks, and I didn't intend to slow the process down five seconds even for the chance to keep my favorite romance. I did a short inspection of the arms locker and it seemed that most of the wonderful weapons we'd been gifted with were still there; the spook could have them, too.

None of us had ever been in full battle gear before on the mountaintop, but I had to admit that our three-man detail looked nasty. Largely for show, but also because I didn't want some dickhead to shoot a hole through an important flying part of the Chinook, I had Pauli and Ebersoll port arms and open their breeches.

"Listen up one more time," I said when I took my place back in front of the formation. "Those of us going back to the world, that means rules and lifers and the C.I.D. for a time. My advice is not to do anything that'll fuck it up. If you got funky stuff, drop it in the jungle before we get to Vung Tau, let Charles party with it for a while. Those of you staying on the mountaintop, thanks for your help, and good luck for the rest of your tours. That's it, that's all I got to say. If you're too stupid to listen, fuck you and the horse you came in on. Mr. Arkwright!"

Arkwright stood up and walked across the LZ toward the formation. I wheeled around and saluted him. "The station's yours, sir. Good luck."

"Thank you, sergeant," he said. He didn't salute back—which was proper, im being a civilian—but he offered his hand again. I shook it.

"Detail, move out and board the chopper!"

25

When DerHammer walked in, I was in my rack reading what seemed to be a communal copy of *The Autobiography of Malcolm X*. It was very dog-eared and had a lot of comments in the margins, like KILL WHITIE.

"Interesting?" he asked.

"Yeah, it is. Do you know those suckers don't take any money from the Feds? They sell things to the Feds. The Shabazz bakeries and stuff get government contracts. But they don't take any free money, nothing off the public dole. They run their own schools, have their own community security. They got focus, direction. They're not just drifting, waiting around with their thumbs up their ass for word from the Great White Chief."

"Maybe you can join after you get out."

"I don't think they'd have me, and I'm not the joining type. They're a little too structured for my taste. What's up?"

"The colonel wants to see you."

"Oh, God. Let me guess. I got a bad citizenship mark from that spook."

"I assume you're referring to Mr. Arkwright. Something like that."

"How big a sling is my ass in?"

"Not a huge one, I don't think," he said. I pulled on my fatigue jacket and the mandatory steel-toed factory low-cut shoes we had to wear on the ship in case a helium cylinder dropped on our feet, and started down the corridor with DerHammer.

"I've tried to run a little interference for you," he said as we strolled. "The C.O.'s in a ticklish situation. He needs to stay on the good side of these people. Maybe they'll want him to stay on as liaison with MACV after they take over. If not, he needs to ship out of here with his rectum smelling like a rose or he'll never see his promotion to full bird. Our part of the war's winding down. There'll be a big RIF in the army, a reduction in force. Everybody who wants to stay in will have to drop down a rank or two. Some of the officers in temporary company grades, maybe even field grade, will end up as NCOs. Eyerworth's been a light colonel for four years now. He doesn't want to spend the next five years as a major. He sure as hell doesn't want to retire. So if he gets on your case about what happened, I think mostly he's just going through the motions to show Old Lady Barker he's on her side. I suggest you go through the charade with as little fuss as possible."

"Look. I didn't even want to be in the army, but in your infinite wisdom, you turkeys decided I had all this goddam leadership potential to run your balloon-lofting operation. Was I supposed to just turn it over to the first encyclopedia salesman who asked for it?"

"Don't tell it to me. Explain it to the colonel."

"Thanks."

DerHammer knocked on the colonel's door—hatch, whatever—and there was a call to come in. I thought I'd have to endure it alone, but DerHammer came in with me. Eyerworth was sitting at his desk. I did the saluting thing and he beckoned both of us to take a chair.

"Sergeant Becker," he said to start the formalities. "It seems there was a little problem at Highball Niner when you left."

"A little problem, yes, sir. I was under the impression it got ironed out when I left."

"Well, it wasn't entirely. I understand you violated some verbal orders not to make radio contact with the ship."

I looked at DerHammer for whatever guidance he might be signaling me. The best I could decode from his elfish little face was his approval for me to let it all hang out.

"The way I saw it, sir, I was still in command until the formation that passed on the command. I'm not trying to be picky, sir, but I hadn't had any warning that Mr. Arkwright was coming, and it seemed a little irregular. I just wanted confirmation from channels I was familiar with."

"Mr. Arkwright reports he told you there was a new communications protocol effective at that moment, that nothing more was to go out over the old equipment."

"Yes, he did. He also told me he was taking command and that I and two of my troops were coming back here immediately. And I'd never set eyes on the man before. He wasn't even in my army. You're in my army, sir, and so's Lieutenant Der-Hammer. I wanted to hear it from someone like that."

Eyerworth went into deep thought mode, eyes to ceiling, hands clasped behind neck, lean back in swivel chair, sigh.

"He gave you written orders."

"About the change of command, yes, sir. And there were orders in it for me and two other guys to rotate back here, all fine and dandy. If he'd come out of the sky in an army uniform with some rank, I probably wouldn't have made a fuss. But it just struck me as very irregular, sir, and as long as my old, reliable radio channels were still working, I wanted someone I knew to make it regular. Orders have been garbled and screwed up before. I can't say it any clearer than that, sir. I got five words off the box from Lieutenant DerHammer, and I said over and out and thank you very much and I gave Mr. Arkwright his mountain. Look at the alternative, sir—guys can walk around dressed like Bozo the Clown and take over army facilities just because they know how to run a mimeograph machine."

More deep thought from the Cheese. Then wisdom.

"Granted these people do things a little differently from what you're used to in the army, sergeant, but they've taken over now, and we all have to do things their way. This has caused me some difficulties."

I got hot under the collar and spewed the next part out in a torrent. "Look, sir—I've always expected to catch hell for screwing up or goofing off, but I seem to be catching it here for trying to watch out for my unit and my responsibilities. I was turning army weapons and equipment and the safety of about a dozen army personnel over to this masked man. I may not be stellar career leadership material, but I take my three stripes seriously, and I don't turn over my station until I know for sure that's what I'm supposed to do. And now I'm sitting here, and you're telling me not that you expected more of me, but that you expected less. That's the way I see it, sir, and I think it bites."

"It what?"

"Bites, sir. Bites the hairy big one. NG, Not Good. Number Ten."

"Well. The civilian group is very upset about the incident. I think they'd like to see PFC Becker walking around the ship for the next few days. I don't think it's worth that. Let's just call this a verbal reprimand."

My mouth started to open and my tongue was revving up again when I felt DerHammer's hand on my elbow. I looked his way and he was gesturing me to my feet. I stood up. I saluted. The colonel saluted back. I wheeled and left. DerHammer stayed behind. I staggered around the ship for a while and finally found a deserted corner of the fantail to work myself into a royal piss-off. DerHammer caught up with me about ten minutes later.

"Fuck verbal reprimand," I said. "Fuck the colonel. Fuck you. Fuck you, sir."

"Look, relax, Becker. Verbal reprimand is army for words, like sticks and stones. Nothing in your record. In fact, we're cutting all your orders for your standard chestful of medals and a bit more. I stayed to have a little talk with the colonel. He's not—well, he's not exactly used to people who take their work seriously. He finds you a little hard to understand."

"What is going *on* here? One fucking radio message—"

"Okay, cool out. I believe you used the term *spook,* to which I pretended to take exception. Well, congratulations on your insight. That's what's going on here. The new equipment—they call it squirt stuff. All the information and reports you guys used to broadcast for hours every day, they've started encoding it and squirting it over the air in less than a hundredth of a second each transmission. They're very thrilled over their new little toys and their new program. They want it all to go like clockwork. You got in their way. They felt you compromised their communications integrity. That upset them."

"For Christ's sake, it's only the weather!"

He dropped the volume down a notch. "The reason they've taken over is that they're starting to do some very . . . kinky . . . yeah, kinky things with the weather. There are six forward compartments of computers and equipment I can't even go into now without a chaperone. Don't ask me what they're up to. Personally, I understand what you did and I've managed to get that across to the colonel. That's why you got what was really a pretty puny chewing out. Be thankful and forget it. Stay out of everybody's way for the next week, enjoy your awards ceremony and go home."

"What can spooks do with the weather?"

"Don't ask. I don't exactly know, and what I do exactly know, I'm not supposed to know, and that suits me fine. Let it suit you fine, too. Now, look. There's an officers beach club that serves a nice dinner in town. Borrow somebody's stupid Hawaiian shirt and be my guest there tonight. Get mildly shitfaced, listen to some Vietnamese with electric guitars play Holiday Inn lounge music and be happy. My treat. Launch leaves in an hour."

The club was your standard syntho-Huki-Lau thatched roof dining room and mile-long brass-rail bar with an open-air view to the China Sea, no doubt courtesy Brown and Root Construction, like everything else south of the DMZ. I was still in a first-class snit by the time the food started to come, but I was trying to be civilized. It was also the first time I'd ever been in an officers club, and even in civvies I was certain I stuck out like a sore thumb, with a hundred pairs of eyes labeling me: EM, EM, EM. I remembered the traditional remedies and ordered lots of liquor. I didn't worry about it. Alcohol might get to my balance centers, but it never made me get loud and stupid, the way an airborne captain in jump boots on the other side of the room was cursing at the band. That made me feel a little better.

I'd traveled seven thousand miles to eat a large rare hamburger with Heinz ketchup, the only item on the menu that looked like it had a chance of being adequate to tasty. It was adequate. It was much better than LRPs rations.

"This is swell," I said, with some lying. "Thanks. I appreciate it. I could have done a good job of sulking by myself back on the ship."

"Oh, well, what I neglected to mention in all the excitement today was how the unit's appreciated your running Niner. Yours was just about the only station that didn't give us a lot of headaches."

"People had trouble lofting four balloons a day?"

"And calibrating the equipment and reading the data and making the reports properly. I don't think you have a very clear perspective of the personnel we have to deal with."

"They went to metro school, didn't they?"

"Really, Becker, army education is to education what army music is to music. What to you was probably boring common sense completely baffles most of my NCOICs."

"Yeah. Before I crossed one of her pet spooks, that crone wanted me to join her circus after I got out. I gave it a lot of thought. Made sense. Join the army, learn the balloon trade for civilian life. I used to know a lot of spooks and their kids back in Maryland. They drink too much. Not many Jews in the spook business, either, I think. They're all Wellington G. Baxter, Jr., types. Older versions of Arkwright, I guess. So what's your pathetic story? You don't look like you're exactly hankering to be chief of staff."

"Oh, it's pathetic, all right. I was a schoolteacher in Milwaukee. My principal and I didn't get along very well. He managed to get my exemption yanked. So when I got drafted and there wasn't anything I could do about it, I opted for OCS. I see you didn't."

"I get yelled at and mistreated enough. I didn't see the percentage in volunteering for more. And I'm a really primitive team player."

"You are a good leader, though."

"Of what? Fuckups and junkies? Yeah, the greatest. Sergeant to the stars. Boy, all I ever hear in the fucking army is leadership, leadership, leadership. If they're so queer on leadership, how come they can't lead their way out of a paper bag? You know what leadership is to me?"

"No. I'm on tenterhooks."

"Leadership is being too fucking bored or jaded to be a follower. Following is real boring. Well, apparently I expressed that clearly enough so that even the army made me a leader. Outstanding. Back on the block I'm sure my attitude will take me straight to the top."

"What will you do when you get back?"

"Ha! Wow! I don't know. I haven't given it much thought. Try school again, maybe. I figure six, seven more years I ought to be able to score some kind of degree somewhere. Or maybe I'll try to grapple with some woman again. I never could figure out what that shit was all about to save my ass. For me, it's like drowning but still breathing. Maybe this time I'll check her teeth, see if she's old enough. Or check the bra label. If it says 'Littlest Angel,' that's a tipoff. You married?"

"I have someone back home."

"Sounds like you have her in a long-term boarding kennel."

"It's an arrangement. I don't know what'll happen when this is over. We get along well, though."

We caught the eleven o'clock launch back, got some coffee from the galley and found some breezes up on the bow. I'd stopped the suicide drinking halfway through the evening and managed to soothe down. In fact, I was feeling pretty good. I realized what it was—a civilized evening with an intelligent human being, probably the first one of those I'd had for eight or nine months. DerHammer had talked about the Lutheran college he'd gone to in Minnesota, about books we'd both read, movies we'd enjoyed—*That Man from Rio* was one of them; the first time I'd seen it I hadn't been able to stop laughing. The theaters had been mostly filled each time I saw it, but Der-Hammer was the first person I'd ever met who'd seen it and liked it.

"Where'd you get your low-life streak?" he asked out of the blue. "It's really very strange."

"It's my ruin. Beats the shit out of me. My people are genteel as all hell. They go crazy over the appearances. Had one of those living room museums that was off limits to the whole family. It was just there to be cleaned and reupholstered now and then as far as I could figure. I'm just an atavism, I guess."

"I told you I had an arrangement back home."

"Indeed you did. How is your arrangement, by the way?"

"He's fine."

The waters weren't lapping so loud against the hull that I could have misunderstood.

"Your arrangement's a he." I tried not to put a question mark on it.

"Yes. His name's Warren. He runs a management training department for some department stores. I hope we can get back together again when this is over. That's all I want."

"Why are you telling me this?"

"Shouldn't I?"

"No, you shouldn't. You don't know me from shit. I could be the C.I.D. or worse. This isn't very smart."

"You're not the C.I.D. You're a decent guy, and you've been around. I needed to talk to somebody about it."

"Well, I am a decent guy and I have been around, so don't do that anymore. Don't ever tell this to anybody else, do you understand? You're being self-destructive, and I hate that. What the fuck are you doing in the army?"

"What choice did I have?" He talked as if he were discussing tomorrow's lunch menu or the geography of the South China Sea. I couldn't detect the slightest quaver of nervousness or fear. "If I'd told the army I was gay, I'd never teach again, not in a public school system. I think my principal knew, and I think that's why he messed with my exemption."

"And if the army finds out, you're fucked. Jesus, and I thought I was in trouble with the army today."

"While I'm in, I don't . . . practice."

"Doesn't that get a little lonely?"

"How much practice have you had since you've been in?"

I laughed. "Yeah, but if I do get lucky, I don't get court-martialed and busted just for throwing a nut off. You do. I'm trying to be angry about this. I don't seem to be able to work up much steam over it, but I am angry. You're laying something on me that's dangerous to you."

"I needed to talk. I knew I could talk to you."

"You could have been wrong."

"I wasn't."

"Bully for you." I looked at him and tried to figure what this was all about. Amazingly enough, I didn't think he had the slightest intention of asking me to dance. "Do you think he'll still be waiting?"

"Who, Warren? God, I hope so. He writes me, but he's not

a good letter-writer, and besides that, he worries about the army mails, so he doesn't say very much that's revealing. But he still writes. You don't have anyone?"

"No. Just a couple of screwed-up disasters, the last one of which got me into this catastrophe. I can't believe the worst of it's almost over. But I don't know what's waiting for me back home. That's the funny part. I know everything about the army. I know what the worst it can do to me is, and it looks like I've managed to miss that. The rest of it I've learned to be comfortable with, the regular meals, a rack with squeaky springs. But what'll happen back in the world—I'm almost afraid to go back to it. It's just vague. I have no family to speak of anymore, just three or four people who think I'm completely deranged. They've practically sat *shivah* for me."

"What's that?"

"Jesus, don't they allow Jews in the Midwest? It's what the family does when somebody dies. Now and then they don't wait for the doctor's certificate, like if you end up drafted to Vietnam. And I got no ladies waiting. Not even skills with ladies. I don't know who my friends'll be or what I'll do. Great life I've wandered into. The army's the only thing I'm not scared of, and I hate it like poison, and I'm ashamed to be in it."

"You should re-up," DerHammer suggested. "The army's crazy about you. I wouldn't worry. You're a smart guy. You'll get along when you get out."

"I don't think so. I can't imagine how. You know, I got so fucking depressed when I was at Benning. The Big Dick had just shot all those kids at Kent State. I didn't tell anybody, but I had a buddy, a medic sergeant, he wrote me out a ticket to see a shrink at Womack Hospital. A real jerk. He told me I'd filled out the wrong form and he couldn't work with me. I told him I'd filled out the only goddam form anybody gave me. He asked me if I wanted to get out of the army. I said no. I didn't, not that way. I mumbled something about Kent State, and he said that had nothing to do with me. That was the Ohio National Guard, right? It just sailed right over his head that I had to put on the identical uniform every day. He asked me if I was suicidal. I said no. So he said there wasn't anything he could do for me, get the hell out. So I got the hell out. I felt so much fucking rage for weeks, I wanted to go back down there and smash his rib cage to shit with a baseball bat. So that's how I feel about being in the army, and I'm afraid to leave it. It makes me nervous that it's almost over."

DerHammer poured the rest of his coffee over the side. "I knew a guy like you. He'd been out for a year and he was freaking out. He went to see a psychiatrist. And he yelled at the doctor. He demanded to know why he was a civilian now and a completely free man, but nothing was working right, but he'd hated the army with all his heart and soul and he'd gotten along just fine in it. You know what the psychiatrist told him?"

"No."

"He told him he did well in shitholes."

26

The Weenie was acting up more than usual. Richard wrote me about how his stay at LBJ had worked out and how my brother's buddy Hart had made the *ipso facto* mumbo jumbo. All things considered, I think Richard and Hart had wrestled the Weenie to a draw just before it moved in for the big final lethal barbed thrust; no doubt Richard and the Weenie both came away with bruises and scabs in the appropriate places. Of course after that came Richard's wholly unexpected episode with the Fort Lewis pay clerk, which I thought was just the dandiest fucking thing I'd ever heard, real lightning; I certainly didn't expect it to strike twice when I got to my final pay window. In fact I intended to count my change very carefully in case the word had gone out to make it up from some fuckhead like me by the end of the fiscal quarter.

When my time came to leave the USNS *Taconic* and the Nam (after I got my pitcher took by the information specialist with his 30-pound dry plate Speed Graphic for the hometown paper grippin' 'n' grinnin' with Colonel Eyerworth and Lieutenant DerHammer), I got to fly down to Da Nang in a baby Hughes observation chopper, spooky and dangerous thing, lot of fun, and although I didn't realize it at the time, the Weenie had me in precisely the vulnerable pose where it wanted me. I figured I had everything made in the shade. Technically I had about eighty-four days left in service (I lie—five years and eighty-four days because, again technically, a draftee's minimum burst of two was just the active part of his obligation; everybody Sam caught in the first place owed Sam seven years altogether, two on active, five in a Reserves filing cabinet), and they were booting people out early left and right who came back to the States with that kind of trivial time left. It just wasn't worth it to the army to reassign them; no way could the army get any meaningful work out of people that short and that pissed off. So without thinking what I was doing, I'd managed to work myself up to this steady waking and sleeping fantasy diet of me in comfortable old civvies or entirely naked lying around on a riot of satin pillows with about twenty certifiably post-consent-age honeys stroking my hair (in my fantasy it had grown back already), fanning me and asking me if there was anything lewd and exciting (and forbidden in most states no matter how old they were) that they could do on or for me. (Well, I found myself asking politely, could one of you tie about six little knots in this scarf . . . ?)

So I have to hand it to my last Green Weenie. It was a monster. It must have been waiting for years for this thrust, keeping count of my DO NOT DIVERTs and my sky-chaufferings and all the cutesy things I'd done to lifers here and there. It knew when I'd been sleeping; it knew when I was awake; it knew if I'd been bad or good. Lifer karma, that's what it was, and I'd apparently accumulated a metric shitload of it.

I should have known something was funky when the Pan-Am 727 wasn't bound for a West Coast debark point like Fort Lewis, but for Randolph Air Force Base and then a bus for us army dorks across San Antonio to Fort Sam Houston. All I thought about that was that it would plop me conveniently in mid-America so I could take my back pay and immediately wreak havoc on any geographical sector of the country that appealed to me: Austin, I'd heard, could be nice and freaky if

I didn't feel like a big cross-country trek immediately; when you freaked out in Texas, you *really* freaked out and you had to go to Austin instantly and stay close to U-T, or the indigenous cowboys would just fucking-A blast your brains all over the sagebrush and then get an award from the Texas Rangers. Or Ann Arbor or Berkeley or Marin or Madison—I'd been doing some very careful research about the most bent oases that had sprung up all over the country in my absence, and I intended to sample them all, maybe after a swing back to D.C. to get my Triumph, or maybe not—in my fantasies I seemed to have acquired the mystic secrets of astral projection, like the promises in the Rosicrucian ads in the back of *Parade*. I made Don Juan the Mexican *brujo* look like a paraplegic hitchhiker.

Our green school bus arrived at Sam Houston and pulled up in front of a grand nineteenth-century Spanish stucco monstrosity of a building around eleven in the morning, and a fairly young but clearly lifer-type SFC with the most spectacularly curved cavalry moustache I'd ever seen herded us into a big waiting room with folding chairs, collected all our orders, and told us we'd be called one at a time for personnel in-processing. I nodded off and dreamed of warm moisture and those smells, not perfume—never liked perfume—but just the smells of women as they were. I would be with them soon, in Austin, Madison, Berkeley . . .

I heard my name barked out and I grabbed my kit and diddy-bopped out of the room and toward the office a WAC was pointing to. I sat down in a wooden chair next to another WAC's desk. She was a Spec-4 and had my file open in front of her. She had enormous breasts, not my favorite style, but I made an effort not to fix my eyes on them constantly. She helped—she had a frame and face like an International Harvester Transtar semi.

"Sergeant Becker?"

"Hi. That's me. What's happening?"

She looked at me a little strangely—Jesus, you'd think she'd never met a guy who was getting out of the army before.

"Well, everything seems to be in order with your files. We don't have any slots in any meteorological support units in the Fourth Army, but you wouldn't be doing that kind of work anyway, so we're going to place you with a medical unit here at Fort Sam for your Project Transition time."

I looked at her little wooden desk name triangle. "Specialist Greenough—what's Project Transition?"

She was annoyed. "God, I wish they'd tell you people what's going on back here. You're the third returnee this morning who didn't know about it."

"What is it?"

"It's training. Job training, before you go back to civilian life. You have eighty-two days left on active duty—"

"Oh, FUCK, man! I'm sorry, pardon my French, I've been to a war. Are you trying to tell me I'm not getting out today?"

"No, you're not getting out today."

"UN-FUCKING-BELIEVABLE!" I was on my feet and about twenty other people were craning their necks around and outside their cubicles to see who'd just had the Weenie-reaming.

"It's all right," she cooed, trying to stop the insurrection before any police cars were overturned. "Please sit down. I'll try to explain."

"Oh, yeah, that'll be some try." I sat down, but I was whining. "You mean I got to play soldier for another goddam—what? —three months?"

"Not exactly. Yes and no. Just calm down a little. I know it's not good news. That's why I wish they'd filled you in a little better in Vietnam."

"Oh, that would have helped a lot."

"Listen. It's a new federal program to make sure you get a good start back in civilian life. It says here you weren't employed before you were drafted. If you had been, we'd probably let you out today, because the law gives you your job back. But you weren't, so those returnees with this much active time left, they're putting them in training classes."

"Look, I got skills. I've been to college, great colleges, dozens of semesters. I speak Latin, for Christ's sake. I can go work for my old man or my cousin. I'm not an employment problem."

"It's not for you to determine. You fit the profile. You can take your file up to the warrant officer or up to the major and it's going to come out the same. It's not exactly all for your benefit. The program's a response to a lot of veteran unemployment. That's not good for the country."

"I don't need a civics lesson. I don't believe this."

"Believe it. It's what's happening. Well, you asked."

"What kind of training?"

"At Fort Sam, there's printing technology, machining technology, food service, health care and computer technology. You get your choice."

"What if I want something else?"

"Like what?"

"I don't know—jeez, the last time I was at college I was studying drama."

"We don't have a theater department here. I don't think Project Transition would think that was a good investment."

"Oh, God. Put me down for—what?—yeah, the computer shit, I guess. Oh, God. I'm going to write to my congressman."

"Your congressman probably voted for Project Transition. I'm sorry. Look, San Antonio's not a bad town—"

"Are you kidding? I passed this giant billboard that said *Welcome to Military America*! That's not exactly what I was looking forward to."

"San Antonio's a very nice town. Project Transition's a pretty loose kind of duty. You make your company's breakfast formation and then go to the training center and that's it for the day. Your off hours are your own. A lot of guys have found that it was a good way to get acclimated to the States again."

"They have? You have testimonials?"

"Try to make the best of it. For the next couple of days you'll be doing some more personnel and medical processing, and then you'll take some aptitude tests, but I'm sure with your background, you'll be able to get into the computer classes. Here's the unit you're assigned to. Report there by five tonight. That's it."

"Oh, joy."

I wandered in a daze around the fort, bumping into the wooden signposts that aimed me toward the 73rd Medical Support Battalion, my new home away from home. I got there around three, plopped my duffel bag in the hallway and wandered into the orderly room. Most of the people I saw were dressed in medical whites, but the first sergeant, a thin black somewhere on the high side of forty, was in dress greens and looked sharp without looking terrifying. Infantry lifer NCOs had to look terrifying; it was the only way they could show their job skills when they weren't actually ripping flesh in combat. Specialists like this one, a master medic who could probably perform an appendectomy on you in the woods without complications, didn't have to look like they were about to bite you to prove their career expertise. I handed him my paperwork.

"Okay, Sarge, looks like you're here for a little Project T. I have a permanent party and they pretty much run the company. You don't mess with them and they won't mess with you. Unless something big happens, you're exempt from inspections and CQ. Just keep your bunk clean and make sure you show up to your classes. Got any questions?"

"Yeah. Is there any way out of this?"

"Nope. How's that for an answer? Reason I'm so quick with it is 'cause you're not the first one to ask. Just about everybody bunkin' down in your wing of the barracks asked me the same thing. You have a privately owned vehicle?"

"No, First Sergeant."

"Well, if you get your hands on one, make sure you get it registered with the provost marshal and then register it with me. Any other problems, see me, and I'll see you at morning formation at seven. Right?"

"Right, Top."

The barracks was new, a two-story battalion-sized yellow cinder-block job, solid but nondescript, more like a state college dorm than any barracks I'd seen. My wing of it, the headquarters company wing, had two-bunk rooms for all the ranks, no Zoo, even though I had enough rank now to be above all that. A couple of off-duty Spec-4 medics lounging around in the hall pointed me to an empty room and helped me draw bedding for it. The locker was pretty solid and might even keep my stuff safe after I bought a good combination lock at the PX. I made my bunk, closed the door and fell asleep in my jungle fatigues.

I spent the next day roaming around the main hospital building from clinic to clinic getting all sorts of tests, most routine, a few special jobs at the tropical medicine clinic to see what weird trypanosomes I might be playing host to. There was never any question about waiting around for any of the results. These people just wanted my fluids and then wanted me to disappear. I was mildly cooperative because most of the tests would be part of my discharge physical.

I ate the aptitude tests up with a spoon. Apparently they were designed for a returning horde of sublingual and subliterate veterans. Almost all of them involved mentally folding and unfolding and spatially rotating geometrical patterns on paper to see which templates could actually produce which three-dimensional objects. The tests seemed to have despaired of the right to ask any questions in printed English. The one section which strayed into this heady atmosphere would present a sentence like:

Thomas Jefferson was the third President of the United States.

and then immediately follow up with:

The third President of the United States was:
a. James Madison
b. James Monroe
c. Thomas Jefferson
d. George Washington

and I suppose the spooky part of it was that they probably wouldn't have bothered if everybody got them all right. I spent a lot of the time wondering to myself what the highest achievements of a civilization highly skilled in mentally folding and rotating paper shapes would be, what their ballets and formal music would be like, what the conversation would be like at a party.

On my fourth day there, the morning formation was coming to a close when Top called out my name. "Yo!" I grunted.

"Got somethin' for you. Catch." He threw a jingling little manila envelope over the heads of the first squad. I managed to catch it. I opened it up. It was a set of dog tags.

"I have dog tags," I said.

"Been some kind of change. Check 'em out," he said and dismissed the formation.

Everything seemed to be the same, my service number, name. I pulled out the dog tags I was wearing and compared the two. Then I saw it. The one I was wearing said my blood type was A POS. The one Top had tossed me said B POS. I just stood there looking at the two while everyone drifted away to the parking lot or toward the hospital complex.

"What's wrong?" asked one of the medics in my wing who'd helped me get squared away.

"My blood type just changed," I said.

"Oh, yeah. That happens a lot."

"What do you mean, that happens a lot? Blood types don't change. I don't have to be no fuckin' hematologist to know that."

"No, I mean the blood lab catches a lot of wrong typing on old dog tags. I think the people who do it at the reception stations are drunk or something."

"How do I know this new one's right?"

He thought about that for a second. "You don't. I guess if you want, you could go off-post and pay a private hospital to do it. Or you could learn to do it yourself. We did it in college."

"But if this new one's right, that means I just spent ten months in a war zone with the wrong goddam blood type on my dog tags. That's a little disconcerting."

"Nobody dies in battle, Sarge. In the army, you die statistically. So—you lucked out. You want to go for some coffee?"

I stood there with my finger up my nose for the longest time. "Well, yeah, I guess. I'm supposed to start my classes . . ."

"Tell 'em you got lost. You've had a jarring episode. They'll understand."

27

It was great to be among intellectuals again. In the barracks
nearly everyone, permanent party and Project Transition, could
read. At class my stellar test scores had been rewarded; I was
in the computer program learning to keypunch. The amazing
thing about Mr. Morris, our instructor, was that he didn't seem
bored. He wasn't exactly thrilled to explain data fields, the Hol-
lerith code and gang punches, but it never seemed to bore him.
The mark of the retired, recycled lifer was written all over him
and that made him perfect for his job. In a real school with a
real teacher, there's always the possibility that if enough of the
class bursts into tears or tries to hang themselves from the
rafters out of boredom, teach will eventually get the hint and
spice up the presentation. With a military instructor, there's no
hope. There's the material to be covered, and if the class that
month turns out to be completely deaf or experimentally composed of all scarecrows or kangaroos, it makes no difference—
same material, covered exactly the same way it was covered the

last three hundred times. He reminded me of one of my drill sergeants during the class on the Code of Conduct, how we were supposed to behave as prisoners of war. "You will accept no payroll," he told us. That made sense, except that I'd never heard of prisoners of war being offered a salary. I looked in the trainee's field guide and found what he was talking about —parole. Morris was about on that level; six months ago the Fort Sam retiree career counselor had crammed all this shit into his pickled head and now he was puking it back at us verbatim. As for the pregnant promise of an enounter with a real computer, it wasn't that kind of deal. The classes, about forty of us to a section, were held in World War I single-story wooden barracks just this side of the wrecker ball, with folding chairs and a blackboard and about sixteen ancient gray IBM keypunch machines against the wall. We were all going to be presented to the civilian world as bona fide data entry specialists, which I gathered was to computers what truffle-hunting pigs are to *haute cuisine*. It was worse for me. I'd finish each punching assignment in ten minutes while Morris had to help half the others get theirs together for the rest of the afternoon, but none of us could leave, so I'd turn the printer off on my station and punch lurid, smutty letters on a deck of cards to Richard, with instructions to take them to his college computer center and ask for a deck read. (I found out later that he did, and when the filth started high-speed printing in front of the computer supervisor, Richard was banished from the facility forever.) I sat next to a smiling white junkie named Wermoth, from Detroit, who kept inviting me to a shooters' apartment in town, but I always declined as politely as I could. He stood about 6'1" and weighed around 105—with just the tiniest amount of peeling, he'd make a great skeleton. Once on a smoke break he talked to me not so much about what he liked about smack, but about the needle, about carbureting, pushing and pulling the blood into and out of the syringe, mixing it with the smack, pumping it back into his vein, and I thought, *They're letting this guy out soon? They drafted this guy in the first place? Jesus . . .* But he had a good soul, what was left of it; he had the answer to Project Transition and all he really wanted to do was share it with me.

Morris let us out of class early on Friday and I wandered

back to the barracks and read a copy of *The Light* on my bunk.
I thought about the night and the weekend and decided to
spend it alone in my room in an orgy of self-loathing. After a
while I heard some of the medics talking out in the hall. Ney,
the one who'd helped me through my blood change crisis, walked
in with a hemostat clipped to the hem of his medic's blouse. It
seemed to be the style among the lower ranks in the unit. I had
visions of them going off to a workday that consisted of long
lines of soldiers with bursting veins and arteries.

"How's computer class?" he asked.

"Oh, God . . ."

"Sorry. Decker, right?"

"Becker. With a B. B for Bravo. Bravo Echo Charlie Kilo
Echo Romeo. Yeah."

"How was Vietnam?"

"Stupid," I said. "I don't mean profoundly stupid or histor-
ically stupid. Just stupid. Like a Jerry Lewis movie."

"Yeah. Most of us are going soon. What did you do there?"

"Sent up weather balloons. Sorry. That's just the truth."

"When do you get out?"

"Two, three months. If I don't kill myself first."

"Hey, we're medics. See us first. We got lots of good ways to
do it. Look, there's a party in town tonight. You want to come?"

"A party?" I was stunned, actually. Unless you're a lifer pig,
there aren't any parties in the army. At least there hadn't been
for me. Nowhere to throw them. Nobody to invite. "A party at
someone's house?"

"Somebody's apartment. Lynch, one of the medics. He's going
to Vietnam in a week. Come on. You'll have a good time."

"I don't think I even remember what the concept is. But
thanks. Yeah, I'd like to come. Look—I don't have any civvies.
I don't want to go to a party in jungle fatigues."

"Got any money? I got a car. I'll slide you by the PX. Or
Neiman-Marcus, whatever. Get yourself a pair of jeans and a
shirt, bam! You're in business. Oh. I've been delegated to ask
you—you're not a cop, are you?"

"Is there going to be lawbreaking at this party?"

"We thought maybe you'd be an accomplice."

"Well, okay then. I don't think I'm a cop."

"That's good enough for us. We'll take a chance. We're real

thrill-seekers. Shit, shave, shower and shine and I'll be here or in the parking lot."

Ney had your basic impoverished enlisted transportation, an ancient, rusted-out little Fiat—somebody told me once that stands for "Fix It Again, Tony"—but the engine, the steering and the radio worked and it bounced us over to the main PX where I managed to scare up a pair of tennis sneakers, a black and red striped V-neck shirt and a pair of jeans that said and smelled "purchased within the last ten minutes" all over them; they were so stiff it was hard to walk in them. I wore them out of the store and spent the ride through San Antonio (it was the first time I'd been off-post) cutting all the tags off the clothes.

"How come this guy lives off-post?" I asked.

"He's married. His wife's name's Julie. She's real nice. She teaches typing at a business school in town. Here."

I looked over and he was handing me his hemostat with a nice fat number clipped to the tip. Another mystery of the universe solved. I lit it under the dashboard and took a pull off it and handed it back. It reeked of Rio Grande moisture. It was very good.

"What's your story?" I asked.

"Me? What do you mean?"

"What's the grat-grandson of the Marshal of France doing in a place like this?"

"Who?"

"Never mind. What are you doing in the army?"

"Just lucky, I guess. My lottery number came up. You a lottery winner?"

"No. They drew the first lottery the week I was drafted. Some asshole with a newspaper was walking around the reception station asking us if we wanted to see what our numbers would have been. It wasn't me, but somebody jumped the fucker and punched his lamps out."

"Did you look at your number?"

"Nope. Didn't have a smidgen of curiosity then or now. It'll still be on microfilm at the library if I ever get consumed with desire to know. Maybe I'll peek the day before I die."

"They're talking about going all-volunteer now," Ney said. "Too late for us, but it's a nice idea."

"What? An all-lifer army? Look, I sure as fuck don't like being here, but the idea actually fills me with horror."

"Why?"

"Look at you. Look at me. We can read a book. We've been to the movies. We know that Canada's up and Mexico's down. Would you rape a bunch of Buddhist nuns and then cook 'em and eat 'em 'cause some lifer told you to? Would you cut off their ears and send them back to your sweetie as a souvenir?"

"I like to think not."

"That's the only fuckin' saving grace of this whole war—it was fought by civilians in the ranks. You take every horror story out of this fuckin' war, like that Calley asshole, and it's a lifer story. Lifers doin' lifer-shit. Lifers doin' what comes naturally to lifers. Every good thing that happened or every abomination that didn't happen, it was 'cause pissed-off, disgruntled civilians with a *soupçon* of college who were temporarily in uniform were there and watching and taking notes, and they didn't give a fuck about what their rank would be in five years. It kept the lifers on a short leash. I can't get enthused about an army of nothing but lifers who got no place else to go. They'll rape hydrants and bugger dwarves all over the world. And that's if we're lucky and they send most of 'em to some more little adventures in the third and fourth and fifth worlds. If we're not lucky, they'll post 'em all stateside, and they'll start getting ideas about us."

Ney guided the steering wheel with his knee for a few seconds while he applauded enthusiastically.

"Thank you, thank you," I said graciously. "Now that I'm almost a much-decorated Vietnam veteran, I'm planning to run for office, and I'd very much appreciate your vote."

"You really think all that shit?"

"I know that shit. War's nothing but dwarf-buggering. The lifers are always deranged to begin with—cocksuckers who *want* to be combat career people; what the fuck you expect of people like that?—and even the temporary help gets silly ideas. It's infectious. It's a party. Nobody's watching, and they give everybody loaded guns. What do you think goes on in a deal like that? The only thing you can hope for is something to make it a little better than the standard version. That's you and me. Civilians. Take a bow."

"Hadn't thought about it like that. You got my vote. Here. Smoke this."

The apartment development was about six miles from post, about nine three-story bunkers with some scrawny mandatory bushes and trees planted around the parking lots. It was around dinnertime and a lot of the conflicting smells were laden with chili peppers; I realized I was hungry with a vengeance. We parked in front of one of the bunkers and headed up to the third floor. Ney knocked and in a couple of seconds some locks unclicked and the door opened. A woman in jeans and a simple blue sweater let us in. She was tall, maybe a hair taller than I was, with light brown hair done up in a bun. She wore round wire-rim glasses.

"Julie, this is—hey, you got a first name?"

"No."

"Oh, okay. This is Becker. He's new in the unit. This is Julie Lynch. Where's Paul?"

"He's in the shower. Hi," she said to me. Ney walked over to the stereo and started hunting through the records.

I held up my bag with my jungle fatigues. "Listen, could I put these in a closet or something?"

"Sure," she said and took them from me. "You a medic?"

"No. I send up weather balloons."

"How'd you get in the unit?"

"I'm getting out of the army soon, so I have to be trained for a civilian job skill."

"Oh. Project Transition. What are you going to be when you grow up?"

"Computer keypuncher! It turns out I have a real aptitude for it."

"Have you eaten dinner?"

"No. I didn't know if there was going to be food here or what. Ney just hauled me out of the barracks."

"Spaghetti. It's almost ready. I like your jeans. How old are they?"

"Half hour. I'm tempted to spend an hour sitting in a hot bathtub with bleach. I heard women do that to get theirs to fit right."

"Don't bother. I don't mind the swishing noise when you walk. There'll be a lot of music and people talking. Nobody'll hear it."

People started drifting in not long afterwards and I found a corner and devoured a few plates of spaghetti. I'd seen a lot of the medics before. Some of them brought dates. A couple of them seemed to be one another's date. Two or three of the ladies could have been young WACs. Every other arrival brought a six-pack of beer, mostly Oly. It was a pretty congenial crowd. Ney had the music concession and was playing a lot of Grateful Dead and other blues for White Folk. I was playing wallflower mostly, but after a while one of the suspected WACs plopped onto the couch next to me and started up a pretty spritely conversation. Her name was Denise and she wasn't a WAC, it turned out. She was a civilian employee at the base hospital. She had that sort of pom-pom girl personality I thought most adult women shed when they got out of high school.

"You don't seem terribly happy," she said.

"I guess I'm not, terribly. Sorry."

"Don't apologize. What's the problem?"

"I thought I was out of the army last week. I was mistaken."

"Oh, dear. Where are you from?"

"D.C. Just outside it, Maryland."

"You're a long way from home. How do you like Texas?"

"This is the first time I've seen any of it. It looks remarkably like Maryland."

"You haven't been out in the hill country or anything? Gee, you really ought to. You'd like it."

"I'm just sort of trying to get through the next couple of months, just hanging on. My enthusiasm for that kind of thing—"

"Well, get it back. You are almost out, aren't you?"

"Yeah, I guess so."

"You guess so? Don't you know when you get out?"

"Seventy-seven days."

"Oh, then I guess you do know. What are you? Specialist?"

"Sergeant, three-striper."

"Oh. I wouldn't have guessed. Nobody here's an NCO. NCOs and draftees usually don't mix very well."

"I'm just a draftee. I went to you-know-where. They give out rank pretty quick out there."

"How was it?"

"Marginally endurable."

I heard some kind of commotion start up in the kitchen. "Oh, hot navz! Hot navz! C'mon, let's go!" She pulled me off the couch by the arm and dragged me across the living room into the kitchenette. There were about five or six people standing over the range all yelling, "Hot navz! Hot navz!"

"What—uh, what is going on here?"

"Hot navz!" Denise squealed. "Watch!"

I squeezed my head through some shoulders. Somebody had spilled about eight or nine reefer roaches on the range top and was carefully arranging them on the flat side of a big blunt butter knife. Then he put another knife like it over the roaches like a sandwich—these, I guessed, were the navz. The guy held the knives by their handles with an oven mitt over the gas burner until the blades started to glow red hot. Then smoke started to leak out from the edges of the sandwich, and he pulled the knives away and held them about chest high in front of us. Six or seven noses descended over the scorched knives and started sucking up the smoke. "Get down! Get a whiff!" Denise yelled. I did. Everybody was very excited about the whole thing. Back east we just used to throw the roaches away. I was mildly impressed. When they'd caught their breath again, people kept jumping up and down yelling, "Hot navz, hot navz!"—even the medics who didn't otherwise have Texas accents.

I wandered away from the ritual with the start of a mild buzz on and headed for the john in the back bedroom hallway. The door was closed, so I leaned against the wall and waited. The bedroom door across the hall from me was half open. I heard Julie's voice and Lynch's coming from inside. Lynch's was loud; Julie's was trying to keep her side of things down.

"Goddam it, you're going to go there and like it! They'll take care of you! I don't want you staying here!"

"I don't see why I have to live there. I don't know anybody there," Julie was saying.

"You know my folks."

"Barely. I barely know them. I'm just going to feel weird moving in with them. I know they said it would be all right—"

"Look, it's going to save us a lot of money we'll need when I go back to school! And if you have a kid when I get back, we'll need that money! You're going. I'll help you pack before I leave. Stop giving me shit about it!"

"I don't know anybody in Arizona. I have friends here. I have a job here."

"You'll make friends there and you'll get a job there."

"It'll be like living back at home with my folks, only worse. They won't even be my folks."

"They're your folks now."

"I don't need new parents. I want to live with you or I want to live by myself. I don't want to go."

"What, you want to screw around while I'm gone?"

"That's not it! That's not fair!"

"Fuckin' little whore!"

The bathroom door opened and Ney walked out. He looked at me. I shrugged.

"Yeah, they go at it a lot like that," he muttered. "Nobody knows quite what to do about it. He's got a real shitty temper and it's getting worse now that he's leaving. He's actually a pretty nice guy, but I guess some people are just always going to be like that. Well. The plumbing's yours."

The beer ran out about an hour later and I volunteered to buy if somebody'd help me fly. Julie said she'd drive us to a Seven-Eleven in the neighborhood and we went out to her car, a little cream-colored Dodge Dart a couple of years old with a red enlisted Fort Sam sticker on the bumper. Its automatic shift made that kind of lurching, indecisive grind everything from Chrysler always seemed to make, as if the driver punched in what he wanted to do and then the transmission mulled it over for a few seconds to see if it was a wise idea.

"I saw you talking to Denise," Julie said. "She's a good friend of mine."

"I don't think it's a mate for life. I ain't too cheerful these days, and she's one of your more upbeat personalities."

She chuckled. "I know. She's really a child. She's funny. But I think she likes you. She told me. She thinks you're cute."

"Cute. Oh, boy. I feel like ten pounds of shit in a five-pound bag. Does she wear contacts?"

"She has funny tastes in men. I think that's why she likes working at the hospital. Thousands of them parade in front of her desk every week. She sees something she likes, she turns on the charm. It's like a supermarket for her. She's a farm girl. On Tuesday nights she still gets decked out like Dale Evans and goes square dancing; you ought to see her. She went off to college in Kingsville and told me she was astounded how easy it was to get a man into bed. I guess on the farm she'd picked up the idea it was difficult. Maybe it is out there."

"What are you going to do after Paul leaves?"

She pursed up a little and sighed. "I don't know. We're having trouble about that. Maybe you heard. Half the party probably did. We've been hassling over it for months."

"I didn't mean to overhear."

"It's not your fault. Paul doesn't mind putting on a show, I guess. I can't stand it. It's just a big strain. It was a strain being married in college and now it's a bigger strain trying to keep afloat with Paul in the army. I should have gotten pregnant before his number came up."

"That's not a great reason to have a kid."

"I want to have some kids anyway. It wouldn't have been that bad a reason. We would have had another set of hassles instead of this one. You really don't have a first name?"

"David," I said. "I can't remember the last time people called me by it on a regular basis."

"Here's the Seven-Eleven, David. Let's get some beer."

I drove on the way back (on a Maryland license that had been dead for about a year, but why tell her?) while she wrestled with the top of some kind of pickle jar. When she finally got it open, she held up a little green wrinkly thing that reeked of vinegar.

"What's that?"

"Jalapeño. Try one."

I thrust my teeth at it and bit down. "Christ!" I almost lost countrol of the car. "What the fuck was that? Give me some beer! Some beer!"

She was laughing as she reached down and popped open a Lone Star and handed it to me. I sloshed down a third of it.

"Local snack," she explained.

"I'd like to meet the first fuckhead who ate one of those and told his friends it was edible. That's sick."

Her parking spot was gone by the time we got back and I found another one a couple of buildings down. We got the bags out of the car, locked it up and started up the walk. I held back a little and she looked at me.

"Hey. I just wanted to say before we got back inside—I'm sorry for your troubles."

She laughed a little, at herself. "Thank you. I love Paul, I guess. I just—nobody ever tells you what a grind it is trying to live with another person. In school they teach you to cook and make dresses from patterns."

"We learned how to make little DC electric motors and a lamp."

"That'll be a big help, too, I'm sure." We started to walk again. There were some little Tex-Mex kids, jet-black-haired little boys and girls riding little fat-tired Schwinns in circles under a street lamp.

"You're not married or anything?"

"Or anything."

"Well. Have some fun with Denise. What a terrible thing for me to say! Yes. What do you guys say down in the locker room? Get a little, and then take your discharge and go home."

"Wow. I'm always blown away by you heavy sisterhood-type women. Can you loan me some chloroform?"

"No. Work it out for yourself. Maybe you'll both discover true love. Here. Have another jalapeño."

28

A warrant officer pointed me down the hallway to Denise's office. I imagined the building and the offices were just as they were when Black Jack Pershing was mounting his punitive expedition against Pancho Villa. Denise didn't see me walk up to her desk.

"Goodness! Hello, there, soldier. Where are your medals?"

"I don't like to blind people. How are you?"

"Well, fine, I guess. What can I do for you-all?"

"It's a personal matter. Got a minute?"

"Ten. Twenty. Pull up a chair."

"Well, it's like this. I had so much unexpected fun at the party—"

"You couldn't prove it by me."

"I felt compelled to play things close to the chest. Since I got sent to Project Transition, I've invested heavily in being really bummed out, and I wasn't prepared to give all that up without a good reason. Anyway, in light of all that surprise mirth I had at the party, I've decided to take your advice and make some brief incursions into the Lone Star State. I thought you might want to serve as my guide and native bearer."

"That sure sounds mighty appealing. Where were you planning to go?"

"I don't know. It has to be out in the open with clear night skies away from the city. The paper says there's going to be a good comet visible this weekend. I wanted to camp out and see it."

"What for?"

"I can't answer that until I've seen it. I've never seen one before. I'll tell you after I've seen it. Want to come?"

"When?"

"I've wangled a three-day pass. Apparently there'll still be a future for me in computers if I miss my class Monday. So I figured I'd go wherever it is I'm going tomorrow night, Friday, and come back Monday night. Special Services rents all these real cheap tents and camping equipment, about five bucks for a whole weekend safari."

"Just you and me?"

"You can bring a friend if you want, as long as it's a woman. I got to tell you, I'm real tired of being around men. If you want to bring another man, I'll just go see the comet all by myself."

"Well, that's certainly out front. Actually, I had plans with Julie this weekend. Nothing special, but we were going to get together. You know Paul's gone."

"Yeah, I heard. Tell her to come along. That would be fine."

"Really? I'll bet. Should I bring wet suits and whips?"

"I beg your pardon?"

"Just kidding. You know where it would probably be real nice? Padre Island, the national seashore down by Corpus Christi. It's probably still a little too cold to do much swimming, but the camping would probably be great, hardly anybody there, and the skies don't get any clearer. How's that sound?"

"Great, Bwana says. Look, here's the catch. I ain't got no car."

"Oh, I have a car. You can even drive it if you want. I hope you like it real straight and flat."

"Sounds divine. You like to camp?"

"I guess I'll find out. I think Julie's more the camping type, but I can be a sport. You ain't going to do anything fiendish to us when you get us alone in the dunes, are you?"

"Not without written permission. You don't know anybody with a telescope, do you?"

"This sounds like it's going to be a real thrill-packed weekend. I think my brother's got one he doesn't use anymore. I'll see what I can do. I'll call Julie tonight and see if she wants to go. I think I can get Monday off."

"I'll reserve the camping stuff. See ya."

The next night after class Denise picked me up in her little Pontiac muscle car outside the barracks and drove to Special Services, where I hauled out two tents, three sleeping bags, two Coleman lanterns, a Coleman two-burner stove, mess kits and a whole raft of other shit we'd probably never use unless the Ruskies dropped the eggs over the weekend. I crammed everything into her trunk and jumped in the front seat. We drove out the main gate and headed down the commercial avenue toward Julie's apartment.

"Look in the back seat," she said.

"Far out!" There was a battered and primitive Sears-style telescope and tripod on the floor. "I got the weather report for Corpus Christi over the weekend—fair night skies, sunshine, temperatures in the mid-to-high sixties."

"I brought my bathing suit," she said. "Maybe I can work myself up for a plunge."

"Well, I got some cutoffs. If you've got the balls—figuratively speaking, of course—I'll give it a whirl. Is there anything nasty in those waters?"

"Sharks, but I don't think they'll be expecting Texans this month. And cabbageheads."

"What are those?" I asked.

"Sort of like Portuguese men-o-war, but I don't think they sting much. They just sort of look ugly and writhe around on the beach. Kids like to hang out on bridges and drop rocks through 'em as they float by. It's a beautiful beach, hundreds of miles of it all the way down to Mexico."

"Are you from there?"

"Inland some. Went to school in Kingsville not too far from there. The King Ranch is all around there. You don't venture on there without permission. It's like its own sovereign little country—heck, I guess it's bigger than most countries. They say they just shoot trespassers and bury 'em or not as they feel like it. They never report it or anything."

"Nice guys. Don't forget to point the signs out to me if I miss them."

"You have a gun?"

"A what?"

"Gun. A pistol. Rifle, shotgun, something."

"I didn't know it was that kind of party."

"Well, you got two women with you. What are you going to do for protection?"

"I take it you don't mean from the two women. You mean like from passing strangers, Charlie Manson, that sort of thing."

"Well, yeah. You never know."

"Look. Up to now, except in designated combat zones, I've sort of managed to live by my wits, and it's seemed to have worked out pretty well so far. I'm bringing along a fiendish-looking Air Force survival knife in a buckskin sheath. How's that?"

"Well, you can use my gun if you need one."

"Uh—what are you, uh, packing?"

"Here." She reached into her purse and pulled out a Colt Cobra revolver. I stifled an impulse to scream and took it from her. I found the release spring and swung out the cylinder— five chambers loaded; the hammer had been resting on an empty chamber. I rearranged it that way when I closed the cylinder and put it back in her purse. It was not, as they say back east, a lady's gun.

"No insult meant, but you can use that thing?"

"Around here, most people I know can. Don't you like guns?"

"Actually, I sort of do. They make neat noises and blast the living shit out of soda cans and pieces of paper. I just don't like the idea of aiming them at humans."

"Sometimes you have to."

"This has happened to you often?"

"No, not to me, but it happens."

"Okay, it happens and we've got the right piece for the occasion. I'm loose. On with the picnic."

We parked in front of Julie's apartment and went upstairs. She opened the door and we went inside. The living room was filled with cardboard moving boxes marked *kitchen, bedroom* and *bathroom* with a heavy black marker.

"Hi," she said. "Sorry about the disaster. The movers are coming in a few days. Thank God the army pays moving expenses, at least. They sure don't pay for jack-shit else."

"Hi," I said. "Glad you're coming along."

"Is this going to be a spectacular comet, or what? I mean, do we get any guarantees?"

"Beats the shit out of me," I said. "I've never gazed on one of these wonders before. The newspaper says it's sort of a standard, medium-size one. It's called Larimer-Dixon, or Shapiro-Mendez or something like that. It cruises through the neighborhood once every thirty thousand years. I just got this feeling I might get upset afterward if I missed it."

"Yeah, I can understand that. Well, let me get my stuff. Denise, are there any snakes there?"

"Can't promise not. We're wearing boots. You ought to do the same."

"Okay."

Denise seemed to get a charge out of me doing the driving, so I got behind the wheel and followed her directions out of town and around the circumferential to 281 south. She was right about straight and flat; half the time I was cruising along somewhere between seventy and seventy-five and the Pontiac just hummed. Off to the right and left of the highway every few miles I could see huge flame balls of gas rig burn-offs. Julie spread out in the back seat and she and Denise started passing a bottle back and forth.

"What is that?" I asked.

"Want some?" Denise asked.

"Not until I know what it is. The last time I swallowed an unidentified Texan object it almost scorched my tongue out."

"Mescal. Look. See the worm at the bottom?"

"Yuch. What's that?"

"Agave worm. It lives on the cactus they squeeze this shit out of. When you kill the bottle, you eat the worm."

"Right. *You* eat the worm. Jesus, you people are savages."

"You'll see. Gives you magical powers. It says so on the label. Want a snort?"

"Oh, fuck, sure." I took the bottle and gulped down a quan-

ROBERT MERKIN

tity. It was good—something about it tasted a lot better, or a lot less bad, than most hard liquor. Down in my stomach a few seconds later something burning gripped and shook my frame.

"Here. Bite the lemon."

"Oh, I remember this part from the movies. Where's the salt?"

"Here it is. Stick out your hand." She dumped some salt on my palm and I tongued it up and then bit into a cut lemon half. The mouth, tongue, throat, stomach and torso sensations, from mescal to salt to lemon, made me feel like a wino getting beaten in an alley by street punks with baseball bats, but in a pleasant way, as if an adult theme park had designed a ride around an experience like that. I thought about it for a few seconds and then ordered another round. It seemed very regional. I felt as if I were starting to fit in. Maybe it was time to borrow the Cobra and shoot passing jackrabbits.

I stopped for gas in a tiny little town on the highway about midway to Corpus Christi. No one was at the pumps, so I went into the little restaurant and went up to the cash register at the bar, which was heavily populated by prototypical shitkickers.

"Hi," I said to the lady behind the bar. "I'd like to get some gas."

The woman smiled and began speaking to me in German. That just sort of knocked me for a loop, and I would have stood there like a wax exhibit for the rest of time if the cowboy on the stool nearest me hadn't volunteered to translate for me. "Just pump what you want," he said—and he sounded just like Tex Ritter, at least. "You can pay now or after if you want." Then he turned to the woman and repeated the terms of the transaction to her in German. I pulled a five-spot out of my jeans and put it on the bar. She seemed to accept it as legal tender. "*Danke schön*," I said.

"*Bitte*," the lady said with a broad smile. As I walked out again, I paid closer attention to the small talk at the tables. Everybody was speaking German.

"Bunch of cow-people speaking German in there," I muttered after I'd pumped the gas and driven off. "Is there something I should know about this trip or that stuff I drank?"

"Oh, no," Denise said. "There are lots of towns like that down here—New Braunfels, everybody's German. You can grow up

310

and die and never have to use ten words of English. They have great Oktoberfests."

"Okay, if you say so. It just caught me a little asleep at the wheel, that's all."

"See? You're gettin' the grand tour of Texas you asked for. A surprise at every turn." She knocked back another belt of mescal and we cruised on into the night.

Just when the signs for Corpus Christi started to get thick, Denise hit my arm and told me to hang a left. "Isn't that the wrong way?" I asked. "That's east, or north, or something."

"Nah, let's go to Mustang Island. We'll skip Corpus and stay away from the naval base, go across on the ferry to Port Aransas. You like shrimp?"

"Sure."

"That's all they got there is shrimp. If you needed a steak, you'd starve to death." A few minutes later we were driving over a huge cantilever bridge over Nueces Bay and then, after a dock and refinery town, back onto open highway through flat farm country again. About fifteen minutes later we were at the far side of Aransas Pass lined up behind three other cars for the last ferry to the island shrimping town across the bay. It was a little before ten o'clock. The ferry docked on our side a few minutes later. We got out of the car on the ferry and I looked up at the sky to see if the comet was there, but there was a bright high moon, some clouds and a lot of spotlights on the ferry's cabin; the deck of the ferry was like a huge cube of daylight sailing across the dark surface of the bay. The salt air wrapped around me. The ferry motor gurgled along without disturbing the ride. The other drivers and passengers had walked to their own sections of the rail and weren't making any noise.

"Whoa," I moaned. "This is wonderful. I didn't know we were going to take a ride like this."

Suddenly Julie stiffened, arched out on her tiptoes and pointed at the waves. "Look!"

I followed her arm and strained my eyes to see what she was pointing to on the dark water, and then I saw it and it sucked my breath from my mouth—dolphins, porpoises, five, six of them leaping along in arcs parallel to the ferry. Their wet skins sparkled dark in the moonlight as they leapt.

"My God, I thought they only did that in engravings," Julie

whispered. "Have you ever seen that before? Hey! Are you okay?"

No, not really, I wasn't okay. I was mesmerized. It was the most wondrous sight I'd ever seen, and the beasts just kept leaping again and again, higher and higher, pacing the boat. It was too dark and their leaps were too short to see a whole dolphin clearly and in any detail all at one time, but you put little parts, aspects of them together leap after leap, the eye, the back fin, the tail, the gleaming, lighter colored snout, and they were extraordinary, too extraordinary, too unexpected, and I felt miserably unprepared for them. I felt as if I'd put a dime in a jukebox to hear Brenda Lee, but Enrico Caruso had burst out of the machine, come back from the dead and started singing the entire score of *I Pagliacci* backed by the Turin Philharmonic. For an instant I wondered if I could hold everything inside.

"Hey. Earth to David," Denise said.

"Yeah—I just— That's the most unexpected thing I ever saw. Did you know that was here?"

"Been over the ferry a couple of times, but I never saw that before. It's really grand. Why do they do that?"

"I don't think there's a reason for it," Julie whispered. "I just think they're happy and curious. If they were scared of us or if the boat bothered them, they wouldn't be there."

"Maybe they think we're a shrimper, going to throw 'em some leavings."

"Nah," I said. "I've read about them. They can tell the difference between different kinds of boats. They've seen this ferry a thousand times. They even know to stay away from one boat in a whole fleet of the same kind of boats. Killer whales can, anyway, and they're pretty close relatives. I think you're right. I think they're just out for a moonlight cruise, and sometimes they get as much of a charge out of seeing us as we get out of seeing them."

We all waved at the beasts. The beasts kept leaping, not synchronized, but close to each other—brothers and sisters, kids, nieces and nephews, I fancied—each when it felt like it, all in the same direction as the ferry. The ferry ride lasted about twenty minutes and the dolphins stayed with the boat until close into the Port Aransas landing. Then they stayed under the waves as moving shadows I could just barely make out and were gone. We got back into the car and drove off with the other cars.

We found a little store still open in town and Denise went inside to get some things for dinner. When she came back, she threw a paper sack in my lap. It was heavy and seemed to have something wet in it. I opened it up; there were about five pounds of huge raw shrimp on shaved ice inside and a can of shrimp spice.

"Jesus. We eat tonight. You know how to cook these things?"

"Fuck, I figured we'd just take the heads and veins off and bile 'em down," Denise said. "You got water with you?"

"A couple of big canteens," I said. "I filled 'em at the apartment."

"That's it, then. Head that way."

There was nothing to Mustang Island but an unmarked asphalt road, salt flats to the right and a huge wall of dark dunes on the left between us and the Gulf. We drove under the moonlight until the lights of the town had vanished and then looked for some kind of road off toward the dunes. I found something in dirt and scrub brush that seemed to answer the description and turned off. It was harder than I'd expected, but you couldn't see where its sides ended and the sandy soil began. I parked the car so it was fairly well concealed from the highway behind one of the first baby dunes.

"Okay, ladies, we march from here."

We each took as much of the tents and the other gear as we could carry and headed up into the dunes. We found a little moon-canyon overlooking both the road and the Gulf that was still shielded from most of the chilly, wet, salt wind blowing in from the Gulf. The edges of the whitecaps seemed to be illuminated as they broke on the shore about two hundred yards below us.

Denise started setting up the stove while Julie and I put up the tents. They were so cheap to rent that I'd taken two of them, one for all the equipment and one to sleep in, or one for dining and dancing and the other for lectures and quilting, who the fuck cared? We had to go back down the dunes to the dirt flats to find some stones to help guy the pegs and poles down, but in about a half hour we had the two of them up pretty well and

the sleeping bags and the equipment inside. Denise had the
shrimp and a shitload of yellow rice cooked up. It was near
midnight, maybe a little past it, and the moon was going down.
We washed the shrimp down with Oly and more mescal and
had some reefer for dessert. We were all pretty fucked up,
dazed, gorged and exhausted.

"I have to pee," Julie said. "You bring any toilet paper by
any chance, General?"

I fell back, reached an arm into one of the tents, pulled out
a roll and tossed it to her.

"Well, I'm impressed. What else you got in there?"

"Barrel of monkeys. Malaria pills. Telescope. Oh, yeah, that's
for this comet. Dexter-Baxter. Becker-Decker. Whatever. It's
up there somewhere. I got lots of shit in there. I got a tape
player, underwear, socks . . ."

"Fine. I'll probably need all of it in a little while. How about
a flashlight?"

"Nah, don't take a flashlight, Julie. You'll just attract the cree-
pie-crawlies. I'll go 'long with you." Denise struggled to her feet
and the two of them went stumbling off through the black
shapes of the dune peaks. After a couple of minutes I heard
squealing laughter and then singing.

"la cucaracha, la cucaracha, la dadadadadada . . .
la cucaracha, la cucaracha, marry-wana por fumar . . . "

I rolled on my belly and started to crawl toward the tent until
I found the telescope. I carried it up the highest dune and set
it on its tripod at what seemed to be about a twelve-degree
list—well, fuck it; this wasn't a test. Then I stood up and gazed
around the skies. The newspaper had mumbled something about
low in the southeast, which, the way I figured it, was over the
Gulf and to the left.

"Hey. There you are." It was Julie's voice over my shoulder.
"You see anything yet?"

"Look."

I stepped away from the telescope and let her at the eyepiece.

"It's really there! There's really a comet there! Wow! It's
lovely!" She stood up and tried to follow the telescope's line of
sight. She pointed. "There! Is that it?"

"Yeah. It's hard to see at first without the telescope, just a little suspended fuzzball, like some blurry cotton. But there it is."

"Wow. We thought it was all bullshit."

"What?"

"The comet. Denise and I thought it was all bullshit so you could get her in a tent somewhere and mess with her sacred zones. She didn't mind that much, I don't think, but she thought the line was a little hokey. I brought the bottle."

"Thank you. Where is she?"

"She passed out, I think. She's down by the tents." She put her eye back to the eyepiece, then stood up again. "Well, this is really amazing. Morose Vietnam vet asks the widow to chaperone a midnight picnic on the Gulf with leaping dolphins and genuine comets. Some show. You ought to get laid royally when Denise finds out you really came across with the comet. Of course that probably won't be till tomorrow night, unless you like to have commerce with the dead. Or maybe all you really brought us here for was just to see the comet. That's pretty kinky."

"You want to go down to the water?"

"Sure. Why the fuck not? Bring the jug."

We slid down the dune on our asses and it gave us a drunken running start across the beach. As the sand got wet and dark about ten feet from the nearest breaking waves, I saw what was happening with my feet, my shoes—the tips were kicking up sand and as the sand burst into the air, there were tiny bright little flashes, sparks, like pixie dust, around my ankles. I stopped short and just started to kick the sand.

Julie turned around. "Jesus, now what?"

"Phosphorescent animals, diatoms. Look."

She kicked a few times for herself. She dropped to her knees and started throwing the wet sand and the fairy dust into the air with her hands. She found one tiny patch that stuck together in a wet bead of sand and pasted it to her forehead. Then she stuck a patch on my forehead. It took ten, fifteen seconds for the glow in the center of her forehead to dim down and die completely.

She started to laugh loud into the wind. "Whew! Hand that bottle over here."

We traded deep swigs and that killed the bottle.

"Okay," she said. "You get half."

"Of what?"

"The worm. I'm ready."

"Oh, Barf City! I don't want to eat no fuckin' worm."

"There's magic here tonight, General, and I for one don't intend to screw it up by defying tradition." She tipped the bottle upside down and shook the little white wrinkly pickled caterpillar into the palm of her hand. She put it to her lips and bit half of it, chewed once and swallowed.

"Okay. Your turn." She handed me the ass-end of the worm in her fingertips.

"This is really the most wonderful thing anyone's ever offered me. I'll never forget this." I took it, tossed it way back into my throat and swallowed hard. Then I set the square-based bottle upright in the sand so I could find it and take it back when we left the beach. Then Mandrake gestured hypnotically out over the ocean.

"What?" she asked. "Swimming? You want to go swimming now?"

"Yeah."

"You have a bathing suit on under that? Well, that was a stupid-ass question, wasn't it? Okay. Let's do it."

I kicked my sneakers off and slipped my pants off, then my sweat shirt. She had her sweater off, threw her hair back, then stood up and pulled her jeans off, hopping around on one leg at a time. It was colder than it should have been for this kind of shit. We both started running for the waves. I didn't really look at her hard until we'd both plunged all the way in and surfaced in water a little below our waists bobbing up and down with the incoming waves. She looked fabulous, amazing—hard little breasts that the cold water had firmed up with goosebumps and rigid brown nipples, salt water trickling down her shoulders and her face. I never wanted to see a woman again in any more light than that. Any more light would have seared her, fried her to a crisp; the wind would have blown the ashes away. Moonlight and starlight, cometlight sparkled off her, and some of the diatoms that had been swimming loose in the sea, that had made the waves break bright as the water smashed the animals onto the sand, clung to her and twinkled and glowed pale green near her navel, on her cheek and in her long, wet hair.

She threw her arms around her chest and shivered. "Whoa, this is nuts. You had enough?"

"Yeah, I guess so. It's a little Spartan even for me. It feels great, though."

"Well, I think I'm a little sobered up. C'mon, everybody out of the pool!" She shrieked something that sounded like laughing, cackling, and splash-dashed ahead of me out of the water. A wonderful ass. She reached for her fatigue shirt.

"Here, wait a second." I picked up my sweat shirt and started to towel down her back. Then her ass and her legs. Then her front. All over.

"Now your sweat shirt's wet," she said.

I used it on myself, then put it on. It wasn't that wet. We put our pants on, picked up our shoes and the bottle and headed back for the dunes.

"Denise snores," I said.

"Yeah, that's for sure. Get the other sleeping bags out and put 'em in the other tent."

I found a number I'd rolled for the expedition, lit it inside the tent on a hemostat Ney had liberated just for me, took a pull and handed it to Julie.

"You've still got twinkle-things in your hair," she said. "Wait, there's one in the corner of your eye. There." She flicked it off my cheekbone with her thumb and forefinger. It flew in a tiny light arc through the tent, landed in a corner and finally died.

"Whew! I am *so* glad I got out of town," she sighed. "Thanks for organizing this little pajama party."

"I had to get away myself. I'm back in the States, I'm safe and I'm almost a civilian again, but I was living in that barracks like I'd just been conscripted for five years. I might as well have been back in Nam, in Phu Bai or Lonh Doc or Soc Ninh or Phong Dong. How did things end up between you and Paul?"

She exhaled some reefer smoke and thought for a few seconds. "Not too good. I guess I understood why. How did you act when you got your orders?"

"Didn't bother me that much, I don't think. I didn't have any attachments."

"You make me feel like a vacuum cleaner."

"You know what I mean."

"You didn't mind going?"

"Oh, I minded, a lot. But the orders weren't the crushing blow to me. Getting drafted a year before—that was the big freak show. After that, I just figured everything else was inevitable and I just had to hold my nose and grit my teeth and get through it. Until this fuckin' Project Constipation. That threw me for a loop. I haven't been behaving very well over it at all."

I heard that noise, very faint, and I looked up and tried to see her face in the tent. She was crying.

"What's wrong?"

"Never mind." She choked a little. "I'll be okay."

"What's the matter?"

"Where's that toilet paper?" I handed it to her and she blotted up her nose. She sighed very low.

"It's just that Paul hit me a couple of times, the last fight we had before he left. That never happened before. He really called me all kinds of shit. I knew he was in a panic, but Jesus, I wasn't ready for that. He left on a real bitter note."

"Did he hurt you bad?"

"No, he didn't break anything. He didn't give me a black eye. But he hit me. Nobody's ever hit me before. I didn't like it."

"Too bad you weren't Denise. You know what she's got in her purse?"

"Sure. Just the usual lady crap, makeup, eye shadow, a loaded pistol. Yeah, I know what she's got in there. Haven't you ever heard that song about the way the girls are in Texas? How'd you find out?"

"Well, I think she was very disappointed when she asked me if I was packing a roscoe and I told her I'd just plumb never gotten around to it. But she said I could borrow hers if Satan's Cannibals roared up on their Kawasakis."

"Well, she's got to learn about easterners just like you've got to learn about Texas girls. She took me out to her daddy's ranch one time and taught me how to use it. She's pretty good. I couldn't hit anything to save my life. It just terrified me. She's just about given up hope for me. Then she tried to make me enroll in a karate class. Does all that shit turn you on?"

"I don't know. Up till now, I've managed to make all my

arrangements with women without a lot of bloodshed and mayhem and carnage being involved. Just, you know, straight sex, hold the violence. I guess I have to modify that a little down here."

"I wouldn't worry about it. You ever hit a woman?"

"Don't be a sexist. I never hit anybody."

"You've never been in a fight?"

"Listen to you. Listen to your goddam tone. You'd have been appalled if I said I'd ever socked a woman. Now I tell you I never hit anybody of either gender and you're lookin' at me like I'm some kind of interior decorator. You want me to go out and hit a man for you?"

"Well, no. It's just—unusual, I guess. Guys—they seem to fight, growing up, sometimes after they're grown up."

"I got pushed and shoved a little by the usual playground dorks. I shoved and pushed back. I just never liked it. I didn't want to get hit, and I sure as fuck didn't have a desire to punch anybody else out. Oh, yeah, I hit a woman once. I was in a very excited mood on a street corner talking about something, I don't remember what, and I was waving my arms around like an ethnic, and I accidentally socked her in the nose. I felt awful. I wanted to crawl in a hole and die. I wanted to buy her a new Cadillac. Shit, man, there's pain on the ends of fists. I'm not into that shit. So I'm an interior decorator."

"No, I didn't mean to say that. Maybe a lot of guys have never punched anyone. But they all seem to have to say they did. I never thought I was impressed."

"Ah, fuck, just like they manufactured me to think I should bop people in the teeth, they manufactured you and Denise to be impressed by that shit. Women aren't any more marginally civilized than men."

"Maybe," she grunted. "Well, I got my consciousness raised about it the other night. Words, even shitty words, they can clear the air sometimes, I guess. But getting hit—that's like someone wants to give you pain. Nothing good can come off of that. I just decided. I just knew."

I looked at her and I wanted her badly. Things were pounding around in my head, and I could smell the salt from her. I put my hand around the back of her neck and brought my mouth down on hers. She was hesitant, neutral for a second and then she put her arm around my back and started to kiss me in return, hard, her tongue stiff and pliant at the same time. The instant I realized she wanted me, too, I thought the back of my skull was going to blast out backward. I arched up and grabbed the front of her fatigue shirt and pulled it open from the middle and took her breasts in my palms. She wrapped her legs around one of mine and squeezed all the blood out of it. Suddenly she went rigid and put her arm stiff against my chest to keep me away.

"This is a really shitty idea," she whispered, trying to catch her breath.

"I guess so. I—probably, okay." I could barely think or put words together. "Look, it's not an idea. It's what I want. It's not something I want to talk about." I had my fingers around her shoulders and I was squeezing them as if I'd float away and be lost in the sea wilderness if I wasn't gripping them.

"I know, I know. I want— It's not that I don't want it to happen. Things—things are real confused for me now. I don't want something like this just because I'm confused."

"We're going to kill this with talk. I don't want to kill it. I think I'll die."

"You won't die. You won't."

"I don't even want to find out." I leaned down over her again slowly and found her lips, wet hot breath hissing out of them. They didn't move away. We kissed long again, deep, and her arm moved away and wrapped itself around me again. My eyes were open, drinking in her eyes and her nose and her hair. Hers finally closed and stayed closed as if they'd stay closed forever. I roamed down and pulled open the rest of her shirt and swallowed one of her breasts, licking and biting at her nipple—I didn't know what was going on with me; I was afraid I might lose it and bite too hard. She was pulling my sweat shirt over my back and then I moved to let her pull it off my head, but I wouldn't let her go to take it all the way off me; it bound up like a wet towel between my shoulders. I was kissing her again, and her breasts rolled against my ribs and my skin, hot, and the nipples poked into my skin and I felt the hair on the back of my neck prick up.

She moved me a little away with her belly and had her hand on my pants button; I heard, felt it bust open, and then the flat of her hand ran the zipper down and was moving over my dick and gripping me just firmly enough under my balls. I lost it then. I leaped down at her waist and pulled open her fly and pulled her jeans and her panties down to her thighs and then my mouth was at her hair and her red and juicy flesh—somehow I saw the red not in the darkness of the tent but in a wild flash in my head—and the smells were the salt sea overladen with something: the salt sea and a glacier lake, cold and bracing but warm and welcoming at the same time. She made a noise and I tore into her five times harder. I managed to thrust my hand down to get her jeans down over her knee and she kicked them off the rest of the way with her other foot. I could feel sand flakes crunching under her ass and on my belly, sharp, glasslike, irritating. My tongue shot at her and I had her clit in my teeth. Her legs went around my ribs and I heard her jeans swoosh and flap against my back.

And it just went on like that for what had to be hours, fingernails and tongues and teeth, wet fingers, hot mouths, clawing and gripping skin and hair, wild things, things I'd remembered from before, things she did I'd never had done to me before, things I had to do right then that I'd never heard of or thought of before. I had to squeeze her to me so hard I had images of her moving right through me and out my spine. I wanted everything that second; I wanted everything to keep happening for years. She was hard to bring off. I stayed out of her and held her wrists over her head and her legs spread with my knee while I rubbed and probed with my fingers and moved my mouth and my teeth back to her tight nipples. There was a noisy wind outside the tent and she arched her ass up finally and seemed to want to scream but to want to stifle it, too, and I said *Scream, Scream* and it was fierce and tore through me, and then her head shot up at my arm and she buried her teeth into my shoulder and stifled the rest of it there, and then she was wrapped around my belly and gasping and sighing, and I wanted to give her time to recover, but I couldn't. I pulled her down and was on top of her and for the first time I was ready to push inside her—it seemed she wasn't just moist but was squirting the fragrance and the slippery juice back out at me. And I went in her and hard for all I was worth and she gasped; I could feel (again, red and blood-gorged in my mind) the little round ball all the way up and inside her against my dick's head and I smashed at it again and again and she shrieked backward, shrieked by sucking air in, not blasting it out each time, and I shot my hands down under her buttocks and spread them apart and probed her asshole with my finger and pulled her into me each time I went into her and she started to scream again and I said *Scream, Scream* and then it was the moment for me to scream too and I did, against the wind that shook the tent flaps, and there were crazy pictures in my mind, and I sank my mouth into the soft of her throat. Her chin was tight against the top of my head and one of her hands grabbed my hair and pulled, yanked, held on to it, maybe tried to pull a clump of it out.

We held on to one another for what seemed more hours and I kissed her and smelled and licked her, places I hadn't before, and finally I told her that damn, God, I wanted her, and she breathed low and touched me and kissed me, a place at a time, and finally we rolled one of the sleeping bags over on us and fell asleep that way. The last thing I saw through the front seam of the tent was an orange-pink line of dawn at the horizon far off through the break in the dunes.

29

Bacon and eggs were floating into the tent and driving me insane. I pulled up on an elbow and looked at Julie's face in the tent shadows. Her eyes were closed but she stirred and I could tell she was awake. I leaned to her ear and whispered hello, good morning. She turned my way and opened her eyes.

"Good morning. Oh, Jesus, I don't know if I can take that food yet."

"It'll be good for us."

"Have you been up yet?"

"No."

"We're gonna catch hell from Denise, I think. I don't want to go out there. She's armed, remember."

"It smells like she's just going to feed us to death. You know, it's strange, I'm thirsty as hell, but I don't have a hangover."

"That's 'cause it was mescal. And 'cause you ate the magic worm." She put her hand on my belly and rubbed the hair on it lightly. I kissed her shoulder.

"I *hear* you two in there," Denise called. We heard her walk to the tent and drop down to her knees. She stuck her head inside the tent. Neither of us bothered to cover up and Denise wasn't wearing any top. She giggled and waved coquettishly at my dead unit. "Breakfast time, boys and girls! God, you two do reek of venery. Well, what the hell. My fault for fallin' asleep. Maybe there'll be room for me next time. C'mon out and get some grub."

We pulled on our clothes and crawled out of the tent and into the noon sunshine. It was hot, in the seventies. I took my shirt back off and Julie decided to do the same. I could see a freighter miles off in the Gulf heading northeast, paralleling the beach. Denise was putting three plates together, fried eggs, bacon and toast, and there was coffee percolating. We sat down in the sand and went at it; it was great, the best meal I'd had since I'd been back, and the company was certainly pleasant as all hell. There was a chance I was going to survive resettlement to the States despite Project Transition.

"You really shouldn't have fallen asleep," Julie said. "First of all, you snore, and second of all, there really was a comet, and David found it."

"Yeah, I saw the telescope up there. I guess the wind knocked it over in the night, but it's fine. I watched the shrimp boats heading back in when I got up. What did the comet look like?"

"Great. Strange. White and round and fuzzy. Eerie, just dangling up in the sky like a feather earring. Can she still see it tonight?"

"Sure," I said, "after the moon goes down some, probably around two in the morning. We'll keep you awake."

"I've been getting a great suntan all morning, and I went bare-assed nekkid for a swim. I was right. There's nobody around here. They're all pussies around here. They won't come out on the beach for another two months when the water's in the seventies. I see you killed that bottle."

"There's another one, and some more beer in the cooler," Julie said.

"You ate the worm, too."

"You can have my part tonight," I said.

"Hot damn! Still, the fun part's gettin' to the worm. I sure had fun last night. I didn't do anything too lewd, did I?"

"No, we were all perfect ladies and gentlemen, as far as I can tell."

"Yeah, right," Julie said.

After breakfast and cleanup, we went strolling barefoot through the tops of the dunes. The bigger ones were about four or five stories high and in some of the high moon-canyons between them there were huge round colonies of dry bushes, or maybe each one was a single giant bush, but the branches rose twice as high as a person and the circumferences were the size of big aboveground backyard swimming pools. We crawled between the branches and into the center of one and found a clearing big enough for us all to sit down. We could see out of the plant, but the branches were so dense that it seemed that no one on the outside could possibly see us inside it, like Merlin's enchantment, trapped forever in woods through which some heard him, but no one ever saw him again. It made us all whisper.

We left the tents and camping equipment in the dunes, made ourselves reasonably respectable and drove into Corpus Christi for dinner at a little Mexican family restaurant near city hall and the *Caller-Times* building. I'd never been terribly wild about Mexican food, but then all that I'd had was cooked some two thousand miles from the Mexican border. This was very different, very angry, rude food, very tasty and fresh; it was the first time I'd ever had fresh tortillas with corn flour still clinging to them, and I kept ordering more and more stacks of them. It even made sense to down a few jalapeños intentionally and wash them down with XX Dos Equis. There was a new winner for best meal since returning to the States. When I went to the john, I looked in the little mirror over the sink and decided I was authentically human again.

Everything was as we'd left it when we got back and we all started in on the second mescal bottle; I was surprised at how much I enjoyed it, because I'd really never had much to do with hard or even soft liquor. We had the salt and limes this time, and it was round after round of that one-two-three punch of drink, recoil, lick, recoil, bite, recoil; wham, bam, thank-you-ma'am. Then we all stripped and staggered down to the beach in the moonlight and took a frigid swim. We stayed in longer and played literal and figurative grab-ass with each other, imitating sharks and crabs, and when we got out, Julie and I pasted

Denise all over with splotches of phosphorescent sand critters. Then we kicked the glow-specks up with our feet on the way back to the dune, climbed back to the tents, put some clothes on and built a fire. Denise stayed awake this time and we all climbed back to the telescope for the comet show. When we'd killed bottle number two and trisected the worm—the ladies wouldn't let me get away without eating my third—no one said anything about the sleeping arrangements of the night before, but we all crawled into the first tent and pretty much behaved ourselves until we stopped singing lewd songs and telling vile jokes and stories and fell asleep. I managed to spoon up against Julie and kiss the back of her neck for a goodnight. She seemed to enjoy it. She reached for my hand and gripped it hard around the front of her belly.

Sunday we spent much the same, serious sunbathing during the day, a run into Port A. for resupply at a mom 'n' pop convenience store, dinner of noodles and canned beef stew, reefer and soft-core misbehavior around the campfire and in the tent. Monday morning we packed up and headed north again and stopped for coffee and breakfast on the road. We rolled into Julie's apartment complex around four in the afternoon, and without making too big a fuss about it I stayed at Julie's, with Julie mumbling something about driving me back to base. Denise didn't seem to mind. She kissed me on the lips before she headed off.

I was a little nervous about what to do, about whether or how to start off anything. Maybe I would have her drive me back tonight after dinner, but it wasn't what I wanted. I just didn't want to press her; she had things to think out. I was a hundred and fifty-odd pounds of freight she hadn't anticipated handing over to the movers.

We squatted around one of the boxes she was using for a table and passed a number back and forth. Finally she cocked her head oddly at me and spoke. "What do you want with me?" she asked.

"Well, believe it or not, not to complicate your life. But I want a lot of you. I want all of you I can have."

"Well, you have complicated my life, and it was already complicated. I don't mean to point a finger. I should have been stronger and said no and meant it. But I'll be out-front. I wanted you, too. You're strange, and you're nice, and I guess both of us were feeling wounded and pissed off. But you know I'm married. I didn't intend to sleep with anybody the whole time Paul was away, and that was what I wanted going on in my mind when he came back. I don't feel so hot that it didn't work out a week after he left."

"Okay. I could make it easy on you and call it a big one-time mistake and go back to the base if you want."

"I asked you what you wanted."

"To take a shower with you."

"Oh." She put her elbows on the box and her head in her palms and looked down, and then back up at me.

"Just a shower?" she asked.

"No. Not just a shower."

"No, I guessed not. I wouldn't want just a shower, either. Or if I thought I did now, I wouldn't most of the way through the shower. You know, you're a pretty earthy guy. You bite a lot, too, and you leave marks. Denise told me she thought that was pretty interesting. Even though you don't carry a heater, she thinks there might be hope for you. I think she's willing to wait for me to leave town and then try for sloppy seconds."

"I take back every bad thing I ever thought about Texas."

"Would you be willing to go back to the base now?"

"I told you I would if it's what you want."

"What do you like about me?"

"I can't say things like that in words. You're smart; you're beautiful to me. I liked—making love to you. I want to look at you again. I want some more of it."

"Could you fall in love with me?"

"Yes. It wouldn't be hard."

"You don't know me."

"People don't wait to know each other. They hold each other and stay with each other and hope."

"What would you hope for?"

"I don't know."

"I said the other night this was a real shitty idea, and it is. But I like baths better than showers. Would that be all right?"

"That would be fine."

We just let in the light from the hallway, and I stripped her slowly as she ran the water. She poured in a bubble powder that smelled like an herb garden, but it wasn't overpowering. I liked it; guys hardly ever get a chance to take bubble baths; they won't even take them alone. She had a big washing sponge and we used it on each other until the beach was off us completely, and then a lot more. Out of the bath, I put her over my shoulder in a fireman's carry and headed for the bedroom; she laughed and told me I was going to get a hernia. The legs of the bed had been removed and it was low on the floor. I rolled both of us onto it and looked down at her from my knees as she lay on her back and touched my legs.

"Let me make some love to you now," she said. "Not so violently. It's a peaceful afternoon and we have all night. When do you have to be on base?"

"I have to make a seven-fifteen formation."

"Fine. I'm not working anymore. I'll drive you there. Or near there. We don't have to advertise this shit to Paul's friends."

It was powerful stuff, I suppose in both directions, and for the next week all I wanted to do was punch my last punch card of the afternoon and get the hell over to her apartment as fast as I could. On Wednesday the movers came and took the bed and the boxes; she had her own fat, overstuffed sleeping bag and it was fine. That night I took her out to dinner, to one of the outdoor restaurants down in the little canyon of the river that ran through the city, a French restaurant, and we ate by candlelight and watched pedal boats churn by leaving little gurgling wakes. She wore a simple long green dress and had braided her brown hair behind her neck.

"I talked to Paul's parents today," she said. "They want to know when I'm coming out to Tucson to live with them. I said I'd be coming out there soon, to live near them, but not with them. They didn't seem to mind the way Paul did."

"When are you going?"

"The rent on the apartment's not up for two weeks. Maybe then. I told them I had business to clear up. I feel like I'm in limbo. I'm not too happy about myself. I don't know why I'm doing this. It's not good, not right."

"Well, eat up and take me home."

"I didn't mean to say it like it's your fault. Don't you understand? Some bad things happened to me and I needed— They left me feeling real alone and needy. You didn't move in like a vulture, but you had needs, bad needs, too. But your needs and my needs right now, they're not any part of my life, of my real life. I want Paul to do his time and come back, and I want him to come back to me. I'm not worried he'll find out about us. He probably won't, but if he does, I'm ready just to look him in the eyes and tell him he shouldn't have hit me. He's got to learn that. But I was serious when I married him. We were in school, and I thought he'd just go right on to med school, and nothing would happen to come between us. I don't mean you, David. I mean the war. Because of the war he hit me, because of the war he was angry at me and I was angry at him. The war's so big and we're all just little people. The war rolls over us any way it likes and we have to pick ourselves up and bind our wounds the best way we can, and we'll be lucky if we're alive when our part of it's over. I was really the one who should have hit Paul. I can't tell you how angry I am that everybody just arranged things so he goes off and has to take the risks and I have to sit back here for a year and—what? Weave? Knit sweaters? Maybe wait for a phone call from the Defense Department. That's really an attractive prospect to me."

"What are you trying to tell me?"

"That I'll have to go soon. And when I go, you have to just let me go. I'll be living by myself in Tucson, and if I mess up again, it can't be with you. You can't come there."

"Am I supposed to say okay to that?"

"Somehow you have to agree to it. This is the part we both should have thought better about when I told you it was a shitty idea."

I dropped my end of the conversation and we kept on eating. She'd picked up on something, that I was—oh, hell, I'd been hung up on her since she'd first opened the door to her apartment at the party. I could have passed then and concentrated on Denise, and I guess I tried, lamely; it wasn't even my idea for Julie to come along to the beach. Now I was hung up and getting more hung up, violently hung up, greedy and hungry, and Julie was telling me how it had to stop, exactly how it had to stop. I was mad at Paul for treating her badly. If he hadn't —but, fuck, Paul wasn't that different from me. He was just high-strung flesh and blood getting ready to be a battlefield medic in a war where people, including the medics themselves, were still getting blown to shit. And he probably didn't have my mystic patina of protection and special treatment; if he lived and came home with all his parts, he'd have had to do a lot more active and quick ducking and bobbing and weaving than I had to.

That night I was angry and violent again and held her afterward in more of a lock than an embrace. I could give her pleasure, but the bottom had fallen out of the happiness market. We were clock and calendar watchers now and for the nights and weekend that came after. Sometimes we'd spend the evenings by ourselves, and sometimes Denise would join us for dinner or the movies; Denise could cheer her up a lot better than I could now. And then finally as we lay together on another Sunday afternoon she told me she was turning over the apartment and driving to Arizona the next morning.

"Okay," I said and my lips were tight.

"Yeah, okay," she said.

"What do you want me to say?"

"Think of something."

"You've given me my lines and told me when to leave. I can't fight what you really want."

"Tell me Paul shouldn't have hit me. Tell me you never would."

"That's not the issue. My not hitting people—it's no more a loving gesture to you than it is to strangers in bars. If I wanted to hurt you, I could do it as well, better than Paul. People have ways."

"You're hurting me now."

"How? By trying to help you do what you want? That's not fair."

"Don't be fair. Do you love me?"

"Yes."

"Then marry me. Tell me to get a divorce and marry me."

"If you were free, I'd stay with you. But you're his."

"He doesn't own me."

"He came to you first. He asked for you first and you said yes. That means something to me, too. Granted, I'm a little late doing anything about it, but you said he was what you wanted. I'm just trying to help do what you want."

"This has been really convenient for you, hasn't it? And in a week—oh, hell, you'll probably be screwing Denise by tomorrow night. Maybe you can both wave goodbye to me together. I'll leave you the keys to the apartment, and you can go upstairs and fuck on the floor."

"What you made jokes about a couple of weeks ago, now you're just trying to find things to twist in me. How does that make you different from Paul?"

"I don't have to be different from Paul if I don't want to! Offer me something! Offer me a life! Offer me a try!"

"I'm not ready to. That's what you want me to say, that's what it is. I'm not ready for it the way it would have to be now."

"Then fuck off and get out."

I stood up and started to put my clothes on. She turned to the wall. I walked out of the apartment and caught a bus back to base.

I hadn't been back in my rack for twenty minutes when the C.Q. knocked on my door and told me there was a phone call for me in the orderly room; I could take it in the captain's office if I didn't make a mess at his desk and didn't stay on too long. I figured it was Julie, and it was. She just barely had herself together when I picked up the phone and the C.Q. hung up his extension.

"Oh, God, look. I'm sorry what I said. I'm really sorry. Please come back and stay here tonight. I'll pick you up."

"Uh-uh. No. I don't think it's a good idea."

"Oh, God, don't let it end like this. I feel like trash on the floor. I was just upset. I didn't mean to say what I did."

"You had to say what you did. Because you know you're going back to Paul. I'm not mad. I'm not hurt. Okay, I'm hurt, but I'm trying to understand. You got married, you wanted to be married. I'm sorry I—hell, I'm sorry I'm in love with you. Maybe you are with me. Don't tell me if you are now. I don't want to know. Maybe you don't know, and that's good. But think of me. Stay safe. Get what you want. Think well of me. That's all I want. That's what I'll settle for."

The phone made it easier for her. We spoke for maybe an hour—I bought the C.Q. a couple of Cokes for not throwing me off—and we tried to soothe each other's feelings and nerves and hearts and suspicions and betrayals. I wondered what her feelings for Paul had been when they'd dated in college and married, but I didn't ask her. What I was doing was trying to act like a decent guy doing a decent thing, and it just made me feel like a bigger and bigger shit every time I came up with words that seemed to work. The last thing I told her was that I loved her.

She didn't say it back to me.

30

Dear Richard,

You never write, you never call . . . is this the army friendship you hoped would last the test of time?

Well, fuck you, then, whatever your name is. You were either the tall blond guy at Fort Bragg or the short, fat, Italian guy with hair all over his back in Vietnam, I can't even really remember now. Everybody I knew then is just a blur. I hope this letter doesn't even get forwarded to you, because I called that fuckin flophouse you were staying at the other day and some spaced-out teenybopper said she hadn't the foggiest where the fuck you were now. Something about Florida. Then she asked me if I knew where she could get some Quaaludes, whatever they are.

Well, anyway, so much for venom and spleen. When last you heard from me, The Weenie had grabbed me by the short hairs one last time and imprisoned me for three loathsome months (well, not entirely loathsome, but that's none of anybody's fucking business) at Fort Sam Houston In Texas (Fort S.H.I.T.) to learn how to data-punch. Lucky me; I can data-punch now.

It finally ended. I was a little shell-shocked when it did. They let you stay on a couple of extra days in the barracks if it's inconvenient for you to go home just that day, and I remember telling a guy in the barracks a week beforehand: "Listen, for Christ's sake, if I make up any excuses about not being all packed or anything, just forcefully get me out of here and throw me off the post, please, I'll give you five dollars now. You're a medic; use drugs if you have to." He promised he'd see to it.

Like always, I put everything off to the last moment. On the morning of my last fucking day, I had to check out with the battalion sergeant major, and that motherfucking swine decided I had to get a haircut or he wouldn't check my paperwork out. He didn't really want me to get out. He was begging me to break into the arms room and find an M16 and waste his sorry lifer ass so I'd have to spend the rest of my life in an army prison. But I fooled him and got the haircut. It is now my intention not to get another one or shave for the next three years, minimum.

The last check-off box around four in the afternoon (I almost didn't get it all done in time) was Top, one of those fairly mellow black, stringy, ageless lifer first sergeants. He looked over the clipboard, checked off his box, then looked up at me and said, "Sorry to see you go, Becker. You're a good soldier."

Well I stood there in a little bit of a daze and didn't exactly know how to react to that. I didn't want to screw everything up with a big fight five seconds before I was a civilian again, but I worked up a little umbrage and I said, "First Sergeant, I don't mean any disrespect, but why do you say that?"

And he said, "Oh, that's easy. This is only the second time you been in my orderly room. The first time was when you checked in."

So I ran that around in my head and it seemed fair. Just fair. Just fucking tolerable. Then the fuckhead saluted me, and it seemed to be the thing to do to salute back, so I did and then I left.

I actually didn't know where I was going to go when I left Sam, meaning my avuncular Sam and Houston, too, but I knew the journey of a thousand *li* starts at the Greyhound bus station, and I called a cab from the barracks lobby and had him hie me thither. They had this big fucking map on the wall with big red lines connecting all their major cities from coast to coast, and I had about four hundred bucks in cash on me. Then I saw a poster on the wall advertising San Antonio's big civic Fourth of July fireworks outside the Alamo that was going to be in a couple of weeks, and I thought, by gad, I think I'll spend this next Fourth of July in some Other Country (second one in a row, if you'll recall), so on four hundred bucks and with an expired U.S. passport, that meant either Canada or Mexico. Well, what can I say? I'm a cheap bastard and Mexico was much closer, so I bought a ticket to Brownsville, crossed over to Matamoras, and now I'm in Oaxaca. Don't ask me why. But it's pretty nifty. The food's wonderful. Americans cannot get laid; trying to bop a local would mean instant mob castration, and all the Yanqui girls I've met so far all have yeast infections up their boogies; it's all they talk about to each other. The first time I went to see the ruins at Monte Albán, an amazing flattened mountain-top plain of sacred Zapotec pyramids, all of them perfectly lined up except one that was shaped like an arrow and pointed at the summer solstice sunrise, my mouth just hung open and flies buzzed around it, and these three Yanqui honeys behind me were yakking and yakking about where to get fresh cotton pan-ties and different over-the-counter cures for yeast infections. Maybe that's what killed off the great Zapotec civilization.

When my money runs out, I'll have to leave or they'll throw me in jail, which is the national policy toward their young vis-itors from the North (whom they refer to in the newspapers as "drugaddictos Norteamericanos"), so before that happens, maybe I'll go back up to the border, hang a right and scare you up in Florida. Hope you don't have a yeast infection.

Your old army buddy,
Becker